The Dream of Macsen

Women of the Dark Ages Book Two

by

R A Forde

Although based upon historical events and characters, this is a work of fiction. Some author's notes appear at the end, giving some of the historical background and explaining the place names and official titles used. The time period is the late fourth century, when control of the Roman Empire was disputed between several different rulers and paganism was giving way to Christianity.

This novel was written using British English

ISBN: 9798679590878

Wise Woman

Women of the Dark Ages Book One

A desperate choice between faith and friendship

On the remote edge of a crumbling Roman Empire, a young woman is compelled to make a heart-wrenching choice between friendship, lover and faith.

Brittany, 443AD. Forced to flee a Britain beset by Saxon marauders, Keri and her mother seek refuge at the court of King Gradlon of Kemper. Keri grows up under the protection of the court, forming a strong bond with Gradlon's wayward daughter, Princess Dahut.With Western Europe harried by invaders and divided by conflict between the Church and the Old Religion, the girls shelter in the coastal city of Ys.

They meet Megan the wise-woman, who teaches them her ways. But the priests hate the wise-woman and her ancient religion and are determined to crush it. King Gradlon, newly converted to Christianity, makes a gift of the city of Ys to Dahut, to rule in his name. When Keri discovers that Dahut plots to seize the whole kingdom, she cannot support this treachery, which endangers their lifelong friendship. As war threatens to erupt between King and Princess, their religious and political differences come to a head – and the King's fanatical adviser, Bishop Corentin, is determined to finally destroy this rebellious pagan outpost, whatever the cost...

I

I was only a little girl when I first saw men die in combat. Of course, it was only from a distance, but I knew that men were dying, and that others would kill if they could. Kill us, kill our neighbours, kill our friends. Men who had never seen us and had no reason to hate us. It was an unsettling, bizarre notion to grow up with.

My nurse had taken me up to the hillside above Segontium — Cair-yn-Arfon in the British tongue. The rocky hills rose high above the town. Modest hills, compared with some I have seen since, but to my six-year-old mind huge mountains full of mystery. It was a warm spring morning and Mabanwy thought it would do me good to take the air. My little legs were already sturdy from hill-walking, and I scrambled up the old goat-path, sending pebbles and goat droppings spinning down the hillside behind me. Mabanwy laughed, but called out to me to be careful.

"Don't run so fast, Helena! Your father will be angry if you fall and scrape your legs."

"I won't!" I shouted, and ran on heedlessly.

Naturally, I soon tripped over my own feet and fell headlong. But I was not hurt beyond a bang on my shin. I sat and held the leg while I waited for my nurse, my eyes screwed up tight against the pain. I seldom cried, but if I did she had a knack of making hurts better. While I waited I looked down over the town, a huddle of rough stone buildings, some rendered with coloured plaster in the Roman style. Outside it, and slightly above, our villa showed as a two-story square arranged Roman-fashion around a central courtyard. A shadow fell across me, accompanied by laboured breathing from the climb.

"Another bruise for your collection," tutted Mabanwy, examining the shin which I was clutching. "Still, at least here's no cut, and I've been able to catch you up at last."

She rubbed my leg, and I stared out over the bay.

"Can we see Ireland, Mabanwy?"

"No, not this morning, little one. There's a bit of a haze. Maybe later. Anyway, why worry about seeing that land of pirates?"

I was about to look away when a vague movement caught my eye. Something had stirred out on the misty waters.

"What is it, Helena?"

"I thought I saw something. Yes, there it is again. Look."

I pointed to where a dark spindly shape was emerging into view. At first it looked like a serpent's neck, but quickly resolved itself into the prow of a ship. Above it a white sail flapped. Within seconds two other ships had joined it, one on either side. They seemed to be heading directly for Segontium. I giggled with pleasure, for they looked just like the toy boats my two brothers sailed on the stream behind our villa. I said so to Mabanwy, who turned a troubled face to me.

"No, child, they're not toys. They don't look like good Roman ships, either. I'm not sure, but I think they're Irish."

I digested this information in silence. Irish keels were feared on this coast, and with good reason. Some might be innocent traders, but many were not. The tribesmen of the mysterious land across the sea were great seafarers, but unfortunately great pirates too. If the harvest was bad at home they might make up the difference by raiding us. If it had been bad last year they might still raid us for plunder to tide themselves over until this year's crop was in. One way and another they often had reason enough to attack.

"What are they doing at Cair Gybi?"

"What do you mean, Mabanwy? What's Cair Gybi?"

"It's what they built when they closed the fort here — you know the old Roman fort in town?"

I nodded. Of course I knew it. It was one of my father's many responsibilities as local governor. I had even been inside it once. It had been a great disappointment — no soldiers, no clatter of shining armour, just rooms full of stores, and most of those in dull wooden crates.

"There used to be soldiers at the fort," Mabanwy went on. "Then the military authorities decided it was no use waiting for the Irish actually to land. They moved the soldiers away across to Mona there" — she indicated the great island across the straits — "and built a great harbour with a wall round it. They keep warships there. Then, if the Irish attack, or the Picts from the north, a fleet can sail out and catch them before they even reach the shore."

2

I clapped my hands. "Ooh, shall we see them being caught, Mabanwy?"

"I hope so," muttered my nurse grimly. "There's no garrison to speak of in the town."

I failed to notice the significance of her words, and carried on watching the ships. They were about a quarter of a mile off shore when Mabanwy suddenly gave a cry.

"Look there, my little one! Cair Gybi is awake after all!"

Sure enough, out of the mist came five more ships. They were heavier and slower moving than the Irish vessels, but they had proper decks with strange contraptions on them. Their sails were furled, and the two banks of oars they each had were dipping in perfect time. Across the still water came a faint rhythmic thudding from the drummers who beat time for the rowing crews.

The Irish had realised their danger. The three ships began to swing round as if to make off to sea again, but accompanied by frenzied drum beats the Roman warships put on an amazing burst of speed and closed rapidly. One of the pirate ships swung to our right and made off up the straits with a Roman vessel in pursuit. The other two turned left across the bay. They had more room for manoeuvre there, but so did their pursuers. The drumbeat had reached a hysterical pace now, as the trailing Irish ship was caught up by one of the Romans.

"Oh, gods above," sighed Mabanwy. "They're going to ram!"

I watched as the Roman vessel hit the Irish one amidships, rending timbers and men. It seemed almost to climb on top of its victim. Then it ground to a halt. Several seconds passed before we heard the crash of splintering wood and the agonised shouts of the Irishmen. I remember my amazement that it took so long for the sound to travel over the water. As we watched, the ships began to tear apart again. The Irish one began to fill with water, keeling over towards its attacker as if bowing in submission. The screech of tortured timbers sounded over the bay. The Irishmen took to the water, grabbing the many pieces of wreckage. The water was shallow and most of them were able to wade through it. They were exhausted by the time they struggled ashore. There they faced a rabble of hostile townspeople armed with spears, axes and hoes. The few available soldiers arrived and kept the civilians from finishing them off. The pirates were tired and defeated, and ready enough to accept the slave chains which the guard commander clapped on them. It was better than being torn to pieces by the crowd.

"They're all very brave now," said Mabanwy, meaning the townsfolk. "I'll bet it was different twenty minutes ago, when they thought they might have to fight a proper enemy."

Even at that age I could see that she was right. Looking back, I suppose her healthy scepticism was one of the formative influences of my early years.

The other ships were out of sight around the headland by now. The rammed Irish vessel had settled on the bottom, her mast sticking up through the surface at a crazy angle. The water was littered with all sorts of flotsam, as the Irishmen's belongings drifted on the tide.

"Come along," said Mabanwy. "It's time we went home!"

"Oh, Mabanwy, we've only just got here!"

"Yes, and we've only just got to get down again. My old legs aren't like yours, you know. They get tired out."

Actually, Mabanwy was all of twenty years old. She had been widowed at the age of seventeen, and had been glad to take on the job of looking after me, my old wet-nurse having got herself pregnant again. I took to my new nurse immediately. She was cheerful and really liked children. Together we roamed out on the hillside or the beach, and I learned a good deal from her about the plants and animals of our countryside. My father had talked vaguely about a proper governess, someone who could teach me all the things a mother of good family would normally teach her daughter. My brothers already had a tutor. They didn't like him much, and I was in no hurry to meet the female equivalent. Still, as my father said, there was time enough yet.

I looked for the pirates on the beach as we came down the hillside, but there were trees here and I could see nothing through them. The goat path widened out and became a track that wagons could use to gain access to the higher fields. Walls of dry stonework flanked it, and proper ditches took the worst of the rainwater away. We passed a group of farm workers, who greeted us respectfully. They knew who we were, of course — Mabanwy was a local girl, and they recognised her if not me. A little further down we passed the workers' houses — round hovels of stone with thatched roofs. They were a far cry from my father's villa. Even then I knew how well off we were. I saw the people who came to visit my father on government business, and how most of them treated him with respect, as if he was an important man. Only occasionally did we get a visit from someone still higher in government circles. Then the positions were reversed, Papa waiting attentively on the visitor, and considering his utterances, however fatuous, with great solemnity.

Eventually we reached a place where the track forked, the left branch carrying on down to the town and the right one to the rear entrance of our villa. As we trudged along the stony track I chatted away to Mabanwy, still excited by the events we had seen.

"What will happen to the pirates, Mabanwy?"

"What? Oh, the prisoners? Well, they'll be slaves now. As they were captured by the Army they're the Emperor's slaves. They'll probably end up in the lead mines, poor devils, although any that are too puny for that might be sold off at the slave market, I suppose. For domestic service, perhaps."

"What a terrible thing to happen to them!"

"Maybe it is, but they were all set to do terrible things to us. If they'd stayed at home they wouldn't be slaves now."

This was undeniably true, but I still harboured a sneaking sympathy for the pirates. I suppose a child always favours the underdog, used to being that herself.

"I wonder what happened to the other ships."

"Who knows, little one? If they were sunk too I expect we'll hear about it. Later on."

My father was an educated man who modelled himself on the highborn Romans he met. He spoke Latin as well as British, and had a good knowledge of Greek. He had copies of many books by famous Roman writers — the epic poems of Virgil were favourites of his, and he often had a scribe read them to him at dinner when he was on his own, which he usually was.

On this day it was dinner time before I saw him. He had been called in to supervise the prisoners and their guards. The authorities were put in the odd position of having to guard the prisoners against the local people, who were all set to hang them out of hand. Papa could not agree to this, of course, and in any case would not have wanted to. He believed in old-fashioned Roman values, one of which was the honourable treatment of prisoners. Besides, they were the Emperor's property now, even though the Emperor would never see or hear of them. His governors would no doubt find a use for them on His Majesty's behalf.

As usual I was bathed by Mabanwy and dressed in a linen shift before being taken to say goodnight to Papa in the dining room. My brothers, being older, would have their turn later. The long room was only dimly lit by a few flickering flames. The frescoes on the walls were hardly visible in the shadows, although in the daytime you could see scenes from Greek and Roman legend there, picked out in white and pink. Papa reclined alone on a couch at the far end, the first course of his meal arranged on the low table before him. A slave stood behind him, waiting to take out the dishes when my father was ready. In the corner sat his best scribe, reading from Virgil. It was the opening passage from the Aeneid:

I sing of arms and the man who came first from the shores of Troy, destined to be an exile to Italy and the Lavinian beaches...

Papa let the man read on for a few lines, telling how the anger of Juno drove Aeneas from the ruins of Troy to be tossed on the ocean and made a wanderer without a country. Then he raised his hand for silence and swung his legs off the couch to sit up straight.

"Hello, Helena. You've come to say goodnight?"

"Yes, Papa."

His greying head turned.

"And has she been behaving herself, Mabanwy?"

"Indeed yes, *Domine*. But then, she usually does."

"Yes, that's true. And what have you done today, little one?"

"We went up the hill, Papa. We saw the ships. There was a battle!"

He frowned, emphasising the furrows across his forehead. "You weren't frightened, I hope?"

"No, Papa, we were a long way off. We saw one ship crash into another and sink it. But the men swam to the beach, I think."

"Yes, most of them did."

"Papa, what will happen to them? Mabanwy says they will be slaves now."

"Yes, child. They will be kept at the fort here tonight and taken away tomorrow. They have attacked the Emperor, and now their punishment will be to work for him instead."

"The Emperor? Was he here too?" My eyes must have been wide with excitement, and I looked around, as if I expected to see the Emperor wander in from the hall. Papa laughed.

"I didn't mean it like that. As far as I know His Majesty is safe in Mediolanum. But to attack the Empire is to attack the Emperor."

"Oh, I see." I was disappointed. I had had a brief vision of myself mixing with the mighty.

"Goodnight, then, Helena."

I tiptoed forward and he bent to kiss me, smelling lightly of the wine he drank with his meal, and the funny perfumed oil he put on his hair.

"Goodnight, Papa."

Our nightly ritual over, I was led off to bed. It had been a typical meeting. My father was kindly enough, but mostly rather distant. His work kept him occupied, and this little time in the evening was often all we had. My mother had died soon after my birth, and Papa seemed in no hurry to marry gain. There was a slave-woman called Finella who seemed to have some special kind of relationship with him. She was often in his private quarters, the only one who was allowed here except for the cleaners. I wasn't sure what position she held, and when I asked once Mabanwy grew embarrassed and told me not to ask about such things, so I didn't. I supposed he loved me. I was sure Mabanwy did.

The next day we went into the town early. Mabanwy and I were accompanied by Rhonwen, the housekeeper, and one of the slaves. One of Rhonwen's duties was to buy our food, and we often went with her. The slave was there to carry her purchases home. Today I especially wanted to see the town — and perhaps the prisoners from the rammed ship, who were to be marched away today. One of the other ships had also been captured, so there were a lot of pirates now in the fort.

Rhonwen was not interested in pirates — she had a household of twenty to run — but the market was on the prisoners' route out of town. This morning it was teeming as usual. I loved the hubbub. There were always travellers as well as local people, for the port was a stopping-place for many ships. There were "friendly" Irish with plaids and copper brooches, British Romans like ourselves, and British tribesmen with long moustaches and woollen cloaks. There were some Armorican Celts from north-west Gaul — they were great sailors, and traded far and wide. The sounds of Latin and several British dialects filled the air, with now and again a word from somewhere even further afield. Not only were there wooden stalls in the square, but there were proper shops in the grey stone buildings around it, so the air was redolent with the smell of fresh bread from the bakery, and smoke from the fish-curers. On the stalls were piled vegetables and fruit, and Rhonwen was soon threading her way through the crowd, arguing with the vendors and trying to get value for Papa's money. She had to account for every *denarius*.

We were down in the market place when the prisoners came through. Rhonwen was looking for vegetables, but I had no eyes for such mundane things today. I was running around, looking here and there and leading Mabanwy a merry dance. Then suddenly a silence fell, as if people were waiting for something. Some word had gone around, perhaps. Then, from the road which led to the fort, we heard the sound of tramping feet.

At the edge of the market place there was a commotion as the crowd were made to part. One or two men shouted abuse at the prisoners, and even demands for their deaths, but the guards told them to be quiet.

"These are the Emperor's property now," the guard commander shouted back. "There'll be no incitement to damage it!"

Property! I shuddered. Imagine belonging to someone else as if you were just an object, or a farm animal! And these men strained at their bonds just like animals, and trudged hopelessly by with heads bowed and gaze averted, as if they really were less than human. It's true that my father kept slaves, but at least he treated them like people. These men had iron collars, with a chain linking one to the next. Their wrists were also bound in iron. The soldiers must have stolen their weapons, and anything valuable, like a good cloak or a piece of armour. The prisoners were dressed in the minimum — simple tunics, mainly, some with leggings. They had red or brown hair and blue eyes, most of them. But those eyes were dull now with defeat and regret. One young fellow wept openly as he shuffled past. Someone muttered about cowardice, but I wondered. Was it cowardice for him to mourn his capture, and the homeland he might never see again? I couldn't see why Irish tears were less sincere than anyone else's. Besides, I found it difficult to be angry with such a downtrodden-looking lot.

Whatever could they have been thinking of, to attack the Empire? Surely barbarians like that would never be a match for our smart Roman legionaries with their polished armour?

As the last of the prisoners trudged off down the road the silence was broken. People turned to discussing the attack, or the price of cabbages. Rhonwen went back to haggling with the stall holders.

"Well," said Mabanwy. "Now you've seen what real Irish pirates look like."

I felt a little disgruntled, though I couldn't say why. Perhaps it was the memory of that weeping youth. I had expected sea monsters and discovered unkempt boys.

"They look just like other people," I retorted, "but sadder and dirtier."

"Don't waste your sympathy on the likes of them, *Dominula*," said Rhonwen. "They deserve hanging."

I was tempted to be rude, but if I was it would be reported to Papa. I said nothing. But inside I rebelled. I think that was the first time I ever questioned the established order.

II

My two brothers were older than I — Kynan by two years and Adeon by five. Inevitably, divided by age and sex, we led largely separate lives. Kynan occasionally spent some time with me, but he was always in the shadow of Adeon, who was a tall and muscular boy, athletic and courageous. He seemed destined from birth to be a soldier, and indeed that was all he ever wanted to be. He had been fed tales of ancient heroes by Nestor, his tutor, till he wanted nothing else. He studied his Greek only to read tales of the Trojan War, and later Alexander's military manuals. The glories of literature were lost on him; he was immersed in the supposed glories of war.

Kynan was a quieter lad — not exactly soft, but of a more intellectual turn of mind. When he was made to study great literature he found he loved it, and was keen to improve his Greek because it enabled him to read Socrates and Plato. He was as good an athlete as most, especially on the running track. He ran a lot, and always stayed thin as a result. Rhonwen used to try to fatten him up, but it did no good. When he was older he did well enough at his military training, but he regarded it as a necessary evil. In more peaceful times he would have turned his attention to other pursuits, while Adeon would have gone off to find a war somewhere else.

I often wonder what would have become of them if their little sister's life had not taken an unexpected turn and cut across theirs, as a sea current cuts across the bow of a ship and turns it aside.

Still, that was far ahead in an uncertain future. My life at Segontium was a good one. If great events were afoot in the world they seldom troubled our little corner of it. There was the year of the Great Barbarian Conspiracy, of course. I remember much talk of that when I was small. It had been the year before I watched the sea battle with Mabanwy from the heights above Segontium. Indeed, it was the Conspiracy which had led to the building of the fortified harbour at Cair Gybi, as I later understood. It was a frightening event, because for once the disorganised and quarrelsome barbarians had buried their differences and attacked together. The Picts attacked Britain from the north and the Irish from the west. Two of the most senior commanders in Britain were killed. It transpired that the *areani*, the border scouts on Hadrian's Wall, had actually been working for the Picts, feeding false information back to their own officers. At the same time the Franks and the Saxons crossed the Rhine and attacked Gaul. Towns were burned, crops ruined, temples plundered — the wild men strode across the Western Empire and rocked it to its very foundations.

By sheer chance the Emperor Valentinian was visiting Gaul at the time, and was able to mount an immediate counter attack. The barbarians' basic lack of discipline and organisation let them down, as so often before. They were beaten, but the attack left deep scars in the memories of Roman citizens everywhere in the West. A special task force was sent to Britain to repel the invaders and restore order. It was led by the great commander Theodosius. The following year he came to inspect the defences at Cair Gybi and Segontium.

With him he brought my future husband.

*

"Rhonwen! Rhonwen! Damn it, where is the woman?"

Servants scuttled in all directions around the sunlit central courtyard of our villa, looking for the housekeeper. It was not like her to be missing, and not like my father to be in such an agitated condition. At last Rhonwen emerged red-faced from the latrine block. This was across the courtyard from her usual post in the kitchen, and next to the bath house. My father, usually a considerate man, was oblivious to her embarrassment.

"Ah, there you are, Rhonwen! Now listen to me carefully. I'm sorry for the short notice. I know it'll make things difficult, but there's no help for it. I have just had word that a very important visitor — a *very* important visitor — is coming to Segontium tonight. Both he and his senior officer will be staying with us for two nights, possibly longer. You must provide the best possible food. No expense is to be spared. None whatever!"

"No expense? Good gracious, *Domine*, who's coming — the Emperor?"

Rhonwen could get away with that, being a valued servant and not a slave. My father's sense of humour had deserted him, however.

"What? No, no, no. It's the *Comes* Theodosius. And his deputy, Maximus, a great general. See that rooms are made ready for them, and then come to me in the study to discuss tonight's menu."

With that he was gone. Mabanwy and I, who had witnessed the scene, stood open-mouthed. Papa, taking an interest in the menu! It was unheard of. Usually, as he dined alone, he dined simply, and ate what was put in front of him. Even when there were guests he tended to leave everything to Rhonwen. He realised she knew her business better than he did.

Later, finding myself at a loose end for a few minutes, I contrived to be playing outside the study window. As it was a warm day the shutters were open and I could hear Papa and Rhonwen talking, while she made notes on a wax tablet. She was not actually very literate, but she could write or draw little reminders for herself.

"We have plenty of eggs, *Domine*," she was saying. "I thought an egg salad to start with — the kitchen garden has some lovely lettuces and green vegetables."

"Have we any fish?" interjected Papa. "The *Comes* is from Spain — they like a lot of fish."

Rhonwen sighed. "With respect, *Domine*, maybe they do, but it could still be that *he* doesn't. Or maybe he's sick of fish, because everyone always gives it him, because they know he's from Spain. Perhaps he'd like a refreshing salad, with eggs and Rhonwen's own special dressing?"

"Ah, yes. Now that's a good idea. Very well. What can you suggest for the main course?"

"I thought maybe venison, *Domine*. We have some nicely hung, just right. I'd do my usual sauce, I thought."

Rhonwen's venison sauce was a long-winded recipe with honey, vinegar, herbs, pepper, oil, and Italian *liquamen* sauce, made from fermented fish. I could see the kitchen maids would be busy tonight. She went on to discuss the fried cakes and fruit she would serve as the last course.

12

"And I had another thought, *Domine*. I dare say you'll offer the guests a bath when they arrive?"

"But of course."

"Then, I could serve them some wine and small snacks — olives, shellfish, little bread pieces, that sort of thing — when they first arrive. That would take the edge off their hunger before their bath. By the time they've spent an hour or so in the bath house they'll have a good appetite again."

"Yes, Rhonwen. Excellent!"

So Rhonwen went about her business, and I pretended my presence was entirely coincidental as she came out and saw me. Then, I was nearly seven and thought I was a pretty good actress. Now, I don't suppose she was fooled for a second.

"You'd better run along, now, *Dominula*," was all she said. "Mabanwy will be looking for you to give you your bath."

Mabanwy soon caught up with me, and rushed me off to the bath house so that it could be cleaned up again in time for the guests. We had a very well-appointed bath house. It was fed by a natural stream which came down from the hills above and had been diverted to run into the villa grounds. Just after it passed under the wall by a culvert there was a stone tank where we drew fresh water for the house. Then the water channel led to the baths. There was a cold bath, and another one heated by a furnace, and also a steam bath where people could sit in the heat and sweat themselves clean. After that the water flowed out to the latrines, which were at a lower level, and it was used to flush them out. It was a very ingenious system, and one of the many advantages which Roman civilisation had brought to Britain. My father, who had to deal with all kinds of petitioners, said it was a pity that more of the population didn't appreciate it.

When Mabanwy had plunged me in the warm bath and scrubbed me all over with a sponge I usually had time for some water play, but not tonight. I was hastily towelled and wrapped in my little woollen cloak before being rushed across the yard to the living quarters. Slaves moved in to clean the bath house after us.

Up the back stairs we went to the little room that I shared with Mabanwy. Adeon and Kynan were nominally her charges, too, but they spent a lot of time with their tutor. They were considered too old to share a room with a female, and shared one with each other instead. Tonight, however, they would be inspected and groomed by Mabanwy, for we were all to be presented to the guests. My father was probably hoping to bring his sons to the attention of the great visitors. This would have no immediate effect, but if they were in military or public service later on it might not do any harm to have Theodosius say: "Isn't that old Eudav's lad? I met him once, you know. A good boy." This sort of patronage was my father's dream, as it was the dream of so many other provincial officials.

Mabanwy brushed my hair thoroughly, and then went to see to the boys. Floating up through the window came the sounds and smells of the kitchen. Rhonwen was busy tonight, and to judge by the clatterings and scrapings the kitchen was full of helpers, too. The evening sun was dimming now, but the air was still warm. Leaning on the window ledge I could look out over the courtyard and see the hills of Arfon rearing up behind. High above, swifts looped and fluttered, and blackbirds trilled in the bushes. Here and there a wisp of smoke showed against the skyline, where there stood one of the numerous farmsteads which covered the hillside. What a peaceful scene it was. How could anyone seek to disturb it?

Mabanwy disturbed me at this point. "Dreaming again? You're a great dreamer, young Helena."

"Not really," I said. "I was just looking at the view, wondering what the people in all the little houses are doing."

"Dreaming, as I said. Fine for those who have time for it," she retorted, but without malice. "Now, *Dominula*, we'll have some nice ribbons in that hair before you meet the guests."

"What? Surely they're not here yet?"

"No, not for ages yet. But there's no harm in being ready ahead of time."

She was cut short by the clatter of approaching hooves. We heard the riders trot in by the archway which led almost under our room. I rushed to the window, and peeped out. There were several riders in the courtyard, for such important men always rode everywhere with a bodyguard. The common soldiers would be fed in the kitchen and would sleep in the barn, while their leaders dined on Roman couches and slept on feather mattresses. Mabanwy shooed me away from the window as the grooms took the horses and the guests entered the house.

We ate in the boys' room while the guests were using the bath house with Papa. Both Kynan and Adeon were highly excited by the arrival of Theodosius.

"He's a very famous soldier," said Kynan, chewing his bread.

"One of our Empire's greatest generals," Adeon said pompously.

"Yes," said Kynan, "and a great favourite of the Emperor's. He spends a lot of time in Mediolanum."

Adeon had a more cynical view. "More likely the Emperor wants to see he isn't getting too popular. Emperors don't like generals to be too popular. Too often they decide to be Emperor instead. That's what Nestor says. Many a great general has ended up losing his head for being too well-liked by the troops."

"That really is silly," put in Mabanwy. "It means the general gets killed if he fails, but probably killed if he succeeds as well."

"Ah," said Adeon, "but if he succeeds then maybe he really will become Emperor. After all, it's the Army who decides who's Emperor."

"It's the Senate in Rome that elects the Emperor," said Mabanwy. "I'm sure your tutor told you that, too."

"Oh, yes," sneered Adeon. "The Senate elects the Emperor, but they only ever elect the Army's favourite, or they'd *all* lose their heads."

As I later had cause to know, there was more than enough truth in Adeon's cynical view. Being half a soldier already, he couldn't see why a general might not make the best Emperor. Anyway, in times of barbarian invasion he may have been right.

When we had finished eating, and Mabanwy had made sure we looked tidy, we were taken down to say goodnight to Papa and his guests. They were about to start their meal, later than my father's usual time. That was why he wanted us out of the way so early. I remember being very shy as we filed into the dining room one behind the other, Adeon leading and me bringing up the rear. The three men were sitting in a row like judges at a tribunal, Papa to the left. The strangers were certainly important men — they wore full Roman togas in fine material. One of them, grey-haired and distinguished looking, had a sash of silk. That must be Theodosius, I decided. He also wore several bejewelled rings and a small gold crucifix. The other was much younger, more simply dressed, and his skin was tanned as if he came from a sunny country. Adeon strode proudly up to stand before the adults. He bowed politely to the guests and then spoke.

"We have come to pay our respects to your guests, Papa, and to say goodnight."

"Yes, my boy. Introduce your brother and sister."

Adeon did so, and I curtsied shyly.

"They're fine children," said Theodosius, his voice deep and vibrant. When Maximus spoke his voice was almost like a boy's, but clear and confident.

"They've learned their manners well, Eudav," he said. "They're a credit to you, especially since you've had no wife these several years."

Theodosius nodded gravely and beckoned us forward. "Come to the light, children. Come on, I won't eat you."

"I don't know about that, *Domine*," said Maximus. "You said earlier you could eat a small child, provided only that it was well seasoned."

The men laughed, but I felt very much on edge. I knew it was meant as a joke, of course, but it did nothing to dispel my awe of the *Comes*.

"And what do you want to do in life?" Theodosius asked Adeon.

"To be a soldier, *Domine*, and rid the Empire of the barbarians."

Theodosius smiled and said dryly: "Not a bad ambition. How old are you, boy?"

"Eleven, *Domine*."

"And can you use a sword?"

"Yes, *Domine*, and I am better with a bow than many grown men."

It didn't sound like a boast, and it wasn't; Adeon simply knew his own value, even then. Theodosius turned a sceptical gaze on our father, who nodded. "It's true, *Domine*. He has a gift for military skills, I think."

16

"In that case, young Adeon, when you are old enough, you get your father to write to me, if I am still alive, or to young Maximus here if not. If you go on as you have begun there will be a commission for you in the Imperial Army."

Adeon blushed to the roots of his hair. "Oh, thank you, *Domine*. Thank you!"

"Such ambitions are to be encouraged, young man. The good Lord knows we have need of stout hearts and stout forearms."

"And what of the other two?" said Maximus gently. "Oh, I suppose they're too young yet to have any idea."

Kynan hung back, but I resented being dismissed so lightly.

"*Domine*," I said loudly, "if the men are all out fighting the barbarians, I suppose the women will have to run everything else until they return. That's what I'll have to do, I expect."

Theodosius covered his smile with his hand, but Maximus burst out laughing.

"Oh, Eudav, this one's got spirit! And just look at her, *Domine*, now she's in the light. I swear she'll be a great beauty one day. I'd be putting in a bid for her myself, but I'm married already!"

All three men laughed aloud at this. I smiled uneasily, not quite sure what the joke was. Actually, I knew betrothals of children were quite common, even if the marriage had to wait for several years. But I couldn't see me marrying Maximus or Theodosius, even if they hadn't been married already. We weren't exactly peasants, but we were hardly in their class.

The next day the men went out early to inspect the defences. They were gone all day, and when they returned they shut themselves in my father's study until late in the evening, discussing plans and sharing their opinions. It was the day after that before I saw them again, and even so it was only when they were moving on.

The horses were held ready while the *Comes* and Maximus made their farewells to Papa. Today they had their uniforms on, with armour and red cloaks. The boys and I were lined up with Mabanwy to say a formal farewell. Theodosius stopped before us, his great cloak flapping in the breeze. With his carefully tailored and ornately decorated armour, polished to a shine, he seemed like

17

a figure from one of the epic poems of legend that Papa listened to so avidly.

"I thank you for your hospitality, Eudav. You've done us proud. It's much appreciated."

"You're very kind, *Domine*, but I'm sure you're used to much grander surroundings than this."

"I am," said the *Comes* frankly, "and what a bore such formal grandeur can be. You've no idea what a relief it is to be a guest in a comfortable house for a change, amongst a decent family. Am I not right, Maximus?"

"Indeed you are, *Domine*, and I add my thanks to yours."

Theodosius turned to speak to the rest of us.

"Farewell, children." And to Adeon: "I meant what I said; get your father to write if you want a place in the Army."

"Thank you, *Domine*. I will."

Maximus stepped up to us, and crouched down so as to bring himself to our level.

"Farewell, boys. Keep up your weapon practice. I fear these are times when it's needed. As for you, young lady, you're a sweetheart. For two pins I'd take you home with me."

He rose again and swept me up in his arms. "Look, Eudav, I'm taking her with me!"

Theodosius and my father smiled indulgently, while Maximus held me up and kissed my cheek. Then he put me down and strode towards his horse, which was waiting patiently by the mounting block. I was nearly dead of embarrassment, but I waved after the departing visitors until they were out of sight down the road. For years my ideal remained someone like Maximus — distinguished, successful, handsome and kind. I dreamed the dreams young girls do. Then I would remind myself that he was much older than me — and married already. Someone else would happen along, no doubt. In the meantime, nothing Mabanwy could say would stop me dreaming.

18

III

On holidays we used to visit my mother's grave. Papa might have formed an attachment to a slave woman, but Finella could never be his wife. Besides, whatever his personal feelings may have been, people expected that my mother's memory should be preserved. We were a family of mixed British and Roman ancestry, and of royal descent, but Papa always tried to keep Roman traditions. A small shrine to the household gods graced our entrance hall, and family members continued to be honoured long after their deaths. It was against the law for people to be buried inside towns, but our villa was outside the town limits and so could have its own family cemetery at the rear of the grounds. This little plot, with the stream running nearby, flowers carefully cultivated all around, and with a little shrine in its centre, was a pretty place. Like most Roman citizens, even educated ones, our father had a strong streak of superstition. I think he feared that the spirits of the departed might be angered if their final resting place was not kept properly.

These were the last golden years of the old religions. Christianity was gaining ground fast. For half a century or so, since the days of Constantine the Great, Christianity had enjoyed the status of "most favoured religion". Indeed, so enthusiastic were the Emperors for the cult that they were gradually placing more and more restrictions on all others, although they were not yet banned outright. Strangely enough, it was not the pagans who suffered most at this time, but those Christians considered to be "heretics". Anyone who professed to be a Christian, but not precisely the right sort, was liable to extreme penalties. Even before his own conversion Constantine had started invoking the death penalty against heretics, whose sole crime was to interpret Christianity in a slightly different way from the majority.

To complicate the issue, many Christians of the Eastern Empire were followers of Arius, who had taught that Jesus was the son of God and therefore created by him and subordinate to him. The Catholic Christians considered that the two were equal but separate. The Western Emperors generally leaned towards

Arianism, but were afraid to force the issue because their subjects disagreed. The whole business irritated my father greatly, and did nothing to dissuade him from following his pagan beliefs.

"If you think the son is subordinate to the father you fall into the heresy of Arius," he said to me once. "If you think the two are just different aspects of the same being you fall into the heresy of Sabellius. To be orthodox you have to believe the two are indivisible but separate. It seems a total contradiction to me, or at least a fine distinction, and a damned small point to kill a man for."

Papa had to know about all these religious matters, for they constantly intruded into politics. Disagreements about the nature of the Holy Trinity divided East from West, and Roman from barbarian — most of the barbarian tribes were Arian Christians, having been converted by missionaries from the East. It was mainly the dreaded Huns and Saxons who were pagan.

The Christians also disagreed over which documents were to be accepted as holy scriptures, and people had already been put to death over that issue. These disputes were real to those who believed in them, and all through my growing up they were discussed and argued about by people from all walks of life. There was a growing feeling that Christianity would one day be enforced by law, and I suppose all the different groups wanted to be sure that theirs would be the version which would prevail. My father had his views on this, too.

"How can we tell people what to believe? We can enforce outward compliance, but how can we enforce belief? Anyway, why should we? No-one knows which view is correct — if any — and until the gods write us a letter setting out their requirements in straightforward Latin, I don't suppose we will. All we can do is honour those things which seem good to us, and appease any spirit we seem to have offended."

My father followed a long tradition of religious toleration under the Romans. All that the Roman state required was loyalty, which usually meant the acceptance of the Emperor as an additional god. As the Empire expanded new religious cults were brought to Rome from all over the world. Before Christianity gained acceptance hundreds of them flourished side by side, usually without any serious discord. The main exception to this rule had been the Christians themselves, who were persecuted savagely at one time. Not that Papa approved of that.

"I don't defend it," he said to me once, "but you must remember they brought much of their trouble upon themselves. Their steadfast refusal to tolerate any point of view other than their own made them the natural enemy of almost everyone else, and they were a handy scapegoat when one was needed. That's how the Emperor Nero was able to blame them for the burning of Rome — although he probably did it himself."

When I was thirteen some of these issues came suddenly closer to home, for many other people besides me. In that year the Emperor Valentinian died — died, it was said, in a fit of apoplexy at the behaviour of some barbarian envoys. In general it made little difference to us who was Emperor. Indeed, it made little difference where. The seat of government used to be Rome; then it was Mediolanum. Later in my life it was split between Ravenna and Constantinople. But we were a long way from the centre of things — a remote part of a remote province.

Things changed on the death of Valentinian. His son Gratian, who succeeded him, was a young man in his twenties. And a religious fanatic.

*

I first became aware of the implications when Papa returned home one evening in a dark mood.

"I've often thought of retiring," he growled. "Maybe now is the time. Send for some wine, will you, Helena? I need a little sweetener this evening."

I gestured to a slave, who slipped out at once.

Adeon, who was virtually a man by now, was awaiting a reply to our father's letter to Theodosius. Papa obviously hoped that Theodosius would remember his promise and take Adeon under his wing. To be the protégé of such a great man would give him a flying start in his career. However, Theodosius was away fighting barbarians in Africa, and Papa's letter would have to wait for its reply until he returned to Mediolanum. In the meantime Adeon

21

took a great interest in all public affairs, including our father's work.

"What's the matter?"

"A dispatch from the Prefect. It's going out to all district governors. This damned Gratian means to make his mark."

"Don't all new emperors do that?"

Papa shook his head abruptly.

"If that were all it was... No, he means business, I'm afraid."

"What has he done?"

"In the first place, he is associating his brother, the younger Valentinian, as co-Emperor in charge of Italy. His uncle Valens is still in control of the East, of course. We'll end up as a federation of kingdoms if this keeps up."

"There could be sound strategic reasons for that, Papa." Adeon had lost none of his pomposity as he had grown. He talked like a manual of strategy these days. "There are different barbarian threats to each of those regions. I can see there could be sense in giving each its own commander."

"Hm! Maybe, if that were all. What may have escaped your notice is that this means Gratian can give all of his attention to the Prefecture of Gaul. And let me remind you that that includes not only Gaul itself, but also Spain and Britain. I feel bad enough about that — it's as if the distance between me and His Imperial Majesty has suddenly got uncomfortably small — but there's worse to come. The final section of the dispatch deals with religious practices. Gratian has the thundering impudence to remind us of what he calls our holy duty to combat paganism in all its forms. He urges us to close and demolish pagan temples, and authorises — no, orders — the use of Imperial troops for the purpose! Damn him, half of his officials are pagans themselves! Just by way of encouragement, he is sending officials to inspect the situation for him. I suppose I'll have to close some temples or be retired without a pension!"

Kynan had been studying one of his many Greek scrolls while this discussion proceeded. Now he looked up.

"I suppose the Emperor can decide what he likes, Papa?"

"The Emperor is a child! He's hardly any older than Adeon!"

Adeon bridled at this.

"Well, I'm not a child!"

"No, son, not compared with this idiot. I'm sure you wouldn't deal with so many people so crassly. Why, he must have offended half the Western Empire with this one document. May the gods preserve us, he's young enough to reign for fifty years! What damage he could do!"

He subsided as the slave came back with the wine. Treason was treason, even if spoken by a governor and reported by a slave.

"You can go, now," said Papa. "We'll call if we want anything."

The man withdrew, shutting the door behind him. Kynan resumed the conversation.

"Surely most of the people here are pagan, anyway, aren't they?"

Our father nodded. "Most. The sailors have brought gods from all over the Empire, but there's little mention of Jesus."

"It seems to me that's a much more important fact than anything in the Emperor's dispatch, then."

Papa looked at him with a sort of bemused tolerance. I loved him in that moment. Many a father would have slapped his son down for such presumption, but ours was listening as if he might receive useful advice.

"What do you mean?"

"Papa, you are angry because the Emperor is riding roughshod over the wishes of his people. But that is his legal right as Emperor. We can't change that, so there's no point in getting upset about it. We must simply see to it that his decision has no effect."

Papa paused for a moment. Then a smile spread slowly over his face.

"By Jupiter, you're a cool one. They should make you governor instead of me! Of course, you're absolutely right. I am letting my anger blind me, and it's no use kicking against the law. It's practical measures we need. Have you anything in mind?"

He turned his amused expression on Kynan again, as if he expected little of substance to follow now.

"If you can find out when this official is coming to make his inspection, I think all the temples should be shut on that day to mark the feast of the goddess Arcana."

23

Our father stroked his chin. "I know there are a great many goddesses, but I don't believe I've heard of that one before, son."

"No," said Kynan with a grin. "That's because I've just invented her. Arcana — 'secret', you see. She's the goddess of secrecy and, and closed doors."

"Go on."

"Well, you order all the temples closed and chained up for the duration of the inspector's visit. You present it to the priests as a religious observance, and tell each one to display a notice declaring the temple closed by order of the governor. In fact, you'd better have the notices painted specially, so as to be sure the wording is exactly how you want it. Then you take the inspector round on a tour of the district. Pack him off again as quickly as possible."

"And what if the inspector talks to any of the priests?"

"Is it likely? He's bound to be a Christian, if he's been given a task of this sort. Don't they consider pagan priests to be agents of the devil, or something?"

"Something like that. Do you know, young man, I think you might have something there."

And our father went out chuckling. Adeon was offended — he thought that as elder son it was his place to advise Papa. But such guile was not his strong point. His strength would be on the battlefield. Besides, he cared little for religion. He would follow a man he could see, not a god that he couldn't. He would probably observe outwardly whatever religion was current wherever he was posted, as many of the soldiers did.

Papa visited all the local pagan priests and told them he would be closing their temples for an unspecified period. He dropped them more than a hint of his true intention, and they complied readily enough. They knew there was little chance of getting a pagan Emperor back now. The last one had been Julian the Apostate, who had died twelve years before after a reign of only three. Too little time to undo the work of fifty years of Christian domination. Perhaps, though, a period of toleration might come about, if the pagans kept their heads down. That, at least, was their hope. Myself, I doubt whether the tide of Christian influence will ever be rolled back, unless the Empire goes with it, but in those days I could not look so far ahead. At the age of thirteen I had other things on my mind.

Mabanwy had been my nurse since I was a baby. She had never remarried, although there had been occasional suitors. And why not? She was a pleasant and cheerful woman, and good looking in a wholesome, country girl's way. But she told me she was not keen to marry again.

"Look at the position I have here," she said to me. "I may be a servant, but your father treats us all well. I have my own money, free time of my own, and I don't spend every spare moment attending to the needs of some man, nor his brood of children!"

"Don't you like children?" I asked, surprised and a little fearful.

"My dear Helena, of course I do! You and the boys, even other people's children sometimes. But that doesn't mean I want a horde of my own. Why, I'd have to leave here and look after them, then, wouldn't I?"

I hadn't thought of that. Mabanwy was the nearest I had known to a mother, and I suppose I had thought of her as part of the household, rather than an employee who might leave one day. I had taken her for granted, and it was a shock to realise that what had seemed such a permanent part of my world was so insecure. What else was I taking for granted?

The last days of childhood were slipping away. A few days after that I woke up to find blood on my sheets and realised I had become a woman. I was frightened at first and called for Mabanwy.

"It's nothing to be frightened of, silly," she said, cuddling me. "It's a natural thing. You know what it means. You're not a child any longer."

"But that's just it," I sniffed. "I'm not ready to be a woman. I am still a child."

She held me tight to her. "Don't worry, little one. We won't be expecting too much of you just yet."

"Oh, Mabanwy, I don't know what I'd do without you! Stay with me for always. Say you will!"

She chuckled loudly. "You'll want me out of your hair soon enough, I shouldn't wonder — probably when some nice young gentleman comes along. Don't worry, little one, I'm not going anywhere just yet."

The Imperial official duly arrived. His name was Sestius, and he was a thin grouchy man with a great sense of his own importance. He grumbled about the accommodation Papa had arranged for him. Papa had made some excuse for not having him to stay at our house, in case he noticed the pagan shrine in the hall, or our lack of Christian devotion. Sestius also grumbled about the Welsh weather, which had turned cold and was as wet as only Wales can be. It was soon clear to Papa that, although the man was a Christian, he was not inclined to pursue his duties too assiduously. A drive around the neighbourhood in a covered carriage was his idea of checking upon the situation. He saw the notices proclaiming the temples closed, saw the chains across their doors, and was satisfied. The entire community prayed for rain and cold to drive the visitor away. Whether or not their prayers were responsible, he cut short his intended stay and departed, pleading rheumatism and professing himself satisfied with Papa's measures. We breathed a sigh of relief, but Kynan thought it premature.

"We may have beaten this one," he said, "but he was a lazy and inefficient fellow. What happens when another edict is issued, and more officials come to see it carried out? We can't rely on them all being idiots, nor on the weather always taking our side."

There was no answer to that. Our community's traditions were safe for the moment and that was the best we could hope for.

In fact, there was one tradition that was causing me some anxiety. In the early days of the Empire the government had been worried that there would not be enough Romans to run it. The Emperor Augustus, and others after him, had introduced extra taxes on single men, and advantages for those who married and had children. The tradition had arisen that people married young — girls could be married from the age of twelve years, and boys from fourteen. While a girl would not be married before she achieved physical womanhood, I had now qualified and Mabanwy would have to tell my father that there was no impediment to his seeking a husband for me. Yet, as I had said to her, I still felt like a child. I was not ready for the responsibilities of adult life. It was true that the British had always married rather later than the Romans, but in our very Romanised family it was a rare girl that was not married by fifteen or sixteen at the latest. I almost envied Adeon for being a boy; his avowed intention to seek a commission in the army meant that he would not be pressed to take a wife just yet.

"Now, now," said Mabanwy when I expressed my fears to her. "You mustn't worry about that. What could be more natural than marriage for a young girl?"

"Then why don't you remarry?"

"Well, I..."

"You told me yourself that you weren't keen to marry again. Why not, if it's so natural?"

"Helena, your position is very different from mine. If I married, it would be a poor man, probably, with years of childbearing and housekeeping in front of me. But you? Why, you'll marry a wealthy man of good family, with lots of servants and slaves to keep your house for you. If you have children you'll get the best midwife and the best of help when the babies are born."

She broke off, frowning. "Is it that you're worried about the getting of children?"

"Well, no, that is, partly, I suppose."

"Bless you, child, that is the most natural part of it."

Mabanwy sat back with a faraway look on her face. "To lie with the man you love, to feel his arms around you, your bodies melting together as if they were one — there's nothing to fear about that."

"What is it like, Mabanwy?"

"Like? It's only itself. It isn't like anything, unless it's maybe flying, or riding a sea-wave till it crashes on the shore. Oh, Helena, I don't think it's like anything. But I tell you this — it's the only thing I miss about marriage."

She saw my bemused expression.

"Oh, I'm shameless, aren't I? I don't mean it the way it may have sounded. It's the being together — the closeness. There's no shame in being close to the man you love, Helena."

"But my father will choose a husband. How can I be sure I will love him?"

"You will grow to love him, if he's a good man."

27

"And if he isn't? What then? What if I don't love him, ever?"

"Your father will only choose a good man, you'll see." Then she giggled. "And if the worst comes to the worst, there's always divorce. Only don't marry a Christian — they don't believe in divorce."

I forgot about the conversation for a while, but I remembered it a few weeks later, when Papa came home with some news.

"You remember Magnus Maximus, who visited us with the *Comes* Theodosius? He's coming to look at the defences again — something to do with rumours about the Picts mobilising. It'll be a discreet visit, I understand, with no official functions or anything. He's still in mourning. His wife has died, poor man."

IV

When Maximus arrived he was a different man from the previous time. I knew he would be older, of course, although he was still a young man, no more than thirty. But he was not just older; he had *aged*. His dark hair was greying, and that was part of it. But there was more than that. His face looked more worn — at least, more worn than I remembered. And his eyes had changed. There had been a sparkle in them, a merriness that had faded. They had been open windows on his bubbling personality. Now they were merely organs for seeing.

"Poor man," I thought. "He must miss his wife dreadfully. What a terrible thing to do to him."

It seemed to my juvenile mind almost as if she were to be blamed for dying.

He had arrived on the afternoon of a windswept spring day. I was in the lane with Kynan when I heard his horse's hooves crunching on the stones. We looked up and saw him coming, another officer riding alongside him, as he himself had once ridden alongside Theodosius, the *Comes*. My smile of recognition obviously appealed to him, and he reined in his horse by our side.

"Good day to you."

"Good day, *Domine*," we chorused.

He looked us up and down.

"It can't be," he said. "You can't be Eudav's younger two, can you?"

"Yes, *Domine*."

"Well, well, I don't visit often enough! Just look at these two, Marcus. This young lady was a tiny tot when I saw her last. The sweetest little thing you ever saw. And she still is, though not so little!"

He chuckled, and I blushed to the roots of my hair. He turned to Kynan. "And you're Kynan, of course."

"Er, yes, *Domine*." Kynan was as tongue-tied as I, flabbergasted that this great man had bothered to remember his name.

"Well, you're quite the young man now, Kynan. Is your brother here, or is he away with the army?"

"He's waiting for a reply, *Domine*. My father wrote to the *Comes*, as he asked him."

"Theodosius?" Maximus's eyes clouded over. "Ah, well, I have news for your father about that. Still, that's old men's talk, for later. This is my right-hand man, Marcus Drustanus."

The younger officer saluted over-elaborately and patronisingly, and we turned to walk with them up to the villa. In well-to-do families there were always servants and slaves to wait at table. However, as a sign of respect a particularly honoured guest might be waited on by the host's wife. My father had no wife, and Finella had no official existence, so I took on the role for the first time that evening. Kynan, much to his disgust, had to help, too. Adeon, also to Kynan's disgust, was deemed old enough to join the men at dinner.

I wore a new white linen robe that Mabanwy had made for me after persuading Papa to buy the material at the port. It was very sophisticated for an adolescent girl from a provincial family — elegantly waisted with one shoulder bare. To top it off she had spent ages putting my hair up for me in an elaborate coiffure, piled high on top, but with ringlets dangling at the sides — very Grecian, and very much the fashion at that time. Papa didn't quite approve in a way — he thought it rather too adult a style — but he was proud of me too. I could see that in the way he tutted about the effect, but smiled, and he didn't tell me to undo the coiffure and brush it out.

The men were sitting and talking when we brought in their first course — a dish of seasoned shellfish which had become one of Rhonwen's specialities. Maximus and Marcus complimented Papa on his son and daughter, and Adeon smirked to show his superiority over these mere children. The visitors also complimented Papa on his cook when they tasted the food. I have always born in mind that a good cook is half the battle if you want to make a mark on society!

We had to wait at a discreet distance, so that we would know when to clear the dishes away. Consequently we overheard a lot of the dinner conversation. There was little small talk; it was mostly politics, as usual.

"Gratian worries me," Papa was saying. "It doesn't do to upset people so much, and so soon after getting into office. I know, of course, that Christianity is a growing force at court, but it cannot be imposed."

"I'm not so sure," said Maximus. "We need the pagan aristocracy for now, but there may come a time when their numbers make them insignificant. Then I can see that an emperor — especially an incoming emperor — might simply decide to make a clean sweep."

"But you can't tell people what to think!" exclaimed Papa.

"No? We do it all the time. We tell people to accept the law, to honour His Majesty, to reject the barbarians..."

"But that's just outward compliance," protested Papa. "It's not the same thing as belief."

"I'm not so sure," said Maximus. "We can never tell what a man thinks, but if we control what he does it comes pretty close. After a while people accept what they're used to seeing all around them, especially if their nice government careers depend upon compliance. If paganism were banned, my bet is that there would be no serious educated opposition. There'd be heretical groups, of course, as there are now, and we'd be busy for centuries trying to stop the peasants from lighting their Beltane bonfires and so on. But, all in all, I'd say the ruling classes would accept it."

Maximus was a prophet. It was not until years later, but things happened more or less as he said.

"That's all very well," put in Marcus, "but Gratian could easily make a complete mess of things the way he's going. If he doesn't get himself organised properly and deal with these barbarians there'll be no ruling class, and nothing for them to rule."

"Take care," warned Maximus. "That could be called treason."

Marcus merely snorted, but he fell silent again.

We served Rhonwen's spiced roast beef, and picked up more scraps of conversation.

"These barbarian attacks in Gaul worry me, too," admitted Maximus. "We seem to be dealing with them in a very piecemeal fashion. Gratian's young, he lacks experience, and he won't be told what to do by his commanders. The army ends up running here and there, but not really taking them on and doing something decisive about them."

"Is it the Saxons there, too?" asked my father.

"Yes, they're the worst. But the Franks are on the northern border in force. They take our side sometimes..."

"If we pay enough!" interjected Marcus.

"...if we pay, true. But I don't trust them either. Nor the Allemanni, nor the Suevi. They're all barbarians, and they all want to overrun us. If it were me, I'd hold the border firmly, and punish all transgressions. Then I'd follow a policy of friendly trade on generous terms, so they'd have a stronger stake in staying at peace."

"Do they trade?" asked Papa with a sneer. "I thought they were only pirates."

"Not at all. They farm, they make things, they trade. Oh, there's plenty of opportunity for peaceful interaction. But they must be kept in their place, too. Show weakness and they will turn pirate, because it's easier. But try telling Gratian..."

He leaned back and sighed, obviously convinced he could do the job better. We cleared the dishes, and brought in their fruit. Then we left amid thanks and compliments. But my mind was racing ... treason was being spoken in our house, and Papa was allowing it.

Late in the night I awoke, needing to relieve myself. After a few moments testing the air I decided to go out to the latrine block. I hated using the chamber pot unless it was absolutely necessary, and it seemed quite a warm night. Mabanwy was snoring happily in her bed across the room as I threw my cloak around me and tiptoed down the stairs.

The courtyard was deserted, or so I thought. There was a light, warm breeze blowing, and the trees rustled overhead. There was no light in the latrine block, but I didn't need it. I found my way to the four-hole stone seat, and began to regret my fastidiousness as the cold penetrated. Still, at least I didn't have to use my cleaning sponge this time. The water for this ran in a channel just behind my feet, and at this time of year it would be even colder!

As I got up and left the building I heard another sound amid the running water and rustling branches. It was almost lost among them, but there was a difference in tone which made it stand out. Was there someone there? All alone in the courtyard? Surely not. An animal, perhaps? But no animal would stray so close to an occupied house, even if it could have climbed our wall. Then the wind dropped for a minute, and I realised a man was crying.

I suppose weeping is weeping, whoever does it, but the sound of a man's deep voice trembling through his tears and sadness always seems worse than any to me. Men are obliged to control their emotions all the time; when their emotion becomes too much, and the self-control goes, it can be terrible to behold. I wasn't frightened, though. I remembered the Irish lad I had seen weeping after his capture. The man I could hear now must surely be Maximus, weeping for his loneliness. A lump came to my throat; I wanted to go to him, to press his head to my juvenile breast, to stroke his forehead and soothe his pain. The image was so intimate that I embarrassed myself. I drew my cloak around me and scuttled indoors.

The next morning Mabanwy and I went for a walk down on the shore. The wind was still blowing, though it had grown cooler, and we wrapped our cloaks around ourselves. It was early, and no one else seemed to be up. I had not slept well, and I wanted to blow away the memory of the weeping man.

We strolled along the shingle between large outcrops of rock. The tide was halfway up, and the waves of a size to crash on the shoreline and rattle the stones. We had to shout above the noise to talk at all, which is why we failed to hear the two men until we rounded a crag and found ourselves staring at two sets of masculine buttocks.

"Oh!"

They heard Mabanwy's cry above the sound of the surf, and turned to face us. It was Maximus and Marcus, still wet and with plastered-down hair from swimming. Maximus's chest was covered in dark hair, and his body was lean and muscular, and very tanned. It had been exposed to the sun a lot, then. It had been exposed to violence, too; a long scar ran from his left nipple to his right hip — presumably a sword slash. Then the men threw their cloaks around themselves to preserve the decencies. Both sides muttered apologies and we hurried away, stifling our embarrassed laughter. I had seen my brothers naked when we were small, but this was... different.

"Oh, dear!" cried Mabanwy. "What a thing to happen! The commander and his assistant, naked as babes! Oh, I hope your father won't be cross!"

"Why should he be?" I demanded. "It was an accident."

"Yes, well, part of my duty is to see you are not exposed to things a young lady shouldn't be exposed to. I don't seem to have succeeded too well this morning!"

"Many girls my age are married by now," I pointed out. "Anyway, if it comes to that, I wasn't exposed to very much — not what I would have expected."

She looked at me closely, reddening, as if trying to guess my meaning. Then the struggle to keep a straight face was lost, and she gave an unladylike bellow of coarse laughter.

"Not what you... oh, that's a good one! Give the poor fellows a chance, they were hardly out of the water!"

When she saw my puzzled expression she explained. "It's the cold, you see, *Dominula*. It ... shrinks things!"

She went off into another shriek of laughter.

"Oh, dear, I shouldn't talk to you like this. I'm supposed to lead you in the path of probity and respectability!"

I linked my arm through hers.

"Dear Mabanwy, you only tell me things I will have to know. You're the only mother I've ever had, and I know you'll look after me. I'm in no danger of leaving the path of respectability while you're around."

Looking back I think it was about this time that I began to find Segontium, where I had always been happy, a rather limited world. Adeon was already finding it so, but he had a ready-made way out via the army, in spite of some very bad news which was brought to Maximus while he was with us. He had an arrangement whereby news was brought regularly by Imperial courier wherever he was. On this occasion the man brought a sealed dispatch from Maximus's man in Londinium, with the news that Theodosius, whom he already knew to have been arrested at Carthage, had now been executed there on Gratian's orders.

"It is a terrible thing to happen," said Maximus, visibly shaken.

"Terrible. Not just for his family, or for me personally — I liked him well — but for this province. He did so much to defend it from the barbarians. And Gaul, too. There'll be sadness there at this news."

My father was aghast. "What cause could there possibly be? Theodosius was a bulwark against the barbarians. Has the Emperor gone mad?"

Maximus just shrugged. "Treason is what they say, but it always is. I don't know the details yet. I dare say I'll get those unofficially from my friends, and a version of the truth, too."

"What do you mean, *Domine*?" I asked him. "Don't you believe the dispatch?"

"Helena!"

"No, no, Eudav, why shouldn't she ask? No, young lady, I don't believe my old friend Theodosius was a traitor. He might have spoken out of turn behind His Majesty's back, of course — not far enough behind it if this is the result. These blasted emperors often see plots and threats everywhere, at least until they're experienced enough to use some judgement. A careless remark can cost a man his life sometimes, but a traitor is something Theodosius could never be. I must write to his wife and son. They will need their friends at this time."

"How old is the son?" asked Papa.

"A little younger than me. He's called Theodosius as well. He's doing very well in the army, out east somewhere."

He turned to Adeon. "Well, young man, I said I'd take you on if anything happened to Theodosius. If your father agrees you can go with me when I leave."

Adeon's face lit up. "Oh, yes, *Domine*. Please."

Papa nodded. "Yes, it's time he started his career properly. He can go, and I'm very grateful to you for taking him under your wing."

All well and good! But who would take *me* under their wing?

My dissatisfaction grew steadily as the days went by, turning spring into summer. Maximus returned to Londinium. He and Papa got on well, and he left with a standing invitation to make a private visit any time he was free. Adeon, of course, went with him; Kynan began to mature quickly when relieved of the burden

35

of living in our brother's shadow. Soon I was fourteen, and also growing up. For the first time I began to notice that men's heads would turn when I was out in the town. Mabanwy noticed it, too, and warned me to do nothing to encourage it.

"You've got a reputation to keep now," she said. "You're not a child any longer."

Mabanwy was always with me now. It was as well that I never tired of her company. I think now that she was better for me in many ways than a mother would have been. We got on almost like sisters; I felt no need to rebel against her authority, as I might have done with a mother, but I respected her greater experience. It was a happy combination, especially when there were daunting prospects to be faced.

As when Papa told me one evening he was thinking of arranging a marriage for me.

"Helena, my dear, I've been doing some thinking."

"That sounds ominous, Papa."

He chuckled. "Now, you must be serious a moment, my dear. This is important."

"Sorry, Papa, please go on." I sat down on the couch opposite him. He looked nervous...

"Well, my dear."

And he kept calling me "my dear".

"Helena, the fact is that you're not really a child any longer. Indeed, physically speaking, you are a young woman and have been so for some time. The time is fast approaching when you will have to assume the responsibilities of a young woman."

A pang of anxiety went through me. I could see where this was leading.

"Papa..."

"No, Helena, listen to me. I think I hadn't noticed until that evening when you and Kynan served dinner for Maximus. You looked very beautiful indeed — for the first time I saw that you are a beautiful young woman. You would grace any man's home, and it is my duty as a father to find you a suitable husband. I should have given my mind to it already, I suppose, but I didn't want to stop thinking of you as a child. I'm afraid I was given little option when I saw how Marcus was looking at you."

36

"Marcus?"

"Oh, nothing improper or anything. No, no, just the natural interest of a man in a beautiful woman. He was very taken with you."

"Not Marcus, father, please."

"Oh, no, certainly not him. He is, I believe, spoken for."

Well, I could be grateful for that, at least. Marcus might have been taken with me, but I had certainly not been taken with him. He had seemed a self-important little man to me.

"No, my dear, I thought... perhaps the son of one of our neighbouring noble families."

"Which one?"

"Well, I haven't got as far as that yet. Many of them are betrothed already, of course, but I should ask around my friends. It really is time."

Time! Suddenly Time, which I had thought of as going too slowly, had sprouted Mercury's wings on his feet.

"Oh, by the way, I heard from Magnus Maximus today. He is taking up my invitation."

"So soon?"

"Next month. He's been appointed *Comes*."

"Well, I hope he fares better than the last one who came."

"Ah, poor Theodosius. Well, we must hope that Maximus is a more... careful man."

I went up to my room and sat on the bed, emotions whirling. A minute later Mabanwy came in and was startled to find me crying my heart out.

"Whatever is it, Dominula? What's the matter?"

Between sobs I told her what my father had said. She sympathised, but also chided me gently.

"There, now, didn't I tell you he'd be looking for a husband for you? You mustn't take on so. It's nothing..."

"Nothing to be afraid of. I know, I know. Oh, Mabanwy, why couldn't I have been born a man? Look at those fat society wives we know. They're like brood mares, and about as intelligent. It's men who have the excitement, and the fun. Adeon's off to join the army."

"Well, that's not fun!"

"It is for him! You know he loves all that sort of thing. And he'll go off and see the world. What will I go and see? I'll probably never even see Londinium."

"Don't you like it here?"

"I like fish, Mabanwy, but I don't want to eat it every mealtime!"

Mabanwy argued no further. She just put her arm around me and let me cry it out, making soothing noises until I calmed down.

"I'm sorry, Mabanwy. It's silly to make such a fuss."

"Ah, no. It's just growing up, *Dominula*. It's never easy."

V

They say that young men think old men are fools, whereas old men *know* young men are fools. It doesn't only apply to men.

After my fourteenth birthday, shortly before Maximus's next visit, my father found a "suitable" young man for me. He was seventeen, and the son of a local landowner. His name was Gaius, and his family was every bit as Romanised as his name. Not that I really minded that, but our own family had Celtic ancestry and was proud of it. It seemed natural to me; after all, the Celts were in Britain long before the Romans, maybe since the dawn of time. The Romans had come only three and a half centuries ago. I admit I was looking for faults. I still wasn't used to the idea of being anyone's wife.

I was in my room with Mabanwy when Gaius and his father arrived. She was brushing my hair out into a rather more demure style than the one I had worn for Maximus.

"That'll be them," she said as we heard the horses pass under the archway and into the courtyard of the villa. "Let's have a look at you, then."

She made me face her, and looked me up and down. Plain but well groomed, I looked — plain white overdress, yellow sash, no make-up, and plain straight hair held back with a yellow ribbon. I wore no jewelry except for a copper bracelet with an enamelled traditional design.

"Hmm," said Mabanwy. "Very nice, I think. The father should be impressed."

"What about the son?"

"He'll do as his father tells him. It's the old man you need to appeal to."

"If I like the young one."

"Hmm."

An eloquent grunt. It meant I too would have to do as my father told me.

We went downstairs to the entrance hall, where Papa was greeting Gaius and his father, Maecius, a balding man who had run to fat. He was dressed in a way which was almost too Roman

— toga, sandals — and what hair he had was trained into a few pathetic curls. I disliked him on sight, which was probably unfair to both him and his son. Then again, they say that if you want to know what a boy will look like in thirty years' time, you should take a look at his father.

And indeed, Gaius was dressed in a similar fashion to his father, although he at least had his hair still. It was reddish-brown and naturally curly. His face was round like his father's; he was slim enough now, but I had an instant vision of him with a middle-aged paunch. His skin was both freckled and spotty — a common enough adolescent affliction, I know, but I had escaped it myself and didn't find it attractive in others. I sighed inwardly.

"You'll take some wine, of course," Papa was saying to Maecius. "Ah, here's my dear Helena. Let me introduce you."

My father formally introduced me to Maecius and then Gaius. I curtsied to the old man and nodded to his son. Both looked me up and down appraisingly, so that I felt like a piece of merchandise. This was quite the opposite of the truth — if we arranged a marriage Papa would have to pay them to take me away! Gaius seemed to have difficulty in keeping in one place, and shifted gradually across the hall, looking everywhere but at me.

"Why don't you take young Gaius out and show him the grounds?" suggested Papa. "Mabanwy can go with you."

Mabanwy would have to. A young lady could not go out alone with a man, not even if he was to be her husband. I smiled and tried to put a brave face on it. I felt instinctively it was all going to be disastrous.

40

"Please come this way," I said to Gaius, who appeared to be trying to get me and my thin linen dress between him and the window. I waited for him to go in front, and Mabanwy and I followed him out.

"Where can he have got this one?" I muttered to Mabanwy in passing.

"Don't judge too soon. Talk to him."

"*Can* he talk?"

She shushed me impatiently and we followed Gaius out into the courtyard. It was a pleasant warm spring day, and I invited Gaius to come and view the flower-covered cemetery. There were two slaves working there under the supervision of the gardener, but they withdrew discreetly as we arrived. There was a certain amount of grinning and winking between them.

"Gods above!" I thought. "Even the slaves are in on the secret — the young mistress is up for offers."

With hindsight, this was not the best attitude to take. I showed Gaius my mother's grave. He bowed towards it — it is deemed a wise precaution to show respect to the departed — and examined the inscription.

"So your mother died when you were small?"

He *could* talk!

"Yes I never knew her."

"My mother is always ill."

"Oh. I'm sorry. Is it serious?"

He explained with a patient sigh. "She's not really ill. She *enjoys* ill health."

"Enjoys? Oh, I see." There didn't seem to be much else to say.

I looked around for Mabanwy, but she had sidled off with the gardeners. She would, of course, be just the other side of the wall, but not so near as to overhear every word. What a time she had chosen to be tactful! I turned to face Gaius.

"Look here, do you really want to arrange this marriage?"

He looked startled. "I beg your pardon?"

"Because I don't. Not really. I'm not ready for it, yet. Are you?"

He recovered his composure, and looked me up and down once again.

"Well," he said slowly, "I would *like* to be married..."

41

I thought I knew exactly what attracted him about the idea. Gods above, why has Nature so arranged things that people have the physical needs of a married person long before they are ready to discharge the responsibilities that go with them? Gaius continued, edging closer.

"I mean, it would have its compensations, wouldn't it?"

He looked swiftly to both sides, lunged for my hand, and gripped it firmly. He pursed his lips and lunged at me with those, too. I turned aside and received a wet blot on the side of my face. Ugh!

"Oh, come on, Helena," he hissed. "There's nobody watching! Be a sport!"

I applied my knee forcibly to the spot where I judged he was most vulnerable, and was rewarded by being released instantly. Then I made for the entrance, and found Mabanwy coming in with a falsely nonchalant air. She glanced at Gaius, who was bent double, and raised her eyebrows. I strode past her and headed for the living room, pursued with anxiety by Mabanwy, and with difficulty by Gaius. I stole a glance and saw they were close behind me as I swept imperiously into the room, where both the fathers were taking wine.

"Really, Father!" I exclaimed. "How could you think of it? You cannot seriously expect me to marry a cripple!"

I turned on my heel and swept just as imperiously out again. Gaius hobbled in, acting very well the part in which I had just cast him, while Mabanwy hovered incoherently in the hall. She hesitated only for a moment, and then pursued me upstairs to my room.

All hell broke loose.

*

I lay on my bed, face to the wall. The bruises on my back would mend soon enough; perhaps the pride would take a little longer. Papa had rarely been known to punish any of us physically, even the boys. But he had been angry — angrier perhaps than I had ever seen him. I had not only let him down, but the good name of our family. In vain I had tried to explain what had happened. I had told Mabanwy already, but by the time Papa had seen off his guests rather hurriedly, and with many an apology, he was in no mood to listen to me or to her. Mabanwy was ordered out curtly and banished to the servants' quarters until further notice. Then Papa came in and took his stick to me, vowing to teach me some manners and decorum if it was the last thing he did. His face was so red I was afraid it might be. How terrible I would have felt then. I wondered vaguely whether it would count as patricide — not in law, of course, but according to the gods.

There was a knock at the door. I ignored it, but then the door opened a crack.

"Helena?"

It was Kynan. He had been out at the time of the row. I tried to wipe my tear-stained face on the sheet, but I don't suppose it made much difference.

"Helena, are you all right? It's me — Kynan."

"Oh, Kyn."

I began to cry again. He quickly came in and sat on the edge of the bed.

"What on earth happened? I went out thinking my sister was about to be betrothed, and came back to a battlefield!"

"Have you seen Mabanwy?"

"No. Father's banished her to the kitchen or somewhere. He said she should have kept a closer eye on you. What happened?"

I told him in a few words. When I described Gaius's behaviour he was furious.

"I've a good mind to pay the little rat a visit and take a few of his teeth away for souvenirs!"

"No, Kynan, for Heaven's sake leave well alone! There's been trouble enough. Anyway, I suppose it's not his fault if he doesn't know how to behave. He's still only a boy, really."

Kynan looked puzzled. "What do you expect? Whoever Father chooses it'll be a boy. Anyway, I'm the same age as Gaius. He's old enough to know what's proper. He shouldn't have tried to kiss you."

"I wouldn't have minded that so much, but I didn't even know him, really."

Kynan looked shocked. "You mean you would have kissed him if... if you had liked him better?"

"I might have. Oh, Kyn, don't be so stuffy! I saw you at the last harvest feast with that little Constantia."

"That's different! I'm older than you!"

"*She* isn't," I retorted, "and don't tell me it's different for men. She isn't a man, either."

He opened and closed his mouth like a fish. Then he found his voice.

"I never thought of it like that. I mean, you..."

"I know — I'm only your sister. Kyn, I'm still a woman, I'm not a eunuch."

"Yes. Yes, of course."

"What shall I do, Kyn? What's Papa's mood like now?"

"Oh, he's brooding by the fire, with a cup of mulled wine. I think he's rather ashamed of himself. He prides himself on being an enlightened, educated man, you know. I suppose he feels he's slipped off his pedestal, that he should have retrieved the situation through reason and logic. He reads too much philosophy."

We both chuckled at that — Kynan, as we both knew, was the one for serious reading.

"Actually, Helena, I think it would be good for him if you apologised."

"Good for *him*!"

"Yes, and maybe for you, too. Oh, Helena, you're my sister and I love you dearly, but you are sometimes just a bit dense, when you don't wish to see something!"

"Oh." I was a bit taken aback — as much by Kynan's declaration of affection as anything else.

"Be honest, my dear, might you not have been a little tactless? Gaius obviously behaved like a little rat, but might there not have been other ways of reacting to it? Ways which would not have left Papa so exposed? You know how important it is for him to keep up appearances in society, especially in the provinces like this. I've heard that in Londinium you can get away with almost anything, but this is a small country place."

He was right, of course.

"Oh, Kynan, you're so damnably sensible!"

A few minutes later I crept downstairs to the kitchen and found some water to wash my face. Then I went back and brushed my hair and found another dress — equally modest, but less creased — and finally made my way down to the living room.

There was a log smouldering in the hearth. It was more for appearance than heat, with the weather being so good. Papa thought an open fire attractive, and often had one when it was not really necessary. He sat as Kynan had described him, a cup of wine on a small table beside his chair, apparently staring at the fire, oblivious of the slave squatting in the corner, who stood up as I came in. As I approached Papa from behind I suddenly realised that he was quite a small man. I had always thought of him as tall, but now I was nearly as tall myself, and it surprised me to realise it. He didn't stir as I walked up softly and sat on the floor by his feet. For a moment I just stared at the embers with him.

"Papa, I'm sorry."

He held his cup out to the slave. "Bring us two of these."

The man bowed and went out. Papa did not speak to me directly, but put out a hand and stroked my hair as he spoke.

"I miss your mother. She would have known how to bring you up better than I. I can manage with the boys, but a girl needs a mother."

"I have Mabanwy."

"She's a good girl, but she's only a servant."

I thought he was being uncharacteristically snobbish at the time, but later I realised he just meant their relationship wasn't personal. He could employ Mabanwy to look after his children, but he couldn't share them with her.

"I have my Finella, of course," he went on, and felt my surprise at the mention of her. "Oh, you must be aware of her, my dear, and there's no point in trying to deny the nature of her service to me; you are too intelligent to be deceived, anyway. I have some affection for her — as she has for me, I hope and believe. But she too is not a wife. Nor a mother."

The slave returned with our mulled wine.

"Now, don't drink it all off at once, my dear, although I suppose the heating kills its potency anyway. I was thinking earlier, you know, you grow more like your mother with each passing year. We often used to sit together like this, just talking over the day's events, drinking a little wine."

I leaned my head on his knee and sipped my drink. It was

warm and spicy, and the aroma mingled with the tang of wood smoke.

"Gaius was a bad choice," Papa went on. "I can see that. And you weren't consulted enough — I can see that, too. We'll organise things better next time, not rush things so much. You'll need time to get to know the man — see if he's the sort of fellow you can sit by the fire with."

*

Magnus Maximus arrived a couple of weeks later. It was a private visit this time, so that Maximus could take a holiday away from the cares of office. His job was the defence of the whole of northern Britain, another high-ranking officer having the east coast — the Saxon Shore. Maximus evidently found plenty to do from his base at Cair Ebrauc, or Eburacum as it is called in Latin. I heard him talking about it the night he arrived.

Papa had given a dinner in honour of his guest, with a number of our neighbours — not Maecius — invited to meet the celebrity. It gave a great boost to Papa's social standing to be on friendly terms with such a famous man, although his standing in his own right was already considerable. His guests reclined on couches in the classical Roman tradition, and he himself presided over the scene like Jupiter on Olympus. It was a mixed gathering this evening, and some of the ladies wore the most elaborate coiffures — mainly wigs. Kynan and I were serving, and livened up the proceedings by spotting who had hairpieces. He was particularly pleased to find that one of our more pompous local officials, Rufius the tax collector, had one. I soon lost interest in the game, and started looking at the jewelry. Many of the ladies had amber beads, but some had necklaces of real gold, and one a medallion of carved ivory. I heard her telling a friend that it had come all the way from India — thousands of miles! I could believe it. Many of their perfumes came from as far, I should say, or at least Arabia. They smelled of flowers that never grew in a British field.

Kynan and I were not really in charge of the proceedings. That was Rhonwen's job. We acted as her assistants, and the actual dishing up was done by slaves. There were simply too many guests, and too many courses. There were salads and shellfish, eggs, more fish, beef, pastries and fruit. There was even a bowl of snails, although not everyone liked them. We ate in the kitchen with the servants when we had a respite from our duties. Indeed, for this evening we might have been servants, but for our clothes. Kynan had a fine tunic of linen, with a blue silk sash which had cost a fortune. It was pinned in place on his shoulder with a brooch of enamelled copper. I was wearing the dress I had worn when Maximus was last here — a young girl, even a well off young girl, has little use for more than one fine dress. Mabanwy had done my coiffure again, even more elaborately than last time, with ringlets hanging down all around it.

"You'd better grow your hair and have some cut for a wig," she said. "It's getting to be a full time job doing this. If you had a wig we could just pin it on."

She also painted my face for me and plucked my rather bushy eyebrows to improve their outline.

"There," she pronounced when I was ready. "You'll amaze them."

Whether I amazed anyone I'm not sure, but after the meal Papa invited Kynan and me to join the guests. We pulled up two of the chairs of woven cane and listened. Naturally, it was Maximus who led the discussion. His theme was as it had been before — the lack of government resolve in beating the barbarians — and he found a ready audience here. Those present were of the class which had run the town councils in the old days. Now local governors like Papa had taken over many of their functions, and the towns had declined. My father was forgiven because his family had a long-standing position of honour in the area, and because he sympathised with those who were worried about their future. If the barbarians took over we would all lose everything.

But it was not the conversation which interested me most. Politics were a game played by men. All this jockeying for power was rather like war to me, and I didn't really care who ran the harbour or built the drains. I suppose I was bound to be unimpressed. I was too used to the fact that my father was a senior official, and mixed with others of similar standing. It was the individuals who interested me, irrespective of their government posts.

Maximus dominated the room. Not only was he the most senior official present, and a military commander, but he had a presence that the others lacked. They were like schoolchildren in the presence of a master. He knew what was going on in the Empire. He had travelled its highways, patrolled its borders, and attended its imperial court. He knew many of the famous personalities of whom the rest of us had only heard. He had met the Emperor personally. As he spoke I found myself losing my grip on his words, becoming absorbed in the atmosphere around him. I watched his dark eyes as they flicked around, responding to a gesture here or a comment there. I watched his lips, moist and full, as they formed his words with precision. His hands made flowing gestures which emphasised the verbal points. I watched them in fascination as they traced curves and circles in the air. On his wrists there were dark hairs and others up his arms, becoming darker and longer until they disappeared under his sleeves. Once, while someone else was speaking, he caught my eye and grinned boyishly, making me blush and turn away. But my gaze soon returned.

I excused myself early and went to bed. As I took off my dress I wondered what the men there had thought of me. I had never really studied my body before, but I did so now, wondering how a man might view it. I ran my hands down over my developing curves, and unfamiliar urges tingled within my body.

I hurriedly put on my night-dress before Mabanwy might come in.

The next day Papa had to go across to Mona to meet some local deputation or other.

"Why don't you and Mabanwy go out with Maximus?" he asked. "It's a lovely day. Show him some of the countryside. He's always been here on official business before, and he's never had time to see anything. He was saying he'd welcome the opportunity. Get Rhonwen to make up a picnic."

Rhonwen clucked with disapproval at the request, partly because she "liked guests to sit down to a proper lunch" but also because she would lose two slaves for the day while they carried our packs. Maximus was pleased — it was exactly the sort of informal activity he wanted, away from the bustle of official life.

Kynan wanted to come too, but he was attending school in the town now and Papa would not hear of his cutting it for a day.

"All right for some," he grumbled as he went out of the door with his wax tablets. "I've got oratory today — delivering a speech on the nature of civilised life. Cleanliness and law!"

It did sound dull. Perhaps there were times when it was an advantage to be a girl.

We went out on foot. This was mainly because we wanted to climb the hillside, and there was little ground where it was safe for horses. It made hard work for the slaves, though.

The track led past peasant stone hovels, and then up through some stunted trees. There were few trees on this exposed coast — few types were hardy enough. After that the track zigzagged higher and the going became rougher, with broken jagged rock underfoot. We were soon well above the level from which Mabanwy and I had watched the Irish ship sunk years before. I told Maximus about the incident, as we paused to get our breath back and admire the view. He smiled as I chattered, and seemed to be at ease.

"The Irish are quiet enough at the moment," he said, "but there's no telling how long for."

With that thought we went on, the path levelling off now so that we could walk in comfort. The town was behind and far below us now, a huddle of stone buildings which faded into the landscape. Soon we came to a stream which foamed its steep way down towards the sea. There was a sheltered spot where we decided to eat our lunch. A flat patch of ferny ground had held on to its earth covering where all around it was reduced to bare rock. We sat there on boulders while the slaves unpacked the food.

"This is beautiful," sighed Maximus. "I never realised Britain had such places before I came here. I was brought up in Spain, and I've travelled the Empire. Yet there's no country which is better from the point of view of natural beauties, or for farming. No wonder we have to defend it against so many. Still, British troops too are the best anywhere."

"You think so, *Domine?*"

"Certainly. The best in the Empire, I'd say. Since we started raising native British units and stationing them at home I've got more optimistic. They'll fight like lions for their own land. In the past we always moved legions away from their home areas, in case they were needed to put down rebellions. It's different now. It's the external threat which is greatest."

He smiled to himself. "You know, I have some native British troops in the north, the First Cornovians. They've translated my name into the British language. They call me Macsen."

"Macsen," I repeated it. "Macsen."

"You like the name?"

I nodded. "If you have a British name then you are one of us, *Domine*. I like that."

He bowed his head to me, smiling.

The trouble with being in an exposed place is that there is nowhere to go to perform natural functions in privacy. After our picnic I needed somewhere to go. Not only had we drunk plenty of spring water after our climb, but the sound of rushing water has its own insidious effect.

I excused myself and wandered back along the path again until I rounded the hillside enough to be out of sight. Having found somewhere to squat I was returning when I saw some lovely wild flowers just below the edge of the path. I decided to inch off the path and try to pick them. Below me there was a steep slope, dotted with rocks and gorse bushes, and full of pits and holes. The ground at the edge of the path was crumbly. It was not a sensible idea, but the warm sun and a full stomach and the lazy atmosphere had made me careless.

I couldn't quite reach the flowers at first, so I inched a little further from the path — and my feet slid from under me. With a cry I tumbled down a few feet before grabbing the stump of an old gorse bush and holding on. My cry had alerted the others, who were soon above me.

"I'm all right," I called up to them. "I'll just find my feet and climb back up!"

"Wait!" called Maximus. "I'll come and give you a hand."

"No, really, it's all right!"

It was too late. He was already making his way down. He was a lot better at keeping his balance than I was, but then he had been forewarned. Within moments he was just above me, and within arm's length.

"Well, well, we thought we'd lost you! Are you really all right?"

"Yes, yes. Just a bit surprised, a few scratches."

He reached his hand out to me. I took it, and my gorse stump gave way. My entire weight went on to Maximus's arm and threw him off balance. He fell down on to me, and we both went rolling down the slope. He threw his arms around me protectively, and we bounced off rocks and bushes until hitting another gorse thicket which stopped us abruptly. I came to rest with my legs splayed, Maximus on top of me. My heart was pounding, the blood singing in my ears. His weight had driven the breath from me, but it was not that which kept me breathless. His face was inches away, the sun in his eyes and his silvering hair.

Then his lips were on mine. It was a long, slow lingering kiss. I was light-headed and panting for breath. Between us I felt something move and grow firm. I threw my arms around him. I wanted to pull him closer — so close there was nothing between us. I wanted to tear off my clothes, to feel his skin upon mine, our bodies entwined as one.

I knew it couldn't be, and tears slipped from under my eyelids. He pulled away suddenly.

"I'm sorry, I don't know what you must think — "

"I didn't. Just for a moment I didn't think at all, *Domine* ... Macsen."

He stood up and waved to the others, still waiting far above. And watching, no doubt.

"Please, take my hand. I'd better get you back while your reputation is still intact."

I was crazy with longing. I had to show him, but I had to stay within the bounds of respectability. My hand came up with a bruised yellow flower clutched in it. I put it on his outstretched palm and closed his fingers over it.

"Here," I said quietly. "That is my... reputation. You have made it a burden to me. Let me know when you have decided what to do about it."

Without another word, we made our way painfully back up the slope.

VI

"No!"

"Father, please listen to me!"

"He's old enough to be your father!"

"That's not fair. That makes him sound like an old man. He's thirty!"

"He's still old enough to be your father. It's just that you're a baby yourself."

"If I'm such a baby, how is it that you're trying to marry me off?"

"And that's another thing. Maximus is a rich man. How can I ever raise the sort of dowry he'd expect? We're not poor, but we're not in his class!"

"What *does* he expect? Have you asked him?"

"He's the commander of the North. He's a man of high standing. And that's another thing, you'd have to go and live in Cair Ebrauc. We'd never see you."

"Adeon's gone off to the army, to who knows where. You didn't stop *him*!"

After our return from the picnic I had been washed and ordered to bed for the rest of the day by Mabanwy. This was just a precaution, in case any of my wounds were worse than they seemed at first. Maximus had spent the rest of that day, and the whole of the next, alone and apparently lost in thought. He had gone out for long bracing walks and surprised everyone by his quietness. On the morning of the third day — this morning — he had formally asked my father for my hand before going off to Mona for the day to see another friend. This was clearly a device to give us privacy while we discussed his proposal.

The argument had raged all day. My father thought of Maximus as his contemporary, which was not really true. Papa was much older. He liked Maximus, but he was worried about the age difference. Marrying me to some youth was one thing, but a mature man was another. To Papa it didn't seem quite decent. To me it seemed a release. All my worst fears had been confirmed by the incident with Gaius — a youth with no experience of the world or of women. I quailed at the thought of taking on all the social and economic responsibilities of married life with such a companion. As for the physical side, the thought of spending a wedding night being pawed by an over-eager clumsy boy was not to be dwelt upon.

Maximus, my Maximus, my Macsen was different. Maximus knew the world — he helped govern it. He was rich enough to live comfortably and wise enough to stay that way. He had been married before and wanted to be again — surely proof enough that he knew how to live with a woman. More important than all that was how I felt when he looked at me. I felt that I took strength from his presence. I grew. For him I could be a woman.

"Father, please listen to me. You want me to marry someone like Gaius..."

"We agreed he was a wrong choice!"

"Not him, perhaps, but *like* him. Another youth, a boy with no experience of life. Father, don't you want me to have a husband I can respect?"

"Of course."

"But what sort of man have I learned to respect while growing up in this house? Ask yourself that. Adeon and Kynan are fine as brothers, but I wouldn't want someone like that as a husband. Yet you are expecting that of me."

"Daughter, what is it you are trying to say?"

"Only that... only that if you didn't want me to look towards an older man as a husband, you should have been a much worse father."

He paused for a moment, then smiled.

"You're trying to get round me by flattery."

"No, Papa, I am not. It's true. I didn't realise it myself until this happened. But a woman is given to a man in marriage. She must be commanded by him — even her body is given to him." He tutted a little at this, but said nothing. "He owns her. Well, I want an owner I can look up to and be proud of, not someone who seems a less competent person than myself. I know that's not very modest of me, but I honestly think it's true."

53

Papa said nothing for a long while, but sat with his eyes closed and his hands together, the forefingers under his chin. Then he sighed.

"Very well, my dear. If that is what you want. Heaven knows, I've nothing against Maximus. He's the finest of men. In society terms he's quite a catch. If you think this age difference doesn't matter, you're probably the best judge."

He got up and wandered out into the courtyard. I watched him as he walked over the gravel to the stone wall at the back, and out towards the cemetery plot. A shock went through me. He was going to explain his actions to my mother.

I was married to Maximus the following spring. Following tradition I wore a white woollen tunic and a veil, with a crown of marjoram on my head. The ceremony, in which my bridesmaid would formally hand me over to the groom, was to take place in my father's house with the exchange of marriage contracts duly witnessed. The contracts laid down exactly what the dowry would be, and what arrangements would be made in the event of divorce. Divorce was very common in those days, especially on grounds of adultery, before the Christians made it illegal. Papa tried to discuss it all with me beforehand, but I honestly didn't want to know. He had drawn everything up with the advice of a lawyer, and I was sure they knew a lot more about it than I did. Besides, how could a girl concern herself with such things when she was going to marry Magnus Clemens Maximus, Macsen, *Comes* of North Britain? We had exchanged rings as a token; wasn't that enough?

Papa invited everyone. There were relatives I had never seen, friends whose houses we had never visited. I wondered how necessary it all was, but he was in his element. It was a big day for him as well as me, particularly because of who the bridegroom was. He wanted the whole country to see who his daughter was marrying, and what powerful connections he would now have. He nearly succeeded, I think.

The courtyard of our villa was partly roofed over with canvas for the occasion in case of rain, but it was hardly necessary. The sun shone brightly from the early morning onwards; it was an auspicious beginning. The food was laid out on long tables under the awning, with cloths covering it to keep off the flies. My father had arranged for extra slaves to be ready with wine for the guests. The servants and slaves would be allowed their own celebration in the kitchen. They would also be allowed to view the bridal dress before the guests arrived.

Maximus's friend Marcus came to act as his witness. It was a pity, but I treated him courteously for Maximus's sake. A greater disappointment was that Maximus did not bring his children.

"They would be lost in this crowd," he said awkwardly.

"Surely they are used to crowds?"

"Hmm. Well, to be honest I thought it would be difficult for them — and for you, too — if they met you just before the wedding like this, in a strange place. Better to meet them at home later, when you have all the time you need to get to know each other."

Maximus's father was long since dead, but his mother was not. She was not up to the journey, said Maximus. She was over fifty and suffered from rheumatism.

"The journey would really not have been possible for her," he said. "She's seeing a new doctor. He may be able to help, but I honestly doubt whether she'll ever make long journeys again. She's at my other house, in Londinium — never leaves it these days."

On the morning of the wedding it was supposed to be unlucky for the groom to see the bride. Maximus was staying with the garrison commander in town, and walked up to the villa at the appointed time with his witness and retinue. Mabanwy and I saw them from my upstairs room. You could see them a mile off, because their armour flashed and twinkled in the sunlight. Both Maximus and Marcus had their ceremonial uniforms on, although without weapons, which they were not supposed to wear when off duty. Maximus's helmet bore scarlet ostrich plumes which made him even taller than he already was. As he came closer I saw that the armour was richly inlaid with brass and copper designs — serpents and dragons. Behind him came his friends dressed mainly in the Roman style with full togas in brilliant white. Their slaves walked alongside, many carrying wedding presents which were covered in muslin, or hidden in wooden caskets, until after the ceremony.

"Come away from the window, *Dominula*," said Mabanwy.

"He's not supposed to see you until later."

"Oh, very well, Mabanwy, but just look at him. Isn't he magnificent?"

She came to look. "Yes. Yes, he is indeed. He looks like one of those great heroes of old that young Adeon always talks about. Now, let's adjust that veil before you go down. We can't have you looking less than him."

"Do I look all right, Mabanwy?"

"All right? Don't insult my handiwork. You look like the moon coming out to his sun — white and silver to his gold."

We went down into the living room where we were to await our signal. Papa was greeting Maximus under the archway. He led him forward to the canopy under which the ceremony would take place. Then Papa hurried in to join us.

"You look exquisite," he said softly. "Mabanwy, you've done her proud."

Mabanwy took my arm and the musicians played a fanfare. This was our cue. At a measured pace I walked to meet my bridegroom.

The revels continued until evening. Maximus and I sat in chairs which were garlanded with flowers. We had precious little time to talk. Guests were constantly being presented by my father, or by Marcus, or by other guests who knew us well. It came home to me once again what a sheltered life I had led. I hardly knew anyone. Maximus seemed to have hundreds of friends and colleagues. Many of them had wives, whom they introduced, and whom I would meet again socially. There were so many I forgot half their names. The place was a riot of colours, for weddings are always an occasion for women to dress up. To judge by the gold jewelry we saw, some of Maximus's friends were not, as we used to say, short of a *solidus*. We all ate from the feast that Rhonwen and her specially-hired staff had created. There were dozens of different fish and shellfish, pies, salads, bread — every kind of cold food you could think of. An ox had been roasting all morning over a charcoal fire in a pit just outside the stone wall at the rear of the house. By early afternoon it was being served up, guests helping themselves to slices piled on plates by the slaves. The wine flowed, although I went easy on that. I wasn't used to it, and Mabanwy had warned me strictly not to drink too much.

"It's all right being drunk, but not incapable," she giggled salaciously. Not quite what I expected of her.

Maximus too drank only a little. There was always water if we wanted to stay sober. Many did not. The scene was noisy, what with the music and talk, and from time to time the entertainments my father had hired. As well as the musicians there were jugglers and dancers, and a small group of acrobats. People came up with their slaves to offer their wedding presents.

It had been decided that Mabanwy would stay with me. We had been together so long that it seemed natural for her to come to live with me now as my personal maid. I think Papa also felt that the advice of a woman who had herself been married might be useful to me sometimes. He was still worried about my being so much younger than Maximus. It was Mabanwy herself who suggested we leave. Maximus and I were due to spend a week together in a villa which he had borrowed from someone in the army at Segontium. It seemed the man was to be away, and so his house, which looked out over the Bay, would be a lovely place for us to spend a short holiday before taking up married life in earnest. His own servants were away with him, but Mabanwy and a few slaves would see to our needs. Indeed, the slaves were already in place, airing the house and making everything ready. They would expect us by sunset.

"I really think it's time to go," whispered Mabanwy. It'll take a little while to get there on the coast road. It's just a track, not a proper Roman road. Although you won't have to walk. I think your husband has arranged a surprise."

One of Maximus's friends tapped him on the shoulder, and he turned to me.

"Well, are you ready to go?"

I nodded. We got up, and the guests stopped their chattering. Papa spoke.

"Thank you all for coming, and for your gifts and good wishes. You are all welcome to stay as long as you wish, but the bride and groom are about to leave and will say goodbye at the front of the house."

Maximus took my hand and led me through the arch to the drive at the front. Parked on the driveway were three chariots, each with a team of three horses. They were all decorated with flowers, and streamers of coloured cloth.

"A military send-off," Maximus explained.

"I can't possibly ride in one of those!"

He simply took me by the waist and lifted me up into the first vehicle. Some of his friends piled into the others, cheering. Maximus climbed up beside me, and was handed the reins and whip by a slave standing on the path.

"Wave goodbye, then," he said pleasantly, and did so himself.

There was a chorus of goodbyes from the assembled company, Maximus cracked the whip, and we were away like a shot from a bow.

"Hold tight!" he advised me unnecessarily, as we rounded a curve in the drive and thundered out of the gate into the lane. I glanced back and saw the other two chariots were following. Mabanwy was in one, with two young men. One was driving, but I think she was fighting off the other's attentions. There was a rail on top of the chariot side. I hung on to it for dear life. My elaborate hair style was coming to pieces in the wind. Long straggly hanks of it streamed back, more shaking free as we bumped along.

"Fun, isn't it?" shouted Maximus, cracking the whip.

I gulped and nodded, sending my marjoram crown flying away. Fun! Actually, once you got used to the breakneck speed I could see that there was something exhilarating about it. But I preferred a slower pace. We hurtled along the lane, slowed briefly for a corner, and swung left into another lane, which I recognised as the coast road. I could hear the shouts of the others behind. Exhilarating it might be, but I was not sorry when we slowed and turned into the driveway of a small villa. Maximus drove up to the front door and reined in suddenly. I would have gone over the front of the chariot, but he caught me on his arm and held me to him. My heart leapt at his closeness. For a few minutes I had forgotten why we were coming here.

"Steady."

He got down, and lifted me down after him. The others were

roaring up the driveway now, and skidded to a halt in a shower of gravel. Mabanwy got down, laughing, and came to me.

"Well, and a proper mess that wind has made of you. Excuse me, *Domine*, I think I should take the bride indoors and tidy her up."

"As you wish." He smiled at me, and I warmed inside. Then he turned to his friends.

"Now, lads, I thank you for escorting us. I can offer you a cup of wine, and then I'd be obliged if you'd take those chariots back. I can only offer you the one cup, I'm afraid. You know how it is. I've a lot to do."

There were some raucous cheers at this, and some bawdy remarks. I know men do this sort of thing all the time, but I wished they had let me get out of earshot first. Mabanwy led me upstairs to a pretty room, the plaster painted with garlands of flowers in yellow and pink. There was a candle on a small table at each side of the bed, and the shutters were drawn across. The room was cosy. I tried not to look at the large bed, which was covered with an embroidered quilt. My chest of clothes was there, and Mabanwy opened it. There was a knock at the door. It was a slave with a bowl of warm water.

"Here," said Mabanwy. "Best have a quick all-over wash. I'll sort your hair out in a minute."

Soon I was washed, and changed into a white nightgown. Then I sat while Mabanwy brushed my hair. We heard the guests go, and the crunch of wheels as the chariots went off.

"There," said Mabanwy. "You look beautiful again." She sniffed loudly.

"Mabanwy, you're crying!"

"Oh, not really. Just a sniffle. It's just, well, I've had the care of you for so long while you were a girl. Tomorrow when I see you, you'll be a woman."

"You look like having the care of me for a lot longer yet," I said. "You don't get rid of me that easily."

She smiled. "Well, I'd better go. Good luck. Bless you. Shall I tell your husband you're ready?"

I nodded. My husband! My Macsen! I shivered with nervousness.

I pulled back the covers on the bed and got in. There were large cushions at the head, and I sat leaning against them with my arms around my knees.

Maximus came in softly with a jug of wine and two cups. He held up the jug.

"Would you like some?"

"Just a little, please." Our words were stilted from embarrassment.

He sat down at my feet and poured a little wine. There must be a dressing room somewhere. He was just wearing a white under-tunic. Its sleeves were short, so that his arms were visible. His hair had been combed, and there was a soft fragrance about him — not a flowery scent such as women and fops wear, but something musky and clinging. My heart was pounding. The wine cup rattled as I put it down on the little table and reached out to him. He put his cup down also and pulled me to him.

"Oh, Macsen."

"I've been waiting for this since that day on the hillside."

"So have I."

He kissed me then, and the beating of my heart seemed to grow until it filled my body. I hardly noticed him slip the covers aside and lie next to me. Then the full length of his body was against me. Feelings burst forth within, sensations I had never felt before, but always knew were there. Something inside told me this was what I was made for. Macsen's hands caressed every soft place of my body, inched under my white virginal covering. I ached to be free of it. Suddenly I was wriggling to sit up.

"What is it?"

"I have to take this off!"

We helped each other strip, and fell together again. Unencumbered, his hands roved freely over my skin. I panted as they traced every curve. His lips found mine. He kissed my neck, breast, nipple. My legs parted. When he touched between them I thought I would die.

"Macsen, Macsen, please. Now!"

He pulled himself fully on top of me. Then, on the very brink, he hesitated.

"Oh, please don't stop."

"We must go gently. The first time..."

"Don't worry, my love. Just push. Please."

He moved. There was a momentary pain, and I gasped.

"Is it all right?"

"Oh, yes, yes, yes..."

As we moved together I heard the sea outside. Our rhythm seemed to me like the rhythm of the ocean. Mabanwy had talked of riding a wave to the shore. Now I understood. But it was a warm, caressing wave. As we moved I felt it build as a wave builds. Breathlessly I rode the wave. Sensations tingled everywhere in me, gathering. The tip of the wave began to curl towards its final crash on to the shore...

Maximus cried out suddenly, then again. That first time I knew no better, I thought he was hurt. Then he was thrusting and jerking uncontrollably, moaning as in a fit. But it was ecstasy and not torment that gripped him. I held him tightly to me, afraid we would separate and spoil the moment for him. Then it was past, his gasping subsided, the rhythm dwindled and faded away. He lay in my arms for a while, then gently pulled away. My heat was cooling now, the world returning, the wave merely a ripple.

"Are you sure you're all right?"

"Yes. Don't worry about me."

He lay back, suddenly overcome with sleep. Soon he was breathing deeply again, but in repose this time. I felt his wetness running from me, and reached for the towel Mabanwy had thoughtfully provided. So I was a woman now. I was elated by the fact, but still on edge.

Unfulfilled.

VII

How are you this morning, then, *Domina*?"

"Why so formal, all of a sudden, Mabanwy?"

"Well, you are my employer now, not my employer's daughter."

"I see. More changes. I don't think I can cope with it all. I suppose you'd better observe the formalities in public, but don't change the way you behave when it's just the two of us."

My tired manner couldn't escape Mabanwy; she knew me too well. She sat on the edge of the bed. Maximus was already up and at breakfast.

"What's the matter, *Dominula*?"

"What do you think?"

"Was it difficult? Are you hurt?"

"No, no, nothing like that. At least... oh, I don't know."

"Ah, not hurt; disappointed."

"I suppose so."

"Don't worry about that, my dear Helena. The first time is often like that."

"Really?"

"Why, certainly. They make a lot of fuss about wedding nights, but from the woman's point of view there often isn't much to write home about."

I had a mental image of myself writing home about my wedding night, and burst out laughing.

"That's better. Love is like anything else, you know — it gets better with practice. After all, a properly innocent girl shouldn't know too much before her wedding night, should she? But just think of all the fun you're going to have learning!"

"Mabanwy, you're a wicked woman!"

"No such luck. It's all talk. Now, there's a nice little bath house at the back of the villa. The slaves have been stoking the fires since early morning. Why don't you go and have a nice warm soak? I'll bring your perfumes, scrub your back, and all that."

"Oh, Mabanwy, I'm so glad you're here."

*

We spent a quiet but pleasant week at the villa. During the day we went for walks and occasional rides along the coast. In the evenings we usually sat together and talked. I sewed, while Maximus read. It seemed that even on his honeymoon he was pestered with work. Twice that week mounted couriers arrived with dispatches. There was nothing desperately important, however, so it didn't take up too much time. I remember the week as a haze of warm weather, sea air, and nights very much on the pattern of that first one. One incident stands out, though. It underlined something I had never realised about Maximus, but which came to loom ever more importantly over our life together.

We were walking down by the seaside. The beach here was sandy, and we paddled along the water's edge, sandals in hand, like a couple of children. Our talk was all light-hearted, the weather was warm and the sea calm. It was a perfect day. Presently we came to a sheltered place where a great outcrop of brown rock reared skyward. At the bottom was a shelf of rock, almost as if someone had deliberately carved out a bench for footsore travellers.

"Let's sit here a while," I said. "When my feet are dry I'll put my sandals back on."

Maximus agreed, and we sat there hand in hand breathing in the fresh salty air and watching the gulls wheel and dive. I turned and looked at him. He was intent on the gulls.

"Look at them," he murmured. "What would it be like to be able to soar and glide like that?"

It sounded almost sad, as if he had his heart set on something unattainable. Something tugged at my own, and I found myself suddenly full of desire for him. I reached up and put my arms around his neck, drawing his face down to mine. At first he responded a little. Then he raised his head again and hugged me close to his side. I persisted, putting my hand on his thigh.

"Maximus?"

He looked down at me and smiled.

"No-one could see us here, Macsen."

He chuckled as if I had made a joke.

"No, no. Love is for the bedroom."

Love is for the bedroom! I suppose I was just disappointed that he didn't find me irresistible, wherever it was. But I told myself I was annoyed at his reason. If he had expressed a fear of being seen I would have been less upset about it. Or if he had said — as Mabanwy did when I told her — "Not a good idea; the sand gets in some very uncomfortable places!" I could have laughed it away. The idea that life was divided strictly into compartments like that was foreign to me. I could see nothing wrong with making love on the beach, or in the woods, or even on the living room floor if the servants were out of the way.

At the end of the week we packed up our things — or rather, Mabanwy packed mine — and went to my father's house to say goodbye. As Papa had pointed out to me, we were going to live at Maximus's residence in Cair Ebrauc. At the time I had thought nothing of it, but as our departure drew closer a sinking feeling began in the pit of my stomach. Thank heavens I was taking Mabanwy with me. Without her I think I might have chained myself to the gatepost and demanded a divorce! She kept me cheerful.

"Never mind, *Domina*, we'll be able to visit. And then there's your brother. Perhaps we'll see him from time to time at Cair Ebrauc."

Actually, this was not likely. Adeon had been posted up to the region of Hadrian's Wall and attached to the First Cohort of Cornovians, who were stationed there. The Sixth "Victorious" Legion was based at Cair Ebrauc, which I would have to get used to calling Eburacum if I was to live amongst the military.

It was an emotional parting, in spite of Mabanwy's best efforts. Besides, it was emotional for her. She had relatives in Segontium, to whom she had made her farewells earlier. When we came to leave Papa's villa, late in the morning, not only he but all the staff came out to say goodbye. Even Rhonwen, who was normally rather stern, was in tears.

"I know you will look after my father, Rhonwen. At least while he has you he will never want for good food."

"Oh, there you go, *Domina*, always teasing!" But she was pleased.

The rest of the staff nodded or curtsied and wished me luck as I passed by. The last in the line was Finella. In spite — or because — of what she was to Papa, I had hardly ever spoken to her. Now I felt I had to say something, and stopped in front of her. She curtsied to me, and I found myself taking her by the arm.

"Look after him for me."

She smiled sweetly and looked me in the eye. "Of course. I love him."

The statement startled me by its quiet self-assurance, but I had no time to dwell on it. Papa was there, taking my hands in his.

"Oh, my dear, I hope all will be well with you in your new life." He glanced at Maximus. "Of course, I know Maximus will look after you. He's a good man. You're lucky."

"I know. Oh, Papa!" I had not meant to disgrace myself by weeping, but there was no help for it. I buried my face in his shoulder while he patted my back and made rather embarrassed soothing noises.

When I was over it he held me at arm's length and looked at me.

"Well, my little girl, you'll be mistress of your own house now. There's much to look forward to. You'll soon settle, I know."

We kissed cheeks, and he turned to Maximus to murmur something suitably masculine and unemotional.

"Well, this is it," I whispered to Mabanwy. "There's nothing left to do but go."

We climbed aboard the carriage. It was almost new, with red dye in the wood and a proper roof with seats for servants on it. Such a vehicle bore witness to the position of my husband in society. I thought on this as we settled into our upholstered seats and waved to everyone. The carriage jerked forward, the cavalry escort clattered into a trot behind us, and we were away.

I sighed, and Mabanwy and Maximus smiled sympathetically at me. I looked out of the window as my beloved lane rolled by.

Surely it was this, and not any mere wedding night, which marked the end of childhood?

The journey to Eburacum took several days but seemed interminable. Thanks to the legions there were decent roads, but the terrain in the centre of northern Britain is very mountainous, and the repeated winter frosts damage the roads there, so it was a rough ride. What is more, every mountain that is ascended must be descended again on the other side. When this happened the carriage threatened to run away. We often had to step down and walk some way, while a soldier would assist the driver by holding on to the brake pole to check the carriage's speed. We soon left the lumbering old wagon, and all my goods, behind, but I worried how it would fare with its greater weight. Still, it seemed to be all in a day's work to these men.

Cair Legion was our first stop of any size. Ironically, the British name recorded the fact that the city was home to the Twentieth Legion, while the Roman name — Deva — gave no such clue. We spent one night there, surrounded by all the noisy activities of a large military base, and I was not sorry when we moved on. The other stops we made have slipped my memory now. Their names are mostly insignificant, and I never passed through them a second time. This part of Britain is sparsely populated by comparison with the fertile South, and the place names — where they exist at all — often refer to local history or even the nearest hill or river. After several weary days of poor weather, staying mainly in wayside inns, military forts, and once even in tents, we saw with relief the stone walls and towers of Eburacum, and passed through its West Gate into a far larger and busier city than Segontium had ever been.

"Thank heavens for that," said Maximus. "I can't wait to get a civilised bath!"

The rest of us agreed heartily. We had arrived in the evening, and presumably the slaves at Maximus's — or rather our — house would have the water hot. Maximus had sent a rider ahead to warn the household of our approach.

The carriage lurched through the cobbled streets in the fading light, and we saw that Eburacum was even more extensive than we had at first thought. As I later found out, it was not only the market centre for a large area, but also an important port. There were even warships there sometimes, and a military pilot to guide them down river to the huge estuary which led to the German Sea. One of Maximus's responsibilities was to maintain the coastal defences of the North. There were a number of forts and watchtowers on the coast to watch for the Pictish raiders who sometimes tried to by-pass Hadrian's Wall in ships, and a unit of the British Fleet to intercept them. It underlined for me how important his work really was, and how important it was that I should cause him no additional anxiety.

The house was a half-timbered villa in the grand style. Despite being within the city walls it had its own grounds and outbuildings — not as large as most country villa estates, of course, but they had their farms to run. For a town house it was large and well appointed. At the back there was a walled garden, and down one side ran a wing with the kitchens and bath house. To one side of the main house lay the stables and a coach house with their own separate driveway. Inside the house, the main rooms were all painted with elaborate scenes from Roman legends, not the pretty but insubstantial flowers which were typical. The main living room gave on to a colonnaded veranda with a view down the garden — an ideal place to entertain guests. I hardly noticed all of this at the time, so keen was I to get to my bath. However, before this there was my first official function — meeting the staff.

They were lined up in the hall, the housekeeper and the cook at the head of the line. I was not as intimidated as I might have been — I was used to servants — but they were much older than me and rather grim. They curtsied to me and introduced themselves, while I nodded as graciously as possible and carried on. Mabanwy was close behind me, carrying a bag with my overnight things in it. She introduced herself to her new colleagues, who treated her with caution.

"My dear," said Maximus, "why don't you go to the bath house now? I'm sure you're dying to, and there is a little business awaiting me already."

"Really, Maximus," I chided him, "you work too hard. But if you must, you must."

There was a silence. I was not supposed to show any disapproval of my husband in public, no matter how slight. Well, it was little enough, I reflected, and they would have to get used to it. I intended to speak my mind when I felt like it. With Mabanwy one step behind I headed for the bath house.

The bath house was luxurious. Not only was there a proper separate changing room, there were warm and cold pools big enough for about ten people, and a steam room as well. This was Roman civilisation at its highest! We soon stripped off and sat in the steam room for a while, letting the steam open our pores and work up a healthy sweat while rubbing in the olive oil which prevented our skins from becoming too dry. After twenty minutes of this, thoroughly overheated, Mabanwy bravely plunged up to her shoulders in the cold pool, giggling as she muttered about the supposed benefits of closing the pores against the chills. My own cooling was more leisurely, by way of the warm pool for ten minutes and a drying off in the air for ten more.

"Oh, this is the life," I said. "Where's the bath slave?"

Mabanwy giggled again and clapped her hands.

Instantly a young girl in a linen tunic appeared from nowhere. Mabanwy and I were helpless. I dare say we looked an unpatrician sight — two naked women falling about with laughter for no good reason. The girl smiled uncertainly and awaited instructions.

"Who are you?" I asked.

"Sara, *Domina*. I am the ladies' bath slave."

"And where did you spring from?"

She pointed to a little door at the back of the room.

"I wait there until called."

"Well, Sara, I would like you to wash my hair quickly now."

"Yes, *Domina*." And she went to fetch the bucket.

"I was joking," whispered Mabanwy. "I didn't really think..."

"No. It's funny in a way, Mabanwy, but it scares me a little."

"Why?"

"It's just that I'm not used to being so rich. I don't know quite what's expected."

"*Dominula*, you've just arrived and your baggage is heaven knows where on the road behind us. I'd say you'd be expected to get some clothes."

"You're right, of course. I've hardly got anything suitable for a society occasion, anyway. I must speak to Maximus about it."

*

68

My next shock came when I was shown to my room by a slave. It was so clearly *my* room, not *ours*. There was a bed big enough for two, but the table with my cosmetics and hair brushes left no room for anyone to share. There were no male clothes or shoes around, nothing to show there was a man in the house. Mabanwy was with me, and was equally puzzled.

"Perhaps that's how these patricians do things," she suggested.

I shrugged. "I thought all married couples shared their bed the whole time, not just when... well, you know. For warmth and companionship, not just to make love."

"Well, that's how I'd have it," said Mabanwy, "but then I'm just a peasant. What do I know of how society people live?"

She brushed my hair, which was tangled after its wash.

"My dear, everything is all right between you and your husband, isn't it? I mean, I've no right to pry..."

"You couldn't pry, Mabanwy. I'd tell you if there was anything. No, as far as I know he's happy."

"And you? Are you happy?"

"Oh, Mabanwy, what a question. We've only been married a fortnight."

"Forgive me, *Dominula*. Only..."

"Only?"

"Only, what an answer."

It was all so strange. I suppose I was still very young, really, and it was difficult to cope with so much at once. Had it not been for Mabanwy, there would have been no one that I knew. Even Maximus — and he was still my dear Macsen then — was a stranger in many ways. This city, this household, this position in society, were what he was used to. He was a part of it, and therefore strange.

Maximus came to me later on that evening. He too had bathed, and now wore a plain linen night tunic. We sat on the bed, drinking the wine he had brought.

"How do you like this room?" he asked.

"It's very nice," I said. "The whole house is lovely."

"I told you it was."

"Yes. But where is your room?"

"Next door."

"Ah. I was wondering... well, why you wanted separate rooms."

"Separate rooms?" He looked puzzled, as if the idea of anything different had never occurred to him.

"Yes. I rather thought we would be sharing. Mabanwy said maybe society people do things differently."

He laughed at that. "Not really. I need space to store my uniforms and things, of course. Sometimes I get in very late, and it's better not to disturb anyone..."

"I wouldn't mind!"

"No? Well, why don't we leave things as they are, but agree that I'll spend most nights here? Would that suit you?"

"Oh, yes!"

"Very well." He leaned over towards me. "It's nice to be in demand. I haven't been used to it for a long time. You know, I suppose you're very tired after the journey..."

I pulled him towards me.

"I was tired, Macsen, but my bath did me good. A great deal of good. Anyway, I'll never be too tired for you."

With the wine, and the new bed, it was like our wedding night all over again.

In every respect.

*

The sun was streaming in through the half-open shutters when I awoke. Maximus had gone already — presumably keen to get back to work and find out what had happened in his absence. As I lay there, rubbing the sleep from my eyes, I became aware of a fidgety scuffling noise in the corridor outside. Then there was a high-pitched giggle, and the door slowly swung inwards. I rolled over and propped myself up on one elbow to see who was coming.

A tousled dark head popped around the door. It clearly belonged to a boy of about twelve. His skin was lighter, and freckled, but he had his father's large dark eyes, and that same patrician nose. There could be no doubting whose son he was.

"Good morning," I said. "You must be Flavius Victor."

He smiled, nodded, and disappeared again. There was more subdued whispering and giggling. I couldn't catch the words, but someone was being dared to do something.

"Well," said a small voice at last, "if you won't do it, then I will!"

The door was pushed back firmly, and in strode a small girl with flashing blue eyes and the most beautiful long red hair. She was only about five, but with a look of determination she came right up to the edge of the bed and transfixed me with a stare.

"I'm Sabrina, and I'm not going to call you Mother, so there."

She folded her little arms and glared at me defiantly over puffed-up cheeks which made her already chubby face look like a pomegranate. I was hard put to it not to laugh, but I felt it would scarcely help matters. Instead I kept it to a friendly smile.

"Good," I said. "I'm nobody's mother, and it would make me sound rather old, wouldn't it?"

"You mean you don't mind?" She had obviously been expecting the worst. Hoping for it, perhaps.

"No." I held out my hand. "I'm glad to meet you, Sabrina. I'm called Helena."

She took the proffered hand and curtsied. "Yes, we know. Well, what shall we call you, then?"

"How about, oh, er... Helena?"

She giggled happily and turned to the door.

"You can come in now! She doesn't bite!"

I sat up properly in the bed and pulled the covers around me. The older two children came in. Victor was a shy boy, handsome like his father, and quiet. The middle child was another girl, Fulvia, aged nine. She too had the blue eyes and red hair, and I guessed the girls took strongly after their mother. The girls shared Victor's freckled skin, but all of them seemed well cared for and fit. Fulvia took my hand and curtsied also.

"Welcome to our home," she said softly. "I apologise for my sister's rudeness."

"Think nothing of it," I said. "I'd rather people were honest. Why did you bring up the subject? Has someone told you to call me Mother?"

Fulvia nodded. "Our nurse, Venetia. We hid this morning so we could come and see you. She says you are our mother now, and we must show you proper respect."

"I'm your father's wife. That doesn't make me your mother, may she rest in peace."

"That's what Victor said. He said we must show proper respect, but that shouldn't mean calling you something you weren't."

I glanced at Victor, who blushed and looked down.

"Victor is absolutely right," I said. "I want you all to call me by my name. That's what friends call each other."

"Oh, good!" Sabrina approved, at least, and I had an idea that might be the battle half won.

There came a gentle knock at the door. It was the nurse, a thin woman in her twenties with very dark brown hair, already greying. It gave her a prim appearance, but she was not unfriendly.

"Oh, there you are, children. I've been looking for you everywhere. I'm so sorry, *Domina*, I hope they haven't been in your way."

"Hardly that. We've just been getting to know each other a bit. I think we're going to be great friends. But I don't think I can replace their mother. Apart from anything else I'm not much older than Flavius Victor here. We've agreed to call each other by our names."

She looked a little put out, but I was surprised when she didn't argue. Of course, I had forgotten I was her mistress. She couldn't.

"As you wish, *Domina*. If you don't mind I'll take the girls out now. And Flavius should get along to his tutor."

Flavius went out with his chin on his chest. He seemed a typically shy adolescent, but a pleasant lad. The girls were delightful. Perhaps being a stepmother was not going to be so bad. I suddenly felt full of optimism, and a sense that things were all coming right and I was beginning to find my feet.

I was blissfully unaware that after less than a year we were to be uprooted as a result of war, and the worst military disaster the Empire had ever known.

VIII

"Disaster!"

Maximus paced up and down, the dispatch which had caused the outburst in his outstretched hand. From time to time he looked at it again and reread a passage, unable to believe what it contained.

I came down the stairs, still in my night attire, for the messenger had woken us in the middle of the night. We had all known it must be bad news, of course, brought to the *Comes'* own house, and in the small hours at that. Slaves hovered about with oil lamps which sputtered and smoked and threw a glimmering yellow light. Shadows danced on the walls.

"What is it?"

"It's terrible! It's worse than the Varus business!"

This was grim news indeed. Varus was the commander who had lost three entire legions — thirty thousand men — fighting the German tribes in the time of the Emperor Augustus. Not only that, their standards were lost — the greatest disgrace a legion could suffer. It was two years before a punitive expedition was able to avenge the defeat and also bury the poor soldiers' remains, left in the open for all that time. The standards were recovered years later by an expedition in the time of the Emperor Claudius. This was nearly four hundred years ago, but the disaster was still talked of in hushed tones by old campaigners. The shadows drew in, and suddenly the night seemed chilly.

"Get me my cloak," I said to the nearest slave, who vanished with a silent nod.

"Maximus, you must tell us what has happened. The entire household is awake."

"Yes, of course. Forgive me. It's just..."

To my horror, he lifted a hand to his brow and a heartrending sob escaped him. He turned on his heel and hurried into his study, afraid to show himself up in front of the servants and slaves. My confusion was relieved slightly by the reappearance of the slave with my cloak. I wrapped it tightly around me. It was time for action.

73

"Let's have some wine mulled. We'll all die of cold. Issue a cup to every adult."

"Slaves as well, *Domina*?"

"Yes, why not? They've lost as much sleep as the rest of us. Just one cup, though — let's not have them falling over. Get a fire going here. Stoke the hypocaust as well. Let's heat the place now when it's needed most. I think we're in for a long night."

They hurried to carry out my orders, and I smiled inwardly to think of the inexperienced girl who had arrived a year before to be the new mistress of the house. I had come a long way.

*

No sooner had I arrived in Eburacum than I had been thrown into a round of dinner parties, as local society struggled to ingratiate itself with the *Comes* and look over his new wife. Maximus took this part of his job seriously enough, but he left the planning of it to me. I soon found out that he was content for me to run his social life, so long as he was left to run his army. I suppose this duty is thrust upon every officer's wife, but the wife of a great commander sees more of it than most. I really didn't mind. For one thing, I had all the help I could need. Not only was Mabanwy there, but there was no shortage of assistance or money when it came to having the right clothes made or having my hair dressed properly. Suddenly I acquired a considerable wardrobe, and more jewelry than I had ever expected to own. I also found that I actually enjoyed it all. It had its false aspects, of course; we were often invited to things just because someone wanted to impress the *Comes* — or the neighbours — but I also met a lot of interesting people. Legions are usually based firmly in one place, but officers and administrators may travel considerably, and the Empire stretches from Hadrian's Wall to Persia. The garrison included men who had been stationed in Gaul and Africa, and a few who had been to the East — Judaea, Egypt, and Greece. Their tales filled many a long winter evening. I also met their wives.

Felicia was the wife of Vegetius, a military tribune in his late twenties. This was young for such a senior post — one of the second highest ranks in the legion — and he had got this far by a combination of patronage and extremely hard work. Felicia herself was younger, about twenty at this time, but to me she seemed mature and sophisticated. I met them for the first time at a dinner party given by the *legatus*, the legion's commanding officer. She was seated opposite me, and soon struck up a conversation when the men's talk turned to military matters, as it so often did.

"There they go again," she offered.

"Pardon?"

"These men. As soon as they get together to take time off from work, they immediately start a deep discussion. And what is it about? Why, more work!"

I laughed politely, and gave her a close look. She had spoken as if some genuine bitterness underlay the banter. Her voice was steady and confident, with the drawl affected by leisured women everywhere. Maybe it's because they never have to hurry anything.

She was a pleasant-looking woman, I would have said, but not beautiful. She did, however, have spectacular blonde hair, which was a rarity. It was naturally curly, and lent itself to some of the hair styles which were then in vogue, featuring curls around the edge of the hairline. She was a little plump, but many men like that, of course — it fills out the figure in some rather important places. She was one of those people who speak with her hands. They were always held up in front of her, and used to punctuate her utterances with graceful caressing movements. Her face was just a little too painted, perhaps, but that went with her outgoing personality. It was part of her nature to overdo things.

"You're right about the work," I agreed. "It does take over everything sometimes, doesn't it?"

"My dear, does it ever? I'm always telling Vegetius it's no use working your way up to be *Comes* or *Dux* if you die of overwork on the way. Well, you know what I mean, I'm sure. Your husband works harder than any."

"Yes, we do share the same problem, I suppose. But what's the solution?"

"My dear, is there one? I just let Vegetius make the money. Of course, he has a private income anyway — and he lets me spend it. What else can a girl do?"

She certainly had a fine dress, daringly low-cut. It was silk, which was rarely seen in Britain, and a beautiful cream colour. Vegetius had not bought that on a tribune's pay, so the private income was no idle boast. Her bare arms were adorned with gold amulets, too.

"I've got to go and spend some of Maximus's money soon," I said. "I don't have enough clothes yet for this sort of life. We provincials are very backward about such things."

She leaned forward confidentially. "My dear, I know a superb seamstress. She's easily the best in Eburacum, I swear. You must let me introduce you to her and show you some of the things she's done for me."

"That would be nice. Thank you."

"My pleasure, I assure you. You've no idea how good it is to have someone young to do things with." Here her eyebrows arched suggestively. "Dear me, that could have been better phrased. Oh, I don't know, though... Anyway, it's nice to have a change from these old career officer's wives. I'm sure we shall get on famously."

Actually, we did. Felicia had a tendency to be outrageous, and I think I influenced her not to go too far — in some things, at least. On the other hand, she sometimes persuaded me to be a little more adventurous than I might otherwise have been. She had excellent dress sense, and her advice resulted in my wearing much more elegant clothes than I would have chosen alone. I would have thought them too daring, perhaps, or too brightly coloured. I soon grew to value her as both companion and advisor. Even so, I still remember the shock of discovering certain of her activities.

We had been out to the market in Eburacum. I liked going there; apart from the fact that I liked getting out and shopping, it reminded me of home. The buildings were different — half-timbered brick and plaster in place of stone — but the bustle of the market place, its colours and smells were the same. Though not on the sea Eburacum is the capital of the province of Britannia Secunda, or North Britain, so it has its own importance. I suppose it is the most important city in the North. And its river links it to the German Sea, so it is visited by as many traders as Segontium.

On this particular day we had finished our shopping and were walking back home, taking our time and chatting. A young man came walking the other way. He was obviously a man of some means, to judge by his dress, and I had the feeling I recognised him vaguely from somewhere. I met so many at one party or another. Felicia knew him, though.

"Tertius! You're back!"

The young man smiled handsomely and rushed up to embrace her with remarkable familiarity. I thought he must at least be her brother and waited to be introduced. As it happened he introduced himself as soon as he could tear himself from her.

"Metilius Tertius, at your service," he said with a bow. The way his eyes swept over me I suddenly knew he was not Felicia's brother.

"This is Helena of Arfon," said Felicia. Tertius said he was charmed. "She's the new wife of the *Comes*, so you watch yourself."

He raised his eyebrows and backed away, his manner cooling noticeably.

"My respects, *Domina*." Then he turned to Felicia. "Keeping exalted company, aren't you?"

"Don't be cheeky," she said with a giggle. "Run along now. See you at the old place? Tomorrow?"

He nodded quickly and rushed off along the cobbled street. I watched him go, and then turned to Felicia.

"Who was that man?"

She smiled. "Just a friend."

"A close friend, obviously."

"Oh, very close." The way she emphasised the word "very" was full of meaning. Young and inexperienced though I was, it didn't escape me.

"Felicia, does Vegetius know about this?"

"No fear. At least, if he does he turns a blind eye. I wouldn't put it past him, actually."

"Felicia!"

"Helena, you're a very sweet person, but you're so naïve. Vegetius and I are bound together by ties of dynastic obligation, not love. We didn't choose each other, our families chose us. He's a nice enough man; we rub along all right together. It's just not enough, that's all. Vegetius is too busy working to worry much about me. On the other hand I don't have enough to do, unless I find myself something to pass the time. A little dalliance with a strong handsome young man like Tertius is just the thing."

I was amazed.

"Well," I said at last, "I had no idea."

"Good. Let's hope you're not the only one. We don't want anyone having a word in Vegetius's ear, do we?"

"Isn't it dangerous?"

"Dangerous? Oh, I don't think so. Vegetius isn't the sort of man to make a lot of fuss and show himself up. Even if he found out I think he'd just tell me to pack it in."

*

"And would you?"

"For a while."

"Well, I think you should be careful."

"Oh, I will, you can be sure. I never bring anyone home. That wouldn't do at all. Discreet inns are the thing. There are a lot of those in town, thank heavens."

"Doesn't it... I mean don't you ever think it might be wrong?"

She looked me in the eye.

"Why? It's a contract, isn't it? I give Vegetius what he wants. I value him for what he can give me in return. What he can't I... get elsewhere. What's the alternative? Should I turn into an embittered and frustrated old shrew, always nagging him for what he can't give? He's a good man, he deserves better than that."

"And you think this is better?"

"Yes, I do. Don't be so disapproving, Helena. It's different for you — you married the man you chose. You love him, and he dotes on you — "

"He does?"

" — doesn't he?"

"Yes, you're right, Felicia. It's different for me."

We seldom spoke about her young men again. Sometimes, when I called for her and she was not in, I would wonder about it, but I never enquired too closely. It was rather like a disagreement over religion — if it threatens to come between you and your friends, you just avoid the topic.

Meanwhile Maximus was constantly having to go away. He went to the north-west to supervise the sea defences against the Irish raiders. He fought there once, when a raid coincided with his visit. He said it was nice to know he still hadn't lost the use of his sword-arm. I was worried sick. I had expected a commander to give orders, not fight. He also went up to Cataracta to the large camp there, and to the north-east to secure the coastline against the Picts. He must have travelled the entire length of Hadrian's Wall. As well as this he went down to Londinium once that year, and brought me a present of cloth from his mother, who sent her best regards and hoped to meet me soon. I still hadn't met her, of course. He was away at least half the time, and in his absence I ran the household and learned to be a commander's wife. I had to organise a certain amount of activities among the officers' wives, although I had a secretary to help. I had to organise Maximus's social diary, and see that we invited everyone we were supposed to invite. I saw to the comfort of guests, some of whom were very important. I even had a religious role. The Emperors might be Christian, but many of their soldiers were not. The *Comes*, like all Roman officials, used to be responsible for seeing that the proper religious rituals were observed when the garrison undertook any project or commissioned new quarters or equipment. In Britain things still happened like that, although more because no one had noticed than anything else. Maximus was going on with the rituals, which he had little belief in himself, until ordered otherwise. His men expected it, and they expected his wife to attend similar rituals when their women got married or bore children.

Felicia might be short of things to do, but I wasn't!

And now this. A "disaster" Maximus had called it. And who should know better than a man of his rank?

"Give me the wine pitcher and a cup," I ordered. The slave handed them over. "Leave me now. I will go to comfort my husband."

The servants and slaves dispersed. Even Mabanwy I sent away. Fortunately the children had not woken up — I dreaded to think how they would have reacted to their father's condition. I had my sandals on, and they flapped across the tiles as I approached the study door. The wood smoke from the fire had percolated into the room a little, and the smell of it hung there. For some reason it reminded me of the open air, of the woods near home and the burning of stubble in the autumn. And an image came to mind of my Macsen and me, tumbling down the slope last summer near Segontium, and him landing on top of me, almost pre-empting the marriage ceremony. I smiled to myself and pushed open the study door.

Maximus was sitting at the small table there, his back to the door. He could not have heard me come in, as I gently pushed the door to. He looked up when I put the pitcher in front of him and began to pour some wine.

"Helena, I'm sorry, it was unforgivable to — "

"Hush. I understand. You don't have to justify yourself to me."

He pushed the wax tablets towards me.

"Look. See what has happened."

"Drink the wine; it will do you good."

The dispatch was from the office of the Western co-Emperor Gratian in Gaul. The Eastern co-Emperor, Valens, had taken a large force to deal with an insurrection of Goths in Thrace. These barbarians had been admitted to the Empire as federates in order to guard its approaches against the Huns and other tribes from the East. He had the chance to negotiate with them, but mishandled the whole business very badly. Relations had quickly deteriorated into outright war. There had been a military disaster of extreme proportions. It seems the enemy had fielded unusual numbers of skilled cavalry — not the Imperial Army's strongest point. Not only had two legions been annihilated, but the Emperor Valens himself had been killed in the battle. This was quite simply unheard of, but it indicated the contempt the Goths felt for Valens, and for the Empire. A certain Theodosius, son of Maximus's late friend and colleague, had been appointed *Magister Militum* — Master of Soldiers — and given the task of restoring order before the Goths could lay siege to Constantinople, capital of the Eastern Empire. For the time being, no successor to Valens was to be announced.

Maximus saw himself as the bearer of a proud tradition, both military and imperial, which had now been dragged in the dirt. I did understand. I was sure my father would feel the same when he heard the news. For men like this it was like taking their manhood away. I looked at Maximus, now draining his cup. There was nothing I could do about the Empire, but I could do something for my husband.

I pulled him to me, kissed him savagely. Surprised, he responded at once. I took his hand and placed it on my breast. He hesitated.

"The servants?"

"Dismissed."

He kissed me again, fumbling with my clothes. Fire coursed through my veins. He needed me, for once. I dragged him to the couch in the corner. No time for stairs and bedrooms. We fell on to it, shedding clothing and inhibitions. This hunger had to be satisfied at once. Still half-dressed we came together on the couch, groaning our desire with every thrust, faster and faster, till I really did feel that I was riding that wave to the shore. Only this time I rode it to the end, till it broke its force in a frenzy of kisses, thrusting hips, and staccato cries of ecstasy.

"Oh, Macsen! My Macsen! I love you so much."

Still clinging to each other we allowed our passion to subside slowly, rolled over — and fell on the floor in a giggling heap.

It would be good to record that this was a turning point in our intimate relationship, but it was not to be. Indeed Maximus was plunged into even more work, leaving even less time and energy for his family. The very next day a courier arrived with fresh news. There was to be a reorganisation of the highest levels of the army. The *Dux Britanniarum* — leader of the army in Britain — was being reassigned to the German frontier. Maximus was appointed in his place.

We were to move immediately to Londinium.

IX

If Eburacum was a contrast to Segontium, how much more so was Londinium to Eburacum! Capital of the two Britains, a port, a great fortress, and home to twenty thousand people.

I was dozing in the carriage when the cry went up that the city was in view. There were shouts of approval from our cavalry escort, who had been in the saddle for several weary days. As with our previous move there was a veritable train of wagons on the road, bringing our goods southwards. We had left them behind, as our progress was so much faster, and tonight we were due to stay with the *vicarius* at his palace near the Tamesis River. This man, Paulus Civilis, was the chief of all the Imperial Governors in Britain and therefore my father's superior. Maximus's own house was available, but he wanted to stay with the *vicarius* as a gesture of solidarity rather than anything else. The exact relationship between the civilian and military administrations had never been spelled out in detail, and in these far flung reaches of the Empire the military often had to take precedence. There was little to gain from arguing over protocol if the barbarians were at the gates! As *Dux Britanniarum*, Maximus was independent of the civilian governors, but he knew the value of allies. Civilis had invited us to visit until our own things arrived, and his hospitality would not be refused. Maximus's own house — and his mother who lived in it — would have to wait.

The walls of Londinium stretched away on both sides of the gate. To the right they seemed to go on for miles, grey stone with lines of red brick, the parapet castellated and punctuated with bastions. To the left they curved away towards the river. In the middle distance we could see another gate spanning the road which led to the east, and the so-called "Saxon Shore". If ever the Saxons laid siege to Londinium it was along this road that they would come — if they were civilised enough to know a road when they saw one.

"Well," said Mabanwy in awe, "I'd be glad of those walls if the barbarians were outside."

I could only see the gate we were approaching by leaning out of the carriage. Its twin square towers, topped with pantiles, stood twice as high as the walls, with a short high section of the wall between them. From this, no doubt, the gates could be defended if necessary. The entrance itself consisted of twin arches, one for traffic in each direction. As we came closer I saw that there was a deep ditch running the full length of the walls, with bridges where the roads crossed. The bottom was full of stagnant water, and the ditch added several feet to the effective height of the walls. It would be a formidable obstacle indeed for any attacker.

My attention was distracted by the distant sound of cheering. Men were at the battlements, waving. Our outriders had obviously announced Maximus's presence. He turned to me with a smile.

"The Cornovians," he said, and turned to look again, pride beaming from his face.

And well it might. Commanders often owed their positions to patronage or bribery, and were not always loved by their men. Maximus was of high birth, but he had worked for his position, and fought. Above all he had won, which is what soldiers value most. The sound of their shouting grew louder, and resolved itself into a single chant of two syllables, rising and falling like waves on the sea. Mabanwy and I exchanged glances as we realised what it was.

"Mac-sen! Mac-sen! Mac-sen!"

Macsen swung himself out of the door, and hung there by one hand, while the other was raised in greeting to his men, the fist clenched. This brought more cheers. The wheels of our carriage rolled like thunder across the bridge and through the stone-lined arch of the Severan Gate.

Londinium astonished me. It was a city of wide streets, parks, and rich houses with gardens and fountains. Everywhere there were trees and flowers. The buildings, mainly brick or half-timbered, had proper roofs of pantiles or thatch, and the smoke of hypocausts was always on the breeze. There were imposing public buildings — besides the massive Basilica, seat of the town authorities, and the vicarian palace, there were many Christian churches and temples of other religions. Of course, many of these were now closed indefinitely. There were several great baths, where the many who had no bath at home could steam or soak themselves, often conducting business or gambling at the same time. Notoriously, the baths were sometimes the scene of less respectable activities.

The south side of the city lay along the River Tamesis. Although there was a wall along its full length, the river bank was lined with wharves, and there were gates to allow the passage of goods inside to the warehouses which lined the streets of that quarter. I will never forget my first site of the magnificent bridge — only a roadway supported by a row of stone arches, but there were more than twenty of them! I think a three-arched bridge was the longest I had ever seen before.

And then there was the market. Indeed, there were several in different places, mostly specialised like the fish market by the river. The main central market was held daily in the Forum — a great open square surrounded by the Basilica, so that complaints of short weight or any other dispute could be settled at once by the authorities who administered justice there. Goods of every kind were on sale — home-produced wool and exotic furs and fabrics from the East; fresh farm produce and preserves from as far away as Africa; spices and herbs from every corner of the Empire, and wines from Gaul and Italy. All around there were vendors of cooked foods, and the smell of roasting and frying always hung on the air, although public cooking was strictly controlled because of the fire hazard. Whole towns have been known to burn down because a cooking fire got out of hand, although of course Londinium is much too big for that ever to happen!

As if this were not enough, in the streets around were the workshops of the craftsmen — furniture makers, toolmakers, tailors, masons and plumbers — in short, everything needed to build and maintain the greatest city in the country. I watched as we passed through, and marvelled. The Empire might be going through troubled times, but if even a provincial capital could offer this much it was not dead yet.

Our carriage rumbled down a wide avenue, passing the basilican complex on the right, our escort shouting at the people to clear the way. There were plenty of onlookers; as well as those out shopping or on business there were many who seemed to have come out of their houses in response to the noise of our arrival. We passed a small detachment of soldiers, who cheered and waved; more of Macsen's men. Then we swung around the corner of the Basilica and passed along its impressive frontage, complete with colonnaded portico, before turning left towards the Thames again. We had only been in the city ten minutes, and already we had turned this way and that until I had no idea where we were.

"Not long now," said Maximus, and smiled distantly.

"Thank goodness. I need a bath."

"We all do, I'm sure. That road is filthy. Actually, the streets here are not much better. The Councillors ought to do something about it."

Occupied with such trivia, we failed to notice that the carriage was turning again. Suddenly the rumble of stone cobbles gave way to the crunch of gravel. The background noise of the street faded, and was replaced by the gentle trickling sound of a fountain. A slave ran up and opened the door, placing a small block of wooden steps before it. Maximus stepped down and gave me his hand. I looked around and saw the courtyard was almost surrounded by a two-storey building with a cloister beneath it. In the centre was the fountain, and in front of us was the grand entrance to the palace, with ornamental steps and a stone portico. As I stepped down a distinguished-looking elderly man hurried out, dressed in a fine toga and followed by a retinue of servants.

"Maximus, you are indeed welcome. And this is your wife? Splendid!"

He bowed and kissed my hand, which from someone of his rank was probably overdoing the courtesy. I had a clear view of his bald scalp, surrounded by a ring of grey curls.

"My dear, you must be exhausted! What a journey! Now, let me look at you."

He gave me an appraising glance and seemed to be satisfied.

"You're a lucky fellow, Maximus. Such a beautiful young wife, and British, too! You're obviously learning sense as you get older."

Maximus just laughed at this rather personal comment.

"This is Paulus Civilis," he said to me. "Don't be deceived. He acts like everybody's uncle, but he can be as tough as old boots if the need arises."

Civilis looked slightly hurt at this, and shook his head.

"Ah, me, such times we live in. Cynics everywhere! Come on inside, now, and tell me all your news. We'll have some wine together, and of course you'll want a bath."

The men soon fell to talking politics, which was inevitable, I suppose. I asked if Mabanwy and I might go to the baths, and a servant was sent for to take us there. The palace was sumptuously furnished and decorated. Mabanwy and I gaped at everything like a couple of country bumpkins. Even Eburacum had nothing like this. The walls were painted with exquisite frescoes of flower garlands, and the main rooms had mosaic floors with scenes from Roman stories on them. There were wall hangings and floor coverings of a quality and exotic nature I had never seen before. I imagined they must be from the East — Arabia or Persia, perhaps even India. Through a window I glimpsed another courtyard. It seemed to be over a hundred feet long, with a fountained ornamental pool running almost the whole length of it. Civilis was even richer than I had suspected. The final luxury came to light when the servant brought us to the baths — there were two complete sets, one for each sex!

We soon stripped and sat in the *tepidarium*, rubbing oil into our skin and enjoying the perfumed warmth until the slave came to rub us down. She massaged our shoulders first, to relax them, and then proceeded to our backs and legs until our bodies glowed and fatigue seemed a thing of the past. At last we dismissed her and went to the *caldarium* to let our pores really open in the hot steam. Curved *strigils* were provided to scrape our skin down and remove both the oil and dirt.

"This is the life," was my comment to Mabanwy. "Wine beforehand, perfumed oils and a masseuse."

"Hmm," she murmured dreamily. "I'd settle for a bronzed legionary with rippling muscles to do the massage — and he needn't stop at the back and legs, either!"

"Mabanwy!"

She chuckled through the clouds of steam. "You've been a married woman for a year, but you're as easily shocked as ever."

I thought of how shocked I had been at Felicia's antics.

"You're right, I suppose. That's meant to be normal, though, isn't it?"

"Maybe. Anyway, I was only joking. No one could make love in this heat!"

"Sounds like you're getting too hot as it is, Mabanwy. Come on — last one in the cold pool's a cissy!"

"Oh no! Not the cold pool! The hot pool!"

"No time. Got to close those pores or you'll die of cold!"

With shrieks of merriment we dashed through the door into the cold room.

While we were towelling ourselves afterwards Mabanwy turned suddenly serious.

"Can I ask you a question, *Dominula*?"

"Of course. You know you can ask anything you want."

"Well, I don't know. I'm only a servant, if it comes down to it."

"Spit it out, Mabanwy! You know I won't bite your head off, servant or not!"

"Very well, then. *Domina*, are you happy?"

The question took me aback. That sort of question always implies that there is something wrong, and obviously so. You feel silly if you haven't noticed it, and compromised if you have.

"Of course I am."

"Really?" Her rejoinder was too quick.

"Mabanwy, I am well to do, healthy, and married to a fine husband who is rich and has yet better prospects — and you ask if I'm happy!"

"Well, it's just..."

"Yes?"

"I don't know. I suppose sharing a carriage with you these last few days has put me in your company more than usual, and especially his! I thought things seemed a bit strained sometimes."

"It's just sitting in that damned carriage for so long. I never want to sit down again. I wonder if Civilis would let us eat dinner standing up!"

Privately, I wondered if everyone was as perceptive as Mabanwy.

*

The next morning I went out into the great courtyard which I had glimpsed through the windows on our way to the baths. It was indeed over a hundred feet long, and perhaps fifty wide. It was surrounded on all four sides by the various wings of the palace, and decorated with flower beds, cherry trees and statues. In the centre, running almost the whole length of the courtyard, was a great oval ornamental pool edged with a stone parapet. On the side nearest the main entrance the pool was widened locally into two curved bays, each with a fountain. Between them and the main entrance the ground was covered in ornamental paving, the rest being gravelled. I wandered slowly around the pool, admiring the fish which swam there and the water lilies. The palace all around blocked out the sounds of the city, so that the courtyard was a haven of quiet. The city bustle was replaced by a background of the gently tinkling fountains and the twittering of the sparrows. Apart from these, only the crunch of gravel underfoot and the occasional swirl of water from a jumping fish disturbed the silence. It was a beautiful and tranquil place; I could see how a man with the responsibilities of the *vicarius* might treasure it. I wondered what it looked like in winter, with snow on the ground, ice on the pool, and the fountains turned off.

"Ah, here she is."

I turned as Maximus's voice broke in on my thoughts. He had entered by the main door and stood on the ornamental paving. Next to him was a woman of about fifty; she was rather thin, but the broad forehead and the large dark eyes gave her away immediately. I knew at once that this was his mother. I walked around the pool to them, my heart beating fast. I saw her turn to her son with a reproachful look. Her words were probably not meant to carry, but she didn't allow for the quietness of the courtyard.

"Magnus, dear, she's a child!"

He had no time to reply before I had reached them. I made a partial curtsey to her, and she coloured a little in the suspicion that I had heard her remark.

"How do you do, Flavia Antonina? I am Helena, daughter of Eudav of Arfon."

She raised an eyebrow at the British style, but gave me the customary kiss of welcome — or rather, she pursed her lips and made a kissing sound in the air near my cheek. There was a waft of rosewater as she did so.

"I am pleased to welcome you at last," she said formally. "This son of mine was too impatient to bring you down to Londinium for the marriage. Now I see why."

I wasn't sure how to take this but I smiled at her encouragingly. She might be a slim woman, her skin lined and her hair grey, but I would never make the mistake of regarding her as frail. The character behind those dark eyes was as strong as it had ever been.

"Magnus, get someone to bring us a drink, will you? Helena and I must get acquainted."

Magnus Clemens Maximus, Commander of the Two Britains, went meekly off to fetch his mother a drink.

"So tell me about yourself," said the Commander's mother, and I obeyed.

We talked for perhaps an hour, sitting in that quiet garden while the fountains played. I talked the most. Flavia listened, but gave away very little about herself. I had the impression she was giving me the inspection she ought to have given me before the wedding. There was no clue as to whether I had passed.

"Now, Helena," she said at last, "before we rejoin the others I feel I must say something."

I was all ears.

"You know, of course, that Magnus has been married before."

She said it as if afraid that I might not know, despite the evidence of the three children.

"Now, you are a young woman, but you will need to be mistress in your own house. If you ever want advice I will gladly give it, but I will not impose my presence upon you unless asked."

I started to make some polite disclaimer, but she held up her hand.

"No, no false politeness. This is much too important for that. I occupy a small wing in Magnus's — in your — house. I have my own servants and I am very self-contained. I prefer it that way, to be honest, and it is one of the reasons I stayed in Londinium when Magnus was posted to Eburacum."

I wondered what the other reasons were, but I could hardly ask.

"The arrangement was my idea, incidentally, when Magnus invited me to live with him after his father's death. My own mother-in-law was never out of my hair, and I disliked her heartily on that account. I do not wish to make the same mistake. Have I made myself clear?"

I smiled. She seemed a naturally domineering woman who knew it, and was desperate to be fair to me.

"Indeed you have. And I thank you for your frankness."

"Good. Forgive me for looking you over so obviously, but Magnus is a great man doing great work. It must not be hindered by domestic discord. I had misgivings, I admit, when I heard how young you were."

"I trust they have been allayed."

"I'm sure we shall get on," was all she said.

*

We moved into Maximus's house — somehow I couldn't adopt the *praenomen* of Magnus like his mother — two days later. For the first two weeks or so I seemed to be bogged down in the business of arranging furniture and ordering new decoration. Those parts of the house which had been empty for some time had deteriorated. There were untreated damp patches here and there, and in one place broken roof tiles had let in water which had brought down a piece of the ceiling. Workmen were never out of the place. The tiler and the mason were sent for to make sure the damp would not get in again, and then we had the plasterers and painters to repair the damage it had already caused. Fortunately most of the house was all right.

And what a house it was! Not as grand as that of the *vicarius*, of course, but still grand by most people's standards, and richer than my father's villa at Segontium. Like most of the town villas, it was built in a square around a central courtyard, with the living rooms

91

to the front and the kitchen, baths, and slave quarters at the back. One side of the square formed Flavia's private apartment. At the back there was a second entrance on to the street behind, and a modest stable with Maximus's four horses and a small carriage.

The courtyard in the centre was graced by a fountain and well-tended flower beds. In the corner by the kitchen there was a herb garden. As was customary, a cloister ran all the way round the courtyard to give shelter from the rain or sun according to the season. The main living rooms had under floor heating ducted from a hypocaust near the baths, and the baths themselves featured warm and hot steam rooms with hot and cold plunge pools. Everywhere the walls were decorated with the best in fashionable motifs, and the entrance hall and living rooms boasted superb mosaic floors. I felt like a queen to be mistress of this sumptuous household, and not yet seventeen!

It was only after the house was set to rights that I thought of the other woman who had been mistress here. It was in this house that Maximus's first wife had lived. And died. Yet it was strange that I knew nothing about her. No one ever mentioned her, even her children. Maximus simply refused to talk about her when I tried to raise the subject. I assumed it distressed him, and I was a little jealous to think that the memory of her could affect him still. But I was not one to fear competition from a ghost. She was dead, and Maximus loved me.

But presumably he had once loved her.

Maria. That had been her name. Even that was gleaned for me by Mabanwy. Maria was the sort of name one expected from a very religious family, and Christian of course. It was not as widespread then as it has become since; it seemed comical to Latin speakers, meaning "seas" in that language. Had she brought her children up in her religion, I wondered? There was little sign of it now. Maximus seemed to practice nothing, and although the children were educated about the religions of the Empire, they were not indoctrinated into any of them. In those days it was not such a rare thing. We were balanced on a watershed between the pagan past and the Christian future, between tolerance and orthodoxy, and even then we half knew it. It was a lull before the storms of religious controversy that were to follow. That is what made it surprising that Maria, named unashamedly after the mother of the Christian God, had left no trace of her beliefs.

And no trace of anything else. There was nothing of her — no portraits, no religious objects, no tapestries or other examples of her handiwork. There were no clothes, although they must have been too valuable to throw out. Perhaps Maximus had deliberately tried to remove all traces of her. I thought again of the man who had wept in the night at my father's house in Segontium. Yes, reminders of her were clearly just too distressing. I knew he could weep under sufficient pressure — I had seen that when he heard the news of the disaster in Thrace. He might be Commander of all the armies in Britain's two provinces, but he still had feelings. Once again, I vowed to try to soothe them, to be his comfort when all was confusion and stress.

The problem with that line of thought was that it aroused my own feelings — feelings which were soothed seldom enough these days. After two weeks in Londinium we still had not made love there. I had tried to blot it from my mind, to bury myself in the work I had to do. I told myself that Maximus too was very busy, and no doubt very tired. Still, I needed the reassurance that he still wanted me. The thought came to me that I should take the initiative myself. He was probably being over-considerate, that was all; he had seen how busy I was. Yes, that was it. He would actually welcome it if I made the first move, I felt sure. I would do it, this very night...

"Macsen, would you like to come to my room tonight?"

He looked up from the wax tablets he was studying. "Do you want me to?"

"Yes. I mean, if you want to, of course. I'd like that."

He smiled. "I'm sorry. I've been neglecting you."

"No, no. I realise you're very busy, and often very tired, too, I expect."

"It's very sweet of you to make excuses for me. I've been preoccupied with my own desires. I should remember you have needs too, and not neglect them." He looked suddenly into the middle distance. "It can be dangerous."

"I'll go on upstairs, now. Join me when you've finished with those."

"Off you go, then. I won't be far behind you."

I went straight to my room, freshened up at the water bowl with the flower petals in it, and then crept into bed wearing fresh perfume and a smile. Maximus came in a few minutes later, and we found that not all disasters happen in the East.

He quickly stripped and got in beside me, took me in his arms. I kissed him hungrily, my feelings surging within me. It had been such a long time. For a minute I was unaware of what was happening. Or rather, what was not. Then, when I pulled him tightly to me, I realised. He put a brave face on it for a minute longer, then broke away.

"I'm sorry, Helena."

"Macsen, my dear Macsen, it's my fault. I shouldn't have asked you when you weren't ready."

He slid out of bed and threw his robe around him.

"It's not your fault," he said in a grim voice. "I *should* have been ready. I should have expected this."

"Maximus, what do you mean? What's wrong?"

"Nothing. Nothing is wrong. We will forget about this. Another time it will be all right. Try to sleep."

And he went out, leaving me to another tearful night of frustration and self-relief. It cured the physical ache, but not the pain of knowing that he couldn't love me. And amongst the pain was a little anger also. I was the daughter of a British royal house. I was considered intelligent, young and beautiful — what more did he want?

X

A depression had settled on Maximus. When he came home — and there seemed to be ever more excuses for him not to — he was quiet and morose. His way of curing this was to immerse himself more deeply in his work, so that I saw less of him than ever. I knew his work was important, of course — nothing less than the survival of Britain — but where was the point of bare survival? Without love and family there was nothing worth surviving for, or so it seemed to me. It was in the midst of this despondency that I first became aware of Maximus's female visitor.

I had been out with the children and Mabanwy. Fortunately Maximus's moods had not communicated themselves to the young ones, although Flavius Victor knew that all was not well. Still, he was a sensible boy, and growing up fast. I liked all of them, to their — and my — great relief. Mabanwy was supposed to be my personal maid now, but she had always liked being with children, and I took shameless advantage of her when I wanted another adult to help out. The children's nurse, Venetia, had stayed in Eburacum. There was a new nurse — there had to be, considering how often we had to leave the house for official functions — but she had to have some time off. Servants commanded high wages here in Londinium, and there were plenty of other jobs if our conditions didn't suit them. Actually, this was only one of the reasons I often took charge of the children myself. As I say, I liked them. So far there had been no sign of my becoming pregnant, and I couldn't see it happening while Maximus's affliction continued. I was a normal young woman, and children were definitely part of what I wanted in life.

It was a Sunday. The bells of the Christian churches had been ringing all morning. Now, in the early afternoon, I thought it would do us all good to go for a walk.

"Can we go down to the river?" asked Flavius Victor. "I'd like to see the ships, but I don't want to go anywhere else much."

The other children agreed and we all got our cloaks and outdoor boots as it was a little chilly. All except Maximus, that is.

"I've got a few things to do," he said grumpily. "Besides, with the life I lead I don't think I need the exercise."

"Your children need a father," I said gently. "You hardly ever spend time with them. Flavius worships you. He's growing up, he needs your guidance."

"He'll get it when he needs it. Right now I'm too busy for frivolities."

And he trudged off to his study — to read more dispatches, I presumed.

We walked the fifty or so yards to the city wall. We had to follow this for some way westwards until we came to the great gate where the road left the city and crossed the river. Downstream from the bridge the river bank had been rebuilt into a long wharf made from great baulks of timber with clay packed behind them. Not the elegant stone of Greek or Italian harbours, perhaps, but formidably strong just the same. Flavius liked to watch the ships loading and unloading here. Occasionally we would chat to some old retired sailor who had finished his working life but still couldn't quite leave the river alone. There were always one or two, just sitting there and watching what was happening. Their tales used to fill Flavius with excitement, and I was sure he would be a sea captain one day. Poor dear Flavius.

With its being Sunday there was not much in the way of commercial activity. Many of the merchants and ship owners were Christians, and it was part of their religion to do no work on Sundays. Since Constantine the Great even the pagans were limited, because he had closed the law courts and other official offices on the Sun's holy day. The Christians had found it politic to change theirs from Saturday, which it had been previously. The pagans often found it useful to repair their craft on Sunday, and save the loading until the next. Still, it was pleasant to wander along the quayside and study the ships. They were mostly quite small, many of them just river craft, but some were fully equipped seagoing vessels from exotic places — or at least Gaul. There were even a couple of warships from the British Fleet, which was one of Maximus's commands. They were formidable ships armed with huge rams at the bow and catapults on the deck. Somehow their capacity for destruction made me uneasy — perhaps because of my husband's profession — and I turned away, just in time to see little Sabrina fall headlong into a patch of mud.

She started yelling at once, and got up in the unsteady way that children do when they are not really hurt, but shocked even so. Her dress and face and arms were covered in black mud. On closer inspection this turned out to be partly pitch, used to waterproof the boats. I was angry at the idiot who had spilt it, but I suppose he would have argued it was a place of work, not a public playground. Anyway, it was clear that Sabrina would have to go straight home. There were groans from Flavius and Fulvia when I announced it, but I silenced them at once.

"Come on! She's cut her knee, too. It must be washed in clean water and properly looked after."

They knew how important that was, and their protest subsided. I picked Sabrina up and set her astride my hip. Her little arms went around my neck and she rested her head on my shoulder, still sobbing. Stifling a selfish thought for my own dress, I led the party homeward at a brisk march.

The shortest route home led us to the house by the back way. The entrance there was mainly intended for tradesmen and the horses, and was marked by a tall gate wide enough to drive the carriage through. Next to it was a little door for people on foot, and as we approached it opened suddenly. We were still some way off, but it was plain that the person emerging was a woman. She wore a plain grey dress, but only the skirt was visible. Her head and upper body were swathed in a large blue woollen shawl.

She turned as she heard us coming, and I caught a glimpse of fair skin and blonde hair. Then she turned away abruptly and made off. She was certainly not one of our servants, but she might have been a relative of one of them, paying a visit to the kitchen without permission, perhaps. She didn't look like a servant, though. Not rich, admittedly, but somehow carrying herself as if she was used to being thought a person of substance. She didn't run off like someone who was up to no good.

Our route lay past the kitchen and hypocaust to a rear entrance of the bath house. My first task was to strip and bath young Sabrina, and I forgot about the woman in blue until later. After dinner she came to mind again, while Maximus and I were talking by the fire. We seldom had guests on a Sunday, although two or three dinner parties a week were not unusual.

"Who was the woman who called this afternoon?" I asked him innocently.

He stiffened. "Woman? What woman?"

"As we were arriving home I saw a blonde woman in a grey dress and blue shawl. She made off quickly and I forgot about it while I was bathing Sabrina. I just thought of it again."

"Someone to visit the servants, maybe," he suggested.

"Did you give permission?"

"No."

"Nor did I. In fact, no one's asked."

I was puzzled. Maximus seemed evasive, and I was sure that he was holding something back. His eyes watched me closely, as if trying to gauge whether I was satisfied with his answers. I wasn't.

"Aren't you concerned, Maximus?"

"Not really. Should I be?"

"Well, yes. It might have been anyone. We should speak to the servants."

"Hardly necessary."

"Oh, honestly, Maximus! This is silly. We should know who she was!"

I got up and reached for the hand bell we used to call the servants, but Maximus snatched it away.

"Not necessary, I said!"

"Maximus!"

"You probably imagined it!"

His eyes were angry and yet there was something else there. Fear, perhaps?

"Maximus, what is all this about? Please tell me!"

"Nothing! As far as I am concerned there was no one. You are making a fuss about nothing, and quite spoiling the evening!"

"I shall ask Caradoc!"

Caradoc was the senior manservant, and little escaped him. Maximus sat fuming while I stamped away down to the kitchen, where Caradoc was supervising the clearing up after our dinner. There was quite a bustle.

"Caradoc!"

He turned, and a hush fell.

"*Domina*! This is a surprise."

He might well be surprised. I seldom ventured here, except to discuss menus with the cook. To arrive without warning was almost a breach of etiquette, as if I didn't trust him and was checking up.

"Caradoc, was there a visitor today while I was out — a young woman?"

His face gave him away at once. So did the atmosphere. You could have heard a pin drop. They all knew something, and whatever it was it was being kept from me.

"Well?"

"No one has visited the servants' quarters, *Domina*."

"And did anyone visit the master?"

"Have you asked him yourself, *Domina*?" His manner was calculatedly bordering on the insolent, which was not like him.

"Yes. He says there was no one."

"Then there was no one, *Domina*."

"Damn it, Caradoc, I *saw* the woman!"

He shrugged. His position, of course, was impossible. He couldn't argue with me, but even less with Maximus. I turned on my heel and walked back to the dining room. Maximus looked up.

"Well?"

"He says there was no one."

"I told you so."

But the relief in his eyes gave him away. Pain and anger boiled inside me.

"Maximus, I am not a fool! We have only been married a year and here you are carrying on with some trollop while you spurn your own wife! Right under our own roof! The gods help me, what have I done to deserve this?"

And I burst into tears.

He was on his feet in an instant, and gripped me by both arms.

"Listen to me! I am not carrying on with anyone — under our own roof or anyone else's. You know I cannot tell you about everything I do. You know there are secrets in my work." He paused, and softened his voice. "It's not just the military plans, it's the politics too. I have to keep an eye on people — those who are over-ambitious, or disloyal. A commander in my position must have eyes both in front and behind."

I looked up at him. "You mean, she was one of your agents or something like that?"

There was the briefest of hesitations before he spoke.

"Yes, something like that."

He let me go as I raised a hand to wipe my tears.

"I think I'll go up to my room, now."

He gruffly wished me goodnight as I went out. I had no stomach to fight on, but I had seen the anxious eyes assessing my reaction.

He was lying.

*

And so matters went on. We spent a winter in Londinium — a mild one, by the standards of Eburacum. In the spring the river flooded in places, but we ourselves were spared that. In January came the news that the younger Theodosius had been appointed Augustus, or Emperor, of the East. No doubt this was because of his success in pacifying the Goths after the disaster of the previous year. No doubt, also, it reflected his great popularity among the Army. As my brother Adeon had so cynically observed, the Senate might appoint the Emperor, but by some coincidence he tended to be the Army's favourite!

Theodosius was to prove the most ardently Christian of all the Emperors so far. Like Valentinian I, he refused the title of Pontifex Maximus — "Greatest Bridge Builder" — on the grounds that it was a heathen title, long held by the pagan emperors of Rome. Unlike Valentinian I, he was actively hostile to the Arian heresy, which had been strong in the Eastern Empire for the past forty years. Many feared trouble, and a renewal of the persecutions which had sometimes occurred before. However, Theodosius was for the most part a reasonable man, with a reputation for mercy. Besides, his position was not yet secure enough to risk fuelling the hungry fires of sectarian division.

Maximus was well enough pleased. His family and that of Theodosius were old friends, and had been even through the time when Theodosius's father had been disgraced and executed. Now the emperor responsible for that was dead, and his victim's son was himself elevated to the purple robe and the golden crown of Constantinople. In theory, at least; he was actually still in Thrace, doing a brilliant job of pacifying the Goths, thousands of whom were now joining the Army.

"What a change in fortunes!" said Maximus when he heard the news. "You know, that family is watched over by heaven, I think. Events may do them down from time to time, but they always rise again. I hope old Theodosius's spirit, wherever it is, can see what's happening. He'd be so proud of his son. Now let's see if he can knock the western emperors into shape."

"You think he will?" I asked.

"Well, somebody's got to. Just look at Gratian. A weak youth who gives no attention to the barbarian threat but spends his time chasing heretics. It's ridiculous!"

"Perhaps he feels that unity is an important weapon, too," I suggested.

"Well, perhaps it is. No, *certainly* it is. But I've been a military man for long enough to know that you can lead troops as far as you like but you can't push them at all."

"What do you mean?"

"Gratian's not popular. He can't ever make up his mind about anything; he's so easily swayed by his advisers. Half his army is made up of barbarian mercenaries. They'll have a go at other barbarians for him, but they've no interest in policing jobs like going after heretics and pulling down pagan temples. Anyway, those that aren't pagans themselves are Arian heretics. If he keeps using them for that kind of work he'll lose their support, and we all know what happens to emperors who do that."

"Is he likely to, do you think?"

"Not for the moment, perhaps. He openly favours the barbarian elements in the Army, especially his bodyguard of Alani. Bodyguard, indeed! Blond beautiful boys! They say his body gets guarded a damned sight more closely than nature intended, if you understand me. Anyway, he keeps their loyalty. The trouble is, of course, by doing that he's losing the support of the Roman legionaries themselves. He can't do without that, either. But if he goes, who else is there? Valentinian's a joke!"

The younger Valentinian, Gratian's young half-brother, was co-emperor in Italy, and ruled from Mediolanum. He was still only a youth, having been elevated to the throne by his father at the age of four. He was totally under the control of his mother, Justina, an Arian heretic who was widely disliked. Naturally Ambrosius, the bishop of Mediolanum, did his best to counter her influence. The result was a constant battle of wits, and occasionally blunter instruments. Tales of their plots and intrigues had spread even to Britain. Maximus was right; if Gratian went, who else was there?

There was an obvious answer, but it didn't occur to me at the time. Perhaps I was too busy. Just as at Eburacum, I had a great deal to do. Still a senior commander's wife, I had a seemingly never-ending round of social engagements. The garrison at Londinium was much larger. This actually meant a more distant connection with the army units, but we were invited to dinner parties and banquets given by all kinds of government officials, from the *vicarius* downwards. This was when Maximus was in town, however, and alternated with long periods of relative isolation when he was away. The invitations rarely came then, and I had to refuse them anyway. It would not have been considered proper for me to go to any social function without Maximus, unless it was purely a women's get-together. Sometimes the military and civil service wives organised lunchtime parties, which avoided our having to go out unescorted after dark. Actually we all had stout slaves and servants to guard us, but the laws against carrying weapons meant they might have had to defend us against a cutpurse's knife with their bare hands. Robbery — or worse — was unlikely to happen in daylight, but after dark any big city has its dangers.

I had a letter in the spring. The wax tablets were brought by a slave, who was ushered into my presence one sunny afternoon as I sat in the courtyard. My first thought was for my father, but the missive was not from him. The letters were in a woman's hand, small and ill-formed like a child's.

My dear Helena, you will never guess the news. Vegetius has been posted, and we are moving down to Londinium. He is to join Maximus's staff with the task of reforming the supply system for the three legionary fortresses in

Eburacum and Wales. Isn't that splendid? I can hardly wait to tell you all that has happened since we last met. We should be arriving early in May. I do hope that we can meet soon and swap all the news. There is so much to tell you. Besides, I have a backlog of about three years' shopping to do. Eburacum is all very well, but it isn't Londinium. Now, my dear, just get your strength up for Felicia's onslaught on the capital. May isn't far off. Love to all, Felicia.

I found myself almost tearful. I could hear Felicia's cheerful voice as I read the letter, and hear her tinkling laugh in the fountain. At last I would have a friend here as well as all these damned acquaintances! I turned to the slave and spoke unsteadily.

"You're sweating. Have you walked all the way from the fort?"

"Yes, *Domina*. The *legatus* is visiting the fort here and seeing various officials before he moves down permanently. He told me to bring this letter as soon as we arrived."

"Yes. If you go to the kitchen they will give you a drink while you wait."

"Wait, *Domina*?"

"Of course. I must send a reply back with you."

He went off to the kitchen, and I took my scraper to smooth the wax ready for the return message. What a cumbersome way to write a letter — if only paper and parchment were not so expensive!

Dear Felicia, you have no idea how welcome your letter was, not to mention the news that you will soon be joining us here. It will be wonderful to see you again. If ever I needed a friend it is now. I believe you have been sent to rescue me! Congratulations to Vegetius on his —

I paused for a moment, not being sure whether the move was a promotion or not. Eventually I thought of a safe word —

— appointment. Maximus will value him, I know, and I will value you. Safe journey. Love, Helena.

I closed the tablets together and tied the ribbon to secure them. There! That should drop the hint that I wanted to see her as soon as possible.

XI

"My dear, I don't know what you can do. Vegetius has never been cursed with that particular affliction — not, frankly that I'd notice too often if he were. They do say, though that the cause is usually not physical."

Felicia had recently arrived and we had taken up our friendship where it had left off. With a husband of senatorial rank, she was one of the few women in Londinium who could be considered my social equal. Not that I worried about that too much — I came from a line of British princesses who were used to choosing friends where they felt like it — but Maximus did. Whether it was his recent promotion, or whether he already had his eyes on a higher position still, I couldn't tell. For whatever reason a streak of snobbery had entered his thinking.

"What do you mean?" I asked Felicia. "About the cause not being physical."

"Well, my dear, who knows what goes on in the darkest corners of the mind — anyone's mind? All I know is that, apart from large amounts of strong drink, impotence is rarely caused by anything physical. I had occasion to ask a doctor about it once. He tried to sell me powdered rhinoceros horn, which he swore was a certain remedy, but I'd heard that one before. Eventually, he admitted that all of these remedies are nonsense — except that they may work if people have faith in them. It was the faith, he said, rather than the recipe. Just as well, as it was only ram's horn anyway. Do you think Maximus might try something?"

"I don't think so," I said. "He won't even talk to me about it, let alone anyone else. He's too ashamed."

"Hmm. Well, as I say, not one of Vegetius's problems. Mind you, I did know someone once..."

"One of your young men?"

"Don't say it like that, dear. You make it sound like hundreds."

"Isn't it?"

"No more than dozens. I think. Anyway, this young fellow had a nice new wife, and why he wanted to dally with raddled old me I can't imagine. Anyway, he couldn't when it came to it."

"Couldn't..."

"Dally. Exactly. He just felt so guilty about deceiving her that he couldn't perform with me. And consulting that doctor was no good at all."

"So what did you do?"

"Packed him off back to wifey, of course. He obviously didn't really want me, did he? And in that state of paralysing guilt he wasn't much use to me either. I told him he was perfectly sweet, but he just wasn't cut out for philandering."

"Felicia, you're awful!"

"No, no, my dear, I'm just unsentimental about it, that's all. Anyway, the last time I saw him he had four children and was utterly happy. *And* utterly faithful, I believe. It's not such a bad way to end up."

"It doesn't get me much further though, does it? Unless — oh, Felicia, it's that damned blonde woman!" And I burst into tears.

She leaned over and put her arm around me.

"Helena, whatever is it? Which blonde woman?"

When I had calmed down a little I told her of the woman in the blue shawl, and Maximus's strange behaviour when I challenged him.

"And Felicia, although he promised she wasn't what I thought, I didn't believe him. He was lying to me. I could tell. You know the way people look at you when they're trying to see if you've swallowed the story they've given you?"

"Only too well, my dear," she said slowly, "but even if he was lying, it might not have been about that."

"What else could it be?"

"I don't know. I suppose you're right. It's just that I'd never have thought it of Maximus."

"Once, in Eburacum, you told me all men are philanderers at heart."

"Well, I must have been having an off day. That sounds a bit cynical, even for me. I suppose all of us can stray, given the circumstances. I stray all the time, but then I'm constantly in the circumstances."

"What circumstances?"

"I'm a whore at heart, my dear. All this cosy domestic bliss was my family's idea. In reality it just isn't me. But I'd have thought it was you two all right. I always thought Maximus was dotty about you, and you about him."

"So did I."

*

My relations with Flavia Antonina, Maximus's mother, went surprisingly well at this time. I think that she was disturbed to see how young I was, but relieved when she found I could still make the sort of wife a senior commander needed. My year in Eburacum had been a good training in this, and I was as glad as she was that I didn't have to run to her for advice every five minutes. She had to be invited to all the dinners we gave at home, of course, although she didn't always accept. She used to plead tiredness or headaches quite often, but I think she just didn't want to intrude too much, and I was grateful for her tact. She would occasionally meet me in the courtyard, and it was in our first full summer in Londinium that we met there one day and she confided some surprising news.

"I've decided to be baptised."

"Baptised? You're going to become a Christian?"

"Yes. When you get to my age, you know, you start thinking about the end of your life, and what may happen after. All in all I think the Church has it about right. What's the point of life if there is no assessment of it at the end? It seems so right to me that one should be judged, and the quality of one's afterlife decided accordingly."

It was quite common for people to be baptised late in life. The Church encouraged the view that baptism was a mystical rebirth — a washing away of all one's previous sins. This in turn encouraged people to leave it late so as to get the maximum value out of their baptism. Even Constantine the Great, the hero of Christianity, had only been baptised on his deathbed. Mind you, the sins he wanted washing away included the murders of his own wife and son, so perhaps he was wise. In fact, I wonder sometimes whether this powerful cleansing sacrament is one reason for the

Church's growing strength. No other religion offers quite so much hope to those with grievous wrongs on their conscience.

"I have been attending St. Joseph's Church in the Via Fori," she went on. "My baptism will take place there next month. It would be pleasant for me if you could attend it, and Maximus, of course, but please don't feel obliged. If you have strong feelings about it — "

"No, no. I'd be delighted to come."

"I thought, with not being a Christian yourself, you might not want to. Maximus probably won't. He seems less so these days, but he used to be quite scornful of the Church."

"He's never mentioned it to me. My father was proud to be a pagan, but I don't really have strong feelings about it. I'm not sure what I believe, these days."

"Then why not speak to my priest? He could tell you far more than I could, and I'm sure he'd be glad to."

"No doubt. Well, perhaps I will. Not just yet, though. Let me think about it."

Maximus was not surprised when I told him the news that evening.

"I've thought for a while she was drifting that way," he said. "I don't know if it will do her any good, but it certainly won't do *me* any harm. Most of the senior staff officers are Christians, and most of the politicians."

"Maximus, you're a cynic!"

He grinned that boyish grin at me, and my heart skipped a beat. "In my line of work you have to be aware of these things."

"You seem to be in a good mood. Are things going well?"

"Things are looking up, I'd say. I've developed a whole new system for defending the Saxon Shore — a new line of watch towers, and smaller, more mobile army units which can be moved quickly to reinforce the defences wherever they're needed. Only two days ago it was tested in earnest and came through with flying colours. A large Saxon raiding party was intercepted and totally destroyed before it got off the beach."

"But that's wonderful! Does it mean we can be free of the Saxons for good?"

108

"I wouldn't go that far," he chuckled, "but I think we're one jump ahead for the time being. Yes, we can breathe freely for a while."

A sudden thought seemed to strike him. "Do you know, we could even take a holiday. How would you like to visit your father in Segontium?"

"Maximus! What a wonderful idea. I'd love to! Oh, and the hills are so beautiful in summer. Could we go soon?"

"Quite soon. A couple of weeks' time, let's say. We'll see Mother baptised first, eh? Yes, a break from all this would do us both good. We don't get that many chances. Why not take advantage of the ones we do get?"

I jumped from my seat and put my arms around him, to his great consternation. He had not been used to such extravagant displays of affection recently. But a holiday back home! I hadn't realised how much I was missing the place where I grew up. I had been thinking of it as a small country town with little to offer. Because I had had no prospect of going there immediately, it had been easy to forget the simple pleasure of just walking in the hills and smelling the wild flowers and the salt sea breezes. I knew Mabanwy would be delighted, too. Her parents were dead, but she still had relatives and friends there.

We arranged to go the day after Flavia Antonina's baptism, which we felt obliged to attend. Church services have never appealed to me much; I find them so dreary. This is not a criticism of the Christians — I feel the same about the services of other religions. I think it is the prospect of so many people standing around and taking themselves so seriously. Do they really imagine that their muttered prayers and out of tune anthems can have any impact upon the Creator of the Universe, always assuming that it had one? I can hardly imagine it. They do these things to please themselves, not their god. I have far more sympathy with the quiet devotions of my father before the shrine of his old household gods, or even the revels held by the Celtic peasantry in honour of their Mother goddess and the springtime. There used to be dignity in the one and uninhibited joy in the other. Both are now equally condemned by the Christians, who have the support of the Emperors to give them legal backing.

Still, whatever my feelings, I did not begrudge Flavia my presence on that day. We sat through the service, and watched as she and several others came forward in symbolically pure white robes to be doused with water and received into the community of the Church. When we saw her afterwards she was shaking with cold.

"You're frozen," I said to her, wrapping her in a warm blanket. "I hope this experience doesn't give you your death of cold."

She just chuckled. "Well, if it does, at least I should be well prepared to enter into the life eternal."

It didn't, however. Flavia Antonina was a tough old lady, and was to live many more years and know great sadness before that happened.

*

It took a few days to reach Segontium by carriage, although a rider could have got there much faster. Using the Imperial courier system, which took government dispatches all over the Empire, Maximus had warned my father of our arrival. Maximus himself wanted to pause in our travels at Deva, so that he could confer briefly with the *legatus* of the Twentieth Victorious. From there he sent a courier to Segontium to tell Father we would be arriving the next day. Meanwhile the wife of the *legatus*, a homely woman of about thirty, showed me round their imposing official residence and engaged me in polite small talk. I met their children — three equally polite youngsters who reminded me of my own stepchildren, left in Londinium.

"No children of your own, yet, *Domina?*" twittered my hostess. "Of course, you are still so young, you have all the time in the world."

I reflected bitterly that, if Maximus's problem were to continue, all the time in the world would be of little use to me. I was in for a surprise.

Maximus and I were staying that night in the guest rooms of the official residence. We were sharing a bedroom for the first time in months. I was getting undressed alone while Maximus made some last-minute comment to the legatus. When he entered I was standing there naked, as he had not seen me for a long time. I was so unused to it that I instinctively covered myself with my night-dress.

Without a word, Maximus strode across to me and put his hands on my shoulders. Then he pulled the night-dress away and dropped it on the floor, his arms around me, his lips on mine. It was so sudden I hardly knew what I was doing. But I could feel his hardness between us as I had not done for months, and my body was already responding of itself. With a gasp I pulled him on to the bed. Though his weight nearly crushed the breath out of me I was breathless anyway. There was no foreplay, no gentle caresses. It was like throwing bread in front of starving people. We were starving, we had hungered so long for each other. We coupled passionately, almost violently. I suppose it was all over in three minutes, but what minutes!

We lay entwined on the bed afterwards, content just to lie together and catch our breath. There were tears running down my face. Maximus was alarmed.

"Are you all right? I didn't hurt you? I was a bit... enthusiastic."

"Oh, Macsen, my darling Macsen, we both were. I'm not hurt, I'm happy."

"Mm. I think being on holiday must be good for me."

"Wonderful. You don't fancy retiring early, do you?"

We giggled at this, both knowing that Maximus without his career would be like a fish out of water.

"If it was like this I wouldn't survive. So much passion would wear your poor old husband out!"

"Yes, but what a way to go!"

We fell asleep in each other's arms. I awoke in the first light of dawn to find Maximus's hand on my breast, tracing curves around it, down to my navel and back. This time we made love slowly and lovingly, as if to make up for last night's haste. Starvation behind us, we were ready for a gourmet experience again. Even the climactic moment, when it eventually came, seemed to last and last as if it was happening in slow time.

Afterwards we again drifted into sleep, waking only when the slave came to call us. No doubt she thought we made a romantic picture, the two of us naked under the blankets and cuddled up to each other. We were probably the talk of the kitchen. I couldn't

111

have cared less. For the first time in months I felt like a complete woman again, and there was a real possibility that I might be pregnant, for the time had been right. When we met my father, who had come to meet us on the Segontium road, he remarked on how serene and happy I looked, and that marriage obviously agreed with me!

Father passed another plate of Rhonwen's pastries around, and swirled the dregs of the wine around in his cup.

"I suppose there's no change in court circles?"

"None that I know of," said Maximus. "Gratian is still the same — a poet, a philosopher, an effeminate. Valentinian is still a boy, ruled by his heretical mother. Neither one of them a leader. Theodosius is the only one worth a damn."

"Hmm. Well that's plain speaking, anyway."

Maximus grinned amiably. Last night seemed to have rejuvenated him.

"If I can't speak freely here, where can I?"

"True, but don't assume that all my friends or acquaintances think as I do. Still, you know all this, of course. Londinium must have far more in the way of plots and intrigues than out here in the sticks."

"Yes, but I won't forget. I'll never forget what happened to Theodosius's father. By all accounts that was simply from opening his mouth too far in unreliable company."

"And what's the news from Gaul? Apart from Gratian, that is."

"Very little. The border seems quiet at the moment, although you can never tell. There's a good network of scouts to bring news of tribal movements. They're strange, these German tribes. The whole lot move, you know — wives, children, old people, animals. It's not like a proper army at all."

"Yet some of them make good soldiers."

"Indeed they do, but usually only temporarily. There are plenty of Vandals and Goths in the army now, of course, but a lot of the other tribes are much less civilised."

My father shook his head sadly.

"And why do they move? Why does a whole people suddenly get the urge to wander?"

"They don't. By and large they'd love to settle down and become civilised. The trouble is, there are other tribes coming from further east, and others still beyond them, and so on right into Asia. Rumours abound of a great empire beyond India which is expanding and pushing them before it. They're being harassed from behind, and it's a question of moving on or being slaughtered. They can't move down into the Middle East, because the Persian Empire won't have them. They can only come west, always west."

Father tutted impatiently.

"But we're in the west! And beyond us is Ireland, and then there's nothing! Only miles and miles of ocean. What are we supposed to do — swim until we fall off the edge of the world?"

"I don't know, Eudav, I don't know. This is why the present situation is so worrying, and why the need for strong leadership has never been greater. And what have we got?"

"Gratian and Valentinian."

"Exactly. The useless sons of a useless father, who executed the only strong commander we had on the basis of tittle-tattle about treason."

"That strong commander's son is co-Emperor in the East now. The younger Theodosius, I mean. Is he the same sort of chap as his father?"

"Oh, yes, no doubt about it. I knew him when he was a lad, and you could see it then. Besides, he's got great political skills, too. He did a great job of pacifying the Goths after Hadrianopolis. They've settled along the Danube now and are our first line of defence against the other barbarians."

"Didn't it cost a lot of money?"

"Yes, but doesn't everything? If we want to sleep easy in our beds in times like this we must pay for the privilege. That's another lesson Gratian must learn before it's too late. Anyway, what's the use of talk? The man is what he is. I don't suppose he'll change."

"No," agreed my father, "I suppose he won't. Unfortunately he's young. That means he could reign a long time. Is there any sign of anyone else coming forward?"

"Anyone else? A usurper, you mean? Good heavens, no!"

"Is it such a surprising idea? It wouldn't be the first time. Far from it."

"Maybe not, but there's no one at the moment who's prepared to take such a step. Besides, it would be very dangerous. Gratian is well supported. Quite apart from his guard of Alani, there's also a Moorish cavalry unit assigned for his personal protection. And that's not counting the rest of the Army in Gaul. He can probably rely on their loyalty, too."

"Hmm. I see you've thought about it, then."

Maximus looked at my father for a moment, a smile slowly beginning to spread across his face. He turned to me.

"Helena, this father of yours is a wily old man. You should have warned me." He turned back again. "No, Eudav, I haven't thought about it, except in the abstract. I've no plans to be Emperor!"

"I'm glad of that," I put in. "It's far too dangerous an occupation for any husband of mine!" And I seized Maximus's arm in mine and hugged it to me. My father smiled indulgently.

"Father, if you two men will excuse me I'd like to go to bed now. Please go on with your talking. I'd stay, but I'm really very tired."

"Of course, my dear, I quite understand. You've had such a long journey."

They both stood up, a mark of respect from my father which underlined my transformation from his daughter into Maximus's wife. I kissed him and climbed the stairs to my room as if I had never left home. The difference was that tonight I would not be sleeping alone.

I got undressed quickly, for it was cool. I went to put on my night-dress, and then left it, crawling naked into bed and pulling the covers around me. I dozed off lightly, and it seemed no time before I felt the bed give as Maximus got in. Then I heard his voice in the darkness.

"Are you really very tired?"

I reached for him, and he chuckled as he realised I had nothing on.

"Not that tired," I told him, "but I'm hoping to be!"

*

It was like that every night while we stayed at Segontium. Maximus seemed to have taken a new lease on life, and not only in bed. He seemed more cheerful, his old wittiness had returned. He was once again the man who had won my heart while I was still my father's daughter. It was as if a great weight had been lifted from us.

On the afternoon of our second day there we had a further surprise. We were out in the courtyard, enjoying the sun and chatting to my father, when there was a jingle of bridles under the archway and two riders swept in. They trotted right up to us before reining in their steeds. They were both dusty and dirty from the road, but there was no mistaking them.

"Adeon! Kynan!"

Adeon leapt from his horse and went up to shake Father's hand. Then he kissed me.

"Hello, sister, are you well?"

"Yes, yes, but how did you come to be here? Why aren't you with your legion?"

He nodded towards Maximus.

"Good day, *Domine*. Helena, I believe your husband knows something about it."

I turned to Maximus, who was smiling broadly, like a child who has kept a plan secret until it comes to fruition.

"I thought you'd like to see your whole family again," he said, "so I issued a few orders. What's the use of authority if you can't use it when it suits you?"

I smiled at him, a lump in my throat. Then Kynan too came to be kissed.

"Hello, Helena. Oh, it's good to be home for a while. I tell you, those Picts are welcome to their land. It's freezing. We still had snow on the ground a month ago. Yet here it's like the Mediterranean."

He went on to greet the others, but I had eyes only for Maximus. He could be distant, even thoughtless. He was not the most passionate of husbands, but he could arrange something like this and not breathe a word, just to show he cared. I made my mind up there and then. I did love him. Whatever the problems

115

had been, I would make this holiday a new beginning. He was worth whatever it took.

But there were more surprises in store.

XII

After two weeks at Segontium we had to leave again for the capital. By this time I had realised that neither Adeon nor Kynan were returning to their posts. Maximus had arranged for them to be transferred to Londinium. This meant that I would see a lot more of them, of course, but Adeon in particular was not as happy about it as I was.

"It will be good to be nearer my sister and brother," he said. "But it will be further from where things are happening."

"But surely Londinium is where everything happens, isn't it?"

He turned that pitying look of his upon me.

"I'm not talking about politics. Soldiering is what I joined the Army for."

"You mean fighting."

"Of course. What do you think soldiers do?"

"But you don't fight all the time. Most of the time we're at peace!"

"Certainly, but then we are still patrolling the borders of the Empire, and helping to keep civilised values alive. Why do you think they give retired soldiers a grant of land in the border areas? It's not just to keep a reserve of fighting men available, you know. It's to set an example of civilised living to the barbarians."

I sighed.

"Adeon, the Army has done nothing for your pomposity while you've been away. Civilised living, indeed! Can you really describe our leaders as civilised? What is civilised about Constantine, who murdered his own wife and son? What is civilised about Old Theodosius being put to death because the Emperor feared his popularity?"

He shrugged. "I do not say we are all perfect. But our way of life is far superior to the barbarians'. I have seen them, remember. Would you really like to live like they do — in a hut of mud and wattle, no baths, no art, no culture?"

"Oh, don't listen to him, Helena," cried Kynan. "I for one will be glad to be in Londinium. I don't know what art and culture Adeon's been experiencing up on Hadrian's Wall, but it can't be much above the level of the barbarians, I'd say. Come on, Adi, be honest. You really don't care much for art and culture. You're at your happiest when you're knee deep in mud and gore. All the rest is just to give yourself an excuse!"

Adeon snorted angrily and stamped out of the room. Kynan controlled his laughter with difficulty.

"Oh, dear," he said. "He's awfully easily offended sometimes, our brother. I hope Maximus gives him something on the Saxon Shore. Then at least he can go and help kill people!"

"Kynan!"

"I'm sorry, but it's what it comes down to, isn't it? Adeon likes the outdoor life, the spartan living arrangements, the danger. He'd fight whatever the cause."

"And you wouldn't?"

He considered a moment. "Well, I suppose once you're in the Army you fight where you're told. But the rightness of the cause would matter to me. I don't think Adeon's so choosy. Just put a sword and shield in his hand and point him at a barbarian!"

Later that evening, our last before heading back to Londinium, Maximus and I walked in the garden by the cemetery. The dying sun was covering the sky in pink and mauve. High above, the swifts were still wheeling and dodging in their restless dance of the air.

"Thank you, my Macsen. It's been wonderful here. And thank you for arranging for Adeon and Kynan to be here too. It was a lovely thought."

"I'm glad it pleased you so much. You put up with enough inconvenience for the sake of my work. It made a change for me to use it to your advantage for once. Of course, it may not do me any harm in the long run to have my two brothers-in-law about me."

"What do you mean?"

"Just that I know I can trust them. They are both good men in their different ways, and as my relatives now their fortune is bound up to some extent with mine."

"Oh. And I thought it was all to please me!"

He chuckled loudly. "Of course it was. I'm just saying that it has occurred to me that I may benefit, too."

118

I squeezed his arm. "Why should I mind? If all the men in my life are together and looking out for each other, then perhaps they'll all come through these troubled times."

"Did you think they might not?"

"Oh, I don't know. It worries me sometimes when you all talk about the Emperor the way you do, and the barbarians, and the wars on our borders."

"All the more reason to surround myself with people I can trust, eh?"

"Macsen, tell me truthfully. Do you really have political ambitions, or is *Dux Britanniarum* good enough for you?"

He hesitated. "I have no real ambitions now, only a dream. I dream of seeing the Empire freed from the threat of invasion, her citizens going about their business and helping others to better themselves. If we stay strong we can do it, but if the Emperors are weak we shall go under. I would rather die than see that happen. God knows, the Empire has its faults, but taken altogether it is a civilising influence in a world of meanness and misery."

"So you might make a bid for power, if it were the only way — the only way to fulfil your dream?"

"I suppose it's possible. If it were the only way."

I shuddered. Suddenly the evening had turned cold.

*

Our return to Londinium was marked by another of those peculiar demonstrations of affection which the soldiers seemed to make whenever they saw Maximus. The walls of Londinium rang with their cheers, and the cries of "Mac-sen! Mac-sen!" Adeon and Kynan were riding alongside the carriage, but I saw their faces; they were impressed. Adeon in particular always had a weakness for hero-figures, and Maximus's popularity qualified him. His prowess as a soldier was well known, but this was the first time Adeon had witnessed such a spontaneous outburst of goodwill from ordinary fighting men.

"You can't fool them," he said to me later. "These are trained and experienced men, hardened in battle and in life. If they rate Maximus so highly he really is someone special."

"Oh, he is," I assured him.

119

Alas, special men have special problems. The next time we attempted to make love Maximus's problem reasserted itself, to his utter mortification. We persisted for a while, but it was no use. He returned to his own room, too embarrassed to talk about it. I lay alone and contemplated the years of bitter disappointment, and probably barrenness, that seemed to lie ahead. A very special kind of loneliness comes to the woman who loves but is not loved in return.

Felicia was the only person I could confide in.

"My dear, how awful for you! You know, there's always my solution."

"No, Felicia, not for me."

"Think about it, dear. The world is full of handsome single men who desire nothing more than a nice, uncomplicated, uncommitted bit of dalliance. Yet if they dally with a young single woman they end up getting involved and either breaking her heart or marrying her. Either outcome rather defeats the object. Respectable married ladies, on the other hand, are as averse to commitment and complication as they are. We were made for each other."

"Stop it, Felicia. Respectable, indeed! You make it sound delightfully simple..."

"It is."

"...but it's not what I need. I don't want a roll in the hay from some young stud you've found for me. I want complication, I want commitment. I want love. I want Maximus!"

I tailed off at this point, tears of frustration in my eyes. Felicia knew when to give up, and put her arm around me.

"Oh, my dear, sometimes I think you are so innocent, and you make me feel like something off the streets."

"No, Felicia, I didn't mean — "

"I know, I know. It's your damned purity. Anything else is bound to look a bit shabby by comparison. Mind you, it's the love that complicates things. Looking at you I'm not sure I envy you your capacity to love."

"Well, as you always say, each to her own."

"Yes." She brightened on a sudden thought. "You know, there is one solution to your problem."

"What?"

"Take plenty of holidays — as long and as frequent as possible!"

I managed a smile, and she stood up, hauling me up with her.

"Now, my dear, you must be cheered up. Have you any money?"

"What? Well, yes, a little."

"What does it matter, anyway? As the wife of Maximus you should be good for credit anywhere."

"What are you talking about?"

"My motto dear — 'When in doubt, go shopping'. Come on, let's find you something nice — a new dress, perhaps? Jewellery?"

"I'm not much of a one for jewels."

"I've noticed. You ought to cure that, you know. You have a position to maintain. Anyway, there's the Emperor's birthday banquet coming up. A new dress would be just the thing. You can't let Maximus down, now, can you?"

"You're incorrigible, Felicia!"

"Oh, gods above and below, I hope so!"

Maximus was pleased when he heard that I had been out.

"I've thought recently that you were moping around the house a lot," he said. "It's good to see you getting out. Even with Felicia."

"Even?"

"Well, I'm not sure she's all she should be. One hears rumours, you know."

Rumours? Who from, I wondered? Blonde women with blue shawls? No, I must bury thoughts like that.

"She certainly has an original outlook on life. But you needn't worry — I won't let her corrupt me."

He looked at me unhappily. "No, of course not. I didn't mean to imply any such thing. Actually," he went on, changing the subject, "I was thinking I ought to make you a proper allowance — for dresses, and such things. You shouldn't have to come to me every time you want money."

"But you never refuse me! You're very generous!"

"Well, it's good of you to say so, but it's the principle of the thing. Besides, you might need money when I'm away."

"You always leave me plenty."

"That's for running the household and so on. In future you'll have an amount of your own. You don't spend much on yourself, you know. I'm a rich man. You could afford to indulge yourself a bit more."

I resisted, but he had made up his mind, and would not discuss it further. Felicia, I knew, would not have needed to be persuaded. With me it was different. I felt as if Maximus was trying to give me money because he could not give me affection. But money would not solve the problem, and if giving it made him feel less guilty he himself might lose the will to solve it. I did not dare to think through the possibilities beyond that. But I felt angry with myself for giving in too easily.

I am not sure when the custom began of holding a banquet in honour of the Emperor's birthday. The governors of Britain have certainly done it for over a hundred years. It was not done everywhere in the Empire, and I think it probably started here because Britain was a remote province and eager to demonstrate its loyalty for fear of being abandoned to the barbarians. This was not an idle fear in the old days — Britain was not only remote but rebellious. It was an ideal place for usurpers to start a campaign for the Imperial throne, and several had already done so. Carausius and Allectus had actually kept an independent Britain outside the Empire for some years before their eventual defeat. Their mistake was to be content with too little. By staying at home they allowed the Imperial Army to gather its forces for an invasion. Constantine the Great simply declared himself Emperor at Eburacum and then sailed with his army to the Continent, eventually defeating his rival Maxentius outside Rome itself. Even then it was a close thing. Maxentius and his army were retreating over a pontoon bridge across the Tiber to regroup. His engineers drew the bolts too soon, and Maxentius was drowned along with many of his soldiers. The fate of empires hinges on such details. The Christians hailed it as a miracle, which just goes to show how success can go to people's heads.

At all events, it seems the British governors were keen to show their loyalty, and the banquet was one way of doing so. Not only was it held in honour of the Emperor's birthday, but His Majesty's health was toasted at set points in the evening. Before the festivities began Christian prayers were said for his well-being and the length of his reign. It was a strange combination of the religious and the secular, the more so since most of those present had little regard for the man. Still, as Felicia put it, it was a good excuse for a blow-out. And it was at the expense of the *vicarius*, for he paid for the proceedings out of his own pocket.

"At least," said Felicia, "he finds the cash for it himself. I sometimes wonder where the money actually comes from. Civilis is a wily old bird."

"What do you mean?"

"Oh, come, now, Helena, you aren't that naïve. You know that all our governors use a little of their power to line their own pockets. And you must know that the Emperor tolerates it, so long as it isn't too blatant, and so long as the taxes keep coming in."

It was true, of course. Every area was assessed for tax purposes by the tax collectors in Rome. If any area fell short in its payments, the local government officials there had to make the difference up themselves. It encouraged them to be most diligent in their tax collecting duties, to the extent that they usually collected a bit too much! The extra money disappeared quietly, of course — it actually had to, for the books to balance. The practice was widespread and officially condoned, and it had made some public officials rich men.

"I'm sure my father never did such things. He had very lofty ideals of honesty."

"And he never got beyond district level? Then you're probably right. He'd have got much further if he'd been dishonest."

"He isn't exactly poor now."

"I'll bet he is by old Civilis's standards."

"Do you really think Civilis is so corrupt? He gives the impression of being such a nice old fellow."

Felicia guffawed loudly. "Oh, Helena, you really are priceless! Do you expect him to go around with a notice on his head saying 'Favours sold; pay here please'?"

I felt a little resentful at this imputation of naïvety. "Of course not. I just thought he seemed an old-fashioned, courteous man."

"My dear, it is old-fashioned courteous men who have brought the Empire to where it is today — run by corrupt officials, protected — if at all — by army commanders who dabble far too much in politics, and ruled over by idiots and perverts. Don't speak to me about old-fashioned virtues."

"Like marital fidelity, you mean?"

That might have been a wounding comment, but Felicia knew at once why I had made it.

"Let's not quarrel," she said. "I didn't mean to be patronising. I'm sorry. You're probably right. I am cynical, and it saves me a lot of hurt. You always want to believe the best of people. It makes you a nicer person than me, but it opens you up to all sorts of pain, too. Just be careful."

The Emperor's Birthday Banquet was a magnificent affair. Maximus and I arrived early, for we were amongst the most honoured guests. The *vicarius* had arranged a little get-together for a select few before the main event. Felicia was there, with her husband Vegetius. She could not, of course, bring one of her young men to a society occasion like this. Even so, I thought I recognised one of them in the crowd. But then, anyone who was anyone would be there.

Paulus Civilis greeted all the important arrivals personally. Slaves, immaculately dressed in matching white tunics, carried goblets of wine to anyone whose hand was empty. The great entrance hall of the palace was decorated with flowers and plants. Their scent filled the air. There seemed to be fountains in every corner, and in the background somewhere a band of musicians played gently. The whole effect was delightful, and I warmly told Civilis so.

"Ah, how kind of you. One does one's best, of course. We can hardly do less for the *Dux Britanniarum* and his charming young wife, now, can we?"

I smiled dutifully at this gallantry.

"You do the other ladies an injustice," I chided him.

He looked around absently. "Oh, were there others?"

"You're a rogue," I said cheerfully. "You really shouldn't be flattering married ladies."

"Habits of a lifetime, my dear. No harm meant, you know."

"Of course not. We're delighted to be here, but I must let you greet your other guests."

Felicia took my arm as Maximus excused himself and slid off to talk to some official or other.

"Helena, my dear, I've just seen the most gorgeous young officer. He's new."

"You should be all right there, then, Felicia. He won't have heard about your reputation yet."

"Don't tease, dear, that's not really fair."

"I'm not so sure, Felicia. Maximus has heard whispers, you know. Vegetius could, too."

She shrugged. "Well, what's a girl to do?"

"Take her pleasures elsewhere, I should think. If a scandal broke over you and some young officer you might be all right, but what do you think would happen to *him*?"

"Hmm. I hadn't really thought about that."

"Well, perhaps you should."

She nodded towards a young man who had appeared at the edge of the crowd. "That's him."

I followed her gaze. A man of about twenty was standing a few feet away. He was tall, with the strong chin and aquiline features popularly attributed to the Roman nobility. Still, he must have had some other ancestry, to judge by his surprisingly fair hair and large brown eyes. To add to this unusual colouring he wore the most magnificent ceremonial uniform. The breastplate was of brass, and inlaid with copper and enamel figures. His red-plumed helmet was being taken by a slave, who also took the scarlet cloak which was standard for most legionaries. The man wore heavy leather sandals with brass and copper fittings. His powerful legs were partly covered in greaves of brass, inlaid with figures of serpents.

"Isn't he beautiful?"

I nodded. He was. I could not deny it. My mouth had gone dry. My heart was beating fast. I felt a twinge in my belly, almost a pain. Oh, gods above, I never felt so excited at the mere seeing of a man! At the same time I felt great fear. I was not Felicia. I could not treat love as a game. If this was love — and how could it be? I fought my feelings down. No, I told myself. You cannot love a man you don't even know. It is just so long since...

125

"Are you all right, Helena?"

Felicia's voice broke through as if from a long way off.

"What?"

"You've been standing there for ages, dear. You've gone pale. Do you want to sit down?"

I was still staring at the man. He suddenly realised he was being watched and turned to meet my eyes. He smiled, his wide mouth parting to show perfect gleaming teeth. Then he bowed slightly towards me, obviously not knowing who I was, and walked into the crowd, leaving me disappointed and relieved at the same time. My heart somersaulted. I took Felicia's arm.

"Quickly, my dear," she said. She beckoned to a slave. "Here, this lady is feeling faint."

"Please come this way, *Dominae*. This room is cool and quiet."

He opened a door and led us into a small sitting room. I sat down on a couch while the slave went to fetch some water. Felicia sat beside me and pushed my head down between my knees until my head cleared.

"You're not pregnant, are you? Oh, Helena, I'm sorry, of course you aren't. There I go again, only opening my mouth to change feet."

The doorway darkened. It was Maximus.

"They said you were ill."

He sounded far away. I sat up straight again.

"No, no. I'll be all right. Just a little faintness. It was probably the warm day, and then the excitement and everything." Yes, and lust for another man, and the feverish guilt that went with it.

"Please don't worry about me. Felicia's here with me."

He wanted to be away again, talking politics and making heaven knows what plans. He nodded.

"Very well. But if you want to leave early just say the word and I'll have the carriage brought."

"Thank you. I'll be better after we've eaten." He nodded again and went.

For the first time I felt completely cold towards him.

Felicia was still fussing.

"Now, Helena, are you sure you're not ill?"

"No." The world had stopped spinning. The wool which had seemed to be stuffed in my ears was being pulled free. The sounds of the music and the chattering guests began to impinge on my consciousness again.

"Well, my dear, I wonder what could have caused you to have such a turn?"

"Guess." I felt irritated with her. I was sure she had a very good idea what had caused it!

"Oh."

"Exactly."

"Oh dear."

"You're my only real friend, Felicia. Advise me."

"My dear, if the young man has this effect on you at first sight, there's nothing I can do."

"Felicia!"

"Helena, if your feelings are this strong already no advice in the world will stop you doing what you want. Go on, I say. Don't wallow in guilt. Have a good time. You have ample cause."

"No, Felicia, I can't do that!"

"Why not? I do."

"I am Maximus's wife. Scandal would ruin him."

"It wouldn't do Vegetius much good, either. That's why I take damned good care not to let it happen. It is possible, you know. I'm not the only society lady who likes a little fun on the side. There's a well-established system for letting it happen without wrecking careers. Or marriages."

"Felicia, I don't want you to tell me how to get away with it. I want you to tell me how to avoid it altogether, and how I get through this evening."

"Well, my dear, if you insist on such a moralistic approach then cold baths are said to be very effective. Apart from that, just avoid seeing him. As for this evening, I'll stick with you. After all, you are feeling fragile, so the company of a friend would be in order. Vegetius will just have to wait. Why not? — it's what he does best."

We got up and went into the great entrance hall. The cause of my discomfiture was nowhere to be seen. Maximus was just disappearing into one of the side rooms with several other distinguished looking men. I knew one of them was a visiting senator. No doubt politics would dominate their evening.

"Ah, Helena, my dear, feeling better?"

It was Civilis himself, two other guests in attendance.

"Yes, I don't know what came over me. The heat perhaps, and the fact that I've been starving myself in preparation for your incomparable table."

"Flattery will get a young lady everywhere with me," he responded pleasantly. "But when you get to my age there's nowhere very much for her to go."

His companions laughed politely at this, and we joined in.

"Well, I must go. Glad to see it's nothing serious."

"Nothing serious!" I muttered to Felicia. "It could be very serious! *He* probably thinks I'm pregnant, too."

"Well, it could be a useful excuse, my dear. It could even be true; Maximus isn't always indisposed, is he? You don't have to produce anything in the end — pregnancies fail often enough, even by accident, sometimes."

I looked at her closely. Abortion was common enough, though it was a risky procedure. Had my friend been caught out at some time? But she just smiled sweetly at me. Then we were interrupted by the sound of a loud gong which reverberated around the hall. Civilis's chief manservant was on the stairs, and used them as a podium to make an announcement.

"Most honoured Magnus Maximus, *Dux Britanniarum*, senators, distinguished guests. My master, Paulus Civilis, welcomes you all to his house, and invites you now into the main hall, where your food awaits."

We all began to file through into the great banqueting hall. I found myself anxiously scanning the crowd, but I saw no sign of the young officer.

Eating from couches in the traditional Roman style was not practical when there were so many. None the less, Civilis had not adopted the barbarian habit of eating at tables while sitting on wooden benches. Instead, there were long tables in the centre of the hall. They were covered with food of every kind — shellfish, salads, vegetable dishes, pies, joints of meat. Slaves stood at the ready to give every guest their choice, and we simply took a plate and approached the food of our fancy. Somehow I couldn't look a shellfish in the face at the moment — perhaps the result of my recent faintness — so I tackled some smoked meat, carved in a trice by a slave. Green salad of several kinds, cabbage soused in vinegar and a round cake of rough wheaten bread completed the first course. It was only when I lifted the first morsel to my watering mouth that I realised how hungry I was.

"Gods above, Felicia, I'm famished!"

There was no reply. Felicia had slipped away and was now talking animatedly to a young officer in similar ceremonial dress to the one "my" officer wore. She saw me and winked. I felt a little put out. She was supposed to be looking after me, or was it chaperoning me? Either way, she had promised to stick by my side. I wandered off and found a cane chair by one of the pillars.

The room was now filling with people, yet it didn't seem crowded, partly because of the high roof. Just under the roof there were long windows, through which I could see the darkening sky and the first stars. The slaves were lighting large candles now, which added a cheerful touch to the scene, although they threw shadows behind the pillars and in corners. I ate busily, and found my appetite sharpened rather than dulled. I sent a passing slave off in search of cheese and fruit, and was tucking into my third course when Felicia found me.

"There you are! I've been looking everywhere for you. The jugglers are performing outside in the courtyard."

"Good for them. I'm still eating. Not much else to do when you're abandoned by your friends."

"Hmm. Well, my dear, I was actually trying to help you."

"I noticed. It looked as if you were trying to help yourself."

"No, no, I promise you. I was just asking that charming young chap for some information. I wanted to find out who your young officer was."

"Felicia, someone will hear!" I hissed, sending crumbs in all directions.

"No fear, Helena, I'm an old campaigner. Now listen, there's good news and bad news, though knowing you I'm not sure which you will regard as which."

"Explain."

"Well, your young man's name is Julius. A very distinguished name, my dear. He should go far. Unfortunately it seems he is already about to."

"What do you mean?" Already my heart was beating fast, and my appetite had vanished.

"He's only in Londinium briefly. His friend didn't want to say too much. I think there may be something hush-hush going on. Anyway, this Julius is off in two days."

My heart sank. Yet, at the same time, there was a feeling of relief. At least the cause of temptation would not be there. Oh, if only...

"His last name is very funny. Rodobertus, or something. I had to ask the chap to repeat it once, but I still didn't get it. Didn't like to ask again. Still, I don't suppose it matters if he's going so soon."

"No," I said slowly, "I don't suppose it does."

It was very late when Maximus tore himself away from the political discussions and remembered me. He was fairly drunk, although he never behaved badly through too much wine. Instead, he had got quite mellow and affectionate. My heart sank again. Tonight of all nights I didn't want to try to revive our moribund love life. Maximus had other ideas.

He followed me into my room when we got home. I turned to make some excuse, and his lips met mine. I thought how ironic it was that the boot was suddenly on the other foot. Whether the drink had dulled his usual tensions or not I couldn't tell, but his manhood had risen strongly to the occasion. There would be no putting him off now. That pain began low in my belly again. Suddenly I pictured Julius there in my husband's place. I could see his muscular body, the fair wisps of down on his chest. I could feel his arms around me. It was his hands that undid my sash, stroked my breast; his lips and tongue that teased my nipples, his thighs between mine. It was for him my body eased and opened like a flower. Poor Maximus was as delighted by my tempestuous response as by his own capabilities. But afterwards I felt like a whore.

We made love three passionate exhausting times that night. And as many times in the next two years.

XIII

The next two years were not marked by dramatic events in our personal lives, although the rest of the world had dramas enough. In Constantinople Theodosius revealed the intensity of his religious orthodoxy by appointing a new bishop of the city — a post second in importance only to that of the Bishop of Rome. Gregory of Nazianzen had long been an opponent of the Arian heresy, which had flourished in Constantinople for forty years, and his appointment gave him unique influence over the most powerful of the three co-emperors. For the rest of his life, Theodosius issued periodic edicts against the Arians, and other "heretical" Christians. I thought of my father, with his pagan tolerance of other faiths, and wondered how he felt. As the Christians say, the writing was on the wall.

To emphasise further the importance of religious orthodoxy, Theodosius declared the Bishop of Rome to be the guardian of the true faith, and reserved for his followers the title "Catholic Christians". The other co-emperors agreed, although Valentinian of Italy was actually an Arian heretic himself. His people were not, and he was unwilling to offend them. At least, not yet.

In my nineteenth year was held the Council of Constantinople. This put the finishing touches to the official doctrines of the Church, begun at the Council of Nicaea nearly sixty years before. Strangely — and significantly — Damasus, the Bishop of Rome, was not invited! Still, the Council did acknowledge his supremacy over the Church, while claiming second place for the Bishop of Constantinople. Constantinople, they said, was the "New Rome", and afterwards it was often called that. It was a clear attempt to limit the powers of the Bishop of Rome, who tended to assume the leadership of the Church, given the slightest chance.

Then suddenly we *were* affected. There was trouble on Hadrian's Wall again, and trouble too from Irish raiders. Maximus, fearing a repeat of the Great Barbarian Conspiracy, acted without hesitation. The first I knew of it was when he arrived home at midday.

"Maximus! What's the matter? Why are you home so early?"

He looked at me from under his lowered brows. He hardly noticed me these days, or avoided noticing me perhaps. I was a constant reminder of his inadequacy.

"I must go north at once!"

"At once? What is it?"

"There have been attacks in the north and the west. The accursed Irish as well as the Picts. I've had an intelligence report, and it looks as if there's a new Conspiracy. At all events, I must go up there straight away. Have the servants pack my clothes. I'm going to have a bath. Heaven knows when I'll get another."

With that he walked straight through the house and out to the baths at the back. I busied myself harrying the servants to pack for him. Mabanwy pitched in to help. It was not her job, really, but she knew we were all needed when Maximus was in this sort of mood. My heart raced, and butterflies flew in my stomach. He was off to face the danger personally, I knew. He would not stand by while other men died at his command. Maximus was the sort who led from the front. That was one of the reasons his men respected him so, even loved him. It came to me that I was jealous of them. He basked in the light of their adulation, not noticing the feelings of others. I hated it when he seemed to need their love more than mine.

I wondered vaguely what he meant by the intelligence report. Surely it would be difficult to get much information about the plans of the Pictish or Irish kings? But then, I knew that Maximus had agents — spies, really — who could do such difficult things. He never said so in so many words, but I had an idea that many of them were working in Gaul to keep an eye on the Emperor Gratian. Maximus would want to keep his back covered.

"Helena!"

It was Flavius Victor, now a fine figure of a young man and a member of Maximus's officer staff. He entered the front door wearing his duty uniform with breastplate and greaves, buckles and scabbard jangling. He looked happy and excited.

"Have you heard?"

"Yes. Your father has just come home. He's in the bath house. Oh, Flavius, I hadn't thought. You're going with him?"

He beamed at me. "Yes. Isn't it exciting?"

So exciting a person could die.

"Flavius, be careful. You're not an experienced soldier."

"Oh, you needn't worry about me. I don't suppose father will let me within a mile of a barbarian."

"You can never tell what may happen on the battlefield. No heroics, now. We want you back in one piece. Have you heard whether Adeon and Kynan are going?"

"Yes, I think they both are. Almost everyone is. There's not much need for a large force here at the moment, father says. The fortifications are so good now, and there are so many catapults on them, that a few men could hold off a legion. Till a relief force arrived, anyway. He says we have to smash the Picts and Irish now, before they can mount a repeat operation of the last time. They did enormous damage then, you know."

I smiled at his enthusiasm. "Yes, I know."

"Of course you do. Silly of me. You were there."

"Here, I'm not that old. You were there, too."

He bent and kissed my cheek. "Sorry. You're father's wife. Even if you're not really my mother, I still think of you in that sort of way."

He went to pack his things, too, leaving me feeling confused but pleased, as people are when they think they've received a compliment.

The house fell silent after the frantic preparations. Bathed, uniforms and weapons packed, all the men in my life were suddenly on the road and gone. I hadn't even seen my brothers to wish them luck. I prayed for their return. And for the return of my husband. I agonised about our marriage, I was frustrated by his incapacity, but the thought of him lying cold and mutilated on some windswept heath was unbearable.

"Whatever gods there are, send him back."

"You'll never guess who I saw." Felicia wiped the crumbs of one of Mabanwy's oat cakes away from her mouth. "My dear, you must give me the recipe for these. Delicious. Are they a local speciality from Segontium?"

"All over that area, really, yes. Mabanwy sometimes makes them when the cook allows her in the kitchen. Well, who did you see?"

"Your young man."

"My young...?" She could only mean one person. I still had dreams about the fair-haired man in the magnificent inlaid armour. I had no other young men, and was not likely to.

"You know, Julius Thingummy. The one you nearly died over at the Emperor's birthday banquet that time."

"Yes, I know. It must be two years ago. I never expected to see him again."

"Well, he's back, my dear."

"How strange. Everyone else is moving out to risk their lives in battle, and he's here in Londinium all of a sudden."

*

"Don't sound so disapproving. I believe he's done his bit already." She leaned towards me in a confidential manner. "Rumour has it that he's got a lot to do with why everyone's rushed off."

"What does rumour say exactly?"

"Rumour says that he's the chap who's provided your Maximus with his secret information about the enemy's plans. You remember when we saw him last he was supposed to be engaged on something hush-hush? Well, rumour has it that he's remarkably fluent in Irish, especially the dialect they speak in the north on the island — the nearest bit to the Picts."

"Rumour is a very dangerous thing."

Still, I couldn't help but bring the image of him to mind. Other images, much more disturbing, seethed at the lower edges of my mind. I struggled hard to keep them there.

"Well, you know, dear, Maximus might be away some time. While the cat's away..."

"No, Felicia, not me. Especially not now. Maximus might be killed. Do you seriously expect me to carry on with someone else when my husband is out risking his life for us all? Credit me with some loyalty, if nothing else!"

"Sorry, Helena, I didn't mean to impugn your virtue. You've made your bed, and if you want to lie on it alone I suppose it's up to you. Still, if that's the way you feel you won't mind if I try to, er, improve my acquaintance of the young man in question."

"You?"

"Well, why not, my dear? After all you don't want him."

Didn't want him? Didn't mind?

"Oh, do as you like. The whole thing's silly anyhow. He doesn't know either of us. He probably wouldn't like us if he did. Certainly not if he could hear this conversation."

"Helena, my dear, you really must decide what you want to do."

"Do?"

"Well, yes. This life is driving you mad. Maximus doesn't seem to want to change, and it simply isn't fair. Marriage is a relationship, a partnership. And don't look at me in that sceptical way. You may not approve of my private life, but Vegetius and I have an understanding. In public we're respectable and we're together. I tell you about my little pursuits because you're a friend. I don't spread them about generally, and I never give Vegetius cause to be ashamed of me. He knows he can appear with me at the palace or the law courts or a banquet and be proud of me. And when I'm called upon to perform some official function myself I'm always there and I always do it properly. Damn it all, we do *like* each other. But that's as far as the arrangement goes. It was never a love match. If Vegetius never came near my bed again it wouldn't worry me unduly — it doesn't happen often, anyway, he's got some little piece of his own down near the Western Gate. But your marriage is different. It was supposed to be a love match. Your bed should be somewhere you take each other in joy and affection. I should be envying you your good fortune. Instead... well..."

She tailed off, and I finished it for her.

"Instead you pity me."

I was right on the mark, and Felicia had the grace to look uncomfortable.

"I'm so sorry."

"Why be sorry? It's not your fault. You're quite right. But what can I do? I fought Papa for the right to marry Maximus. How can I go back home now and say 'Sorry, you were right. Can I come back, please?'? You don't know my father. He'd tell me to get on with it. It's not as simple as you make it out."

"All human problems are simple to solve, Helena. It's getting people to accept the solutions that's difficult."

"So solve this one for me."

"It really is simple. You have only two choices — divorce or stay married. If you divorce, Maximus will have to make a settlement — at least return your dowry, but probably much more. You mightn't need to go back to your Papa. On the other hand, if you stay married you must make a further choice — between soldiering on as you are or finding some way to make it bearable. I honestly don't think you can soldier on as you are, not indefinitely. It's killing you with resentment and self-doubt. You need something to look forward to. That's why I suggested young Julius, or someone like him."

"Love where I can find it."

"I suppose so."

"Not for me, Felicia. I can't treat love as a game the way you do. Besides, it isn't just the physical affection. To be honest I wouldn't mind that if I could get pregnant some other way. But Maximus just doesn't seem to *need* me. He's wrapped up in his work the whole time. I hardly ever see him. Just occasionally he does something marvellous — like that holiday in Segontium — but it's so rare and so unpredictable that it doesn't solve anything. It just makes me feel guilty for criticising him. Oh, damn it all, I don't know what I want!"

"Yes, you do. We all know what we want. It's just that to get it you must do something you don't want first."

There was a long silence then. I knew she was right. The solution was simple. I just didn't want to accept it. I thought of how I would survive alone — well, not quite alone, Mabanwy would come with me. Actually, I would probably survive well enough. I would stay in Londinium, find a little house. Eventually, I might even find another husband. I might have children of my own. Oh, the children! Maximus's children had grown to love me, I thought. How would they take it if I left? Well, they were not infants now. They would survive, too. Perhaps we could even see each other. No, I realised that was impossible. They would regard me as a traitor, deserting them. I would have to harden my heart. I had my own needs, my own life to live.

It's funny, but when you have to look at something unthinkable it gradually becomes thinkable. I found it was possible to imagine a life without Maximus. It was a miserable prospect for me, but eventually it would get better. Other people got divorced and survived. It was quite common, in fact.

I sighed heavily and looked at Felicia.

"You're right. I'll speak to Maximus when he gets back."

As it happened Maximus was gone for a long time. We heard news. I had letters from him, and also from Adeon and Kynan. It proved they were alive and well, at least when the letters left. They told of numerous skirmishes, but no decisive battle, and of intrigues between Maximus and various different tribes of the Picts and Irish. Some of the latter had landed north of the Wall to reinforce their friends, but there was a possibility that some would change sides. Kynan in particular was full of praise for Maximus, but he predicted a long campaign. The letters came by Imperial courier from wherever the legions happened to be, and a messenger would bring them to the house. It was on one of these occasions that fate took an unexpected turn.

I was sitting in the courtyard with — as usual — nothing much to do, and trying to improve my sewing skills. Fulvia and little Sabrina were with me. Indeed, it had started out as a lesson, but I soon felt they could teach me more than I could teach them. The fact was that there were servants to do almost everything, including day-to-day needlework. The only sewing we ever did was the ornamental type — pretty but useless. We were working together on sashes for Adeon and Kynan, who were of course uncles to the girls. There was a crunch of sandals on gravel as a slave came out.

"*Domina*, there is a visitor."

"Who is it? I'm not expecting anyone."

"It is an army officer, *Domina*, with a letter from the Master."

"From Maximus? Show him out here at once, and bring some refreshment for all of us."

The slave went back in, and a few moments later the messenger came out.

It was Julius.

He was not in his ceremonial armour this time, but in the customary workaday leather tunic and plain round helmet. He carried the bundled wax tablets in his hand, and strode across the courtyard with his eyes fixed on me. Those big brown eyes. I didn't trust myself to stand up, my knees were shaking so much. Fortunately, as his commander's wife I didn't have to.

"S-Sabrina, let the messenger have your chair, please."

"All right, Helena, but may I go and play now? I've been doing this for ages."

"Yes. Fulvia, you may go too, if you wish."

"Oh, I want to hear what Papa has to say."

It was her birthday soon, and she wanted to know if Maximus had remembered it.

"Of course, if you want."

Sabrina stayed too, then, and they watched Julius, the same question on their minds as on mine.

"Why did they send someone as important as you?" demanded Sabrina with her usual bluntness.

He smiled, and unstrapped his helmet. I was bewitched! I had a wild urge to trace that smile with my forefinger, but he handed me the wax tablets, and a small package wrapped in cloth

"I just happened to be there when they arrived, and going off duty. I was coming this way, so they asked me to drop the tablets off."

"P-Please sit down," I said, indicating the chair. "There is a drink on the way."

"Thank you, *Domina*. It is indeed warm."

He sat, and smiled at the girls. They were quite taken with him too, but who wouldn't be?

I fumbled with the ties on the tablets. They were knotted hard, and my efforts just seemed to tangle them more. I giggled nervously.

"I'm all f-fingers and thumbs today."

"Here," he said, in a deep and even tone. "Allow me."

He took the tablets back, and seemed to have no difficulty at all. They were undone in seconds and handed back. As I took them our hands touched. I jerked my hand away as if burnt. Shivers went through me. There were goose pimples on my arms.

I read the tablets quickly.

"There's not that much news," I said. "No more battles since last time, but a lot of parleying with the local chiefs. Your father thinks there is a real possibility of a lasting peace, now the Picts have seen our strength. He sends his l-love to all of us, of course."

"You said 'lullove'," commented Sabrina helpfully. I was not surprised that I had stumbled on that word.

"He sends birthday greetings and wishes for a happy year to Fulvia, and says the little parcel is for you."

"Oh, may I open it? What is it?"

"I don't know what it is. You had better open it now, I think, or there'll be no peace."

The girls giggled, and Fulvia started to unwrap the parcel.

"He says your uncles Adeon and Kynan are well, and Adeon is fretting to attack the enemy again as soon as possible. That's... that's about all the news, really."

The slave brought out the drinks and set them down on a little table. Fulvia's present lay revealed at last. It was a beautiful golden brooch, with a very Celtic pattern of intertwined vines and serpents on it.

"Oh, Helena, isn't it lovely?"

"It is. There is a note about it at the bottom of the letter. Your P-Papa says it is made by an Irish goldsmith, and he bought it from an Irish trader."

"They're very good with gold," put in Julius. "I've seen a lot of it."

"I'm going to try it on my green dress!" exclaimed Fulvia. "Do you want to come, Sabi?"

The two of them rushed off chattering, leaving a heavy silence behind them. I tried to lift my cup to my mouth, but my hand was shaking so much I was afraid I would spill it. Julius was looking at me strangely.

"If you wish to write a reply a messenger will call tomorrow morning," he said.

"Thank you. Yes."

"Are you all right, *Domina*?"

I managed to look at him, but I could feel myself reddening.

"Not... not quite."

"The last time we saw each other you were also unwell."

"You remember?"

He nodded. "I'd better keep away if my presence makes you ill."

I looked at him sharply, but he had that maddening smile on his face again.

"You don't make me ill," I said stiffly.

"Ah."

He looked away. I sneaked a look at him. His skin was smooth and evenly tanned, as if he had spent a lot of time out of doors. There were powerful muscles in his bare forearms. The fingers were long and slender, the nails clean and manicured. Wicked thoughts crowded in.

"Well, if you have no further need of me I'd better be going," he said. "My thanks for the drink. It was very welcome."

"N-Not at all."

He rose to go, and I felt an irresistible urge to make some move. Anything to prolong the moment.

"Will you be long in Londinium, now that there's this trouble in the north?"

"Oh, quite some time, I believe. I have already done a little for the present campaign. The Irish High King has put a price on my head."

"Oh no!" My heart had turned over.

"Oh, there's nothing to worry about. The Irish don't even know my real name. I posed as a sea trader and spied on their ship building arrangements."

"How brave of you!"

"Perhaps. No braver than those who risk their lives on the field. Perhaps less so."

"How did the Irish discover you?"

He gave a low chuckle. "The whole fleet was on the slips waiting for the final tarring when a terrible fire started. The tar had somehow got daubed over all of them. Terrible stuff to put out once it catches fire. Even water isn't enough — it just spreads the fire. The fact that my ship was the only one to sail off safely was a bit of a give-away, though."

"Goodness, what daredevil stuff."

He looked at me levelly. "I don't mind taking a risk. If the stakes are high enough."

It was a proposition. In code, but a proposition! I was totally confused, not ready. I decided to speak the truth.

"I don't know what to say to that."

He stepped forward and formally took my hand in his. His grip was warm. When he kissed my hand his lips were soft. His nails scraped my palm and sent a shock wave through me.

"Then say nothing," he advised. "I will be here for some time. We shall see each other again."

"You think so?"

"I am sure of it. Good day, *Domina*."

"Good day."

I watched him walk back into the house. It was as if fate was taking over. I no longer felt in control of myself.

XIV

It was a terrible winter. Maximus and his forces were camped up near Hadrian's Wall, in a temporary fort and conditions of some primitiveness. Sometimes the snow was so deep even the couriers couldn't get through, and we heard nothing for weeks. It snowed heavily even in Londinium, and I took to going out as little as possible.

I heard from Felicia, who seemed to know all the gossip ("My second most important hobby, my dear") that Julius had been sent out of the capital on some duty or other, but was not expected to be away for long. I had not told her of our meeting. My feelings were still in turmoil. It was wonderful to be thought attractive by someone again. To contemplate adultery was quite another thing. Yet I did contemplate it. I wondered about the practicalities of it — where could we meet, how could we avoid discovery? I always felt very guilty about this. I remembered Felicia saying to me once that when you started wondering how to do it you had already made up your mind to go ahead.

Then again, I felt angry with Maximus sometimes, for being the cause of my torment. If only he could be a husband to me, none of this soul searching and guilt would be necessary. He couldn't help it, of course, poor man. Well, at least he could have sought help. Maybe a doctor would have been of no use, but at least he could have tried. He simply refused to admit there was a problem. Perhaps for him there wasn't. Besides, he had other things to fill his life — his career, his campaigns, while a woman has only her home and family. For me, besides the physical frustration, there was the humiliation of being rejected, and having no chance of a family if things went on like this. I loved his children, but I wanted to have some of my own. *Our* own. And there was the hopelessness of seeing no end to my plight.

A strange story came from Rome at this time. Well, perhaps it was not so strange, considering the politics of the Church at that time. Damasus, the Bishop of Rome, was furious at not being invited to the previous year's Church Council at Constantinople, so he held a synod of his own at Rome. This declared that the primacy of the Bishop of Rome was not due to any mere council, but to the powers conferred by Jesus upon St. Peter — supposedly the first Bishop of Rome. This interpretation was not accepted by all the Bishops, especially Ambrosius of Mediolanum. Since Mediolanum had replaced Rome as the Imperial capital, some years ago, the Bishop of the city had become more powerful because of his closeness to the Emperor, and Ambrosius wanted to keep it that way. Rome was not to be dismissed so easily, however. After the synod, Damasus began to address the other bishops as "sons" instead of "brothers" as before, and to use the royal plural in all official utterances. I might have thought all this jockeying for power rather childish, but for the fact that men's lives could hang on the result. As it happened, though, these events were tame in comparison with what was to follow.

In the early spring a detachment of the army came home. With them came the news of victory. The Picts had been beaten soundly and their Irish allies forced to an agreement. It even looked as if some of the Irish might settle western Caledonia, where the Picts lived, and help us to keep them in order. Apparently one of the lesser Irish kings had fallen foul of the High King and could do with the support of Rome. Maximus would no doubt be well pleased. He had achieved a great victory at little cost in the end. We all rejoiced to hear the news, but I couldn't help wondering whether a victorious Maximus would be any more successful at home than he had been before. There was another anxiety. He was now getting to be a very powerful man. It was after just such a victory that the elder Theodosius had suddenly been declared a traitor and executed by the old emperor. Gratian, whose domain included Britain, was very much his father's son in most ways.

According to the Roman tradition a person became an adult at the age of twenty-one. This was to be the year of my majority, then, but also of far more significant developments. My life was to change in ways that far outweighed the addition of one more year.

The spring came suddenly, and caused widespread flooding because the snow melted so quickly. Still, within a few weeks the damage was repaired, and the fine weather brought with it a sense of expectancy. Londinium was waiting. Maximus's victory was talked about all the time. If I went to social gatherings people fell silent when I entered the room. I knew what they were thinking. They knew what the history was as well as I. They were waiting to see whether Maximus had overstepped himself. It was a grisly spectacle, like watching the crowd at an execution. Half the time I hated them for wishing his life away. What right had they to wish his downfall, just to provide them with diversion? At other times I hated myself, for that pernicious whisper at the back of my mind — "Let them take him away; then your troubles will be over."

Even Felicia's normally bubbly character became subdued. She confided in me that she was thinking of giving up her young men. Normally I would have approved, but coming at this time it seemed like another bad omen.

"I'm getting too old," she said, but when I laughed at this obviously ridiculous statement she explained further. "Too jaded, anyway. You know, after a while one young man is very much like another. Other things start to seem more enduring."

"Such as?"

"Oh, loyalty, perhaps. Family. Social standards. That sort of thing. I don't know, I'm still thinking about it."

She carried on as before while she thought, so perhaps it was just a passing philosophical phase.

I received a most unexpected visit from Paulus Civilis the day before Maximus was due to arrive. He caught me just finishing a lunch with my mother-in-law, and we all retired together to my favourite place — the sunlit courtyard. The slaves brought us sweet wine and pastries.

"Ah, how hospitable!" The governor shifted uncomfortably in his chair and broke a pastry in two on his plate. "You know, I rather envy you this house."

"This one? But it's nothing to your great palace."

"Ah, my dear, you are right as far as you go. But my palace is a huge place. It's too big for an old chap and his good wife. No, I'd love a smaller place. Somewhere to retire to, perhaps."

"Retire?" put in Antonina. "You'll never retire, Civilis. You're too addicted to politics."

He smiled. Behind the smile was a gleam of annoyance, as if he had been found out. He probably had been. Antonina had known him for years.

"You didn't come here to discuss your retirement plans," she went on.

"Indeed no. Since you obviously wish to come to the point I will respect that. The fact is that I have some news from Gaul. News that Maximus ought to have without delay."

"Then why not send a courier?" I asked. "He's only a day's march away on the Eburacum road. A rider could be there within hours."

"Ah, I'm afraid news of this sort cannot be entrusted to the normal channels. One never knows who is working for whom."

A chill clutched at my heart. "What is this news?"

He cleared his throat. "Well, I understand that Gratian is in two minds about Maximus's victory. Now, don't panic. I have this news a little ahead of its official release. But it seems I am to be ordered to arrest Maximus upon his return."

"What?" Antonina spat the word. "For the love of God, Civilis, what is that supposed to mean?"

"It means that the official sealed order is on its way. My own sources have brought me the information early, thus giving me the chance to circumvent the order before it actually arrives."

"And to avoid being forced to state your loyalties in public when it does," added Antonina waspishly.

He shrugged, a man indicating that he doesn't make the rules. "As you say."

"Damn the Emperor!" snapped the old woman. "My son has served this Empire well. He has risked his life time and again against the Emperor's enemies. Is this to be his thanks? An arrest for treason? His head on the block?"

145

There were tears in her eyes. Tears of rage, I thought. Who could blame her? There was a lump in my own throat. Perhaps all my guilty feelings were collecting there.

"Well, now, dear ladies, I feel there may be another way. If Maximus were to be warned early then he would have time to think. I anticipate that my official orders will arrive at about the same time he does himself. Indeed, the timing is deliberate. Now, the manner of our meeting can only be decided by Maximus himself."

"You mean you would arrest him if he was not forewarned?"

I couldn't believe it, but Antonina could.

"He would," she snarled contemptuously. "It's all a game to him. It's not his fault if Magnus loses."

"Not a game. I know and respect Maximus, and would not wish him ill. But I can't disobey orders without placing my own head on the block, as you put it. And yet I will give him what chance I can," said Civilis. "If he doesn't want to be arrested there are other choices."

"No," said Antonina. "You know perfectly well there is only one choice."

At the time this passed over my head, though I remembered it later and wondered how I could have been so naïve. Civilis merely shrugged again. In the meantime I had made a decision.

"If he must be warned, and you cannot trust the couriers, then I will do it."

They both looked at me in bewilderment.

"Who else?" I snapped. "Neither of you can go."

"Well," said Antonina. "I thought maybe a servant..."

"No. 'One never knows who is working for whom' — it applies here as well as in the Palace."

She stood and bent over me, looking closely at my face.

"You have courage," she said. "You're a good girl. I had my doubts, but I was wrong."

*

I set off on horseback within the hour. Advance couriers had brought news of where the army lay, and we knew that a carriage would take too long. At Antonina's insistence I had dressed in men's clothing, purloined from one of the servants who had been sworn to secrecy. I still remember the look of bewilderment on the poor man's face as he was shown into my room. Antonina looked him up and down.

"He'll do!" she pronounced. "Young man, get some of your clothes — clean ones, mind — and bring them here!"

"My clothes, *Domina*?"

The poor man looked scared, as if he had been indecently propositioned by both his employer's wife and mother at once.

"Don't stand there gaping like a carp. Do as I say!"

"It is much more important than you know," I said to him. "Your master will certainly reward you for your help."

"Well, if you say so, *Domina*." Of course, he had no choice.

"At once!" bellowed Antonina, and the bewildered man went to fetch his clothes.

My mother-in-law cackled at the sight of me when I was all dressed up.

"I hope no one takes you for a pretty boy," she said. "That would destroy the whole point of this pretence."

"I'll think ugly thoughts," I said.

"We shouldn't joke about this, anyway. Oh, to think of that damnable Paulus Civilis! He's known us for years. How could he do this to us?"

"He hasn't," I reminded her. "He's actually given us the only chance of warning Maximus. It's all he could do, really. As he said, his head is at stake too."

"That's a very understanding approach."

"It's the way of the world. He isn't *my* old friend."

Antonina merely grunted and pretended to adjust my belt.

So, barely an hour later there I was, dressed in the servant's clothes, a hood over my head to disguise my face, and German-style leggings. For, as Antonina had put it, "Not even a pretty boy ever had legs like those." I suppose I should be pleased that my femininity took so much disguising.

The afternoon was already drawing on when I rode through the Severan Gate and the horse's hooves thundered hollowly over the short wooden bridge across the ditch. Then the open road was ahead of me, and I urged my mount to a brisker pace. I was terribly out of practice, not having ridden since Segontium, but it soon came back. They say you never forget it entirely. The weather remained warm, and the horse and I created our own cooling breeze as we sped along.

I knew the army was on the main road, so there would be no trouble seeing them. In fact, I suspected they would find me. There would be plenty of sentries looking out for trouble, and no one ever travelled at night. Any rider would be suspect.

There were no large towns on this road for some distance. I was struck by how little Romanised life was outside the towns. I trotted briskly past farms and through villages, watched by peasants whose way of life had not changed since long before Roman times. They still lived in windowless round hovels of wattle and daub, with a central fire whose smoke found its way out through the thatch. No wonder they liked to spend so much time out of doors.

The sun drew low on the western horizon. My behind was numb and my legs chafed by the saddle before I realised they must be near. I did not see them at first. The army had many horses, and many cooking fires. It was the smell of horses and wood smoke borne on the wind that told me my journey was almost over. Then I topped a rise in the road, and there they were. The light was dim, but the fires were clear enough. They stretched for a mile at least, like a flickering necklace catching the sun's last rays. Near them, by the road, there were countless dark shapes. The weather was so good they had not bothered to raise tents, except for the officers. But, fair weather or foul, there was still the rough palisade of sharpened stakes which they always erected at night. The front edge of it was right beside the road.

"Halt!"

I reined in the horse, panting with excitement. Out of the darkness came a figure, a tribune, probably inspecting the guard.

"What are you doing on the road this time of night?"

"Night? The sun's barely gone down."

"At this time of year it's night."

"Well, I'm looking for the army of Magnus Maximus."

"You've found it. What is your business at such a late hour?"

"I have private business with your Commander."

148

"Oh yes?" The young officer stepped forward, flanked by two soldiers. "What sort of business could that be?"

"*Our* business. I am his wife."

"His wife?" They all three laughed heartily at this joke.

"That's what I said. Now, are you going to take me to him, or am I to have further grounds for complaint?"

"Complaint? Well, I don't know about that." He reached forward as if to grip my arm.

"Lay that hand on me," I hissed, "and my husband will cut it off!"

There was a brief pause while he hesitated. I exploited it.

"Take me to your superior officer if you don't believe me," I suggested. "Let him take the responsibility. If you disbelieve me, and you're wrong, you're in deep trouble. If not, well the officer can deal with me."

The officer nodded. He could see the logic.

"Very well, er, *Domina*. Please dismount and come with me. One of my men will look after your horse."

I did as I was bid. The tribune led me in through the entrance of the temporary fort and past the ranks of men, mostly already asleep. We passed hundreds. He was leading me towards a large white tent with a fire before it. As we entered the circle of light thrown by the fire the men sitting there looked up. One of them was Maximus, but it was another that my escort approached.

"Excuse me, sir. This person has just arrived and claims to be... well, *claims* to be the wife of the Commander."

I stepped further into the light, drew back my hood, and shook my hair down. Maximus started up as if he had been stung.

"Helena!"

The others stared in amazement.

"Maximus," I said, "is there any way a woman can get a bath in this camp?"

*

You may imagine the reactions of the assembled officers. Some thought it highly amusing and perhaps a tribute to his virility (would that it were so!) that Maximus's young wife could not stay apart from him for one more night. Others sensed that something more serious was involved, although they could only guess at what. My appearance in men's dress should have given them a hint that my journey was not only secret but desperately important. Still, some of them just thought it was some sort of prank — a dare, perhaps. As if I would have risked my life on deserted country roads at that hour for a game! Maximus, to give him credit, knew at once that something dangerous was afoot, but he pretended it was all a joke.

"Get my bath set up!" he yelled into the darkness, and there was an answering obedient shout. He put his arm around me and steered me towards the great tent which stood behind the fire. As soon as we were inside he drew me to him and hugged me tightly.

"Oh, Maximus, you are in great danger!"

"I thought as much, or you would hardly have made such a journey, and in such a way!"

He laughed quietly. "God, Helena, what a sight you made! I thought some of their eyes would pop out."

"Maximus listen! Civilis came to see us! He is expecting orders to arrest you tomorrow on your entry into Londinium."

"Hmm. Come and have your bath. We have no women here, so decency dictates that I must be your bath slave tonight. Not that you haven't earned it. You can tell me everything while you soak."

He led me through into an inner compartment of the tent. A large metal bath had already been put there, and two soldiers were bringing pots of water to fill it. As soon as it was full Maximus dismissed them. It was so long since I had been unclothed in front of my husband that I felt quite shy. But the warm bath water was too inviting to let that stop me. Soon I had stripped and climbed in. Maximus produced a sponge and began to wash my shoulders and back.

"You poor thing," he said. "You must be exhausted."

"Rather. But Maximus, that is the least of it."

I told him everything that Civilis had said. When I had finished he paused in silence for a while, his hands still dipped in the water.

"Wait here a while," he said at last. "I must confer with my commanders. But I think I know what they will say. They are all loyal men."

All loyal men! I pondered on what he meant by that. They had all sworn an oath of loyalty to the Emperor, I knew that. Indeed, so had Maximus. Did loyalty include submitting to arrest and death? For a Roman it might. There were generals who had done just that rather than risk splitting the Empire. Of course, that was in the days before the Empire was already split.

The water was cooling by the time he returned. I turned to ask him what had happened, but he just knelt by the bath and took my face in his hands.

"You risked your life for me," he said quietly. "I will never, never forget it."

Then he kissed me — a long slow kiss, filled with suppressed passion. I could feel his heart racing. He reached for the large towel, wrapping it around me and pulling me to my feet in one movement. I hardly needed to be dried, we were making so much heat between us. He picked me up lightly and carried me into the neighbouring compartment of the tent, where his bed was. He laid me down and threw off his uniform.

"Here," he said, "let's get you dry."

Getting me dry involved rubbing me all over — not all of it strictly necessary, but unexpected and delightful. Then he wrapped us both up in the blankets and held me close to him for a long time. I could feel his excitement, but we were in no hurry. We both knew it might be the last time.

Ironically, it was also one of the best.

*

The next morning we rose early and breakfasted simply in the tent. I had to dress in my servant's clothes again, as they were all I had. As we went out into the camp the scene was one of unrelieved industry. The men were making ready not only for the march, it was clear, but also for war. Weapons were being cleaned and sharpened. Men were practising in odd spare moments. I saw horses with chain mail coats — a trick learned from the Persians, I believe.

"Maximus, what is going on?"

He had never actually got around to telling me the night before.

He smiled. "Patience. I told you my men were loyal."

151

There was an expectant air about the camp. As Maximus walked around, nodding to junior officers and men, speaking to some in low tones, I realised that his popularity had not waned. They were respectful, of course, but not servile. He in his turn showed them the respect they merited — he was almost deferential to one old bewhiskered campaigner. Later he told me it was the *primus pilus* — the "first javelin" — the most senior centurion. Centurions were often oldish men of much experience, and the *primus pilus* would take command if the senior commanders were away, or killed in action. It was a highly responsible post — and highly paid — and perhaps the highest that a soldier could aspire to if he had no aristocratic family connections. This old soldier was British, and what struck me was that I heard him address Maximus by the British title "Amherawdyr".

That might be translated as "Supreme Commander".

Or "Emperor".

*

It was late afternoon when we sighted the walls of Londinium. Maximus and his immediate retinue were meant to go in by the Severan Gate, but the rest of the troops were supposed to enter the fort at the north-west corner of the city. In fact, Maximus had couriers sent there to alert the garrison to the situation and demand their obedience. Then, as we slowly advanced on the capital at the rate of the marching men behind us, we saw ever more clearly that the walls were heavily manned.

"Damnation!" muttered Maximus, at whose side I was riding. "Don't say we have to fight! Not for Londinium!"

My heart sank as I watched the armed men, tiny black dots at this distance, swarming along the battlements. Londinium had not been attacked seriously since the days of Boudicca's rebellion, three hundred years ago. The Queen of the Iceni had massacred ten thousand people there. I knew Maximus's men were not the sort to do such things, but the thought of Britain's foremost city under siege sent a shiver through me. Besides, Maximus was set on his path now. He must secure Londinium at once, and head for Gaul to attack Gratian before he was ready. There was no other course open to him now except to fall on his sword in the old

Roman style. Even so, those old Romans usually waited until they had lost the battle before taking their own lives.

One of the officers rode up at a gallop and hailed me.

"Hello, sister!"

"Kynan!"

"We have heard what happened. Your brothers both salute you!"

And he raised his arm to me. I laughed, but I was happy to see him. He looked every inch the army officer now, a tribune on Maximus's personal staff. His battle armour shone in the sunlight, and the legs which showed beneath his tunic were muscular and athletic.

"Will you need to fight?" I asked anxiously.

He shrugged. "We hope not. Maximus has built up the defences of Londinium too well, because of the Saxon threat. A small force could hold us off for weeks. If necessary, we shall leave some men behind to guard our rear and take the rest on to meet Gratian. That would be unfortunate, though; we need all we can muster."

The walls loomed close now, barely half a mile away. They were thick with men. Then I noticed the worst possible sign. Kynan noticed it too.

"They have closed the gates against us."

The Severan Gate's twin arches were closed by their great iron-bound doors. No doubt the other gates were all closed as well. Maximus spoke to the messengers riding near him, and they galloped off to take his orders to the various commanders. I had not heard what they were.

Gradually our column ground to a halt, only a hundred yards from the great walls. Maximus rode forward, and as he did so a familiar figure appeared on the tower above the Gate: the Governor, Paulus Civilis. At the walls on either side new men came to the front. The round shields with their red dragons made it clear who they were — the Cornovians, units of British soldiers raised by Maximus himself. It was the first sign of hope.

"Greetings, Magnus Clemens Maximus," called the old Governor.

"Greetings, Paulus Civilis? What sort of a greeting is this? Am I, commander of a victorious army, not to be allowed into the capital city I have risked my life to save?"

Civilis produced a large document and waved it in front of him. "Well, that depends. I have an order direct from the Emperor ordering your arrest. My duty is clear, unwelcome as it is. This order can only be countermanded by another from the Emperor. I would dearly love to receive such an order, but so far I have waited in vain."

Beside me, Kynan suddenly began to giggle. "You've got to hand it to the wily old bastard, he knows how to play both ends against the middle."

Maximus was also grinning. Then he dismounted, and walked across to a cart which had been brought up. Climbing on to it, where he could be seen by the troops, he cupped his hands before his mouth.

"You heard the Governor, lads. So tell him: Who is your Emperor?"

"Maximus!" they shouted as one. "Maximus! Maximus!"

The ensuing silence was deafening. Softly into it fell the sound of tearing paper. The warrant for Maximus's arrest was torn into tiny pieces and flew away upon the breeze. A babble broke out among the Cornovians.

"Macsen! Macsen Amherawdyr!"

"Maximus Imperator!" shouted the legionaries outside.

All along the wall the soldiers raised their swords in salute, and crashed them flat against their shields with a sound like a thousand anvils. Civilis was grinning all over his face. He had arranged the result he wanted, but in such a way that he could not be blamed if it all went wrong. There were thousands of witnesses to the fact that he had had no choice, and that Maximus had usurped his authority.

Amid the cheering, the gates creaked slowly open, and in through them rode my husband, Magnus Clemens Maximus, Emperor of Britain — Macsen Gwledig Amherawdyr.

XV

Maximus departed with his entire army the next day. The north was still garrisoned against the Picts, and secured by his new Irish allies on the other side of the Wall. The south was loyal to him. As far as the soldiers were concerned Maximus was one of their own, while Gratian was the incompetent and effete son of a vicious father. They would be happy to depose him. Maximus had to act while the mood lasted, and before Gratian had time to move first. Their forces were evenly balanced, if not slightly in Gratian's favour. The outcome would be close, whichever way it turned out.

"I pray that God will smile on his enterprise," said Antonina. "He will know what little choice my son had. He did not seek this confrontation. It was forced upon him. His hands will be clean of the Emperor's blood."

"Blood?" I asked, shivering. "Must the Emperor die?"

"There will be two Emperors in Gaul now," she replied. "One of them must die. I am Maximus's mother. Though it goes against the grain to pray for anyone's death I must pray for Gratian's."

"Let us hope that Theodosius will accept the result," I said, worried lest the impending conflict might spark off a greater one.

Antonina shook her head. "He must. He has no love for Gratian, and Maximus is an old friend of the family. Besides, he is busy in the east cleaning up the mess left by Valens and pacifying the Goths. He will accept whatever will give the west peace and stability."

"And Valentinian? He is Gratian's brother, don't forget."

"Yes, but what a brother — an immature youth Dominated by his ageing mother, and her a heretic, and in charge only of an Italy riven by factions. Little danger there, I should think. No, the next few days will decide it all. In a week you will know whether you are a widow or an empress."

I shuddered at her cold-blooded summary. Widow or empress? I wasn't sure which was preferable. Maximus had, true to form, left me in a rush, too busy organising troops to worry about his private life. Our last night together was no more than a tender memory. I sighed to think of how our marriage seemed to lurch from one remote bright spot to another through a wilderness of politeness.

Then there were my two brothers to consider. They were both with Maximus's army, although I had only seen Kynan this time, and I felt partly responsible for the danger they were in. They might have been in it anyway, but I felt sure that Maximus had them near him partly because they were my brothers and he knew he could trust them. Even if they were not killed in battle, they might be executed as traitors if Maximus lost. Or even as a precautionary measure, simply because they were his brothers-in-law.

"He must win."

The thought was spoken aloud, and Antonina smiled approvingly. If only she knew!

Felicia came to see me a couple of days later.

"My dear, your young man is back in Londinium."

"If you mean Julius, he isn't my young man."

"Oh no? Well, he's back in the city anyway."

"How do you do it, Felicia? You seem to have an unerring nose for gossip."

"Simple, my dear, I keep my ears open, and I mix a lot. You, on the other hand, spend far too much time cooped up in this mausoleum."

"It's a very nice house."

"The Emperor's palace would be like a mausoleum if you never got out. You should mix more. The officers' wives expect it, you know. They'll think you very aloof if you don't, especially when their husbands are off fighting for yours."

It had been on the tip of my tongue to say that I didn't give a damn what the officers' wives thought, but this last comment of Felicia's stopped it. She was right, as usual. The other women's husbands were away at war out of loyalty to mine. Of course, we all knew Maximus would be a better leader than Gratian, but some of the women would never see their husbands alive again. I owed them something.

"Where do you suggest I begin?"

"Serena Servilia is at home tomorrow afternoon. You must have had an invitation."

"Yes, but I wasn't going to go. I'll go if you will."
"Of course. I never miss a chance for news."
"You mean gossip."
"Of course."

*

Serena Servilia was related to one of the oldest families in Rome. She never tired of reminding everyone of this, although they soon tired of hearing it. The fact is that her connection was remote and brought no wealth with it, but was all the more important to her for that reason. Her husband was an unpretentious man who worked in the Imperial Revenue Service. He was, therefore, a glorified clerk, but one with a good deal of power and money. The Emperors had always conferred great legal powers upon their tax collectors, as a means of ensuring the success of their efforts. If they also made a little for themselves that was just the way the world worked. He was not at this gathering, of course, as it took place in the afternoon. Most of the guests were women whose husbands were away with the army — "grass widows who may soon be real widows" as Felicia put it. Most, but not all.

I stood with Felicia and chatted idly to some of the women we knew. Fruit and little pastries were passed around, and slaves did the rounds with drinks. There were fruit drinks as well as wine, as it was rather early yet for alcohol. None the less, Felicia was not above a cup or two in the afternoon, and I found myself keeping pace with her. The warm weather and the alcohol soon brought a flush to my face and a pleasant, relaxed feeling everywhere else. There was still that recurrent pain low down in my belly, though. Mabanwy had suggested purges, but while these worked horribly well they failed to cure the problem. The pains were never crippling, and never got any worse, so I doubted if anything was seriously wrong. I had confided in Felicia, who had given a somewhat coarse explanation.

"You're not getting enough," was all she said.
"Really? I didn't know it could have that effect."
"Certainly. Physical love is healthy, you know. Human beings were not meant to lie alone all the time. We're not designed that way."

157

"There are celibate people, though. Monks, and so on."

"And just look at them! I think that rather proves my point."

I glanced around at the other women, and wondered if their marital relationships were like mine. Perhaps I had an idealised image. Perhaps they too felt as useless. I realised suddenly that that was one reason why I had been avoiding company. It hurt to mix with people who seemed so much happier than me, but who envied me my position so much. I felt like shouting at them, telling them to be content with what they had, telling them the truth. It was impossible, and I turned away with a sigh.

And came face to face with Julius.

He smiled, and bowed slightly. "Good afternoon, *Domina*."

The alcohol had fortified me a little. No fainting this time. Just the pounding of my heart, the melting feeling inside.

"Good afternoon. I had no idea you would be here."

"No, well, a few of us have duties which keep us in Londinium, and Serena Servilia was kind enough to invite us."

"I'm surprised you're not working."

"Frankly, *Domina*, my duties here are not very arduous. I am often free at unusual times."

I gazed at his fair skin, his deep brown eyes. God help me, a girl could drown in those eyes! He was wearing civilian clothes — a simple linen over-tunic and sandals of leather. He looked very cool for this weather.

"And are you not bound to Gaul?"

"Not yet, at any rate. I might be sent for, of course, but there's no word of it so far."

I became aware that Felicia was watching the encounter from across the room — mentally cheering me on, no doubt.

"I wonder what you find to do with your spare time, then?"

"Oh, you might be surprised, *Domina*. There is really quite a lot to do. I have to keep fit, of course, so I go to the baths in the Via Fori. They have a good gymnasium there."

A mental picture of him came to me, clad in only a loincloth, sweating from his exertions, muscles rippling.

"And w-what else?"

"There's the theatre."

"Oh, you don't go to those awful prize fights?"

"I go for the plays, not the fights. Have you not been?"

"No. My husband is — was — so busy most of the time, we hardly ever got out to such things. Now, heaven knows what the future may bring."

He nodded. "We all wish Maximus well."

"Do you?"

He looked me in the eye.

"Oh, yes, *Domina*. The entire army knows who would be the best leader. I should say support is total. Even over there, I reckon a lot of Gratian's men would rather not fight for him."

"But they will, won't they?"

"Possibly. I wouldn't be surprised if some of the auxiliary legions defect to Maximus, though."

Julius glanced around the room.

"I don't think I'll stay too long here. I seem to be the only man."

"Duty calls?"

He smiled at me conspiratorially.

"Not really, although it's a splendid excuse. No, I think I'll sneak off home."

"Where do you live?"

"I have a little house down in the Via Fabrorum. It's small but comfortable. Just right for one person. Far better than living in a barracks. There's no privacy there at all."

"I suppose not. Do you have servants?"

"Just a woman who comes in the morning to clean. I generally eat in the barracks. I dress for ceremonial occasions there, too, so I have a batman. No one at home, though."

"Isn't it l-lonely?"

He looked me in the eye again, an unnerving habit.

"Sometimes it is." He dropped his voice. "Especially when you find someone you'd like to share it with."

I looked away, terrified of betraying my feelings. But of course, the act itself betrayed them.

"I think I'll go now," he persisted. "May I escort you home?"

His home or mine? I tried to bury the thought, but it refused to die.

"I-I came with a friend..."

He nodded across to Felicia, who smiled back at him.

159

"She will understand."

Only too well! Then she was at my side.

"Going so soon, my dear? I don't blame you, frankly, it's a very dull party. I'll come with you."

"Oh, well, I..."

She lowered her voice. "Just as far as the corner dear. Just for the sake of appearances. What you do after that is your own business."

She turned a bright and cheerful face towards our hostess, and invented an excuse for leaving early. It was a conspiracy; I was being carried along on a tide of events which were not of my own making.

We went out into the street, Julius offering me his arm. I took it and held it against my own, warm and firm. True to her word, Felicia went with us to the first corner, and then bade us good day with a twinkle in her eye. Julius grinned conspiratorially at her, and then turned to me.

"You'll walk a little further with me, *Domina*?"

I nodded, unable to utter a word. He led me away down a side street. I knew it was not my way home, but I made no protest. It was all beyond me now. We took several short cuts through back streets, eventually emerging in a quiet tree-lined avenue. We stopped outside a narrow-fronted house in the middle of a terrace.

"Let me show you my house," he said pleasantly.

"Yes." I could hardly speak.

Mesmerised, I saw him produce a key and unlock the door. He ushered me in to a small darkened hall and locked the door behind us. He turned to me and placed his hands on my shoulders. They slid up my neck until they held the sides of my head.

As he drew nearer our feelings erupted in a surge of passion — if that's what it should be called. Together we tore at each other's clothing. It was impossible to undress like that. We simply lifted our tunics high and pressed ourselves together. His hands went under my bottom and lifted me right off my feet, my back to the wall. As our bodies slid together I wrapped my legs about him as if to pin him to me. Then all was a frenzy of thrusting and gasping and kissing. It was an explosion of lust, almost animal, and utterly wonderful. And when the final explosion gripped both of us, all too soon, we clung to each other while our bodies arched and twisted, oblivious of the noise we were making, and the bruises we were getting from hitting the wall. Lost in each other till the last panting sigh, and the slow return to reality.

"Are you going to put me down?" I asked him, and he drew away and set me down with a rueful smile.

"I'm sorry. The situation isn't very romantic, is it?"

I giggled.

"It was what I have wanted since the first time we met."

"Yes. Me too."

"I suppose I ought to feel guilty, but I feel wonderful."

"It's for me to feel guilty. Your husband is my commander-in-chief."

"And do you?"

He paused, and then shook his head with a smile. "No."

We went into his little living room. It was comfortable, but sparsely furnished. It had an empty feel to it, as if it was not lived in very much. There was none of the clutter and the personal touches that make a place look inhabited. I supposed it was because Julius was away such a lot, but it gave it a lonely air. I sat on a couch. Julius sat down too, and put his arms around me. I snuggled into them, and we sat there for a long time without a word.

*

I arrived home alone and unobserved — I simply let myself into the house and went to my room without anyone seeing. That was not so unusual. As it happened, Mabanwy came to my room soon after.

"Ah, so you are back. I wondered. What was the party like?"

I grimaced. "Not so much of a party. There were a lot of other officers' wives all talking nonsense. You know the sort of thing — dresses and hair styles, and what the latest fashion is."

"Really? You stayed long enough, considering it was so bad."

I nearly jumped. I had almost given myself away at the first opportunity. I would have to be more careful if I was to see Julius again — and I would die if I didn't.

"Oh, well, Felicia was there, you know, and some of our friends. I enjoyed talking to them."

"So it wasn't so bad, then."

Mabanwy seemed satisfied. I felt a twinge of guilt for the first time. I wouldn't have minded lying to the servants, and one need not explain oneself at all to slaves. But Mabanwy was different. She had cared for me since childhood. Our relationship was much closer than that of mistress and servant, and I hated deceiving her. Still, I could hardly tell her the truth. It would be unfair to load such a responsibility on her.

For the first time, it occurred to me that having a lover might be a lonely business in some ways. I went to my room and looked around at it with new eyes. It was a nice bedroom, but that was all. Just a room. Why on earth could Maximus not make love to his wife in it?

Over the next few days I walked on air. Widow or empress, it seemed to matter little enough now. In some ways it was like my first infatuation with Maximus, but it was better. It gave me a possible alternative to my present life. I didn't know yet whether Julius wanted to marry me, but I felt that he would take me if Maximus rejected me, or failed to come home. He was my rescuer, my champion.

It was Felicia — who else? — who brought me down to earth. She knew very well what had happened, and I couldn't keep from telling her anyway.

"I wish you joy," she said, "and lots of it. But don't go imagining that he offers you a permanent way out."

"What do you mean? I couldn't possibly go back to Maximus now."

"What makes you think you have any choice?"

"Felicia!"

"Listen, my dear. Listen, not just for your own sake but for Julius's also. 'Widow or empress'; wasn't that how Antonina put it?"

"Yes, but..."

"No, let me finish. If it's 'widow' then you can do what you like, I suppose, although you must hope that Gratian's vengeance doesn't extend to Maximus's family."

162

"His family?"

"His children. And you, too. Just because you don't think of yourself as belonging to Maximus any more, don't imagine others will share your view. If Gratian wins you may find yourself arrested."

"Oh, gods above and below, I never..."

"No, well, it may not come to that. On the other hand, if Maximus wins you will be an empress."

"Well, perhaps I had better pray for him to win."

"For heaven's sake, Helena, are you witless as well as besotted? Or is the one caused by the other? Helena, how many empresses do you know of who have been divorced?"

"Well..."

"Save yourself the trouble. The answer is that empresses don't leave their husbands, except in a coffin!"

"Felicia!" I was close to tears. I felt as if she were attacking me, destroying my world around me.

"Oh, Helena, I don't want to be brutal, but someone has to make you see. Maximus might divorce you, but you can't count on it. Marriages are very political for people in his position. Then there's the Church."

"Oh, but Maximus doesn't worry too much about..."

"He will if he's on the throne. He'll have to. Just look at the trouble there's been over young Valentinian. The Church is terribly important in politics these days. And the Church doesn't recognise divorce."

I sat miserably, my eyes filled with tears.

"Oh, Felicia, what can I do?"

"You can only enjoy your good fortune while it lasts. Julius is a nice young man, handsome and strong and loving. Be grateful for that, but don't expect it to last forever."

Of course, as soon as I thought of him the tears cleared. My heart leapt within me. What did it matter what happened? Together we could beat the world!

Not original thoughts, I'm afraid, nor any more true for me than for the countless other young lovers who have thought them.

*

If Antonina was surprised at the sudden increase in my "shopping" trips she showed no sign of it. Maybe she thought I was just keeping myself busy out of anxiety. Maybe I was. I needed Julius every day. I needed him physically, more than I had ever needed Maximus ("The more you do it the more you want it," said Felicia prosaically). There was something in that; he seemed to know exactly what pleased a woman, and how to draw from her the capacity and the desire to be pleasured. Hardly surprising if I longed for more and more. But there was more to it than that; I needed to talk to him, to hold him, to laugh with him. All the things that Maximus hardly ever did. To start with he was reluctant to talk about himself, but gradually he unwound with me, and told me about his background. Part of the reluctance, it turned out, was because he was not a true-bred Roman.

"My father was a soldier too," he said. "But his father was a barbarian mercenary, a Goth named Hrodobert. He fought for the Romans for years, and took citizenship when he retired. He Romanised his name to Rodobertus, and my father gave me the name. My grandfather had settled in the east, close to the Saxon Shore, at Venta. My father moved away and came to Londinium. He wanted me to learn a trade and get rich. He said the army was all right, but after two generations the family ought to look for wealth elsewhere. It was a disappointment to him when I enlisted. My brothers went into the army, too. They're both dead now, and my parents."

"My poor love, you're all alone in the world."

He kissed me. "I was."

I snuggled up to him in the bed. "Go on."

"Well, I soon found I had a talent for learning languages. Most of us learn a smattering of all kinds, because the army is full of so many different nationalities, especially the foreign auxiliary units. But I had more than that. Anyway, someone recognised it and suggested I should be specially trained and sent to gather intelligence."

"To spy?"

"If you like."

I shuddered. "It sounds terribly dangerous."

"Not really, not usually. The last time was a bit awkward, but it isn't usually like that. Mostly I just pose as a trader or a religious pilgrim, or whatever seems useful, and keep my eyes open. You'd be surprised how many of us there are. The Empire has enormous borders, and most of those on the other side are not all that friendly to us. They need to be watched."

"So that's why you're not attached to any of the legions?"

"That's it. Officially I'm a staff officer, attached to the headquarters."

"And although you joined the army you still didn't end up exactly poor."

"What makes you say that?"

"This house. Your uniforms. You looked superb that first time I saw you at the governor's house."

"Hmm. Well, the uniform was my grandfather's originally. He wasn't a poor man in his tribe; he was actually a chief. But I have made some money of my own. Posing as a trader is no good unless you actually trade. I found I had a talent for that, too."

I moved against him lazily. "Julius?"

"Mm?"

"There's another talent you've got..."

*

The news came unexpectedly one morning. I was at breakfast with the girls, who had hardly realised what their father was up to, or how dangerous it was. There was a clatter of hooves outside, and immediately someone banged on the front door. A pang of fear went through me. Somehow I knew that this was it.

Widow or Empress?

I shuddered. Caradoc, our senior manservant, was answering the door. Voices rang in the hallway, and I rose to go to the messenger.

A tribune stood in the hallway, a parchment scroll in his hand. The Imperial seal adorned it. I looked at it with a start. It was the appearance an arrest warrant might be expected to have. My insides turned to jelly.

"*Domina.*"

The officer bowed formally and handed me the scroll. It was not an arrest warrant, of course. That would have been opened by whoever was to execute it. It could still be a demand for my surrender, or even my suicide, as an alternative to a treason trial.

My hands trembled. I fumbled with the wax seal. Bits of it fell on the floor, shattering the silence like a breaking jar. My mouth had dried. Don't let it be bad news — I will never see Julius again. The thought stilled my heart for a moment.

"Helena, what is it?"

Antonina had come in. She saw the scroll, which I was still trying to undo.

"I heard the riders." The tribune bowed to her, too, but she ignored him.

"Your hands are trembling, child," she said to me, but not unkindly. "Here, we old ones have less to fear."

She took the scroll from me and unrolled the top section, squinting because of her short sight. Nobody breathed. Then she handed the scroll back and shook her head in disbelief.

"God be praised."

I looked at the scroll. It was not in Maximus's hand, but he would have dictated it to a scribe.

Honoured mother, dearest wife and daughters, may this letter find you, as it leaves me, in good health.

Great things have happened here. We landed safely and our army marched straight away to meet Gratian, who had assembled near the capital of the Parisii, on the Sequana river. We met within two days and joined battle at once. I hate doing things this way, preferring to have a proper battle plan, but both armies had moved, and came upon each other unexpectedly. There was some indecisive skirmishing and I feared we might lose the day. Gratian's forces were fresher and more numerous than ours.

Suddenly, and unexpectedly, a large unit of the enemy broke away. These were his Moorish cavalry, who had been offended by his favouring of the Alani in his bodyguard. They sent forward an officer who immediately hailed me as Emperor. The entire contingent changed sides and began to fight their former comrades. Gratian's force was quickly split, and we moved in to complete its disintegration. Seeing which way the wind was blowing, several other units also defected to us, and within an hour Gratian had fled the field with a few loyal retainers. We believed he was heading south, and sent fast riders to cut him off.

Word has just come that he has been apprehended and is being held at Lugdunum by troops loyal to us. He was, as we supposed, making for his brother's territory in Italy.

There seems little doubt now that our victory will be accepted by Theodosius, and I will be formally invested with the rank of Augustus before the summer is out. The men here use the title already. They are cock-a-hoop, of course, especially since casualties were very light.

Dear Mother, I took the advice you gave me on our parting. I prayed to God and His angels to give me victory, and no one can doubt that my prayers were answered. We march tomorrow for the capital at Augusta Treverorum, and I will be baptised there as soon as it seems fitting.

Dearest wife, the country is not yet settled. There is still the possibility of insurrection, or even counter-attack by Valentinian's men. Not by Theodosius, I think, for he is too busy with the Goths, and anyway must have much sympathy with us. This means that I cannot yet send for you and the children. I will do so as soon as it is safe, probably in the autumn. You will all be baptised with me at Augusta, and you yourself will of course be crowned Empress to reign alongside me.

With dutiful affection, Magnus Clemens Maximus.

It was typical of Maximus that he should use such a stilted phrase to express his love for his family. Typical also that he should assume the right to tell me when and where I should be baptised — and into which faith. Typical that he should assume I would happily follow him to a foreign country to be a decoration for his palace. I pictured the life before me and burst into tears of bitter despair.

Fortunately, Antonina took them for tears of relief.

167

XVI

"There are grass seeds in your hair," commented Mabanwy, who was brushing it. "Honestly, the mess your hair gets into these days!"

This innocent comment sent a shiver of guilt through me. I was still keeping things from Mabanwy, and still hating it, but the less anyone knew about Julius the better.

We had spent the day in the country outside Londinium. Julius had organised horses and food, and Felicia had organised an alibi. She knew someone who was inviting other army officers' wives for a celebration of their safe deliverance. It was natural that I should be invited. We had done this sort of thing several times now, so that Julius and I might spend his off-duty days together. The summer was glorious, and it seemed a pity to waste it.

Especially as it might be all we would get.

He was teaching me to swim. I had often paddled in the sea as a child, but proper swimming was not a skill that was much taught. Apart from anything else, public nudity was frowned upon. The only exception was at the public baths, and then the sexes were supposed to be strictly segregated, women using them in the morning and men at other times. Actually, I had heard that mixed bathing occurred in some places, but several imperial decrees had been published against it. ("Spoilsports," was Felicia's comment. "Still, if they did allow it, they would only tax it!")

Julius and I had ridden out early to a remote spot on the banks of the Tamesis. There was a small sandy beach on a bend in the river, and trees and bushes to screen us from any chance observer. Not that anyone was likely to pass by — there were no villages or farms nearby. Boats were more likely, but they would probably keep to the other side, where the water was deeper.

"If you're shy you'll have to run into the bushes when they come past," said Julius.

"I'm not shy when I'm with you. The entire fleet could go past and I wouldn't care."

This was true. At the time I didn't analyse the feeling, but with the benefit of hindsight I suppose it was because I felt safe.

Clothes are a protection, and we feel vulnerable without them. Julius, the principal cause of any danger to me, made me feel protected.

We swam, we picnicked, we made love (in the bushes — there were still some things I wanted privacy for). It had been an idyllic day.

And a very sunny one. Later when Mabanwy began to help me undress part of my tunic scraped my back and I started. Mabanwy pulled the cloth aside.

"Gods above and below!" she exclaimed. "What on earth have you been doing? Your back's all sunburned!"

I could think of no convincing lie, and would have been reluctant to utter it if I could.

"I've been out in the sun, of course."

"I can see that." There was a pause, while suspicions raced almost audibly through her mind, and she considered whether to reveal them. Her role as friend struggled with her other role as servant, and eventually won.

"Helena, is there something you're keeping from me?"

My heart was in my mouth. "What do you mean?"

"You must have been out in the sun for a long time. And with no clothes on. It wasn't here, and I don't suppose it was at that party, either."

I sat down on the bed and pulled the tunic around me.

"No, it wasn't. Of course."

"And it wasn't in the company of other officers' wives, I suppose?"

"No."

I felt ashamed, but not of Julius, or our affair. It was because Mabanwy had caught me out in a lie. I felt like a little girl discovered in some naughtiness by her mother — which was almost what Mabanwy was to me.

"Mabanwy, it's not the way you think. It's not like Felicia, with her young men. For her it's a... a sport. It could never be like that for me."

"Oh, dear heavens, that's worse! That means you're in love with him."

"Yes, yes. Mabanwy, I should have known you'd understand."

169

"Understand, is it? Understand? For heaven's sake, Helena, you're married! Your husband is about to be declared Emperor of the West! And you're in love with another man, and sharing his bed! Gods above and below, your husband will need all the understanding he can muster!"

"He is no husband to me!"

"What's that supposed to mean? He keeps you in style. You're accepted by his family. What more do you want?"

I began to cry. "I want to be loved, Mabanwy."

"Loved? Heaven help us, child — "

"I am not a child, Mabanwy!"

The harsh tone quietened her. Seeing her look of alarm I motioned to her to sit next to me. With an effort I brought my weeping under control.

"I am not a child, Mabanwy. I am a woman. I have the needs of a woman. I want children of my own. I want to feel I actually *matter* to my husband. I am not asking for flowers and serenades. Maximus is a busy man, and anyway he's not that type. I understand all that."

"What, then?"

"Mabanwy, since we came back to Londinium from our Segontium trip he has shared my bed on about three occasions. While we were away it was all right, but before that it was the same. When he does make the effort it's only ever because he's had too much wine. What do you think it does to me to know that he can't face the prospect without resorting to alcohol? Am I so repulsive?"

"Don't be silly. You're a beautiful woman, you know that."

"So people say. Only Julius makes me feel that it's true. He would still make me feel like that if I had a face like a horse. But anyway, Mabanwy, that isn't all."

"What more can there be?"

"Maximus has another woman."

"What?"

"I've seen her. She came here once, and I came home early and saw her leaving. Maximus denied it all, but he was very uneasy and obviously lying. Caradoc knows something, too. I'm sure of it. He was shifty and insolent when I questioned him. Mabanwy, it's bad

170

enough that Maximus can't bring himself to share my bed — it's bad, but I could learn to live with that if it were all, and there would still be the chance of children, even though his attentions are rare. The humiliation is a thousand times worse when at the same time he's going to someone else's bed."

"Who is this woman?"

"I've no idea. I thought I saw her in the street another time, and I'm sure I'd know her again, but I don't know her name or where she lives. I do know that while he sees her I owe Maximus nothing — certainly not fidelity."

Mabanwy put her arm around me. "My poor, dear Helena. Perhaps if we could put a stop to this other woman things could be put right?"

I shook my head. "Not now. It's gone too far. I love Julius, and he loves me. Whatever happens now I will never be a wife to Maximus again. I couldn't give up Julius, not if my life depended on it."

"Oh Helena, don't say such things. It so easily might..."

Mabanwy offered to try to pump the servants for information about the "other woman". In the meantime Julius and I went on as usual. I saw him almost every day, and longed to have him with me at night. The bed seemed large and empty, now that there was someone I really wanted to share it with. We often spent days outside the city, as it was the place where we were least likely to meet anyone we knew. I was half afraid that Antonina might notice something amiss — I had suddenly developed a great desire to socialise with everyone — but she continued to keep herself to herself and seemed to notice nothing.

It was on our return from one of these trips that we found the city buzzing with expectation. It was late in August and the weather, having turned rainy for a while, was once again right for swimming and picnics. Inside the gates once more, we noticed that there were more people out and about than usual.

"It's like market day here," said Julius suspiciously, "and there are a lot of soldiers about."

There were soldiers in twos and threes at all the main road junctions, and some outside public buildings, too. It was not a heavy presence, but more than usual, and all strategically placed. Those who knew me stared and muttered to each other.

"There's someone I know," said Julius. "I'll ask him."

He rode up to a young soldier and spoke for a moment, but it seemed the man knew nothing.

"He says they were just told to take up these guard positions. That doesn't sound like trouble to me — more a precautionary measure. I'd better report in, in case there's some news. They may have sent for me at home, anyway."

I returned home myself, and found several soldiers on guard outside the house. They too had no idea why they were there. It was just a routine precaution, they said. Asked which routine this was, they just shrugged. Orders are orders to a soldier.

Mabanwy met me inside the hall. She at least had heard a rumour.

"There's a rumour that the Emperor is dead!"

"What?"

She saw the expression on my face and shook her head.

"No, no, *Domina*, not your husband! Heaven forbid! Oh, I'm sorry, it was stupid of me. No, I should have said the former emperor — Gratian."

A strange mixture of feelings gripped me. Dread, perhaps, and yet relief. Gratian's death would certainly bring the much-wanted stability that Maximus had written of in his letter.

"How did it happen? Was he ill?"

"I've no idea, *Domina*. That's all I know, and that's only rumour."

But it was true. A messenger came with the official news shortly afterwards. Felicia's husband, Vegetius, had received a despatch, and wanted to let us know right away. Gratian had died while at a banquet in Lugdunum.

"That's why they had the guards out," I said to Antonina. "Just in case any of Gratian's old supporters made trouble."

She nodded. "And yet there has been none. It is a measure of his unpopularity. Well, the way will be clear now. Maximus will doubtless send for you soon."

"Yes." I tried to sound enthusiastic at the prospect. But it brought my hour of decision that much nearer.

The next time I saw Julius it was at his own house. He answered the door, and as usual he was alone. He seemed rather subdued. His usual affectionate greeting was reduced to a peck on the cheek, and he turned away and let me follow him inside. I had a sudden sinking feeling.

"What's wrong?"

"It's that husband of yours."

"What about him? Julius, don't be like this with me. I am not my husband."

A grin stole over his features. "I should think not!"

"Well, then, what has upset you?"

We sat together on a couch and he hugged me to him.

"I'm sorry. It's not your fault. It's about Gratian's death."

"He died at a banquet."

"Yes, so I heard. Did you not think that strange? Maximus beats Gratian, and takes him prisoner, and then invites him to a banquet as if he were an honoured guest?"

"What have you heard?"

"A friend of mine has just come home on leave to attend his ailing mother. Actually, the old girl was dead and buried by the time my friend got here. Anyway, he was part of the guard at this banquet. He says Gratian had been under house arrest at a villa in the town, while they decided what to do with him. He had some servants and disarmed Alani guards in attendance. He was invited to the banquet and promised a safe conduct between the two. The idiot accepted. When they all sat down at the table, two officers ran in and killed him."

"Oh, no!"

"They took out their spathas and hacked him to pieces."

The spatha was a slashing sword with two sharp edges but no point. Many of the legions used them for close fighting. Their effect on a man without weapons or armour would be hideous.

I was barely able to believe it of Maximus. The honourable treatment of prisoners was one of those old-fashioned Roman virtues he professed to admire so much.

"Perhaps it was done by one of his subordinates."

Julius shook his head. "I can't see any of them doing anything so drastic without his say-so. Of course, just a nod or a wink might be enough. Then he could always convince himself that he hadn't given the order. It's the coward's way, though. If I wanted someone murdered I'd do it myself, or at least give the direct order. If I felt too guilty to do that, then I'd know it was wrong."

"Antonina said one of them would have to die."

"Melodramatic old woman. Exile would have been enough. It's been done before. Gratian wasn't popular enough to stir up trouble from abroad. No, it's murder, and the whole army is contaminated by it."

"Will others feel the same?"

"Probably. No, don't worry, they won't rebel against Maximus. But some will watch him carefully now. They wouldn't want him to get too big for his boots, like the one he's killed. If an emperor thinks he can get away with murder, though..."

He left the sentence unfinished. For a long time we held each other close without speaking.

*

Mabanwy was troubled when I returned home.

"I don't know what's going on," she said, helping me to change for dinner. "I've got a little information about that woman, though. The slaves have been told not to speak, but I persuaded one of them. She says the woman is not your husband's mistress, as far as she knows."

"Not?"

"No. She says the woman comes here at regular intervals, and that Maximus gives her money. She says she's seen gold coins given to her. Once, when Maximus was away, the woman saw Caradoc and he gave it to her."

"What is she, then — some whore?"

"Hardly likely, is it? If that was Maximus's taste he'd hardly need to bring her home. Besides, the slave says this woman only ever sees him in the study, and stays in the house for only a few minutes."

I could make no sense of this. If there was nothing underhand about his relationship with the woman, why would Maximus not tell me about her? Why had Caradoc so obviously been told to lie? I thought about Caradoc. If only I had some lever I could use —

something to make him talk to me. I asked Mabanwy to keep her ears open for any information about him, too. I was angry and frustrated with my lack of knowledge. Perhaps also I was disappointed; if the woman was neither mistress nor whore it made my own position less defensible. It was time to take the initiative; if Maximus was going to send for me soon, I needed to strengthen my position before I refused to go, and asked for a divorce.

I suddenly realised that I was now taking it for granted. The decision was made — no matter what happened I would not go to Maximus. It was a great relief, though a little premature...

We were in the market at the Forum — Felicia, Mabanwy, the children and I. I was looking for cloth for a dress, knowing that I might soon be a good deal poorer. This had been Felicia's idea.

"Go on," she said. "You might as well make hay while the sun shines. Personally, I think you're daft to contemplate leaving Maximus for a poor young officer, but if you insist upon it — and if Maximus will let you — then you'd better spend a bit first. Maximus can afford it, and the gods know he's given you cause."

I was less sure, but Felicia swept my protests aside, and there we were, looking over rolls of cloth in the market. Actually, a new dress was not all that unreasonable, or wouldn't have been if I was staying. If I were to go to Gaul as Empress I would need plenty. But of course, I would not be going.

The two girls went through every bale of cloth they could. They were both pretty things, now, with the usual female interest in clothes and finery. Indeed they didn't seem interested in much else. They would make good princesses.

The market was as crowded as usual, and we had to struggle down some of the lanes between the stalls. There was precious little respect for rank here, not if a bargain might be lost! The whole scene took me back to Segontium, and the cramped little market where we had seen the Irish prisoners paraded. I slipped into a nostalgic reverie, and my eyes wandered over the scene, seeing only another scene in another market in another time...

Until they passed over a flash of blue in the crowd.

At once I was awake and in the present. The blue shawl. It was the same one. I was sure of it! I could not see the woman's face, but there was a wisp of fair hair poking around the edge of the shawl.

"Mabanwy, look after the children. Take them home when they are tired."

Mabanwy was too surprised to argue.

"Yes, *Domina*."

"Felicia, come with me."

"Yes, *Domina*."

I ignored the sarcasm. "Felicia, it's that woman — the one Maximus sees in secret. I just saw her over there."

I pointed to the food stalls, where the blue shawl could still be seen, wandering amongst the crowds of housewives out shopping for their families. Felicia understood at once.

"Right, let's get after her."

"Wait. She knows me, but not you. You get up close to her first. When she sees me coming she may run off. Then you could follow her."

"Good thinking." And Felicia was off. I waited until I saw her almost next to the blue shawl and then I made my move.

But as I had feared the woman saw me coming when I was still some way off. She turned suddenly and made for one of the archways leading out of the Forum. I saw Felicia go, too. By the time I reached the archway they were nowhere to be seen.

I waited, pacing up and down in disgust, but it was not long before Felicia arrived back.

"It worked! She never realised I was with you. I followed her all the way home. It's only a couple of streets away — a tenement block. Come on!"

Hearts beating like a couple of excited schoolgirls we retraced Felicia's steps through the back streets.

"I trotted along just keeping her in sight," said Felicia. "She must have assumed you were on your own. It obviously never occurred to her that I might be with you. I nearly lost her when she turned into the tenement block, but then I saw her at a window. Here."

We stopped by an old crumbling building. There were many of these in the city — mostly built in brick with timber frames. Many of them were in worse condition than this one. Every so often one of them would fall down, and the owners would have to pay compensation to the victims — or their surviving family. Inevitably, there would be disagreements and lawsuits. Owing to the expense of hiring lawyers it was usually the landlords that won.

"Upstairs," said Felicia. "The first floor."

We climbed the spiral staircase, ignoring the smells — urine, rotting food — and the buzzing flies. It occurred to me that what the city needed was a rubbish collection service. I wondered if Civilis could establish one. But then, who would pay for it? Were taxes not high enough already?

Felicia led me to a door. "I'm sure it must be this one. As I say, I only saw her at the window."

I knocked loudly. After a few moments the door was pulled back, and there stood the fair-haired woman. She tried to shut the door, but we were too quick and threw our weight against it.

"Go away!" she begged, a pleasant voice unused to angry scenes. "Please!"

"I will go as soon as you answer me some questions," I said quietly.

"No, I can't. I daren't."

"Daren't? Have you been threatened?"

"No, but, well..."

"It's the money," said Felicia suddenly. "She's afraid of losing the money."

The woman looked at her in gratitude for her understanding. I could feel for her. If the money was keeping her in this sort of style, she would certainly not want to get any poorer.

"Just tell me what I want to know," I said. "No one will find out you have told me. But I must know! I *will* know!"

She sighed in a defeated sort of way and let the door go.

"Very well, you'd better come in."

We almost fell inside. She motioned us to a table with chairs, and we sat down. The room was sparsely furnished, but clean. Through a door I could see there were other rooms. As these apartments went, it was not all that bad.

"Are you on your own here?" I asked.

She shook her head. "I have two children. They are at school."

School! For a woman of her limited means that was a great expense. That was where some of the money went, at any rate.

"What is your name?" I asked her.

"Rhiannon." A classic British name. "What do you want of me?"

"I want to know why you visit my husband when I am not at home. At first I thought you were a mistress." I raised a hand to stifle her protest. "I don't believe that now. But why do you visit him? And why does he give you money?"

She looked at me disbelievingly. "Do you really not know? He told me you did, but you found the whole business distasteful and wanted nothing to do with it. Well, I could understand that, especially if you were jealous of his first wife."

"What? Where does she come into this?"

The woman shrugged. "I see you really know nothing."

"Why does my husband give you money?"

"It's a... a pension, I suppose you'd call it."

"Were you employed by him?"

"No, *Domina*. Oh, please go away. It's better you don't ask any more!" Tears ran on to her cheeks.

"Tell me, Rhiannon. I already know too much to be fobbed off."

She wiped the tears away. I suddenly realised that the problem was not just the fear of losing the money. She actually found it painful to talk about this — whatever it was.

"Tell me," I urged her gently.

"Your husband... your husband p-pays me money as compensation. Blood money."

A cold grip tightened about my heart.

"Your husband... he killed mine. He murdered him."

We were all silent for a minute, but for the woman's sniffing. It was Felicia who broke the silence.

"But you mentioned Maximus's first wife. Where does she come into this?"

The woman wiped her face again and looked at us.

"He murdered her, too."

XVII

Murder is largely a matter of definition. If a man kills a stranger who has not offended him we call it murder. But in war soldiers do it all the time, and we call it heroism. If they are particularly good at it we heap honours upon them, and sometimes even make them emperors. If the killing results from some great provocation, we recognise that the victim was partly responsible, and call it manslaughter. I dare say it makes little difference to the victim; he — or she — is just as dead whatever we call it.

Rhiannon had had plenty of time to think about it, and to her it was still murder. Under the ancient common law of Rome it was no such thing, for it was a crime of passion. Less than that, it was his right. Maximus had caught his wife in bed with another man, drawn his sword, and killed them both. That ancient common law would hardly have protected him these days, but Maximus was a powerful man. He had used his position to cover up the truth. He had used his money to buy silence. Rhiannon would have taken her husband back, despite his sins. She had lost her breadwinner, and Maximus felt obliged to support her, although in law he was not. Anyway, it helped prevent scandal. Under the circumstances I felt he could have done more. Property was cheap in Londinium at the moment, and Maximus had been rich even before he became Emperor. He could have bought her a proper little house with a garden, instead of which she rented this slum. I could do something about that. I had legal authority to handle his money while he was away.

These were some of the thoughts that buzzed around my head while Rhiannon unfolded her story. Mixed in among them was a growing fear. Felicia had spoken of the power of emperors to get rid of unwanted or errant wives. I now knew that Maximus had had such power for years, and had already used it. Surely he would not think twice before ridding himself of a second faithless hussy? I could almost hear the justifications he would utter as the sentence was pronounced. Not only was adultery a blasphemy against the religion he had so recently embraced, for an empress it was treason against her husband. Previous emperors had killed wives for less. I could see myself dragged off in chains, my husband watching from the balcony as I was forced to my knees in the courtyard, the flash of the sword in the sunlight as it arced downwards to part my head from my shoulders...

I came to myself with a guilty flush. Rhiannon had been speaking, and I had not heard a word until now, when she began to weep.

"My Cadell was not a bad man. He was good to us. He didn't deserve to die for a passing weakness. It was her fault, anyway. She went out of her way to tempt him. He was only flesh and blood."

"Please don't," said Felicia, looking across at me uneasily. "Don't torment yourself. It is no good now. You have your children. You are still young."

"Don't patronise me!" spat Rhiannon. "I am young. I am also lonely, and what man will take on a young widow and her two children? Besides, a woman in my position has no chance to meet decent men, even if she wanted to."

"Please listen," I said. "We don't want to patronise, but we do feel for you. Personally, I think you've been badly treated all round. You've been compensated for loss of income, but you've lost a good deal more than that — lover, companion, helper. Maximus is not really mean, but I'm afraid it's typical of my husband that he would not think of those things. If you could have gone to law, the courts would have given you more. I shall put that right immediately."

"But then your husband will know!"

"He will not. It will be a lump sum, and it will appear in the domestic accounts as something else."

"You'll get into trouble."

I smiled ruefully. "Not so as you'd notice. Don't worry about me."

She looked me in the face. "Well, thank you, then. Perhaps I misjudged Maximus. There must be good in him somewhere if he can attract someone as good as you."

I could hardly keep from trembling, the epithet was so ill-deserved.

*

Felicia and I walked back home together, talking over the afternoon's events.

"What on earth am I to do, Felicia? I feel like a condemned prisoner already."

"I told you before," she said quietly. "I said you could only have Julius for a while."

"And I told you. I can't give him up. I'd die without him."

"And what'll happen to you *with* him, Helena? For heaven's sake think! Come to that, what'll happen to *him*? Have you not thought about him? He's broken military law by seducing his commander's wife. He's broken religious law by committing adultery — not very crucial here, but it would be at Court. And now the whole thing becomes treason, because Maximus is Emperor. Helena, you have no choice!"

"I love him, Felicia."

"Then do what's best for him. Do you know what they do to soldiers who commit treason?"

"No, and don't tell me."

She stopped abruptly and took my face between her hands.

"Helena, my dear friend, listen to me. If you truly love Julius then you will not want to see him humiliated, tortured and killed. If you love him, don't think of the pain it will cause you to lose him. Think of the terrible pains he will suffer if you don't."

We resumed walking, and went on for some time in silence. When I finally spoke it was only with difficulty, and with hatred for every word I uttered.

"Help me Felicia. Help me to do what's right. I will see Julius tomorrow.

"I don't believe you."

Julius looked at me calmly and steadily, and I couldn't meet his eye.

"It's t-true. I don't want to see you again. I've been thinking it over, and... and I've decided..."

"Decided?"

"Decided that, now with Maximus being made Emperor and... and everything, well, the situation has changed."

That was true enough, but it was all that was.

181

"So now you've had enough of your pleasant little diversion and you're calling a halt."

"Yes, that's it."

He suddenly laughed out loud. "Oh, Helena, my darling, never take up acting!"

My heart sank. He wasn't supposed to find it funny! This thing was difficult enough as it was. I tried to be angry, but my voice dried up to a whisper.

"Don't laugh."

"Helena, this isn't you speaking. This is the way Felicia would speak — or the way you think she would. If you were really the sort of person to drop me so casually you wouldn't come and do it in person. You'd write a curt note, or even more likely say nothing. You'd let me find out by seeing you out with some new toy on your arm. Come here."

He held out his arms and I hesitated only for a minute before falling into them. I still felt safe there, in spite of everything. He drew me on to the couch beside him.

"I've lived for years in situations where I need to know what others are thinking — sometimes before they do," he said. "I know what's eating you. You're afraid, now that Maximus is Emperor."

"Yes, but it's not just that."

And I told him all that I had heard from Rhiannon. He listened in silence, seeming unsurprised even at the worst revelations.

"Well," he said at last, "from what you told me it was obvious he had some great problem about women. Now we know what, and we know why it was only in the house here in Londinium. Your Maximus bears a heavy burden of guilt."

"Not *my* Maximus. Not ever again."

"Hmm. The question is, how do we disentangle you from him without giving him any cause for revenge, especially any public cause?"

"What do you mean?"

"Helena, my love, it's all politics. Whether Maximus divorces or not is of minimal importance. You are not a Christian, and neither was he when you were married. The Church does not recognise pagan marriages, so if you refused to be baptised they would probably go along with his renouncing you and perhaps marrying someone else — a Christian woman, of course. So far, so good.

"But if he is seen to be publicly humiliated in some way it's another matter. The Army would lose respect for a leader who was not seen to act decisively."

"You mean, if we — you and I — became public knowledge."

"Exactly. Maximus would come under great pressure to act harshly, to show his strength. The Army would be demanding heads on poles."

I shuddered, and he felt it.

"Don't worry, we're not done for yet. I've a lot of experience of getting out of tricky corners."

"Maybe I should write to Maximus — tell him the truth, ask him straight out for a divorce."

"I think that would be most unwise."

"But why? Maximus isn't really an unreasonable man. He knows he hasn't been a husband to me. He would accept he had been at fault."

"Privately, he might. But this will have little or nothing to do with how he feels privately. I told you, marriage is all politics at his level. Besides, your letter might fall into the wrong hands and even be made public. No, the technique of handling these things is always to retain control in your own hands."

"But we haven't got control of the situation."

He smiled. "Not yet."

"What are you going to do, then — raise an army and fight Maximus?"

He shook his head. "I don't want your husband's blood on my hands."

"Julius, I was joking!"

"I wasn't."

"Oh, Gods above and below, this is madness!"

"No. You meant it as a joke, but it almost is a practical possibility. More to the point, running to Theodosius, or even Valentinian, is a possibility. I would simply be a loyal officer who refuses to serve the usurper. I'd be sure of a job, if not actually promotion! I'll bet either of them would annul your marriage to Maximus, and we'd be free to marry."

"Oh, do you think so?"

"I'm sure of it. Of course, if we were caught it would be treason, I suppose, but then it is already."

"Oh, Julius, let's do it!"

He kissed me. "It'll take some organising, but it could be done. I'll just have to become a trader again for a while, eh?"

When I left him that afternoon I felt happier than I had done for weeks. At last it seemed there was a solution to the problem. Julius and I would be free! It was only later I thought of my family. What would the effect be on Papa? What about Adeon and Kynan? Once again my feelings plummeted.

When I came home I almost ran into Antonina. Her back was troubling her, and she was using a stick like an old woman. But of course, she was an old woman. She nodded at me before going through the door into her own wing of the house. A curt acknowledgment, I thought. As always when one has a guilty conscience, I wondered if there was more to it. Did she guess more than she showed? If so, what would she do? Julius would find a way out. If I clung to that thought it wouldn't matter what Antonina did.

*

Mabanwy was worried. She would follow me whatever I decided to do, but she had no doubt of what she wanted. Like Felicia she felt that the only realistic option was to break with Julius and go to Maximus when he sent for me.

"It's no good, Mabanwy. I've been through it all with Felicia. I can't give him up."

"Like you couldn't give up Maximus, *Domina*?"

"Be quiet, Mabanwy, don't go too far! Julius is a different person, and I'm older now. The whole situation is different."

"As you say, *Domina*."

"What worries me more than anything is what might happen to Papa and my brothers."

"Do you think Maximus would take it out on them?"

"I don't know, Mabanwy. Once I'd have thought not, but now who can tell? All along, I never really knew Maximus. I don't see how he could keep two officers on his staff whose sister was

184

accused of treason. He'd be bound to think they were in on the secret, or likely to seek revenge. The least they could expect is banishment. I daren't think what the worst might be."

I fretted more and more over this problem, but I could see no way out. I could do nothing to warn my brothers and persuade them to escape with us. Any letter might be intercepted in these times, and it would itself be evidence of treason.

"You've got to decide something, *Domina*," said Mabanwy. "This is killing you. Look at yourself. You're not eating properly, and you look as if you're not sleeping properly, either."

I nodded miserably. "It's true."

"Then take a decision. Please! If only to save yourself. I know it will be hard for you, but there is so much at stake!"

I agonised for two more days, I think. But in essence most human problems are simple, as Felicia had once said to me. The difficulty is not that people can't find the solution, but that they dread carrying it out. All the time I knew that there was only one way to get out of my dilemma with some hope of saving my brothers. On the third day, shortly after breakfast, I finally accepted it.

"Caradoc," I said. "I am going to the study to write a letter. See that everything is laid out."

I wrote it on a wax tablet, so that Julius could erase the evidence easily. I made it short and brutal. Then I got Mabanwy to deliver it for me — I could trust no one else.

Then I took to my room and wept for a very long time.

My beloved H, ran the letter. *I read what you sent me, although I don't believe a word of it, and I will cling to that. Believe me, I understand your situation, but I will not give you up so easily.*

Something has happened which may help in a backhanded sort of way. I have been posted to Gaul. I hope this may give me the chance to meet your brothers personally, although I am going to the south at first. If I do meet them, perhaps we can work something out together. Don't give up hope. I shall not.

I love you, J.

The tablet had been brought by a friend of Julius's, who had insisted on delivering it to me personally. It was, he said, a private business letter. This was not altogether implausible, especially as the man was in uniform, but Caradoc obviously thought it a little odd. I could hardly conceal my excitement, and took it away to my room to read. When I had finished I ran downstairs to find Mabanwy and tell her the news. Felicia called while we were talking, and I took her upstairs while I changed to go out.

"I've heard from Julius!"

"Is that a reason to be so excited, my dear? I thought you were going to finish with him."

"Listen, Felicia, all may not be lost!" And I told her what had happened.

"So he has been posted? Well, maybe it's for the best. Just don't pine away for him. There are plenty of other men in Londinium — or in Gaul. Have you erased his letter?"

"Not yet. I'll do it now."

As I picked up the tablet I noticed something strange about it. The letters weren't formed exactly the way Julius usually did his. But then, I hadn't seen much of his writing. It wasn't the sort of letter he would dictate to anyone else, after all. I decided I was mistaken and quickly took the stylus and used the flat end to wipe the wax till it was smooth.

"That's it," said Felicia. "Never leave the evidence lying around!"

Privately I thought what a cynic she was! In a way, Julius's posting was the best thing that could have happened. It forced us to stop seeing each other, with all the dangers that implied. It might give Julius the chance to sort out an escape plan with Adeon and Kynan. Above all, it made our parting much less than final. I could still dream — and I did — that he would return for me one day. The result of all this was that my emotions calmed. There was loneliness to cope with, but not the months of bitter gloom which I had expected. After all, I told myself, our separation might be long, but it was temporary. And it was some consolation that Julius would not be endangered by me.

*

Maximus's men came without warning after breakfast one day. I thought it strange — weren't arrests usually carried out in the middle of the night to catch the victim off guard?

It didn't seem like an arrest at first. The officer in charge asked to see me. When I came into the hall two of his men took up positions behind me. That made me nervous, but the officer was friendly enough.

"*Domina*, we have come to escort you to your husband."

"Oh? But this is extraordinary; there was no advance warning. When are we supposed to leave?"

"At once, *Domina*."

"At once? What nonsense! I have packed nothing yet. It will be several days at least before we can set off."

"Begging your pardon, *Domina*, my orders are quite clear. Your maid may pack some personal requirements and clothes for the journey, and she may accompany you. Anything else must follow on."

"What is this? Who are you to give me orders?"

"These instructions are not from me, *Domina*, but from His Majesty."

His Majesty! I had almost forgotten that Maximus was Emperor of the West now, and officially recognised as such by the other two. My status was clearly indicated by the fact that the officer was not using the royal title to me.

"This is monstrous! Am I under arrest? If so, what for?"

"I have no arrest warrant. I have orders to take you to Gaul under close escort."

It was a matter of words, not law. Maximus was the law. If he had ordered these men to kill me and dump me in a ditch somewhere they would do it, and who would charge Maximus with murder? The chilling thought struck me that he had got away with murder before. My mouth went dry, and there was a shaking in my limbs. Maybe the officer read my thoughts.

"Never fear, *Domina*," he said. "I am ordered to see you safe and sound all the way to the Imperial Palace at Augusta Treverorum."

"All the way?"

"Exactly. You will be reunited with your husband."

I was not to be quietly disposed of, then.

"Scarlet woman!" It was Antonina, but an Antonina transformed with outrage. She stood at the bottom of the stairs, leaning on her stick like the hooded figure of Death. A bony finger pointed.

"I hope my son has the courage to deal with you as you deserve!"

"It was you who betrayed me." Not a question.

"I am proud to say it was! Myself and Caradoc here. Did you not think I had the sense to see what was going on? All these sudden social engagements? Did you think I was blind because I was old?"

"Antonina..."

"Don't even speak to me! I have the evidence here."

And she held out the wax tablet from Julius.

"But I erased it!"

"So it's true! Condemned out of her own mouth! No, you didn't erase this. You erased the copy which Caradoc made and left for you to erase. He pocketed the one you left lying around and brought it to me. A very unwise piece of untidiness, and one which will bring you just retribution for your faithlessness!"

"Antonina, Maximus was also to blame!"

"I don't want to hear!" And she turned away as if to mount the stairs again.

"Your son was no husband to me!" I shouted. "He is not a man, Antonina! Not a man in the proper sense! Did you not wonder why I was not pregnant after so long?"

But Antonina was an old hand. She turned, and turned the comment back on me.

"So? The attentions of *two* men, and you still can't get a child? Huh!"

She turned up the stairs again. "I hope he has the courage..."

At that time I didn't know the bible story of the woman being stoned to death for adultery, or I might have asked Antonina if she was without sin. But it would have made no difference. She would hear nothing against Maximus. I felt the officer's hand on my arm.

"Please. We must go at once. We have a ship waiting on the River."

I fought for a minute to bring my feelings under control. Then suddenly my anger subsided, and I felt very calm. What could I do? Once again I was in the hands of Fate.

"Very well," I said. "If the mother has no conscience let us go to Augusta Treverorum and see if the son has any."

XVIII

From my upstairs apartment I could look out upon the city in every direction. To the east and north the city wall was only a couple of hundred yards away. The great Mosella river washed the western walls of the city, but I had never seen it, having arrived through the open country of the south. There was no eastern gate, but on games days I could hear the crowds at the amphitheatre, less than half a mile away. A few miles to the north lay the mighty River Rhenus, greatest of all the rivers in Europe and the northern border of the Empire. I had never seen that, either. The rich countryside around was (so they told me) dotted with estates and villas, and many pagan temples which were now falling into disuse or being consecrated for Christian worship. I had seen nothing of all this. I had arrived in Augusta Treverorum at night, and had not set foot outside my private apartment in a wing of the Imperial Palace ever since. These few rooms had been my prison for nearly two years.

I had realised that Maximus might have me put to death, or divorce me, or even banish me to some remote island. There were precedents for all of these. What I had not anticipated was that he might refuse to see me. True, he had been away fighting the barbarians again for a large part of the time, but there had been ample time to pronounce a judgment on me, or even to forgive me and resume our married life. It didn't happen. Mabanwy was allowed out from time to time, to buy me things at the market or to take clothes to the palace laundry. Twice a week we were both allowed out to the palace baths — not often enough for my taste. Mabanwy had tried to see Maximus for me, but had been refused by the court officials. Our apartment was guarded day and night, and locked for most of the time. I had no chance of slipping out, and I was reluctant to try in case we were caught. This apartment was prison enough without giving Maximus cause to think that a proper dungeon was indicated.

At first I had expected to see Adeon and Kynan, but it seemed both were away. Perhaps Maximus had arranged it deliberately. They were not in disgrace, apparently, but they had been given duties which took them far away — Adeon to Spain and Kynan to Africa, the western part of which also came under Maximus's rule. I suspected that Adeon, conservative and strait-laced as he was, would have had little sympathy for me. Kynan was another matter. He was more tolerant of human frailties. But there we were — me at the northernmost tip of Maximus's Empire and him at the southernmost. Apart from Mabanwy the only person whose sympathy I might have relied upon was Julius.

And of him there was no sign.

"I told you not to depend on him," said Mabanwy. "He may have the best of intentions, but he's only one man against an Empire. You really can't expect too much."

I knew she was right. But my mind would not accept it. Felicia's cynical words came to me, telling me that solutions were easy — only accepting them was difficult. Perhaps I was refusing to face facts, too, but I would not lose faith in Julius. It was all I had to keep me going.

I was not entirely without outside contact. Letters were allowed to pass. A few months after arriving I had got one from Felicia. As usual, it had been brought along with an official despatch by a military courier.

Dear Helena, I don't know quite how to address this letter. Should it be 'Your Majesty', or is that a sore point? I was amazed when I heard of your abrupt departure. Then I began to hear whispers of armed escorts and you may imagine the terrible things that went through my mind. However, a friend who visited Court recently said all the gossip was that you were officially an invalid. Unofficially, the word was that you were under a sort of house arrest, accused of nothing but not free. Either way, I hope this letter will reach you and   perhaps   the memory of your daft friend will cheer you a little. Vegetius is still trying to wangle a promotion, but without success. If he gets it eventually, he will probably be posted to Lower Germany, which is very much your area. I do hope so. I miss you here. No one else among all these officers' wives has a sense of humour.

Antonina is getting very frail. She misses the children, of course, but equally doesn't feel up to a strenuous overland journey. I do hope you can write back soon, and let me know you are well. All of your old friends here are thriving. Rhiannon has moved house — she has a sweet little place at the western end of the city now. Her brother Julius is abroad again but no one knows where. He's a strange fellow. You never know where he's going to turn up next.

My heart leapt as I read this. Calling Julius Rhiannon's brother was, of course, meant to blind anyone who intercepted the letter. It seemed an obvious ploy to me, and I hoped she hadn't underestimated my potential enemies. Still, it meant there was no news of Julius's having been arrested, and he was now abroad again. My head filled with fantasies of rescue. They remained fantasies. I replied to Felicia, but I was never sure how open I could be, so I tended to gloss over my present circumstances. She made no further reference to my "house arrest" when she replied, but tried to slip in little items of interest.

There were some Saxon coastal raids not long ago, but those new defences of Maximus's put paid to them. No doubt there will be more. Apart from that, life goes on much as before. Vegetius keeps on at me to be baptised a Christian. I think he feels it would further his career. These days religion is so important, and of course your husband is widely known to be devout.

Devout? Maximus? If so he had changed a lot. But then, the last letter we had had from him in Londinium had mentioned his baptism. Perhaps he had been more affected by his conversion than I realised. It came to me how out of touch I must be and I nearly wept.

Well, that's most of the news that's really important. Let's hope that we meet again soon. Give my love to the children. I hope they had a good journey.

Your loving friend, Felicia.

I read the last line again in astonishment. Having heard nothing I had assumed that the girls were still in Londinium. Felicia's letter made it clear that they were now in Augusta too, and I had not even been told! We had not been as close as we might have been, but we had got on well enough. Surely Maximus didn't mean to deprive me of their company, too? But if not, why had I not been told, and given the chance to meet them? Mabanwy had heard nothing, but then she had not asked, and was never allowed close to Court circles. I resolved to make sure they were brought to me for a visit.

It was a resolution that nearly cost me my life. Mabanwy found out that Sabrina and Fulvia were staying, not in the palace, but in a government-owned villa outside the town. She was not under the restrictions which I faced, and simply intercepted the children's nurse — perhaps "companion" would be a better title at the age they were now — on a visit to the city. The nurse, a pleasant local woman, was happily oblivious of the trouble surrounding me, being recently recruited and having been told only that I was too ill to be visited. She was suitably delighted to be told that I was better and capable of meeting the girls now. Maximus and Flavius Victor were away, although due back imminently. Neither the nurse nor Mabanwy asked anyone's permission, and my guards had had no instructions on the matter. They knew the girls as my stepchildren and simply let them in.

"Helena, Helena!" Young Sabrina at least was pleased to see me. Fulvia, rather more reserved by nature, hung back a little as her sister flung herself at me.

"Oh, Helena, they said you were ill! It was such a long time I was afraid you were dead, and they were just being kind. You look fine now — well, a bit pale."

"I am fine," I said, laughing, and indeed I did feel good to see them. "You must tell me all you've been up to. You know, I've hardly seen the place since I arrived. I've... well, I've not been able to go out."

"Poor thing," declared Sabrina. "Now you're better you must come out with us. We've been everywhere. We went on the Mosella River on a boat the other day. The day it was so hot, you know. It flows north all the way to the Rhenus. Father says it's the biggest river in the world."

"In Europe," corrected Fulvia. "The Nile is bigger, but that's in Africa."

"Well, anyway," Sabrina went on unabashed, "it's big."

Fulvia was not to be so easily dismissed. "You haven't seen it yet, though, so you haven't been everywhere."

"Oh, don't quarrel, you two," I said. "You haven't changed a bit — not in that respect anyway. Tell me, how is Victor?"

"He's well," said Fulvia. "Father says he's going to declare him Caesar soon."

That was news indeed, and it reflected how secure Maximus now felt himself to be. The rank of Caesar — virtually the Emperor's deputy — was normally not conferred on men as young as Victor. It meant that he was effectively to be marked out as heir to Maximus's throne. Antonina would be delighted.

"And your grandmother? Has she joined you here in Augusta?"

"No." Sabrina shook her head. "She says she's too old for all this gallivanting about the place. She wants to stay in Britain."

That news hardly distressed me.

"Helena?" Fulvia was looking at me strangely. "Helena, do you know the rumour that's been going around?"

"Rumour?"

"Well, I heard two of the guards talking about you."

I thought it best to squash this before it got started properly.

"I shouldn't listen to gossip and rumour if I were you. It's usually only at someone else's expense. People can be ruined by rumour and scandal. Even perfectly *innocent* people."

She caught the emphasis and glanced at Sabrina.

"Hmm. I expect you're right."

Not that I wouldn't have liked to know what the rumour was. It was me that might be ruined by it, after all. Maximus must be a fool if he thought he could put me under guard and not have it known all over Augusta, and probably much further afield. I wondered if Antonina was sending him letters exhorting him to "have the courage". Probably.

"Father has forbidden us to talk about it," said Sabrina.

"Then don't."

Fulvia chipped in.

194

"That's what Flavius Victor says. He says we must obey Father. To disobey him is supposed to be a sin."

"So people say."

"But Victor does. He's been told to stop seeing someone, but he still does, in secret. I know."

"Seeing someone?"

Fulvia reddened a little. "Well, you know. A girl."

"What girl is this? Why doesn't your father want Victor to see her? Isn't she of a good family?"

"Oh, yes. Well, good enough for most people. Her father's a senator from an old patrician family. It's not that, though." Her nose wrinkled. "It's religion."

"Ah, you mean she's not a Christian?"

"No, nor likely to become one. Her father is dead set against it. Flavius Victor says the old man still hopes for the return of the pagan gods."

I smiled. "Small chance of that now, I'd say."

"That's what Father says. And Father Petros, too."

"Who's Father Petros?"

"Goodness, you are out of touch, aren't you? Father Petros is Father's — Papa's — priest. Being Emperor now he has one all of his own."

"I think it's funny," said Sabrina. "Father Petros is much younger than Father, but Father — Papa — has to call him 'Father'. I said that to him once, but he said he is Papa's father in Christ."

"What does that mean?"

"I don't know."

We were interrupted at this moment by Mabanwy, who had gone to fetch some cakes from the kitchen.

"This is lovely," she said. "Just like old times."

"Mm." Sabrina was working her way through a mouthful of cake. "Now you're better I want to see you every day."

I had opened my mouth to reply when I saw something which made me stop in the act of taking breath.

Maximus, still in his fighting gear, covered in mud and horse sweat, was standing in the doorway. His sword was drawn, his face like a storm looking for somewhere to vent its fury. When he spoke it was through gritted teeth.

"What is the meaning of this?"

The girls jumped up and made as if to run to him, but his appearance intimidated them.

"Leave us!"

Fulvia scuttled away, but Sabrina lingered.

"But Papa, we only — "

"Silence!"

She too ran out, bursting into tears. Maximus glared at Mabanwy.

"Are you deaf, woman?"

"You won't hurt her!"

He swung his sword at her. She dodged back, but he had turned it sideways. The flat of it hit her on the backside with a resounding slap. I leapt up.

"Maximus, please! Mabanwy, you'd better go. I shall be all right."

Mabanwy gave me a sceptical look.

"What can you do? Go, now."

She shuffled out, also crying. I turned to Maximus.

"Well, brave soldier, you've put three females to flight. What are you going to do now — murder the fourth?"

He strode forward with his sword raised, and for an instant I thought I had pushed him too far. My insides churned. But he stopped a pace away and thrust his face forward towards my own.

"Murder?" he hissed. "You dare to call it murder, you faithless bitch?"

"In cold blood."

"Do you know the penalty for treason?"

"Don't be ridiculous. You know perfectly well I would never plot against you."

"Never plot?" He turned away and paced the room as he spoke, his naked sword still gleaming its threat. "Never plot? Adultery against an emperor is treason! It undermines him. It undermines his standing with the troops. If a man can't control his wife how can he control an army?"

196

"That's crazy."

"It's how they see it. Manliness to them is very simple, and it is the quality they value most. If I once appear in public branded a cuckold I assure you I will not last long."

"Then why did you not kill me as soon as you knew, or have me quietly disposed of in Londinium?"

There was a silence. He broke it with an embarrassed cough, turning half away.

"Because I felt that I might have been partly to blame."

"I believe that. You are a just man at heart."

"At heart? What do you know of my heart, woman?"

"As much as you let me, Maximus. You refused to talk to me. You kept me at a distance. You could have confided in me. I loved you, but you rejected me. You spurned me, and for years I never knew why."

"It was not my will to do so," he said quietly. "It was a penance imposed upon me by God."

"Maximus, have you taken leave of your senses? A penance on you? What about me? Your... disability was a penance for me too, but what had I done to deserve it? How could I face a life without affection, without a place in your heart, without children of my own?"

He turned on me again.

"You showed what you deserved when you crawled into the bed of that young filth and started playing mare to his stallion!"

I got to my feet and faced him squarely. "Damn you, Maximus! Damn your disability, damn the guilt which drives it, damn your self-importance and damn that scheming old witch of a mother of yours! Damn — "

I'm not sure what I was going to damn next, but he suddenly swung his sword. I fell backwards in avoiding it and felt my ankle twist painfully. He advanced again. I spun away as the sword fell again. It clanged on the tiles by my head and gritty fragments stung my earlobe. I scrambled half way up. I was in the corner of the room. There was no escape. I had to sit there while he stepped up and put the point of his sword against me, just below the left breast. He pushed gently, and I felt a searing pain like the touch of a firebrand. I felt the blood flow.

197

What an ignominious end. I thought of my father, grey-haired and lonely in Segontium. I thought of Adeon and Kynan, keen soldier and statesman in the making. Julius. Dear, sweet Julius, wherever he was.

"My sword is an inch from your heart," growled Maximus. "Give me one good reason not to push it home."

I gabbled the first thing that came into my head. "Manliness."

"What?"

"If you wanted to kill me the time was when you first found me out. Kill me now and they will realise the truth."

He chuckled very unpleasantly.

"No, whore! I have told them for two years that you were terribly ill. What could be more natural than your death now?"

He gazed in fascination at the spreading stain on my dress. Suddenly he shifted the sword and made a matching cut on the other side.

"Maximus!"

He leered at me.

"Your death after a long illness. I'm afraid you were in torment, poor thing."

He moved the point to my belly.

"In many places they torture whores to death, you know. Especially adulterous whores!"

"Maximus, please!"

"You never bore me a child. What about him? Did you give him any bastards? Shall I open you up and see?"

The sword point moved. My inside was twitching and churning.

"Do you know, I still don't even know his name? Tell me. Tell me who it was."

He twisted the sword point, sending fire through my chest.

"For pity's sake, Maximus!"

"Pity? You chose the wrong man for pity. The law is the law, and the law of God is the highest law."

I was trembling so much I could make no reply. The sword point moved, and I bled again. I was in a state of terror now, knowing I was in the power of a madman. A madman who could kill me with a flick of his wrist. Still, my voice returned, albeit in a half-strangled tone.

"Does the law of God permit the torture of defenceless women?"

"It does not!" boomed a voice from the doorway. "Maximus, in God's holy name restrain yourself!"

Hazily, through my tears, I could see past my tormentor to the doorway. There stood Flavius Victor with a stocky middle-aged man in priest's clothes. Maximus turned to face them, and trembled for a minute as if struggling with himself. He began to croak something, but stopped. Then he flung his sword into the corner and stamped out of the room, rudely shoving past my rescuers.

"Sweet Jesus!" gasped the priest. "Look at the blood! Fetch a doctor, my boy."

I was dimly aware of struggling upward, and then falling into strong protecting arms.

IXX

Flavius Victor and Father Petros probably saved my life. Not only that, the priest gained me a degree of freedom. He apparently had no fear of Maximus.

"After all," he said to me the next day, in tones of the utmost joviality, "the worst he can do is have me killed."

"You seem very unperturbed at the prospect."

The priest's brown eyes twinkled, and his short grey beard waggled as he spoke.

"Why should I not be? Death is but the doorway to the life eternal." He grinned at this a moment. "Mind you, I don't actually seek it. I'm sure I can do something useful in this life before I go."

He and Flavius Victor had come to see how I was recovering, but in fact there was no need for concern. My wounds were slight. The shock had been the worst thing. After my rescue I had suddenly begun to feel cold, and by the time the doctor arrived I was shivering violently and uncontrollably. He was an elderly man with a straggly beard, but richly dressed and scrupulously clean.

"Blankets," he said laconically. "A hot drink. A heated brick under the feet. Get her warm. Wash the wounds. They're not serious, but they must be cleaned."

He was off again almost immediately, saying he had a birth to attend. Mabanwy looked after me lovingly, as she had done since I was a child. After a while the shivering subsided and I went to sleep.

It was the next day when Victor and the priest came. They told me that Maximus had been under severe strain for many months. There had been a plot by some senior officers, which he had dealt with by having them executed. Some he had thought of as old friends, and it was hard to say whether their treachery or their loss had been the greater blow. Then there had been an incursion by some German tribesmen from across the Rhenus, and a small but fierce battle north of the city. On his return Maximus had mentioned the children to someone and been told where they were. It was the final straw, and he seemed to have gone temporarily mad.

"He is more himself today," said Victor. "Father Petros and I took him to the state apartments last night and sat him down in his room. Then we stayed up for hours, arguing with him. It was Father Petros who got through to him. Papa feels great remorse for what he did yesterday, Helena, and what he nearly did. Father Petros pointed out the Christian duty of forgiveness. Papa cannot bring himself to forgive what he calls your great sin, but he does accept that things must change."

"Does he?" The news was a relief, if it meant that I need not live in fear.

"But where exactly does that leave me? Does he want a divorce?"

Father Petros tutted disapprovingly, and I remembered the strict Christian attitude towards marriage. It was Victor who spoke, though.

"He says that is impossible, but he will lift the restrictions on your movements. As soon as you are well enough you may leave this apartment and live normally in the palace. If you will agree to appear as the Empress he will ask nothing more."

"He wants nothing in return?"

"Nothing, as far as I know. Discretion, perhaps."

"Then things have changed indeed. I thank you both for everything you have done. I would not be here today without your timely intervention."

Father Petros went out, murmuring some sort of blessing, I think. I turned to Flavius Victor; I had no idea what he thought about all of this, and he was a decent young man in a difficult situation; his opinion mattered.

"Victor, what do you think?"

"Of what?"

"Of me, I suppose. I'm sorry, I'm a bit of a failure as a stepmother."

He took my hand in his.

"You mustn't feel you have to justify yourself to me."

"Victor, I was unfaithful to your father. Doesn't that disgust you?"

He thought for a minute. I could see that he was torn, as if he disapproved of me, but still wanted to like me.

201

"Helena, who knows what goes on between people? I know you loved my father when he first brought you home. I know he blames himself partly for your, your... lapse. He said as much yesterday, although I didn't understand the details. He was a bit incoherent, but his general meaning was obvious. I'm sorry for the trouble between you, but I don't want to take sides."

After a pause he went on: "Did you love this other man?"

"Yes. I still do."

"Ah." He waited a moment. "Well, then, what can I say to you? I know I'm only young still, but I understand that people do strange things — maybe wrong things — when they're in love."

And he coloured suddenly.

"If it comes to it, I suppose nobody's perfect."

There followed the most bizarre time in my life. I was allowed out of my rooms and into the main palace. I had a room of my own, and Mabanwy one adjoining. Maximus slept in another wing, and the pretence of a normal married life therefore ceased at bedtime, for which I was grateful. I knew I could never share a bed with Maximus again; too many ghosts would lie between us in it.

I didn't hate Maximus, but I feared him. He seemed remote and preoccupied in my presence. He spoke politely enough, but formally, without any sign of personal feeling. For my part I couldn't forget the day when he had nearly killed me, and it overshadowed everything we said or did together.

Not that there was much. Maximus had made it clear — mostly through Flavius Victor — that he would rule alone. There had to be an empress for social reasons, but that was all. I would attend state functions, I could lead an active social life, but I would have no involvement in politics. Of course, this was very much a Roman tradition anyway, but Maximus was going to carry it to its logical conclusion. Perhaps he thought me morally unfit to make any contribution to government.

It mattered little to me. Mabanwy and I gradually recovered from our long isolation and began to venture out. The angry scene with Maximus faded a little in our memories. Young Fulvia was less lucky. She seemed unable to shake it from her mind, and I noticed that she had begun avoiding me. There was little to be done about it. I would not make her feel comfortable in my presence by forcing myself upon her. Patience was indicated. Fortunately, Sabrina, who was growing into a delightfully irrepressible girl, allowed nothing to cloud our relationship. She led her own life to a surprising extent, but she was always welcoming when she saw me. Even so, with Fulvia hiding from me in corners and Flavius Victor a grown man, my role as a stepmother appeared to be shrinking.

Although I didn't realise it at first, those world events which had been the background to my life were about to move centre stage. During my captivity the Bishop of Rome had died, and his place had been taken by a man called Siricius. Siricius was a politically aware prelate who was determined to halt the flow of ecclesiastical power away from Rome to Mediolanum and Constantinople. He underlined this determination by declaring himself Pope, or Father of the Church. Other bishops promptly adopted the title too, but in them he discouraged it. Another politically-minded bishop was Ambrosius of Mediolanum. He was still locked in a struggle with Valentinian, the Emperor of Italy. This was the poor youth with the heretical mother, Justina, who was still plotting to bring back the Arian form of Christianity. Ambrosius had taken the precaution of coming to Augusta to meet Maximus. Ostensibly this was to act as go-between for the two Emperors, and that was probably true as far as it went. However, few doubted that Ambrosius was also enlisting the support of Maximus in case Valentinian moved decisively against him. Ambrosius mostly stayed in Mediolanum, preferring to send Martin, one of his bishops, to speak for him. On one of these visits I remember waiting at the table — Martin was an honoured guest — while Maximus and the bishop argued theology together. It was a far cry from the days when we first met, when Maximus seemed to care little for religion, or indeed for politics. Now religion and politics were the same thing, or at least inextricably entwined. Defiance of religious authority was the same as defiance of the emperors. On this occasion Maximus was proposing the use of government troops to hunt down heretics in Spain. Not Arians, this time, but Priscillians. I never did quite understand what their offence was, but it seemed to involve a disagreement over which texts were to be officially accepted as Holy Scripture.

The books which made up the Bible had been decided in the days of Constantine the Great. Many others, including several different versions of the Gospels, were still in circulation, some giving a very different picture of Jesus from the one promoted by the Church. This appeared to be the main reason why the Church had banned them; there was as much — or as little — evidence for their accuracy as there was for the officially approved texts, but the Church had no use for a text which portrayed Jesus as a revolutionary, or a man with a liking for women, or even married, whatever its provenance. The Church wanted one sanitised holy book, and Maximus was prepared to kill heretics who refused to accept it. Martin, to do him justice, argued against such ferocity. For the time being Maximus agreed to hold back. The troops were needed, anyway. The barbarians were never quiet for long, and the Western Empire would be in a poor state if the Army was under strength when they next invaded. Most of the barbarians who were not actually pagans were Arian Christians like Justina, and they were arguably a greater threat than any Priscillian. I think it was this, rather than any spirit of liberality, which caused Martin to urge tolerance. He was certainly not slow to attack pagan temples at other times, nor to use troops to do it.

Meanwhile, of Julius there was no sign. I wrote to Felicia, guardedly asking her to find out what she could, but I knew it might take months to get a reply.

*

My official duties as Empress were limited — deliberately limited by Maximus, who wanted me to play as small a part as possible. I had to appear at social functions, to honour visiting ambassadors and heads of state, but there were few of those. Many other rulers regarded Maximus with suspicion. He was, after all, a usurper. In the old pagan days there would have been religious ceremonies to perform, but these were now in disrepute. Christian ceremonies were performed by priests, and my attendance at these was not requested, my absence discreetly ignored. I thought Maximus was probably noting my absences down to use against me later. Perhaps too my lack of religious enthusiasm discouraged anyone from trying to involve me further in politics.

I was not sorry. I had had enough, both of religion and politics. The previous Easter in Mediolanum had seen some extraordinary events brought about by the mingling of church and state affairs, which had exposed Valentinian's weakness and the growing power of the Church.

The dowager Empress Justina had begun the trouble herself by persuading her son to demand a church from Ambrosius in order to celebrate Arian rites at Easter. Ambrosius refused angrily, going so far as to say that he would rather be martyred for his faith than hand over a single church for heretical worship. Summoned before Valentinian and his Imperial Council, he agreed to attend, but was followed by an enormous and angry crowd of Catholics. Humiliated officials were forced to ask Ambrosius to intercede with his followers for the very safety of the Emperor and his retinue. This he did, but the peace was short-lived and was soon broken by riots. Arian priests were attacked in the streets, and mobs rampaged through the new Basilica being prepared for the Emperor and his heretical mother. Gothic auxiliary troops were sent to recover the building, but were met by the bishop himself in fiery mood. Although they were Arians anyway, he declared the soldiers to be excommunicated. Some might have thought this to be asking for martyrdom, but such was Ambrosius' charisma that he succeeded in intimidating the troops and holding them off. Faced with a near mutiny Valentinian had no option but to give in. The plans for a public celebration of Arian rites were dropped, but Justina's hatred of the wily bishop was all the greater. She still plotted his downfall and waited only for another opportunity to bring it about.

Maximus's attitude to all this was scornful in the extreme.

"What can we expect?" he snarled derisively at dinner one night, surrounded by his chief advisers. "Who is in charge of Italy? A boy and an old woman. They don't make an empress between them!"

The guests laughed. They were given to laughing at Maximus's derisive statements about Valentinian. We had once laughed in similar vein at my father's table, but then Maximus had been concerned and questioning. Now he was certain and condemnatory.

"And they're heretics too," he went on. "The double-damned! Isn't that so, Father?"

Father Petros shrugged.

"Perhaps," he said. "And yet Christ himself tells us not to call any man a fool for fear of our own damnation."

Maximus smiled. "You're too charitable, Father. Doesn't the Church hold that heretics are more damned than pagans, for pagans have merely not heard the word of God, while heretics have heard it and rejected it?"

The priest looked uncomfortable.

"The great Augustine certainly wrote to that effect. Far be it from me to take issue with the great men of the Church."

I smiled at this; he was reminding the company that the pronouncements of the Church were only made by men, however great.

"Still," he went on, "I believe my first duty to the heretic is not to damn him a second time — or is it a third, I've lost count — but to save his soul by bringing him back to the right path. Surely both God and man will be better served that way?"

Maximus frowned. He was clearly not amused.

"As I say, Father, your charity does you credit, and I know how keen you are to save sinners" — he glanced at me here, a gesture which was not lost on the company — "but if it's all the same to you I'd rather make an example of them to teach any other waverers a lesson."

There were mumbles of assent. Valentinian's antics were as unpopular as his brother Gratian's had been. The mumbles were subdued, though — these days there were ears everywhere. Valentinian was still officially recognised both by Maximus in the West and Theodosius in the East. Technically to speak against him was treason. No one pointed out that this applied even to Maximus.

Not long after this there was a momentous event — momentous for me, at any rate. I had a letter from Felicia. Much of it was filled with the usual gossip, but in the middle, couched in the usual disguise, was a mention of Julius.

You remember Rhiannon's brother, Julius, of course. He is back in Londinium. My dear, you would have been shocked to see him. He has been abroad on Imperial business again, and was apparently ill for months with some dreadful tropical fever. Despite living in the most primitive conditions he survived and is now on the mend. I have urged him to ask for less dangerous work, but he seems very downcast and I feel he badly needs something to live for. He has been granted a lengthy leave, and intends to go to Gaul to stay with friends and recover in their warmer climate. Who knows? Perhaps you may see him.

See him? See Julius? Oh, I would have given my right arm to see him! At last I knew he was alive. What was more, there was an explanation for his lack of contact. He had been away working undercover again, and then very ill. For months. Now he was coming to Gaul! I laughed aloud as I reread the passage. "Stay with friends" be damned. He was coming for *me*! I knew it! By the gods, I would give him something to live for!

Of course, Mabanwy soon spotted the fact that I was unable to keep a smile from my face, and had to be told.

"Well, I hope this time he stays near," was her reaction. "But I hope your husband doesn't find out."

It was a sombre thought, but nothing could dampen my spirits at the prospect of seeing Julius again. Somehow we would sort things out, I felt sure. Surely Maximus, however devout he had become, would not consider himself bound to a wife when the marriage was not a Christian one? It might be a positive advantage to him to put me aside and marry some good Christian woman. He must know I would happily go without demanding any financial or property settlement. All I wanted was my freedom. With thoughts such as these I filled my days, waiting for Julius to arrive and Maximus to see reason.

"The idiot! The backslider! Heretic's pawn!"

It was Maximus who was shouting, and once again Valentinian who was the object of his wrath. He jumped down from the dais which supported his throne, and paced the floor of the audience chamber. Usually I was not party to such scenes, but on this occasion I had been drafted in to entertain the wife of an envoy, and an urgent despatch had arrived while we were actually being introduced. All eyes were on Maximus now, as he vented his rage at the news.

"The madman! He has actually passed a law guaranteeing freedom of worship to all faiths, and mentioning the Arians by name!"

Freedom of worship didn't seem such an unspeakable thing to me, but it was hardly the time to say so.

"Those who seek to undermine the new law are to suffer death! Death, no less!"

Maximus turned back towards the dais and threw himself into the large throne, which squeaked backwards on the floor.

"Death is an appropriate sentence for a heretic! This spawn of Satan intends to apply it to followers of the true faith! Why, laws condemning Arianism have been current for years now. Some of them have Valentinian's name on them! We all agreed our religious policy — Theodosius, myself, and Valentinian! Does the boy want to tear the Empire apart? How can we present a united front to the barbarian enemy at the door if we cannot unite ourselves with God? God must be our shield, our sword! The barbarians themselves are tainted with Arianism. Can we really overcome them if we adopt the same heretical doctrine? We are no better than barbarians ourselves in that case!"

He picked up the despatch again and read further.

"God have mercy! The great and saintly Ambrosius has spoken out against the new laws, and Valentinian has sentenced him to exile!"

A buzz went around the room. This time it looked as if Valentinian meant business. With Ambrosius out of the way his principal opponent would be gone, and the way left clear for his mother's heresy to be restored at the very heart of the Empire.

"He won't go! Ambrosius has taken refuge in the bishop's palace. Troops have surrounded it, but a large mass of ordinary people has gathered there and will not let them through. I am asked whether I can lend my support, and that I surely shall!"

He leapt to his feet and thundered away to his private office, followed by the most senior officials and military leaders present.

Shortly afterwards, by one of those "coincidences" which sometimes favours the unscrupulous, Ambrosius discovered the bones of two martyrs which supposedly had magical powers. The common folk believed this, if no one else did, and their resolve was strengthened. Faced with another stalemate, and strongly advised by Theodosius to give in, the weak Valentinian did so. It was not enough for Maximus. He saw Valentinian as a threat to the integrity of the Empire. He saw his dream of One Empire Under One Emperor Under One God severely threatened. Just after Christmas he called a War Council.

"This boil on the Empire's backside must be lanced," he told his commanders. "We must sweep the heretics into the sea. I want to prepare a plan for the immediate invasion of Italy!"

XX

Hannibal crossed the Alps with elephants during the Carthaginian Wars. He was a brave man. We crossed them with nothing more cumbersome than horses and wagons, but it was an uncomfortable enough experience. It was springtime, and the streams were swollen with melt water. On top of that, we had some late snows high in the mountains, and the going became treacherous. The horses often fell, and some had to be destroyed when they broke legs. A few of the soldiers were also crushed in falls, and died without ever reaching the battlefield.

If I had had my way I would not have gone at all, but Maximus insisted. We had a stormy interview at which he made his feelings plain.

"I want you where I can keep an eye on you," he informed me bluntly.

"And what is that supposed to mean?"

"It means I will not leave you behind, either to plot against me behind my back — "

"Maximus, you know that's nonsense!"

"I thought so once, but not now. You are obviously a weak woman, easily led away from the path of righteousness. I see now that I should never have left you before, not without a chaperone of considerable character."

"You left me in spirit long ago, Maximus, when you ceased to be a husband to me. For goodness' sake, you don't need to drag me along on campaign!"

He waved his hand dismissively.

"Say what you will. I will not leave you behind, either to plot or to disgrace me a second time. You will come with me to Italy. There won't be much of a war. I don't expect much resistance from Valentinian. He's a weak man, and his army has no love for him. I shall keep my capital at Mediolanum, close to Ambrosius. Now there's a man with a following. Imagine a rabble of civilians keeping Valentinian's army at bay, armed with nothing but their faith!"

I snorted at this. "Faith, indeed! They are armed with ignorance!"

He glared at me, but said nothing. We both knew they had also been armed with cudgels, rocks and swords.

"Maximus, what do these people know of obscure theological arguments about the nature of the Holy Trinity? They can't read or write, let alone appreciate the finer points of logic. They defend Ambrosius because he tells them what to believe and threatens hell fire if they don't. A hundred years ago the same common people were upholding the old pagan gods, and demanding death for those who refused to worship the Emperor. In another hundred years it may be some other faith."

"How dare you! Are you wishing the Church away?"

Actually, I cared little for the Church, but Maximus's pride in it was not to be contradicted.

"I didn't wish anything away," I said. "I'm only pointing out that nothing lasts for ever, not the faith of your forefathers, and not yours."

"This conversation is serving no purpose," he replied stiffly. "You will come with us, and that is that. You may bring Mabanwy."

"What about the children?"

"They will stay, of course. There is no place for girls with the army. Victor, of course, will stay as Caesar to govern in my absence."

"Poor Victor. You realise that by raising him to such a rank you have made the boy party to your actions?"

"What do you mean?"

"Maximus, if you fail they will kill you — "

"You'd be happy then, I suppose?"

"I will not even deign to answer such a remark. As I say, if you fail they will kill you, and then they will come looking for your deputies. You might have waited till the outcome was clear. Fail now and Victor's head will roll as well as your own."

"We shall not fail."

"Damn your arrogance, Maximus. All human endeavours can fail, even yours."

"We carry the cross of Christ upon our shields."

"So does Valentinian. So does Theodosius."

"This is not Theodosius's fight. He will not interfere to protect Valentinian. Theodosius too follows the true faith, and he is the son of an old friend. He would remove the heretic himself if he were not so preoccupied with the defence of the East."

This was less true than it had been — Theodosius had done a good job of pacifying the eastern Goths — but the East remained uncertain enough. January had seen fierce rioting in Antioch in protest against a special tax, levied to pay for the forthcoming celebrations of Theodosius's tenth year on the Eastern throne. The mobs had smashed up the public baths — almost a symbol of the Roman way of life — and destroyed statues of the Imperial family. The local governor had overreacted, and the result had been a massacre, with many women and children among the victims. There was general uproar after this, and it was to be Easter before order was restored after a visit by Theodosius's own personal emissaries. Following this there was a resumption of the old dispute with the Persian Empire over the ownership of Armenia. Theodosius was busy for the moment, but he had a habit of concluding such business quickly and decisively and leaving himself unexpectedly free.

But there was no reasoning with Maximus these days. I went to pack my winter clothing for the Alps, and my summer clothing for Italy. By the time summer was upon us we were over the Alps and camped in Northern Italy. The weather was warm but dry, and it seemed the perfect setting for an outing. War seemed a long way off.

Actually, it *was* a long way off, as we soon discovered. It seemed that Valentinian's will to resist was even weaker than Maximus had supposed. When he knew that Maximus was over the Alps, the youth fled to Aquileia on the northern Adriatic coast. His heretical mother went with him. So far as we knew, they were in no position to mount any effective campaign. We overlooked the fact that wars are not always won on the battlefield. There was still Theodosius. The fact that Theodosius's wife had recently died seemed, however, to rule him even more firmly out of the conflict.

"It is God's will," said Maximus, "and even Emperors must bow to that. Clearly, He has approved our expedition to rid the Empire of the taint of heresy."

The extreme religious devotion he was displaying by this time of his life was well known. Some have suggested that it was a matter of political expediency, to justify his invasion of Italy, but I don't believe it was. He had undergone a genuine conversion, I think, unlike the conversions of many of his officials, who would cheerfully have adopted tree-worship if they had thought it would further their careers. Maximus's problem was that he had, like Constantine before him, confused religion and empire, rule and divinity. Constantine in his day had made remarks which suggested religious madness more than piety, and at times Maximus seemed to be going the same way. He certainly had the same obsession with religious unity — he saw one orthodox Church as the key to divine approval and the survival of a divided Empire. I remembered how Bishop Martin had had to persuade him not to use troops to pursue heretics in Spain. It was strange, considering how militant the Church tended to be towards heretics at this time, that the Church's envoy should have been counselling moderation. But they were strange times.

I must admit these global considerations were not much on my mind at the time. I was miserable at having to go on a dubious military expedition just when I had found that Julius was alive and once more fit to pursue the matter of my release by Maximus. I did not weep, but a depression settled on me.

"It's like a conspiracy," I said to Mabanwy as we rode the last few miles along the road to Mediolanum. The land here was fairly flat and the going easy. If only the mental going was as easy as the physical. "Just when I thought there was some possibility of an end to all this we're on the move again. Sometimes I doubt if we'll ever be free. Perhaps Maximus is right, and it's a judgement for being sinful."

"Is that what he says?"

"He doesn't know. He never found out who my lover was. Oh, Mabanwy, it seems so long since I saw Julius, or held him. Sometimes I feel I never will again. What if he's forgotten me?"

"Surely not."

"Why not? He must have known many women. Why should I be special?"

Mabanwy chuckled. "My dear Helena, I can't tell you what you should believe, but I tell you this. If you weren't special to him, your young man could have found plenty of willing women who weren't married to his commander! Why risk his career and maybe his life, if you weren't special? No, I'd say that he'll appear again. Probably when you least expect him. After all, isn't he used to travelling secretly and spying out the lie of the land before he makes his move?"

Unconsciously I cast my gaze over the surrounding countryside, and Mabanwy laughed again.

"Well, maybe not right this minute!" she said. "But soon, perhaps."

"Soon."

I could live with "soon".

*

Bishop Ambrosius met us outside the city. He was on foot, and followed by a crowd of monks and ordinary people, who had come to greet what they regarded as a liberating army — a true Christian army, come to drive out the forces of evil and purify the throne.

I didn't like Ambrosius. It was not just the odour of sanctity about him, but his unshakeable conviction that he was right, and that he could read the intentions of God in his own mind. I often think the worst people in the world are priests. They think they know what is good for people. It makes them dangerous.

Ambrosius was in his late forties. His once black hair was greying now, and thinning on top — quite apart from the ridiculous tonsure which is the badge of office in the Church. His thin face was youthful enough, though, and I would probably have thought him handsome without the ill-kept full beard. His eyes were held open wide, as if with wonder, but the pupils always looked like pinpoints. I thought cynically that he might be keeping his eyes open for divine inspiration, but his pupils closed against those things he didn't wish to see. Whether or not this was true, I must admit he was friendly to us and delighted at our arrival.

"Maximus, my son! We heard you were almost at the gates. What a happy day this is!"

Maximus reined in his horse and his servant ran up to help him dismount. Once on the ground he went forward and took off his helmet. Then, as Ambrosius approached, he went down on one knee and accepted the bishop's blessing.

"Father, it is my honour to be here, and to fight the forces of heresy with the sword and shield of Christ."

"Well said, well said. Rise up, Maximus, let me look at you."

"I'm no different from when we met in Augusta, father. I am well, and ready to fight if need be."

"Well, my son, it looks as if it will not be needed. The painted Jezebel has fled, and her whelp with her. The gates of Mediolanum are open. Italy is yours. Oh, you should have seen them. They rushed out at crack of dawn three days ago — Justina, Valentinian, and a few guards. They took the minimum of baggage so as not to be slowed down. No one turned out to bid them goodbye."

"No one but you, father?"

"I turned out to wish them God speed on their breakneck gallop to Hell. The followers of Satan make good time when they are in retreat!"

They both laughed at this, and some of the monks with them. I dismounted while their attention was taken up.

"You have brought your daughter?" said Ambrosius in surprise.

Maximus's face darkened sharply. "My wife."

"Ah, of course, forgive me. We have not met before, but I was told how young and beautiful she was."

He held out his hand, and I curtseyed politely. He returned his hand to his side.

"And what brings you here with such a gathering of men, *Domina*?"

"My place is at my husband's side," I said — ambiguously, I hope.

He nodded approvingly. "Of course. Such devotion is most seemly."

I thought Maximus would choke.

The two men talked for a while, and then we all set off again, a horse having been found for the bishop.

"What a strange man," murmured Mabanwy to me.

"What did you expect?" I asked. "Anyone who could stand up to Valentinian and Justina the way he has must have something unusual about him. After all, his life and liberty were seriously threatened, and he never wavered. Whatever else you may think of him, he must be a man of tremendous courage and principle."

"You sound as though you admire him."

"I'm not sure I'd go that far. There's no denying his steadfastness, though, and his leadership. He obviously managed to appeal to the common people far more than Valentinian did."

"How many Emperors appeal to the common people, *Domina*?"

"True. Impudent, but true."

Maximus lost no time in getting firmly ensconced in the Basilica, that same Imperial palace which had been occupied by the mob, and from which they had defied the might of Valentinian's Gothic troops. The Goths themselves stayed in barracks mostly, and kept their heads down until it was clear that Maximus bore them no malice. All he demanded was loyalty, and he soon got it, Arians or not.

He also made strenuous efforts to win the goodwill of the people, and in this he succeeded as far as anyone could. He heard grievances and gave judgments, and if he was firm he was at least fair. The corruption which so often tainted the occupier of the Imperial throne was absent in his case.

As things went well his mood began to lift. He was cheerful and his smile returned — sometimes even directed at me. His enthusiasm for his new faith was undiminished, and he often sent Father Petros to talk to me about it.

"I'm sorry, Father," was my invariable response. "I know you mean well, and I know that Maximus wants me to adopt his faith. But faith is a matter of conscience, not of politics. I will not convert hypocritically, for you or for him."

"No, no, of course not, Empress," he would say, "but may I not spend a little time in telling you more about the faith you reject?"

Sometimes I would let him, but it made no difference. Perhaps it was my mood at the time — trapped in a miserable marriage, and with the one person who might help far away and maybe sick, I could not be very receptive to the "Good News". There were times when I even contemplated suicide. I could hardly mention that to the good Father, though, as it was one of the greatest sins in the Christian calendar. Yet he understood something of how I felt, and made it his business to visit me often simply to try to cheer me up. He was so relentlessly good-humoured himself that it often worked, especially when he brought snippets of news. He was a kind man and he liked me — he seemed to like everyone. He never spoke badly of people, and if he disliked their actions he would say so to their faces, whether the offender was a slave or an Emperor. I never forgot that he had risked his own life to save mine. His example came closer to converting me than his preaching ever did. There were times when the refuge of religion seemed to offer a way out of my misery, but they were few. I always came back to the contemplation of a life without love, and for me the love of God would never be enough. I don't despise the needs of the spirit, but I at least am a creature of flesh and blood as well.

So, as it turned out, was Theodosius.

*

Since the death of his wife he had hardly had time to mourn her decently. King Shapur of the Persians had come to the throne only that year, and sent an embassy to the Eastern Emperor in Constantinople — an embassy which brought rich gifts of jewels and even elephants. In the talks which followed, however, he showed that he wanted more than just goodwill — he wanted Armenia. Theodosius was not perhaps at his strongest. At all events, he drove a swift bargain with Shapur, ceding him four fifths of Armenia in return for guarantees of peace.

The dowager Empress Justina knew just what the tired Emperor needed to refresh him now that the crisis was over. He needed a new wife. Theodosius had shown no sign of taking arms against Maximus, who had been his father's friend. He seemed to believe, along with everyone else, that Justina and Valentinian had brought their troubles on themselves. But the wily old woman was an expert at manipulating men. Theodosius was supposed to have

217

a weakness for beautiful women — what man has not? — and so she exploited it. Instead of going to him to state her case personally, she sent her daughter, Galla, reputedly a young woman of great charm, intelligence and beauty.

Theodosius was smitten. Galla was so successful in her pleas that she soon won, not only his heart, but his armies too. Theodosius was in no hurry, but his marriage to Galla made him a close relative of Maximus's enemies. Soon he would have to support their cause with more than words.

"How sad," was Maximus's comment on hearing the news, which was brought to us at lunch one day. "It's a black day for the Empire when the Emperor himself is diverted from its welfare by a bitch in heat."

I don't know why, but the disparaging statement irked me. Perhaps I felt sympathy for anyone whose bereavement had been lifted by a new love, as I had once thought to lift his. Perhaps it was just that anything Maximus did tended to irritate me now.

"Since the laws against unnatural practices are very strict, I presume you are referring to the Imperial Princess."

"Princess!" Maximus seemed outraged.

"Well, she is one, or was. Actually, she's Empress now."

"She's a royal whore," he fumed, "sent by Her Majesty The Heretic to charm her way into Theodosius's bed and make him plot against me!"

"Oh, really, Maximus! Can't you just accept that the man was bereaved and lonely, and he found it easy to fall in love with her?"

"Sentimental nonsense!"

"To you, maybe. I can see that you'd find it difficult to sympathise. But I don't suppose Theodosius killed his first wife!"

I wanted to reach out and grab the words back as soon as they were uttered. For a moment Maximus sat there, his face reddening, a muscle in his left cheek suddenly twitching. Then he leapt to his feet, brandishing a table-knife.

"Get out! Get out of here! Don't strain my patience too far!"

His fist crashed on the table. I did indeed leave my couch and the room in some haste, memories of another stormy episode flooding back to me. I hurried away to my private quarters. There I sat and wiped away the tears which had stubbornly formed in spite of all my attempts to hold them back. I was still there some time later, when Mabanwy came looking for me.

"Oh, here you are — whatever's the matter?"

"It's all right, Mabanwy. Don't fuss. Just a row with Maximus."

"Another one? My poor Helena. Oh, dear, what are we going to do?"

There was an edge to her sigh that made me look up.

"What can we do? Anyway, at least we are out of those rooms and fairly free. It's progress. And we are together. I don't know what I'd have done without you."

I decided to make a firm effort to lighten things up. "Mabanwy, it's a fine afternoon. Let's not waste it. What can we do to cheer ourselves up?"

"Well, er, *Domina*, there's a travelling pedlar in the servants' quarters. I was there just now and he asked to see you. That's why I was looking for you."

"Oh, I don't mean buying things, Mabanwy."

She looked disappointed, or perhaps perplexed. Anyway, it was a strange look she gave me.

"Very well, what's he selling?"

"Er, silverware. Fine chains, jewel mountings, all that sort of thing. And of course he's looking for commissions."

"Mabanwy, I don't care that much for jewelry, you know that. Maximus may not think much of me, but even he would have to admit that as empresses go I'm very cheap to keep. I'm not sure I want to see pedlars today."

She giggled at that. Then she looked me in the eye and spoke very firmly.

"*Domina*, you *will* want to see this pedlar."

"Oh, go on then. It's obvious you'll give me no peace until I've seen him. If he doesn't smell too badly I'll see him in my private sitting room; if he does I'll see him in the garden."

"Oh, no need to worry, he's quite presentable." And she went hurrying off while I adjusted my hair a little and went through to the sitting room. I usually saw private visitors here — there were state rooms enough for the official variety.

I saw them coming well before they reached the sitting room — the door was open and the corridor leading to it was long and straight. The man was scuttled after Mabanwy, looking bent and old. He had a slight limp, and although his bowed head was obscured by a hood, the end of a straggly beard was visible. Altogether an unprepossessing figure. They came in, and the man shuffled up silently to make his obeisance and lay a wide but shallow box before me. He raised the lid to reveal a selection of silver items, not very well displayed, and some of them not particularly good examples. I rifled through them, slightly peeved with Mabanwy for wasting my time.

"You know," I said to him, still looking at the silver, "I'm not sure that this is the sort of thing I'd be interested in. Some of the pieces are all very well in their way, but my need — so far as I need any jewelry at all — is for fairly showy items. I really only wear much jewelry on state occasions, and then it needs to impress. It's not for my own personal glorification, you see, but that of the Empire. His Majesty needs to create an impression for some of our visitors, and my job is to help him. Otherwise, personal adornment is not of great interest to me. These pieces are pretty enough, but they're not ... impressive. I really think — "

He interrupted me then. Just one word.

"Majesty."

The voice was so out of place that I jumped. It was a young man's voice, warm and sensual. Shivers ran through me. I looked up as he drew back the hood and stood straight.

A gash on his left temple had healed badly, leaving a scar. He was thin. There were new lines on his brown face, lines of care and illness. His carefully cultivated beard had streaks of grey. But the eyes had not changed. There was still the cold steel, with the hint of fire inside. The room seemed to quiver. I could hardly see it through the tears which had once again sprung into my eyes.

"Oh, Julius..."

"Alas, no, Majesty. I am Julius's cousin, Beornardus. We look very alike — we have our grandfather's face, as they say in the family. All his grandsons do."

I felt rather foolish, but the mistake was understandable, after so long, and knowing how much thinner Julius must be. I had expected him to be different. Sheepishly, I wiped my eyes and tried to recover my voice.

"And what brings you here, Beornardus? Have you news, news of Julius?"

"That I have, Majesty. I promised him I would come to you in person, after I last saw him."

"When is he coming?"

The man looked embarrassed.

"Well?"

"Majesty, I have to tell you that my cousin cannot come to you. That is why I am here. He insisted I must come to you."

"Yes, yes, you said that! What's wrong? What's happened to him?"

A cold hand had settled on my heart. It was hardly necessary for him to explain further. I knew what he was going to say.

"I am sorry, Your Majesty. It was a recurrence of the fever. I happened to be in Londinium and stayed with him until the end. He was ill for a week, and then, just when he seemed to be getting better, it turned to pneumonia and he was gone by the next day."

The man's voice faded until it seemed to be coming from a long way off. A rushing sound filled my ears. I heard Mabanwy's voice.

"She's falling!"

Strong hands gripped me, and the world swayed giddily as they turned me to lie full length upon the couch. Mabanwy raised my head and a cup of water was put to my lips. I was suddenly, irrelevantly, conscious of her perfume, and the motherly softness of her arms as she cradled me. The man seemed to have gone.

"Should I fetch a doctor, *Domina*?"

"No, no. What good can a doctor do?"

And I wept bitterly, not just for the void which had been opened up in my affections, but for the removal of hope.

*

Mabanwy gave out that I had a headache and would skip dinner. She helped me to bed and soothed me to sleep. Later, when she was ready for bed herself, she looked in on me. I had slipped into a sort of half-wakefulness. When she sat on the bed and asked me if I was all right the tears came back again.

Tenderly, like a mother, she slipped her arms around me and cradled my head against her, stroking and soothing. I clung to her, the comforting softness of her against my cheek, and wondered whether the love of men was worth all the heartache.

XXI

When I awoke it was already late in the morning. Strangely, I found that I could think of Julius with little pain. It was not that I was indifferent — over the weeks that followed I often thought of him with renewed anguish, and I had not finished shedding tears for him yet. But the truth is that I had not seen him for over two years, after knowing him for only a short time. It is difficult to go on loving someone who is never there. Had that not been one of the problems with Maximus? Oh, they say that absence makes the heart grow fonder, but I wonder. Surely love is something that has to be worked on, not neglected. Absence, even if it is not the loved one's fault, still prevents him from demonstrating his love, or doing any of the things that bring a couple closer.

No, when I thought about it rationally, I realised that it was not Julius the lover that I mourned so much as Julius the rescuer. I had harboured a fantasy that he would one day appear and whisk me away. Only now that he was dead could I admit that a fantasy was all it had been. The practical difficulties were just too great — no matter how I did it, any escape would be a threat to my family. I thought of my poor father, amongst the last of the pagan aristocrats, and my two brothers, young men of ambition starting on their careers. There was nothing to be done.

At least, perhaps there was one thing. All my life I had let other people — mainly men — plan out my life for me. Now at last perhaps I could take hold of my own fate and at least try to steer it in the direction I wanted.

"Mabanwy, lay out something impressive. I want to look like an Empress today. I will also need all my make-up, and the best efforts of your artistry."

Mabanwy raised an eyebrow, but did as she was told. She chose a magnificent dress of yellow silk which, along with many others commissioned for me, I had never worn.

"I want to look good today," I told her. "From now on I may want to every day. Maximus needs an Empress, and an Empress he shall have. Do you know where he is?"

"I believe the Emperor is in the garden by the goldfish pool. You know how he often sits there on fine days, and reads the documents they bring him and receives guests."

"Yes. Well, he will have an extra guest this morning — his wife. Oh, jewelry, Mabanwy, if you please. What do you think?"

"The jasper, *Domina*?"

"Ideal. It'll match beautifully."

"*Domina...*"

"Yes, Mabanwy?"

"Are you feeling all right?"

*

I found Maximus as Mabanwy had said, sitting at a table under the shade of the cherry trees while he read through documents of state and occasionally signed them. Nearby sat a scribe, ready to take dictation at a moment's notice, and a slave ready to fetch refreshment. There were no guards here — the outer wall was well enough guarded — and for the moment no official visitor. Maximus heard the rustle of my dress as I approached, and glanced up for a moment. Then he sat up sharply and took a much longer look.

"Are you going to a party?" he said at last.

"Don't you like it?"

"Well, yes. It's a beautiful dress. You look, well, it's not often you dress up so much."

"It's not often I need to. Maximus, may I have a word with you — a private word?"

He glanced down at his work.

"It's important, or I wouldn't bother you."

He shrugged, and spoke to the two men. "You may go. I have the bell. I will ring if I need you."

They bowed and went back to the building. Maximus motioned me to sit down at his table, and gestured at my clothes.

"What's all this about?"

"Just to prove that I could do it, I think. I know I've not been much of an Empress, but at least I can look the part. Perhaps the rest may follow."

He sighed, apparently in one of his better moods. "You're still young. Too young, inexperienced. A lot of this is my fault, I know. Your father was right. I should never have married you."

"It's not an insoluble problem, Maximus. Marriages can be ended."

He shook his head. "I cannot get divorced."

"Why not?"

"You know perfectly well why not. I am a Christian Emperor. Divorce is out of the question."

"Maximus, do you really think our marriage was made in heaven?"

I hurried on as I saw him start to protest.

"Wait, hear me out. We married according to the rites of pagan Rome. Our marriage has no standing in the eyes of the Church. If you were to set me aside now, who would complain? You may be a Christian Emperor, Maximus, but I am not a Christian Empress and never will be."

"It doesn't work like that. The Church regards even pagan marriages as binding."

"How can it, Maximus? It doesn't recognise any rite other than the Christian one. Oh, I know it fosters the traditional Roman values of family and marital fidelity and so on — but, if it came to it, who would argue that you must bind yourself in perpetuity to a woman who is damned?"

His eyebrows shot up. "You don't believe that!"

"The bishops do, though. If you told them that I steadfastly refused to convert — which is no more than the truth — they would not protest if you decided to put me aside in favour of a Christian. They want a Christian Empress too. I'd stake the Treasury on it."

A smile spread slowly over his face. "I admire your confidence, if not your fiscal policy. But, as you know, there are other considerations apart from the religious ones. The fact is that this is a bad time for anything to affect the stability of the Imperial family. You know it will come to war with Theodosius?"

"Oh, no! Are you sure?"

"It can hardly be avoided, I fear. Damn Justina! She knew what she was doing when she sent her daughter to him."

225

"What will you do?"

"What can I do? I must fight. Even if I wanted to, there's nowhere an Emperor can run."

"And if you lose?"

"If I lose you won't need a divorce," he said bluntly. "If I win ... well, the time might be right. A new start, a new commitment to our religion. Yes, then I think you could have what you ask."

"Thank you. And in the meantime?"

"What do you mean?"

"I don't support you the way an Empress should support her husband. We decided I would not take part in official life."

"You want to change that?"

"It would be fair, in return for your promise to me. I don't mean anything involving policy decisions, of course, but if you thought I could pull my weight more..."

He looked me up and down. "Very well. I'll think about it. If there's a way you can help I will surely call upon you."

It was all very formal and polite, but that was an improvement on some of our other interviews.

*

Maximus soon found he could use an Empress who looked the part. He was by nature a reserved man, and found socialising difficult. Yet, to a surprising degree, positions of power demand conviviality of a man. He has to throw parties and dinners, invite the right people, and impress them. In Maximus's case, he had to impress them with his determination in the face of the threat from the East, and his ability to lead men. Emperors cannot be voted out of office, but they can be removed, as Maximus knew only too well. Therefore, he used me to do the things he was not so good at himself. I organised social events, as I had done for him when he was merely *Comes*. I met and cultivated the wives of important men, side-stepping questions about my health and why it had kept me out of circulation for so long. I entertained visitors — usually anxious provincial governors who wanted to see which way they should jump. I did my best to encourage them to jump in Maximus's direction.

"Of course," as one commander's wife said to me, "Theodosius is much the younger man."

We were at a large banquet for senior military men and their wives. I glanced across the room, to where Maximus, impressive in his purple-edged toga, was talking animatedly to some of the most high-ranking guests. He looked distinguished even to me, despite or because of his greying hair. He had not run to fat at all, no bulging waistline swelled the lower half of his toga. Where his arms and legs showed they were still lean and muscular. He was no fop, unlike some other emperors, and still exercised with the soldiers. I turned back to my companion.

"Yes," I said. "Theodosius doesn't really have the experience, does he? To be a real emperor takes more than a youthful face and a weakness for the ladies. Anyway, Maximus is only middle-aged. And it might be thought treason to suggest the Emperor is no longer fit for his duties through age."

"Oh, I didn't mean ... I hope you don't think — "

"Of course not," I said smoothly. "Though these days one must be so careful. There are those whose loyalty is in doubt."

"No!"

"Indeed there are. Naturally, Maximus has no fear of them. He is confident that Right is on his side, you see."

"Of course," twittered the woman. "Naturally. And of course, we all agree. I know my husband is totally committed to His Majesty."

"How very reassuring. I know His Majesty will be delighted to hear that."

The doubts of a silly commander's wife were merely irritating. More worrying were the doubts of those whose opinions I valued.

Whether it was coincidence or not I never knew, but shortly after Maximus and I had come to our accommodation with each other my brother Kynan arrived in Mediolanum. Not only that, he had seen Adeon recently and was able to tell me how well he was. I, of course, had not seen either of them since before my departure from Britain. When I had got over the initial shock, for his arrival one evening was quite unexpected, we sat before the fire with Mabanwy, drinking mulled wine and swapping news. He whistled in disbelief to hear of Maximus's treatment of me, even though I had to tell him of the reason.

"My poor sister, what a terrible tale. How does he treat you now? Things must have improved if you are allowed to move freely and preside over his banquets."

I explained our agreement — my support now in return for a divorce when Theodosius was beaten. Kynan nodded.

"Fine. If he is."

"Don't you think Maximus can beat him?"

"Well, I'm not sure. Maximus is, well ... I hardly know how to put this ... I mean, I'll follow him to the end, but he's not a military genius. He can lead well enough, plan a campaign, organise. It's not that. But he's stuffy, you know — he lacks the spark that makes for greatness."

"What do you mean — stuffy? He always gets on well with his commanders." It was all very well for me to criticise my husband, but other people were a different matter.

"Yes, that's not quite what I meant. I mean he can fight a good enough campaign from the book, but he won't know when it's necessary to depart from the book and strike out on his own. He nearly lost to Gratian, you know, and Gratian was a military idiot. It was only the Moorish cavalry changing sides that did it."

"Well, I think he's set on his course now."

"Oh, yes, he can't change. It's not him now, anyway, it's Theodosius. I would say that war is inevitable unless he dies. Now, there's a thought. What if Theodosius had an accident, eh?"

"Don't."

I shuddered, t.hinking of the deaths of Gratian, and of Maria. I didn't want to see another burden of guilt fall upon Maximus. "Let's talk of other things. Tell me about Father. How long is it since you saw him?"

"Just a couple of weeks. I've got a letter from him for you. It's with my baggage. I'll have it brought to you. He's getting old, you know, Helena. I'm sure he'd appreciate seeing you, if it were possible."

"I don't see how I can — not while the war is threatening. Perhaps afterwards."

He nodded. "Yes, whichever way it goes. Father's rather rheumatic now, you know. He's often in some pain. But that girl looks after him very well. You know the one I mean."

"Finella. Yes, I know her. She's a good woman, I always thought."

"You know what she is, of course?"

"Our father's mistress. Yes, I know, and good luck to them. They're actually very fond of each other. I think they'd marry if it were possible. Don't look so prim, Kynan, mother's been dead for years now. What would you do in his position?"

He grinned. "You may be right. He could marry, of course."

"Marry whom? How many eligible women does he run across? And how many would marry a man old enough to be —"

I stopped short.

Kynan cleared his throat awkwardly.

"Well, enough of speculation. It isn't what he has in mind, and that's that. Tell me about your stepchildren. Do you get on well?"

"Well enough, especially with Flavius Victor and Sabrina. The middle one, Fulvia, isn't so keen, I think. I also think she's got some sort of idea of the reason for the trouble between Maximus and me."

"And what about Flavius Victor? Surely he knows?"

"He knows, but he doesn't condemn, the dear boy. It's a strange family, Kynan. They're all very reserved. They don't tell anyone what they know, or what they feel. Maximus's mother is the worst, I think. Young Sabrina's the most open, though heaven knows how she'll go on as she gets older. Victor's a nice boy, too. He likes me, and he doesn't care what I've done."

"Does he know what happened to his mother?"

"I don't know. Maybe he does, and that's why he's tolerant of me. But it doesn't seem to be the sort of subject one can raise. 'Did you know your father killed your mother?' It's hardly parlour talk, is it?"

He shook his head. "I suppose not, really. Tell me, how important is religion to Maximus? I thought he was relatively unconcerned until recently, you know, but he seems to have changed."

"It's getting to be an obsession, Kynan. It worries me. Gratian lost his support in the army by pushing the religious issue too far. Maximus could do the same. He seems to be convinced that the world situation can be solved if we all get behind the same bishop, or something. He's imprisoned a lot of heretics, and even had some executed. There's been no time since we moved to Mediolanum, but back in Gaul he was going at them hammer and tongs. In the end, even the bishops were asking him to ease off. A lot of them are narrow-minded, but not to the point of killing their opponents off."

"Not all of them, maybe, but there's a group who would skin their own grandmothers if they lapsed into heresy. The whole thing's crazy. The issues are so trivial, and no one really knows the answers. Besides, what's orthodox and what's heresy keeps changing, depending on which faction gets the majority in the synods. If you ask me the whole thing has little to do with worshipping God, and a great deal to do with earthly power for bishops."

"I'm sure you're right. They say that Theodosius is nearly as bad, too. Everyone seems to think that he will eventually outlaw pagan worship altogether."

"I know. The world's going mad. We're going to outlaw the worship of pagan gods, yet we have a large army of foreigners, many of them pagans, whom we depend upon to fight off the attacks of other foreigners, largely Christian."

"They're Arian heretics," I put in with a smile.

"Oh, of course. They're Christians, all right, just not the right type of Christians! Oh, well, I suppose the real test will come when we have some good Catholic barbarians, and have to decide whether to welcome them because they're Catholics, or fight them because they're barbarians. Which outcome would you bet on?"

I thought of Maximus, and then Bishop Ambrosius.

"I wouldn't."

"Nor me. You know, if I survive this war — no, don't protest, we know it's coming — if I survive this war I think I'll leave the army."

"Leave? What would you do?"

"Well, I'd retire from any sort of public life. I can't see me as a politician, working my way up from city council to the Senate in Rome or Constantinople. No, it'd be worse than the army."

"You're a bit young to retire."

He smiled. "And a bit too poor. Father might want someone to run his estate for him, of course, but I actually have something else in mind. When I was in Gaul I had to go and inspect the defences in the north-west, in Armorica. It's a rugged sort of country, you know, not unlike the hills around Segontium. But it's a long way from the Saxons and the rest. They've never been a problem there. There have been some rebellions among the peasantry there, and a lot of them died in those, but it's peaceful nowadays. The population's a bit sparse, though. There's lots of cheap farm land, and quite a few derelict houses that would be easy to repair — very fine, some of them. A bit of capital would set me up nicely. I might be able to manage that."

"Sounds idyllic. A gentleman farmer in a land of peace. You don't want a lodger, do you?"

He grinned boyishly. "I know it's only a dream at the moment. But that's the dream I'm aiming for, and if I fail, there's no harm to anyone else."

*

Kynan stayed for a week, and then had to go to join his new unit. He was on the staff of one of the commanders, helping to administer the supply lines — any army needs another army behind it, one of caterers, armourers, blacksmiths, farriers, carpenters, engineers and all the myriad occupations which enabled it to live. He grumbled that he was only a civil servant in uniform, but I knew that really he had no great liking for battle. It was a duty when danger threatened, that was all. He was not like Adeon, who had earned himself some renown already in his battles against the barbarians, and had an appetite for it. Adeon was too busy to come and visit me. He was now stationed in Italy, but actively training barbarian auxiliaries in Roman methods of warfare. Maximus might not want war, but war was probably coming, and he was not altogether confident of the quality of his auxiliary troops.

News came that Theodosius was wintering at Thessalonica, a favourite place of his. There was nothing unusual in that, except that Valentinian and Justina were going to stay there with him. Such a cosy picture of family unity did nothing to dispel Maximus's fears. Indeed, it concentrated them.

"Can it be that God does not smile on our undertaking?" he asked Father Petros one day in the garden, not realising that I was sitting on the other side of one of the ornamental shrubs.

The priest sighed, as if tired of dealing with such questions, or perhaps worried about which answer to give.

"My son," he said at last, "we cannot know what is in God's mind. We can only follow His laws and obey His commandments. At the end, if we have followed Him with a pure heart and a genuine desire to do His will, He will forgive us the human frailties that make us fall short."

Maximus was not the man to be satisfied with that.

"Is that it, Father? Is that all there is? Is there no certainty?"

Father Petros chuckled. "Certainty? My dear fellow, God protect us from men who are certain!"

"What do you mean? I should have thought there was nothing wrong in wishing to be certain of what is right."

"My son, the worst acts of cruelty are committed by men who are certain. They believe they know what's right for humanity, you see. They 'know' the divine will, and in seeking to bring it about they believe they are justified in doing anything, anything at all, because if it furthers God's will it must be good. No, I'll settle for men who try to love their neighbours. The Lord knows, that's a difficult enough task sometimes..."

They wandered away, leaving me to ponder on the requirements of Maximus, and the requirements of his God, and whether the two might ever coincide.

XXII

All through the winter — not a particularly cold winter, but very wet — the army sat in barracks and perfected the instruments of war. Swords and spears were made razor-sharp, armour was repaired and chain mail forged. Some nights the sound of hammers on metal went on into the small hours. Maximus was not taking his victory for granted. More soldiers had been drafted in from Gaul, and arrangements made to guard the walled cities of the West in the army's absence. With the standard of modern defensive walls, and the long-range catapults which were mounted on them, it was judged safe to leave a city with only a handful of defenders, where in previous centuries only a full garrison would have done. It was progress of a sort, and with the threat of barbarian invasion always present the West could not be left altogether without soldiers. There were still a few large garrisons, too, so that they might go to the aid of any towns that were besieged. Flavius Victor had been supervising the strengthening of town defences in Gaul, and he came to see us in Mediolanum to consult with Maximus before he left on his eastern campaign. He brought news of considerable flood damage.

Around Mediolanum, in the valley of the great River Padus, the land was a quagmire. Fortunately there were good military roads to the east, west and south. Maximus's army was due to march out eastwards, along the Via Postumia, but the reports were that the road had been flooded in places, and bridges swept away.

"It makes no difference," he said to me. "We have splendid engineers. They can put a pontoon bridge across the Tiber itself if need be, and not take all day about it."

He had a spring in his step these days, striding about giving orders and being a general again. The darker moods were gone. It was not, I think, the fighting which he liked, although I suppose it was exciting. It was the sense of purpose, heightened by the presence of his son. He loved the business of organising everything, of solving the problems which arose, and seeing everything ran smoothly. The ponderous pace of state occasions and diplomacy had always irked him. In many ways it was like seeing the young Maximus again, the dashing young officer on his way to campaign, sweeping a little girl off her feet and kissing her cheek. Leaving an indelible impression on her heart.

"Now, listen carefully," he said to me one day, not long before his departure. "If the worst should happen you are bound to get word before Theodosius and his army arrive. In that case I'm not sure you'd be wise to stay here and trust to the honourable intentions of your conquerors."

"Surely you don't think Theodosius would vent his anger on me?"

"No, no, not him. He's an honourable enough man. It's those around him I distrust. It would be better if you and the children made for the coast, and took a ship for Britain. Victor will, of course, be standing in for me while I am away with the army, and he knows well what I want of him. If anything should happen to him you will have written authority to do whatever you think fit to safeguard yourself and the girls."

I thought, but did not say, that his written authority would be worthless if he was dead.

"Your father's place might be best," he went on. "I don't think you could trust old Civilis in Londinium. Your father could protect you, though."

I shuddered. "That's enough detail, Maximus. If I have to do it I'll do the best I can. We must just hope and pray it doesn't come to that."

They marched out at dawn one morning in early summer. Maximus himself took the lead, with his mounted guard of Moorish troops around him — those same troops that had swung the tide against Gratian five years before. Behind them came more cavalry, including a squadron of the strange *clibanarii* — helmeted horsemen who fought with long lances, both rider and horse being covered in chain mail. Cohort after cohort of foot soldiers followed them, including Gothic mercenaries and auxiliaries from all parts of the Empire, each with their own styles of dress — some plumed and feathered like peacocks. Then came the long train of wagons containing the supplies and the special equipment of the engineers. The rear was brought up by another cavalry guard. The column took hours to form up and get under way, and it was early afternoon before the last hoofbeats were fading on the stone-dressed highway. I had watched it all from the city walls with Mabanwy and the children. Flavius Victor, resplendent in ceremonial uniform, watched the whole column, waving and cheering with the rest of the populace. Bishop Ambrosius was there, too. He had been made aware of my lack of religious faith, and kept his distance as if afraid it might be infectious.

At last we turned away, and Victor walked over to me, his face looking careworn.

"Well, that's it, for better or worse."

"Cheer up, Victor, we need you to keep our spirits up while your father is away."

"Hmm," was all he said.

Within the week Victor had to return to the governing of Gaul, and I was left almost as regent in Mediolanum. Not quite, and not officially, regent, however. Maximus might be prepared to trust me a little, but I had his promise of release, and either way it didn't look as if I would be Empress for much longer. Strangely, now that I was about to get what I wanted, I found myself hesitating. But when I thought about it again I knew it was the only way. I could not be a Christian Empress. Perhaps if Maximus had been less devout I might have been able to pay the right kind of lip service, but that would never satisfy him, or Ambrosius. As Empress my future role would be almost like that of chief nun. And I was never meant to be a nun.

"My dear, I just knew you'd be pleased to see your old friend, and I do mean old."

"Felicia, you will never be old, but it is wonderful to see you. You couldn't have come at a better time!"

She had set off to visit me as soon as she knew the army had departed.

"I knew you'd be lonely, my dear, and perhaps just a little worried?"

"A little. Maximus seems confident enough, but you can never tell. Even Kynan wonders about his generalship."

She had, typically, arrived unannounced and simply breezed into the palace. The servants and officials, who usually had plenty of notice of visitors, were thrown into confusion. The wife of Vegetius could not be insulted, but they really didn't feel very welcoming. Of course, as soon as I was informed I rushed to see her and we embraced like long lost sisters. I rattled off a few orders and Felicia soon had rooms for herself and her servants. Her baggage taken away for unpacking, we retired to the palace's private baths. We had had a session in the steam room, and now wallowed comfortably in the warm water bath, a flagon of wine on the stone steps with a cup for each of us.

"Ah, this is the life," she murmured. "My dear, if this is what being Empress means I'll convert at once and make a play for your Maximus as soon as he's free. I could get used to this. I'd put up with it for the sake of the Empire."

I laughed. "You're welcome to have a try, but somehow I don't think you're Maximus's type. He prefers his women meek. Then there's always the small matter of your being married already."

"A detail, darling, a detail. Ah, that Vegetius, he spoils all my fun!"

She sipped from her cup. "This is good stuff, Helena."

"Best Falernian."

"Actually, my dear, I'm not really being truthful. The fact is, these days Vegetius *is* all my fun."

"Really? No more young men?"

"No. I think it's age. I began to wake up and look at myself."

I looked at her. She looked all right to me, and I said so.

"Yes, but age is beginning to show. Look at the bosoms, my dear. I mean, they're not as bad as if I'd had children, but they're definitely sagging a bit, aren't they?"

They were. I told her they weren't.

"Well, we can't go on for ever. The fact is, I realised I was getting older but my young men weren't. Now, an age difference of a year or two doesn't matter, but when it's getting to ten years or so you suddenly think what it's going to be like when you're fifty. I think it would be rather pathetic, really."

"So, the young men are out?"

"Yes. Old Vegetius hasn't had so much attention in years. He doesn't know himself. He had to give up his young thing when we moved to Lugdunum, but he hasn't found it necessary to replace her. In fact, I think it's made him younger."

I giggled, and swilled some warm water over myself. "Ah, well, for such an old boot you're not doing too badly."

She splashed water at me. "And what of *your* young man?"

I started at her question, and tears came unbidden into my eyes. Of course, she was no longer in Londinium. She hadn't heard. I told her what I knew.

"Oh, my dear, I'm so sorry. I never thought."

"How could you know? Well, he's gone and there's nothing I can do about it. Only face up to things, I suppose. I think that's why I tackled Maximus about the divorce and everything. I realised at last that I could only get out of this situation by my own efforts. In one way it's almost a relief. At least now I'm not waiting and wondering all the time."

Felicia turned her dark eyes upon me. "You've certainly changed."

"In what way?"

"Well, you're tougher, I think. More self-reliant."

"Isn't that a good thing?"

"Oh, certainly. I didn't mean it to be a criticism. Only, don't let it cut you off from things. You're young, you're beautiful, you will soon be free, and not badly off I'd say. I'm sure Maximus will make some honourable sort of settlement. There will be plenty of chances to start afresh with someone else. If that's what you want, of course."

"Felicia, you're getting sentimental in your old age."

"Dreadfully, dear, dreadfully."

"You've changed too, then. You used to be so cynical."

"Yes, well, isn't it good to be improving so much? We'll be damned perfect if we keep it up! I tell you what, though, this water's changing, too. It's getting cold. Be a dear and ring for the bath-slaves."

Maximus's first despatch came soon after. It seemed that there had been no resistance to the army's progress through Italy, unless you count the resistance of the elements. The roads were definitely not at their best and were not much improved by the passage of so many men and horses. They had forded some rivers and bridged others, and were now based near Aquileia at the northern end of the Adriatic. Ahead lay the mountain road into Pannonia. He went on:

Word has come to us that Theodosius is on the move. I do not know exactly where we may meet up, but Southern Pannonia looks the most likely place. It is not the best country for fighting, being rocky and mountainous, but that could work to our advantage. Perhaps we may ambush the enemy. I commend you to God's care. In any case, it is His will, and not ours, which will be done. I pray that I may soon be able to send for you, so that you may accompany me on a triumphant entry into Constantinople. I have not forgotten our bargain; help me in this and you will have what you desire.

I showed it to Felicia, and we congratulated ourselves over my good fortune. It seemed as if my freedom was in sight, and as if it would come on more amicable terms than had seemed possible a year ago. I wrote back at once, promising to be ready to join him as soon as the call came. Uncharacteristically, I resolved to make a gift to one of the churches. I suddenly felt as if I had a lot to be thankful for. Two weeks passed, and another despatch rider came. I was in the garden, enjoying honey cakes in the midsummer sun with a few notable ladies. I had invited them to meet Felicia. She was due to go soon, but she might need friends in the capital if Vegetius was posted there, as he would be if he prospered. They used to say that all roads led to Rome, but these days it was Mediolanum.

A slave approached and told me that the rider had arrived. There was an immediate buzz of excitement, and I had the man sent for while we speculated upon the possible news.

"This could be it, my dear," said Felicia quietly. "They could have met by now."

"By the gods, I seem to spend half my life waiting to see if I am widow or Empress."

The man walked in, still stained from the road, and went down on one knee, offering me the wrapped despatch. I took it and bade him rise.

"You'd better report to the barracks for a bath and refreshment," I told him. "I'll have you called for when I'm ready to send a reply"

"With respect, Your Majesty, His Majesty the Emperor ordered me to return as soon as possible, and in any case without waiting overnight."

"Really?" This was most unusual.

"Perhaps if I might obtain some refreshment in the servants' quarters, *Domina*, I would be on hand then when needed?"

"Very well."

I motioned to a slave, who led the man into the building. "My, my, I wonder why Maximus is in such a rush." I soon knew.

My dear wife, great news! We met the Easterners on the Savus River yesterday, and drove most of them back into it. They were tired from their

*march, yet they waded the river to attack us as soon as they arrived. The effort
was fatal for them, and we cut them to pieces! The survivors are being rounded
up now, but we have promised to treat them well, and we shall. It pains me to
report that Theodosius, who was once, after all, a friend, fell in the battle.
With him fell the Frankish* Comes, *Flavius Arbogastes, and many other
commanders. We are to march at once on Constantinople, and hope to take
the Empress Dowager and the former Emperor Valentinian on the way. They
are reportedly on the road with only a small detachment of guards. The
moment has come for you to join me on my triumph. You will need only a
small guard. The roads are safe.*

Everyone cheered when I read the letter out. I sent criers to
proclaim it on every street corner, and sent word to Bishop
Ambrosius. There would be wild rejoicing in the city tonight.

"Wonderful," murmured Felicia. "I feel so happy I almost feel
like breaking my own rules. Know any nice young men?"

"Felicia! It's time you went home to your husband!"

"Oh, Helena, I'm only joking. And I hope you are, too!"

"What do you mean?"

"My dear, I want to come with you, if you'll let me."

The thought staggered me, but when I thought about it there
was absolutely no reason why not.

"Of course, Felicia, there's no one I'd rather have with me."

And so we sat down to plan the journey in detail. Quinctilius,
the guard commander, was not terribly happy about the trip. He
had few men left now, and didn't want to leave the city short.

"I know there's not much chance of barbarian attack, Your
Majesty, but I'd rather not have to take such chance as there is.
Communications to the north are not that good, especially after
the wet spring. If they came we might get very little warning."

"I understand, Quinctilius, but His Majesty says there's little to
guard against on the Via Postumia. A small detachment should
do."

"Small? Well, I suppose I could spare fifty men."

"That will be ample."

"I certainly hope so, Domina, though it doesn't sound much to
guard the Empress of half the Empire — well, all of it now, with
Theodosius gone."

"So it seems." But not for much longer! "I'll take the fifty,
Quinctilius. I'm sure it will be enough."

He agreed in the end, as he had to, of course. The despatch rider was prevailed upon to stay one night at the palace, and set out with us the next day. I had promised to speak up for him if Maximus was angry at his waiting one night. For some reason it seemed to amuse him.

Felicia and I rode in a carriage, each with a personal servant. In my case, of course, this was Mabanwy; the name of Felicia's girl eludes me now. I remember her vaguely as a fair-haired, timid little person who seldom spoke. There was a baggage cart behind, and a couple of slaves rode with it. Apart from that there were fifty mounted soldiers under the command of two officers, a centurion and a tribune. In deference to my august presence these were well above the usual ranks for commanding such a small force. Quinctilius had wanted to send someone of even higher rank, but I had refused. As I pointed out, it would deprive the city of one of its most senior defenders for no better reason than to flatter me. I had insisted on taking only those people who would be indicated by a purely military assessment of the party's needs, and in the end we had compromised. Quinctilius was relieved, as every man counted at this time. This way, if anything went wrong he would be covered. To make sure of it I left a letter recording the decision.

The going was surprisingly easy. We had about three hundred miles to go, which at the pace of the baggage cart would take us five long days on a good road with no hills! Of course our path had been cleared by the army, which we were following. Thousands of feet had tramped flat any small obstruction, and thousands of hands had cleared any large ones. The engineers had made temporary repairs to a couple of broken bridges, and left in place a pontoon bridge over one river, where the original stone bridge had been washed away in the floods. Anything which could take the weight of an army would have no trouble with our little band, and the waters were slack now, so it was easier than we expected.

"I still think I should have dressed as a man again and gone on horseback," I said. "The travelling might have been harder on my backside, but it would have been over more quickly."

We stayed at the small towns which lay on or near the Via Postumia. Many of them had a *mansio*, the Imperial inn where government couriers stayed on their important journeys. They always gave me the best room, which often meant turning someone else out. I felt uncomfortable about this, but Felicia would chide me.

"What's the use of high rank if you can't claim a privilege or two, my dear?"

Even the best rooms were usually not all that good, so I consoled myself with this thought. We saw a few travellers coming from the east. Mostly, however, they had come from the Illyrian coast, well out of the way of the fighting. They had no news, except that there were indeed rumours of a battle, or perhaps two.

"Two?" mused Felicia. "Maximus made no mention of a second battle, did he?"

"You know he didn't. I hope the Easterners haven't managed a counter-attack."

"Never. Not with Theodosius dead. His main supporters will be off back to Constantinople to pass on the news and try to make themselves out to be loyal Maximus supporters before he arrives there!"

"I hope so. It's having no facts that makes it difficult. There's only rumour, and you know what that's like. Stories grow in the telling."

"Never mind," said Felicia. "We're making good progress. We'll soon be there, and if Maximus has moved on Constantinople you know he'll have left an escort to give you the news and help you the rest of the way."

"Yes, you're right, of course. We'll soon have something more definite to go on."

As it happened we did, but it was not quite what we were expecting.

*

It was on the fifth day that it happened. We were on a stretch of road that ran through dense woods. The trees were so high that they would normally block out the sunlight, but it was morning and the road ran eastwards. The sun shone down the avenue of trees and half-blinded the horsemen as they rode; it made the dark forest seem even darker and more impenetrable. We were off our guard; Maximus's letter and assurances of the peaceful nature of the countryside had soothed our fears. Besides, we had had no indication of trouble anywhere on the route. Otherwise we might not have forgotten that a bright road between dark trees makes an ideal spot for an ambush.

There was no warning — not even a whinny from a horse. The attackers must have hidden their own well away. There was only a shouted command, the musical twang of bowstrings, and death hissed through the air to bury itself in the chests of several of our men.

The bodies had not hit the ground before the centurion, an old soldier, had jumped down, shouting orders. The tribune ran to the carriage. We were cowering in a heap on the floor.

"Keep going, man! The safety of the Empress comes first!"

The carriage lumbered along a little faster, but no arrows came near it.

"They know who it is," muttered Felicia. "They're not attacking us, just the soldiers." We raised our heads a little.

Behind us the air was filled with screams, as men and horses were injured. Two riderless animals galloped past, terrified, and bleeding. There was the clang of metal on metal.

"Swords!" I cried. "Those poor men!"

There was a great shout.

"That's in front!" gasped Felicia.

She was right. The carriage ground to a halt. We heard running feet, the sounds of a scuffle. Then there was silence around us, broken only by the sounds of the battle still in progress a hundred yards behind.

Footsteps approached. We saw the plumes of a helmet over the half-door of the carriage.

"Well done, men," said a cultured voice in Latin.

The door was opened.

XXIII

The man was a Roman officer, not some barbarian auxiliary. That at least was a relief, although the insignia of his legion were unknown to me. I had time to notice that he was a fairly young man, perhaps in his late twenties. His hair and eyes were a deep brown, and his expression gloomy. He bowed his head to me.

"*Domina*, please! There is no need to huddle on the floor. You have nothing to fear from me."

We all got up and uncertainly resumed our seats. I felt the heat rising in my face.

"What is the meaning of this? You are clearly a Roman officer. Those are good Romans dying back there. This is murder!"

He looked troubled for a moment. Then he shrugged. "I don't like it either. The problem is, *Domina*, there are Romans and Romans these days."

"Kindly address me in the correct fashion. I am the Empress Helena of Arfon, wife of the Emperor Magnus Clemens Maximus."

He nodded with brisk politeness, but not a trace of deference.

"I am sorry. My understanding is that your husband is now considered a usurper. You will, of course, be treated with respect, but as a gentlewoman."

"This is intolerable! Who gave you such instructions?"

"The *Comes* Flavius Arbogastes."

"But he is dead!"

"Is he? Your information must be recent indeed. He was alive and well at dawn this morning."

I had a terrible sinking feeling in my stomach.

"Can you stop this fighting? Aren't there enough dead already?"

He turned to look down the road. "It seems not, as far as those taking part are concerned."

His complacency angered me beyond all endurance. Hardly knowing what I was doing, I leapt through the door. He made as if to stop me, but slipped as I careered into him. He almost righted himself, but Mabanwy, hot on my heels, pushed him in the ditch. I lifted my skirts and ran.

"Helena!"

It was Felicia's voice, but there was no time to debate matters. Besides, I felt no danger. My own men would surely not attack me, and the enemy was obviously under orders to capture, not kill.

There were about thirty bodies on the ground already, about ten of them my men, including the tribune in charge. We were outnumbered, but the enemy were auxiliary troops, neither so well trained nor so experienced. It mattered little. They were all some woman's son, someone's brother, or someone's father, or lover. All human beings with lives, emotions, loves and hopes. It was unbearable that they should die fighting over me. I stopped a few yards away, aware of the running feet behind me.

"Stop! All of you stop this at once! At once, do you hear?"

Like a school teacher, Mabanwy said afterwards. And like naughty boys they stopped and drew apart into two lines, eyeing each other warily.

"*Domina*, for Christ's sake!"

It was the enemy officer, now at my side once more.

"Not here," I gasped, still panting. "Nothing here is being done for the sake of Christ. He was against killing. I may not be a Christian but I know that much!"

My old centurion was still standing, though bleeding from a wound. He was now the senior officer.

"Your Majesty, we can still beat them."

"No, no. Enough. If you beat their swordsmen the bowmen will cut you down. You know it's true."

He nodded slowly, then shrugged. "I can't surrender my Empress. I'd rather die than live with such shame."

They all muttered their agreement. There was a general shuffling of feet. Another second and they would be at each other's throats again. I strode between the lines, the officer protesting but not daring to touch. A good sign.

"Damn your chivalry! What about *my* shame — the shame of knowing that I let a half a hundred men die uselessly? If you have any respect for me at all then see reason!"

I turned to the enemy officer. "What happens to them if they surrender?"

He shrugged. "What happens to any soldier who surrenders? Slavery, I suppose."

"Let them go."

"I can't do that!"

"You can! You know you can. They pose no threat."

I strode further into the lines of panting men. The air was filled with the smell of sweat and blood, and the appalling stench of punctured entrails. I fought the nausea down.

"Let them go, or risk losing me to some random sword thrust when they start up again."

"Your Majesty!"

This from the old centurion.

"Well?"

The officer stared, and his lip twitched in the beginnings of a faint smile. Slowly he nodded. "Very well, if you will give them a direct order to retire from the field."

"Certainly."

I moved over to the enemy line and faced my men.

"Go, all of you. Find your horses and go home!"

The centurion protested again, but I stopped him short.

"That is an order! Disobedience is treason!"

Old habits die hard, and an old soldier's habits die hardest of all. "Form up, men."

Just before he gave the order to march he turned back to me.

"I hope God knows what He's doing. You make one hell of an Empress. Begging your pardon, Your Majesty."

"Go!"

He smiled and gave the order. I turned to our captor.

"Very well. Now tell me what the hell is going on here."

*

He introduced himself as Lucius Gabinius, and sat with us in the carriage as our journey was resumed. This time the escort was a good four times as strong.

"Tell me what you are doing here."

"I am a tribune in the service of the Emperor Theodosius. I am here because I am assisting the *Comes* Arbogastes."

"Don't be evasive. I meant what were you doing on this road at this time of day?"

"Waiting for you, of course, <u>Domina</u>."

"But you can't have been. No one knew we were coming."

He shrugged easily. "With respect, someone must have. Otherwise I could hardly have been given orders to intercept you."

262

I didn't know what to think. Until then I had assumed our encounter had been more or less accidental. As for Lucius, a tribune might have many different duties depending upon circumstances. His rank was no guide.

"The courier," said Felicia. "We thought his manner was odd, remember?"

I wasn't thinking straight. "What?"

"He was an agent of Valentinian's. The letter was a forgery, in response to yours. They must have intercepted that, too."

"But the Imperial Seal..."

"Valentinian's an Emperor as well. Besides, a competent craftsman could make something good enough to forge that with, too. You're a valuable hostage, Helena; it was worth the risk to them. And it worked, didn't it?"

I could hardly take it all in. I turned to Lucius again.

"You were given orders that I was coming?"

"By the *Comes* Arbogastes himself."

"But surely Arbogastes is with Theodosius's army?"

"I shouldn't say too much, I suppose, but you'll know soon enough. Arbogastes is with the army of His Majesty the Emperor Valentinian."

"Valentinian is in Illyricum with Theodosius!"

"That is the First Army. His Majesty Valentinian now commands the Second Army. We crossed the sea from Illyricum to Italy four days ago, and have made camp at Aquileia."

"Oh, my God!" That was Felicia. "Helena, you see what they are doing?"

I nodded miserably. Theodosius had created this second force and sailed it across the Adriatic to place it to the rear of Maximus's army. Now they could advance from both sides to crush him between them.

"But Valentinian's a boy," I said disparagingly. "He can't command an army."

Lucius chose his words with care. Criticism of *his* Emperor was treason too.

"No doubt the *Comes* Arbogastes was chosen to, er, give His Majesty the benefit of his extensive military experience."

"You should be a diplomat. Anyway, when my husband beats Theodosius all your preparations will be in vain. You may advance on him, but he will be in Constantinople. You will see, you'll end up having to let me go as part of some political bargain — to gain your own pardon, probably."

He raised an eyebrow. "You think so? I doubt it, personally. Tell me, how up to date are you with the military situation?"

Something was wrong. He was too confident. "What do you mean?"

"*Domina*, your husband has been defeated on the River Savus."

There were gasps of disbelief from all of us.

"It is true, I assure you. His army was put to flight, regrouped, and was defeated again. We are not advancing to meet him. *He* is retreating to meet *us*."

*

"His Majesty will be pleased to see the prisoner now," intoned the steward.

"Prisoner!" I spat the word. "Does that limp-wristed flunky know who I am?"

"*Domina*," said Lucius gently," it can hardly be denied that you are a prisoner."

"It makes me sound like a common criminal!"

"You could never be that." Tactfully, Lucius refrained from further comment. The flunky, who wasn't really particularly limp-wristed, drew aside the flap of the Imperial tent, and in we walked.

Inside, the tent was almost like a small palace. There was a wooden floor, laid in sections which locked together. The roof was lined by a ceiling of expensive crimson silk. At each side there were tables with scribes and secretaries. Straight ahead was a raised dais with a wooden throne, and upon it sat the young Emperor, so recently deposed but now enthroned once more.

"Please come forward," said Valentinian. His voice was gentle, almost friendly — a contrast with the ceremonial armour which he wore, but which could never survive on the field. I had been right — this was no commander of men. I curtsied, and he smiled.

He was slightly built, with short curly brown hair and brown eyes, restless eyes that darted glances here and there constantly. To say that they were shifty makes him sound like a thief; they were wary. This round-faced young man had had to watch those around him minutely, always alert for signs of disloyalty. It was easy to imagine him being dominated by his mother, the redoubtable Justina. She would be able to feed his insecurities with stories purporting to show the disloyalty and ulterior motives of anyone she wanted to smear. By all accounts, this was exactly what had happened.

"So you are Helena, Empress of the West."

This was so obviously true that I didn't bother replying.

"Well, well, you are just as beautiful as they told me."

He paused. If he was waiting for me to thank him for his fatuous compliment he could wait for ever.

"And it seems, Your Majesty, that you are just as devious as they told me."

There were sharp intakes of breath all round. Valentinian stiffened.

"And what exactly is that supposed to mean?"

"It means that I was lured here by means of a forged letter — a shabby trick, hardly worthy of one who aspires to Imperial greatness. You must be hard up for ways of proving yourself to your men if you've stooped to kidnapping defenceless women!"

"That will do! A woman with an escort of fifty armed men is hardly defenceless. Besides, you have aided and abetted the usurper Maximus. You could hardly expect anything else but arrest."

"Of course I aided him. He is my husband. It is my wifely duty to support him." And if I doubted it myself I would certainly not reveal that to Valentinian.

"No doubt," murmured the young Emperor. "Really, though, it doesn't much matter what you say. The fact is, you are important because of who you are. You will remain under my protection."

"Protection! This is captivity!"

"That is up to you. Will you give me your word not to attempt escape? If so, we need have no recourse to chains and cages."

"And my companions?"

"Their conditions will be as yours."

"Small choice then. I can hardly choose chains for my friends."

"Good. It would have distressed me to imprison a woman, especially one of your gentle breeding. My steward says there is a small villa nearby. We will billet you there with a small guard detachment. For your protection, of course," he added hastily. He glanced at a wax tablet in front of him. "Now, this companion of yours."

"Which one?"

"I don't count servants and slaves. I mean this Felicia woman. She is, I am told, the wife of a legionary commander."

"Yes, but he is no longer with the legion. He is a staff officer."

"Yes. Well, she too may have her uses. Can you accept responsibility for her behaviour?"

"I'm sure of it. We are old friends, apart from anything else."

"Good, good. Then that is all for the moment. I don't anticipate any need to call on you for the next couple of days. After that, who knows?"

I was dismissed.

*

I had wondered why Valentinian had not ensconced himself in the "small villa", but when I saw it I stopped wondering. It was indeed small — too small to satisfy any Emperor's ideas of what would suit his status. I think it was someone's second home — a place to take a break from the cares of the city and maybe go and hunt in the surrounding forests. Valentinian would have had more space in his tents. Felicia and I had a room each, but our maids had to share. The guards lived in their tents outside. They had left us the small garden.

"I suppose it's better than a tent," said Felicia on our first night there.

"Yes. What surprises me is that Valentinian is in a tent at all."

"Why? What should he live in when he's on campaign?"

"On campaign this close to Aquileia he should be in the town's largest public building. He must effectively have the place in his hands. Why isn't he there?"

Felicia pondered for a moment. "I should think it's because his army is more out of sight in the forest. If he stays here he can defend his position easily and block Maximus's retreat. Besides, if Maximus occupies the town he'll soon find that it can't cope with thousands of extra people — the water supply alone won't be up to it."

I could see that made sense, though I shuddered to think of Maximus being driven inexorably back into a trap.

"It's terrible!" I burst out. "He's being hunted like a dog!"

Felicia raised an eyebrow. She was not used to seeing me show much concern for my husband.

"It's not fair," I went on. "He never wanted to be Emperor. He just has a dream of unity — a dream that the Empire can continue, can uphold civilised values against the invasions of the barbarians. That's what this religious business is all about, you know. He was never that devout before. It's all part of his wish for unity."

"One Empire, one ruler, one God, I suppose," said Felicia.

"That's it."

"Constantine's dream."

"And now Macsen's."

"Ah, yes, the British name. I wonder how his Cornovians stood up for him on the field."

"Unless we find a way to get out of here and warn him I don't suppose we'll ever know."

"You gave your word."

"And how much use is someone's word when it's given under duress? For goodness' sake, Felicia, don't go all moral on me now."

"Never mind me. What about Valentinian? He'll expect a Roman lady to keep her word, you know. It'll be chains and cages for all of us if you're caught."

"Maybe. And maybe there's more to honour than keeping your word. Like not letting people down when they depend on you."

She was sceptical. In the morning I realised she had every right to be; Valentinian might have put guards around the villa for our "protection", but they would effectively prevent any escape. They were camped in a ring of tents all around it, leaving only the little walled garden free. Short of becoming invisible I could see no way out. For a while I toyed with the idea of becoming at least close to invisible by repeating the trick I had used in Britain and dressing as a man to get through the lines. Then I realised that a strange man out of uniform would soon be arrested if spotted, and anyway we had no male clothing. It seemed there was nothing we could do but wait.

The weather had turned unexpectedly cold. We went out to walk in the little garden each day, an autumnal feel to the air well before time. Crows nested in the trees behind the villa, and their constant harsh cries added a sinister note to the gusting wind and the patter of rain on the tiles.

"Even the elements are against us," I said broodingly to Felicia.

"Nonsense. You're just feeling depressed, and small wonder. Surely something will turn up soon."

Something did — or rather, someone. A week after we had been billeted in the villa Lucius, the officer who had captured us, arrived with an escort at breakfast time.

"Good morning, *Dominae*," he said as he cheerfully breezed into our little kitchen. "How are we all today?"

"I don't know about *you*," muttered Felicia acidly. "We're all right. Impatient, but all right. More or less."

"Good. I am required to escort you to see His Majesty. I believe he has some important visitors he wants you to meet."

"Is there any news of my husband?" I demanded.

He shrugged. "His army has arrived in Aquileia. I don't know much more than that."

"Oh, gods above and below. He's in the trap!"

"I do believe so, *Domina*. I can't expect you to see it our way, of course — "

"I should say not!"

" — but at least it means there should be an end to the killing soon. I know that concerns you, after your amazing ... well, after what you did the other day."

I had almost forgotten that. He was right in a way, of course. The sooner the war was over, the sooner the killing would stop. Mothers' sons, all of them. I shuddered. Lucius misinterpreted it as a retrospective sign of fear.

"It was a dangerous thing to do, *Domina*, but it was magnificent."

There was such warmth in his words that I turned to look at him. He coloured slightly, but stood his ground.

"It is good sometimes to be reminded what this is all about. And what doesn't need to happen."

"What will happen to the... to my husband's men?"

He shrugged again. "I don't know, *Domina*. Truly, I don't. It's up to the authorities, I suppose. Of course, usually in such matters prisoners are sold for slaves, and officers executed."

"Oh, no!" Tears leapt unbidden into my eyes — Adeon and Kynan were both officers.

"Well," he said gently, "it's treason, you see."

"Stop it! I don't want to hear any more! Take us wherever you've got to take us."

A few minutes later our little carriage trundled back out through the gate and along the narrow lane between the trees. The crows rent the air with their hungry screaming. They ought to be patient, I thought.

It was only a short ride — just back to Valentinian's tent. When we stopped and looked out things had changed somewhat in the week since we had last been here. There were more tents, huge ones. There were flags flying, couriers running in and out of the tents, servants with jugs and plates. Officers also hurried to and fro, some carrying scrolls with the Imperial Seal on them. Presumably it was genuine this time. Unusually there were some female servants, too. Only the presence of high-ranking female guests could justify their presence here.

Lucius helped us down. He called a servant over, and muttered some instructions to him. The man disappeared into the largest tent, presumably to announce our presence. A few moments later he returned, and bowed towards us, holding the tent flap open.

"There we are," announced Lucius cheerfully. My own spirits were as low as they could be as we trudged across the clearing and entered the enormous tent.

Inside it was like Valentinian's had been, only larger. There was a wooden floor, and heavily shod feet rumbled all over it. There were tables with secretaries, and a large table in the middle with a great plan laid out on it. It seemed to show the outline of a piece of coast, with a town — presumably Aquileia — detailed on it. There were little wooden figures representing different army units, and symbols whose meaning was unclear to me. The officers gathered around the table seemed to know, though, and were arguing about which units should be moved where. The ridiculous thought went through my mind that it would save a mountain of misery if they could conduct the whole battle with the wooden soldiers on such a table and leave real men alone to die in bed.

The officers turned to stare as we came in. One of them came forward. He looked somehow familiar. The handsome face with its thick brow and dark eyes struck a chord. So did the proud bearing and the boyish smile even in such circumstances. Even then it was only when Lucius bowed to him that it penetrated — this was Theodosius! Enemy or not, he was a lawful co-Emperor, and I showed him the respect due with a curtsey.

"Your Majesty."

He took my hand and kissed it, raising me up while I was still curtseying. He nodded to Felicia.

"My father was *Comes* in Britain," he said. "I've never been there, but perhaps I may go some day. I am truly sorry that Fate has placed us on opposite sides. There was loose talk of using you and your companions as hostages of some kind, but I really could not have that. Others may make war on women, but not if they want my assistance."

"I met your father when I was a girl," I told him. "If you are anything like him it is what I would have expected of you."

He seemed to find the answer acceptable, although one or two of the others plainly thought it presumptuous. What of it? I was still Empress, and officially Theodosius's equal.

"What is the position?" I asked. "Is there news of my husband?"

Still holding my hand, he drew me across to the table.

"Look," he said. "That is the position. Maximus's men are in the town, and entrenched on the landward side of it. They have prepared a stockade and ditches, and are ready to make a stand. We are all around on the landward side, and our ships are blockading the harbour. There is no chance of escape or of being relieved. He must know this. I am sending envoys to ask for a surrender."

I was dimly aware of someone else coming in, but gloom had descended on me.

"So it really is all up with them?" I said.

"Yes, indeed," said an elderly female voice. "Right has triumphed!"

I turned to see the regal figure of a woman in late middle age. She was dressed in the finest silk robe I had ever seen — minutely decorated with embroidery and sewn with pearls. She wore enough gold to sink a ship, and enough face paint to decorate a fair-sized church. Behind her trotted the sheepish figure of Valentinian, and she could only be his mother.

"The Empress Dowager," murmured Theodosius. "My mother-in-law."

Was it imagination, or did I detect a rueful note in his voice?

"Yes," I said. "I knew it must be."

She moved to stand in front of me.

"So you're Maximus's wife? Come to see him die, have you?"

"You know why I am here," I said. "You tricked me into it."

She nodded towards the war table. "Well, we will soon have them all. And then their upstart blood will flow in torrents until the very sea turns red! It's death for every single one of them if I have anything to do with it!"

XXIV

For a moment no one moved. Then Theodosius put his hand on her arm.

"Mother," he said briskly, "you know my views on that. I have not yet decided what to do with the rebels, but a massacre is out of the question. Who am I — the King of Persia? Such barbarities are commonplace enough outside the Empire. Inside, we have a duty to exemplify the Christian virtues of forgiveness and mercy."

She snorted and turned away. "An emperor who values his throne will deal sternly with those who oppose him."

"And an emperor who ignores the sensibilities of his subjects will soon have no throne to value. Have you forgotten what happened to your stepson?"

This reference to Gratian, ironic in the circumstances, kept her quiet for a while. Theodosius turned to me.

"I cannot promise anything about your husband, but if the war has spared your brothers they, at least, will have nothing to fear from me."

He turned to Felicia. "Neither, when we return to Gaul, will your husband."

I knew it was the most he could promise. "Thank you. I regret more than ever that my husband and yourself were unable to agree terms."

He shrugged. "Such is the way of the world. We mortals do our best, but it's never enough."

"How did you know about my brothers?"

He smiled. "This is a civil war, in effect. Both sides are led by members of the same social classes — the same families in some cases. Everyone knows everyone else. It's not hard to discover intelligence about personalities. Someone always knows."

We were interrupted by the arrival of a courier from the front line.

"Your Majesty, the commanders respectfully request your immediate presence at the front. Fighting has begun at the north side of the town, and they would like to know your views on how to proceed."

"Tell them I'll come at once! In the meantime, there is no change to their orders. They are to hold the line, but concentrate on containing the enemy, not counter-attacking. We'll get a surrender without a bloodbath if we show we won't be budged. They've nowhere else to go."

He nodded to me and strode out, followed by the other leaders. Nervously aware of Justina's baleful eye on me, I turned to find Lucius at my elbow.

"Can we see the battle?" I asked.

"If that's what you want, *Domina*."

What I wanted was to be out of Justina's stifling presence. Besides, I still harboured some hope of an escape for Maximus. Perhaps there would be a breakout through the besiegers, and a breakneck gallop into the hills? Perhaps, on the other hand, the naval ships would be misled by fog, or a decoy, and allow him to escape by sea? Surely there were a dozen ways it might happen? There were, of course, but none of them was very likely. Still, I clung to the thought that he might yet get away. Now that our marriage was so nearly over, it seemed even more important to me that he should live. Guilt, according to Felicia. Whatever the reason, it was how I felt, and if it happened I wanted to see it, to cheer him on as he sped away.

Freshly-cut logs showed where the army had widened the old path. Now a broad column of men could have marched along it easily. If the churned-up mud was any guide, several had already done so. Lucius led us along it at a brisk pace, occasionally exchanging greetings with officers who passed the other way. We came out of the woods at the top of a gentle slope. Below, only a couple of hundred paces away, was the stockade which protected Aquileia. It was sparse, being composed of the pairs of sharp stakes which every legionary carried. Behind it hundreds of soldiers milled in feverish activity. Some seemed to be building barricades, as if they expected Theodosius's cavalry to storm the stockade and try to enter the streets of the town. It seemed pointless to me, as likely to hem in the defenders as to keep the attackers out. Others were going from tent to tent, or caring for horses, or even cooking. My spirits plummeted. The scene looked undisciplined to me, even chaotic. There was no sense of common purpose. Lucius also saw it.

"They are not well led," he murmured. "They can't last."

"Where is the fighting, then?" I asked him, for it all looked peaceful enough.

As if in answer, a yell issued from the town. Through a gap I had not noticed before a troop of cavalry galloped out from the stockade and made for the tree line. All at once the innocent-looking trees became a hive of activity. Men appeared at the edge of the wood, bowmen like those who had ambushed us on the road.

"The cavalry are Moors," explained Lucius. "I'd guess they're hoping to break through and escape — they dropped Gratian in the mire when they changed sides in Gaul. A lot of our men have never forgiven them. If they had kept faith all of this war need never have happened."

"Can they get through, do you think?"

"I doubt it. Those archers are Syrians. Good men with a bow. The Moors will never get close enough to strike, and if they do they'll have to dismount to fight in the trees. No, it's a crazy idea. They must be desperate."

He spoke as casually as he had done on the road, when I had wanted to stop the fighting. I found the same anger rising in me, but there was nothing I could do. I watched helplessly as the horsemen galloped up the slope until most of them were within easy bowshot of the trees. Then the Syrians stepped out and let fly a terrible cloud of arrows. Their finned shapes filled the air. They fell like rain upon the men and horses, until only a few were left unscathed. I thought suddenly of the Irish raiders I had seen as a child. They too had died suddenly and violently, and I had watched from a distant hillside. The cavalry reined in, and the survivors turned and headed back to the town, pursued by more arrows. Many of the horses were riderless now, and galloped along with the others as if out for exercise.

With a yell a troop of infantry ran out from the trees and fell upon the helpless wounded who lay on the grass. I cried out loud as the dreadful chopping of sword upon bone echoed across the field.

"Lucius, do something! This is murder!"

"So is inviting a man to a feast and having him stabbed," he said evenly. "Anyway, what can I do now?"

It was true. It was all over. The infantry were already stripping the bodies of weapons and armour, and anything else of value. I shuddered.

"Is it all like this?"

He nodded. "Yes. It's just skirmishing here and there along the line. I don't think anyone's really directing them from a proper plan. Their leaders have given up."

He spoke with disdain. According to Roman tradition you were supposed to fight to the death. Anything else was dishonourable. Saving lives was less important than dying correctly. Well, there was one thing that the bishops and I could agree on — life was worth more than death, however honourable.

"I've seen enough," I said.

*

The same sort of stalemate continued all day. There were more skirmishes, more useless deaths, but no resolution of the situation. When dusk fell Theodosius had us escorted back to our little villa, promising to have us fetched in the morning if we wished. He was a strange man, unfailingly courteous to us even in these times. In his position many a man — and at least one dowager empress — would have treated us far worse. I slept badly that night, anxious about what was to come.

At one stage I got up and lit a rush light from the smouldering fire in the hearth. There was water in the kitchen, and I took a cool draught of it, hoping to settle my nerves, but it failed. There was a scuffling on the stairs, and Felicia came in.

"Not sleepy?"

I shook my head. "Well, sleepy enough, but I can't."

"Nor me. Poor Vegetius. Theodosius said he'd spare him, but it's Valentinian who will rule in Gaul."

"If they beat Maximus."

"I think they already have. We're just waiting for him to admit it."

"Is that what you think?"

"It's what everyone else seems to think. I'm not a military strategist, Helena, are you?"

"Of course not. But I am Maximus's wife. I can't bear to think of him losing."

"Yes. You've come rather late to that feeling, haven't you?"

It wasn't spoken critically.

"I suppose so. Rather like you and Vegetius, perhaps?"

"Yes. I was married to him for years before I... well... fell in love with him, I suppose."

"Ah, well, I wouldn't go that far with Maximus. Besides, he doesn't want it. You're lucky, Felicia. You could say you've had your cake and eaten it too."

I saw her smile in the flickering light. "Perhaps you could."

After hours of tossing and turning I eventually got to sleep, but not for long. We were called at first light by Mabanwy.

"The soldiers have come for us," she said. "Lucius says there's a fierce battle going on."

"What?" I sat up, instantly awake.

"He says our men are trying to break out, and attacked just before dawn."

I threw my clothes on, and then calmed a little. With Justina and her son to be faced, I would take a little time to dress and make up properly. Felicia was ready when I had finished, and we rushed out to the coach, where a guard of only two men waited. A sudden elation gripped me as we set off. This was Maximus's chance!

"That's what the fighting yesterday was about, I expect," I said to Felicia. "He'll have been testing the enemy lines to find their weak spots. You'll see, it's not over yet."

As we neared the tents we saw several fires raging in the woods. The trees were not particularly dry, but the fires had caught well, and forest fires do their own drying out. There was a sulphurous smell on the air as well as the reek of wood smoke. Through the trees we could hear the cries of men and horses in combat. As we approached Theodosius's tent there was a strange sound overhead, like the beating of huge wings. I looked up to see a ball of fire spinning through the air, curving down towards the trees. Greek fire! The ball struck the treetops, leaving blazing smears on every branch as it fell. It bounced away and into the side of a nearby tent, setting it ablaze in seconds. Men ran out like disturbed ants, and started beating at the flames and running for water. I smiled. Maximus had a few tricks left yet! Perhaps a part of the delay had been to gain time to build catapults. Lucius saw my smile.

"It makes no difference, *Domina*," he said, shaking his head. "You'll soon see. We have them."

Another fireball whizzed its way overhead and crashed into the trees close by. Another team of men ran to it, and a bucket chain was set up to bring water from a nearby stream.

"Many more of those, and they'll have you — or at least your headquarters."

"I told you, *Domina*, it doesn't matter. They're in a hole. They'll have to do more than burn down a few tents to climb out of it." But he looked a little less confident.

A troop of cavalry thundered out of the forest and wheeled in the clearing, going on in the direction of yesterday's battlefield. The sound of steel beating on steel was borne faintly upon the wind. Lucius was very restless. He obviously resented his role as our custodian. Perhaps he felt it was demeaning when there was a battle to be fought. He was constantly looking this way and that, trying to catch a glimpse of action through the trees.

The flaps of Theodosius's tent opened, and Valentinian stood there. He took a deep breath of fresh air before his eye fell on us.

"Why not bring the ladies in, Lucius?"

"Of course, if Your Majesty wishes."

"It's better than standing out here in the cold."

He took another deep breath and then went back in. We followed. The map table was surrounded by a throng of officers, and couriers who came and went constantly. There was a subdued buzz of conversation, which rose and fell as one development after another was discussed and dealt with. Theodosius was there at the centre, his firm command of events evident in all he did. He gave orders, he heard couriers, he moved models on the table, all in the same tone of voice, unhurried but decisive. He barely had time to nod to us.

Slaves brought us food and drink as the day went on, but there was no slackening of activity around the table. There was no crisis, either. It was clear that the deadlock was continuing. There was no breakout. A courier was brought to Theodosius, who briefed him in hushed tones. The officers looked this way and that, either staring at me or avoiding my eye. I wondered what could be wrong now, but nothing was said. The man was sent out.

It was with hardly any surprise that I saw the courier come back in, late in the day, and saw Maximus's personal seal on the parchment he carried. Theodosius tore it open feverishly.

"That's it, gentlemen! It is as we expected. On our promise of lenient treatment for his men, Maximus will surrender at dawn tomorrow!"

A cheer went up from the assembled men, but I ran out into the twilight, brushing the tears from my face.

*

Again I hardly slept. A sense of gloom and foreboding rested heavily upon me. Felicia was nearly as bad, although Vegetius was not in danger. Mabanwy stayed up most of the night, getting us drinks and trying to soothe our nerves. It must have nearly been time for the surrender before we fell asleep. We were woken almost immediately by the guards, who had been ordered to call us early. We quickly washed and allowed ourselves to be escorted through the forest, cold and wreathed in mist like something out of a nightmare. The first cold light was creeping its way across the horizon, but the sky overhead was still dark. As we got out of the carriage by Theodosius's tent a cry went up from one of the escort. They were German auxiliaries and I couldn't understand a word, but my eye swiftly followed his pointing finger upward to see the last dying traces of a shooting star.

Compared with many I am not superstitious, but I shivered to see that omen. Not with cold, either.

When we entered the tent we found the place cleared. A large throne had been set up, and Theodosius was on it in ceremonial uniform, with a purple cloak and a golden coronet. In his hand was the sceptre of office, and on his finger a solid gold signet ring. He would greet his vanquished enemy like the emperor he was. He did not look like a victor somehow. He looked as if he had spent much the same sort of night as we had. It raised him in my estimation that he worried so. I assumed it was about his responsibilities. In part it was, but only in part.

Lucius was there as usual. He ushered us to wooden seats at one side, among the commanders who were there to observe the proceedings. Opposite sat Valentinian and Justina, but there was no doubting who was the senior emperor. Without him, of course, Valentinian would not have been an emperor at all by now.

The tent flaps were thrown back, and a big man in the uniform of a high-ranking officer came in. He had long hair and a beard, not the Roman style at all. Amongst Romans in general, and the military in particular, the fashion was for short hair and shaven chins. This was surely one of the barbarians who were achieving high office in these strange times. He strode forward with a heavy footfall, and bowed rather perfunctorily to Theodosius. There was almost a token nod to Valentinian.

"Your Majesties." The voice was gruff and the accent foreign. "The surrender is under way. The enemy soldiers are lining up under the supervision of their officers and piling up their weapons and armour. Some two hundred have already been taken into custody."

He was interrupted by a courier who rushed in.

"*Comes*! Your Majesties! Fighting has broken out!"

"What?" Theodosius was on his feet.

"More a massacre, Your Majesty. It's the Moorish guards. Some of our men are taking it out on them for the way they abandoned His Majesty the Emperor Gratian."

I glanced at Valentinian and Justina. They seemed unperturbed, and somehow I sensed that this was not news to them. Theodosius turned to the big man.

"Arbogastes, see it is stopped!"

So this was the famous *Comes* Arbogastes, a Frankish auxiliary risen to the highest military rank!

"Inevitable," he said, but he went out. He was not hurrying. There were some bellowed orders in the distance.

"That barbarian probably started it," piped Valentinian. "I don't trust him."

Theodosius gave him a look that plainly said "Not in public."

For a few moments we listened to the rain which had started pattering lightly on the tent walls. There was an atmosphere of growing expectancy. I was not so naive that I didn't understand why.

The Frankish *Comes* returned.

"I stopped it. Not that it makes much difference now. They'd practically finished the job by the time I got there. I've given strict orders."

"Thank God for that," said Theodosius with a heavy voice. "There has surely been enough killing."

Arbogastes said nothing. He obviously didn't agree. He took a seat next to Valentinian, who shifted uncomfortably in his chair and leaned away from him. Then there was the sound of marching feet approaching the tent. They squelched in the mud, but there were enough of them to sound like a substantial force. The party stamped to attention outside. Then the tent flaps flew open and two soldiers came in. Between them was a prisoner, shorn of his armour and weapons, stripped of his cloak and his emblems of office. He wore only a coarse linen tunic and sandals. His greying hair was straggly, as if it had not been washed properly for a long time. His face was lined deeply, and he had lost weight. My voice escaped me in a loud whisper.

"Maximus!"

He turned his head towards me as they half-dragged him forward and forced him to kneel at the feet of Theodosius. There was a wan smile on his face. Then he looked up at the son of his old friend.

"I am sorry it came to this," he said.

I thought Theodosius would weep. He controlled himself with obvious difficulty.

"I too, Maximus. Old friend. They say that when you crossed to Gaul you told them I had approved your rebellion."

Maximus nodded. "It's true. Forgive me."

Arbogastes snorted. "Forgive? Your Majesty, stop all this nonsense and call the executioner now."

Theodosius shook his head. "Wait."

"I am in your hands," said Maximus quietly. "God is watching us. I am ready to die if it is His will."

"No, Maximus!"

But my shout went unheeded. Whether he knew how I came to be there I couldn't tell. Did he think it was treachery at the last? I don't know.

Arbogastes stepped forward. "Take him away."

The guards dragged Maximus away, scarcely giving him a chance to get to his feet. Theodosius leapt up in a rage.

"Arbogastes, what do you think you're doing!"

The commanders too were on their feet. They blocked Theodosius's path. They all spoke at once. Vividly I saw how true was Adeon's boast that the military controlled the Emperor.

"Your Majesty, think what you are doing."

"Our men have fought hard for this!"

"Think of the dead!"

"Think of the living. They must have satisfaction now!"

Suddenly the babble faded. We all became aware of a multitude of voices. They seemed to be chanting a word. There were just two syllables that rose and fell rhythmically.

"Mac-sen! Mac-sen! Mac-sen!"

"What is that?" asked the Emperor.

"Your Majesty, it is the British soldiers in my husband's army. The Cornovians."

"What are they chanting?"

"It is his name, in the British language."

He turned away, and I walked with him. The chanting continued and grew even louder.

"Your Majesty, please do something. It is not too late. Maximus was never disloyal to the Empire. It is the Dowager Empress who is the cause of all this, not him. She is the one who espoused heresy and split the church and state."

He shook his head sadly. "Dear lady, I wish I could help you. Your husband is an old friend. If only there were a way out. But even emperors must bow to greater forces."

"No, no, you can do something — "

He held up his hand.

"Listen."

There was near silence. The chanting had stopped. Dimly I was aware that there had been a sort of sigh, as if a thousand people had breathed out together. I still didn't realise what had happened, as the mind will block out those things it doesn't wish to understand.

The tent flaps rustled and the two soldiers ran back in with a triumphant cry, followed by a crowd of others. One of them carried a heavy stick which he raised and lowered in time to his insane cries. My eyes were full, and I blinked them clear to try to see the object which adorned the stick. Theodosius's cry of horror seemed miles away.

"For Christ's sake, man, have you no feelings? This is his wife!"

The soldier moved into the light of the rush lamp hanging down. His face was distorted in a grimace of cruelty and crude triumph. The face next to his was expressionless as it moved up and down, the eyes staring, the lips bleeding, the neck ending in a hideous crimson stump which dribbled blood and mucus down the stick which held it aloft.

It was the head of Maximus.

XXV

The long lines of men seemed to go on for ever. They were used to the endless marching — used to doing it with heavy armour and packs of equipment, what's more. This was easy by comparison. Besides, the exercise was good for them. It banished their dull spirits, got the blood flowing. And every mile they marched was a mile further from Aquileia and their sorry defeat.

This was not my analysis of the situation, but Kynan's. He should have known. He was their leader. After the removal of a few senior men for punishment, and allowing for those already dead, he was in the next rank. His relationship to me meant his appointment was certain. It was justifiable in any case. He was a popular officer, and efficient, and he could be relied upon to keep his word. It was fitting, as the solution to the problem had come from him, albeit indirectly.

*

I had been lying in my bed in the little house they had given us. Mabanwy had looked after me as always, after my collapse in Theodosius's tent. The sight of Maximus's severed head had been too much. Not only was I physically ill, but for a short time I think my mind went as well. At any rate, I seemed to fall into a pit within myself, and not venture out for two days, which I passed in weeping, and dreaming waking dreams of horror. Theodosius was very concerned. He felt responsible, since it was his men who had caused my decline. He was hard on himself. I think my collapse had been coming for a while already. It was inevitable. He sent me a doctor, but the man, though kind, achieved little. It was the Emperor himself who ordered that Kynan should be sought out and brought to me, and that did more good than anything. We wept a lot, but we comforted each other.

Adeon lay in a mass grave in Pannonia, struck down in the second desperate battle which Maximus had fought there.

"Don't be sad for him," said Kynan. "He had the life he wanted, and the death. Not many can say as much. Personally, I'd rather die in bed, old and infirm, with my sorrowing and respectful grandchildren gathered around me. But that wasn't for him."

I knew it was true. If we could have asked him, Adeon would have been pleased with his lot. More pleased than Maximus.

"What will happen to you all?" I asked Kynan.

"No one seems to know. We're all sitting around in the open at the moment, praying the rain doesn't start again. They say that Theodosius intends to be lenient, but still doesn't know what to do with us. He doesn't want to send us back home, apparently. You can't blame him — we're the third rebel army in a century to have started out from Britain. The question is, where else can we go? Assuming the sulphur mines have been ruled out, of course."

It was then that the idea came to me. It was simple and obvious, but compelling enough to make me drag myself up and dress and prepare to face the world again.

*

"Armorica?" mused Theodosius. "It's an idea with possibilities."

"I think so, Your Majesty. My brother Kynan says Armorica is underpopulated. There is plenty of farming land, plenty of fishing. The British are good at both. There are good sea links with Britain, so the married men could easily send for their families to join them, and the single men could send for wives."

He nodded pensively.

"Yes. Of course, they'd have to swear a new oath of allegiance — this time to me, personally. The Armorican coast needs defenders — Saxon pirates have raided it recently; they are getting bolder. These men already have the training to defend it. There could be a civilian militia, to be called up in times of danger. If they agreed to all that they could have grants of land for farms."

"Then you agree to the idea, Your Majesty?"

"I'm not sure yet. I'll think about it and take advice. We'll work something out. I'd have to send a governor to administer it, allocate the land grants, and so on. But it's the best idea I've heard yet."

And he scowled at Arbogastes and Justina, who seemed about to speak but thought better of it. I already knew what their ideas on the subject were.

"Where did the idea come from?"

"My brother Kynan said he wanted to retire there after he had seen it. I never gave it another thought until now."

"Hmm. If he knows the area well we'd better send for him and have the benefit of <u>his</u> advice, too."

So it was that Kynan was put in charge of the emigration, together with Lucius Gabinius, who had apparently requested the post. And so it was that I found myself watching the lines of marching men file past an inn near Lugdunum, in the middle of Gaul. Felicia, Mabanwy and I could not march, so we still travelled by carriage. We also stayed at inns along the way, whereas the men camped out, just as if they were still an army. We stood at an inn window now, watching them as they filed past to spend the night in the nearby meadow. Felicia was hoping for news of Vegetius. She had sent word to him, and knew he would be able to find the column of emigrants easily enough. She would rejoin him when he sent for her.

It was early evening when the messenger arrived. We were dining at the time, and saw the new arrival come in and speak to the landlord, who pointed us out to him. The man, dressed in military uniform and well cloaked against the cold, approached the table and bowed politely.

"*Dominae*, I apologise for interrupting your meal. I have come with despatches from Lugdunum. Which one of you is Felicia Lentula?"

Felicia was all agog. "Do you have news from my husband?"

The man hesitated, and a cloud of anxiety passed over my thoughts. There was something he did not want to say.

"News *concerning* him," he amended, "and a letter."

He presented a wax tablet and she undid the ribbon feverishly. After reading only a few words she suddenly put it down and looked at me. There was a catch in her voice.

"Vegetius. The poor, dear fool. Oh, the great, noble fool!"

And she lowered her head to the table, sobbing. I reached out my hand for hers, and with a lump in my throat read the tablet.

My dearest wife, The news has come from Aquileia. Since the hunt will now be on for all of those who supported Maximus, there is only one honourable course of action left to me. Valentinian is a weak boy, and Arbogastes a vengeful barbarian. My removal will also be the best protection for you, and the best hope that my possessions will not be confiscated. It grieves me more than I can say that I must die without seeing you again. I have set all my affairs in order, and the lawyer M. Viennanus is empowered to hand you all that is mine. I hope you will observe the proprieties for me, but know that if you wish to marry again you do so with my blessing, and with sincere hopes for the happiness I was not able to give you. Farewell, With love, Vegetius.

A weariness settled on me. Was there no end to it? And how unnecessary it was. With any other conqueror Vegetius might have been right, but Theodosius was different. The evidence of his humanity was camped in thousands just down the road. I became aware that the man was still there.

"*Domina*, there is a despatch for you also. It was sent from His Majesty at Mediolanum, and caught up with me as I left Lugdunum."

A wax tablet for me, too. I didn't want to open it. I could think of no one who would write to me with good news. But it had to be done. Good news or bad, it would not improve with keeping. Then I saw the Imperial seal.

It is my duty to inform you that a force led by the Comes *Arbogastes recently encountered your fugitive stepson Flavius Victor near Arelate in Gaul. After a short skirmish the Comes and his forces were victorious. With deepest regret I must tell you that your stepson was killed in the battle, although I had requested that he be taken alive. The exact circumstances are not clear, and I have asked for an investigation. Of course, I cannot command it as Valentinian now rules Gaul again, with the help of the* Comes. *The Dowager Empress Justina is ill and may not survive the winter. I would like you to know that your other stepchildren are reported well. They have returned to Londinium to their grandmother Antonina, to whom I have granted a pension. Both your stepdaughters will be educated as gentlewomen at my expense. With deepest sympathy, Theodosius.*

I sighed and put the tablet down. I had half expected the news — had I not warned Maximus of it? Felicia's grief was greater than mine. Eventually I would weep for Victor too, but not now.

*

"Armorica" means "The land that faces the sea", and it is aptly named. This corner of Gaul is one giant headland which has the Narrow Sea to the north and the Atlantic to the west. Much of it is high moorland, riven by valleys which run down to the sea, providing scores of natural harbours for fishing craft. The coast, especially in the west, is rocky and stormy. It is really very reminiscent of Western Britain, and a good place to be exiled if we had to be exiled anywhere. Even the climate is similar, although a little warmer. We have made a good life here.

Many of the men who fought with Maximus married local women rather than sending back to their families in Britain for a bride they would not be able to approve personally. The much-vaunted shortage of people seemed mainly to be a shortage of men. Many local women had been trying to run farms or fishing boats single-handed, or with the help of children. The influx of marriageable young men was a godsend, especially as they were soldiers, and therefore physically very fit. Fishing and farming are both strenuous occupations. The tendency has been for men who fought together to settle near each other too, so that whole districts are now known by the names of the army units which settled them.

There has been a trickle of emigrants from Britain ever since we arrived. They are mainly relatives of the settlers here, or others who have suffered too much at the hands of the Saxons or the Irish. If there is a total collapse of Roman rule in Britain — which seems quite possible now — I can see that many more will come. Already the British language is widespread here, alongside Latin and the Gaulish tongue, which is related to ours anyway.

The rest of the world has not stood still while we rebuilt our lives, of course. The year after we came here there was a terrible incident at Thessalonica, where rioting crowds murdered the captain of the garrison. Theodosius, urged on by his generals, ordered a wholesale massacre of the population. Later, having cooled his temper, he sent a second courier countermanding the order. It was too late. Seven thousand men, women and children had been butchered as they gathered to attend games in the local arena. Bishop Ambrosius was outraged and risked his own safety by excommunicating the Emperor. After some careful negotiations, the excommunication was lifted in return for a public act of penance by Theodosius in the cathedral at Mediolanum.

Kynan was amazed.

"It is the end of an epoch in history," he said wonderingly. "You realise this is the first time any Emperor has acknowledged any authority as being higher than his own? The bishops will never be out of politics now."

Two years later Theodosius finally outlawed all forms of pagan worship, and ordered the destruction of the last pagan temples and statues. It is now a criminal offence to practise any religion except so-called "Catholic" Christianity. I must say, it will take more than an imperial edict to stop our local people from worshipping whatever they like. Armorica is a long way from Mediolanum, and in spring and autumn the hills are bright with the sacred fires of the old religious ceremonies. I have even been there myself, although I shy away from some of the more extravagant rites, which always produce a crop of midwinter babies of doubtful parentage!

It is the custom of the pagan British to drive their cattle between a pair of bonfires at Beltane, the spring festival. It is supposed to purify them and ward off disease during the coming season, although it seems a strange idea to me. Still, they believe it. Anyway, it's a good excuse to have a good time, and we can't have too many of those. The year after Theodosius's capitulation to Ambrosius I was at the local Beltane festival. My father was also there. He was old now, but still sprightly, due largely to his habit of taking long walks among the hills, I feel sure. He had retired finally on the death of Maximus, and had promptly sold up everything to move to Armorica to be with his son and daughter. Finella was still with him. Kynan used to let his men drive his cattle between the fires, for they swore it made their year easier. Like me, he had his doubts.

It was uncomfortably hot near the fires, for the weather was warm anyway. I wandered away for some cooler air, and saw a man sitting on one of the stone walls which the local men used to mark their land, just like the farmers at home in Arfon. He seemed lost in thought, and I was about to turn away for fear of disturbing him. Then I realised that it was Lucius Gabinius, who had been my unwilling jailor at Aquileia and was now a neighbour as well as a government official.

"It's cool here. Why don't you join me?"

"Oh, er, well, just for a moment."

I clambered up on the wall and sat next to him, thinking how unladylike it undoubtedly was, but how like my childish escapades around Segontium. The memory made me sigh.

"Surely not sad on a night like this?"

"I was just thinking about my childhood home. Segontium."

287

"Ah, a beautiful part of the country. But it's good here too." He paused, as if unsure of himself. "I was thinking, too. I was thinking of Aquileia."

"I prefer to forget it. It has only miserable memories for me."

"Of course. I understand. Forgive me."

He paused again, as if he wanted to say something but didn't know how to express it. "I, er, I don't want to distress you by bringing up the past ... it's just that, well, for me there are one or two memories that stand out, that make it worthwhile remembering."

"Well, you were on the winning side."

"Not military memories, *Domina*."

"What, then?"

"The sight of you striding down the road to stop those men fighting. You did it, too. You treated them like small boys, and they loved you for it. There wasn't a man there who wouldn't have died for you."

"Lucius, I was trying to *stop* them dying for me."

"Of course. You put us all to shame. You were magnificent. Then, in Theodosius's tent, when they brought — when you knew Maximus was dead — "

"Please don't say any more!"

There was an uncomfortable silence. Then he cleared his throat and spoke.

"Helena, perhaps you'll think it impertinent of me, but would it be acceptable for me to call on you?"

"To call on me?"

I looked at his dark eyes, which now reflected the first rays of the dawn. I had seen him quite often since our resettlement in Armorica, but he had never come out with anything like this before. Indeed, it was the first time since our arrival that anyone had shown any interest in me as a woman. The thought warmed me.

"Please don't think it impertinent. I'd be glad to see you again."

"Then you shall, *Domina*, you certainly shall."

*

From such small beginnings great things can grow. We soon began spending a lot of time together, and Kynan and my father exchanged knowing looks when Lucius's name was mentioned. I think they saw how the wind was blowing even before I did.

On first acquaintance I had thought Lucius insensitive to the sufferings of war. I soon found that was a misjudgement, the opposite of the truth. In fact his sensitivity had made him adopt a protective cloak of indifference. When that was set aside it revealed a kind and considerate man with hidden depths, intelligent and cultured. When, in late summer, he took me to his bed for the first time, it was everything those earlier times had not been. Lucius was no inexperienced youngster; he understood women, he *liked* them. So many men don't really, and resent the fact that they still can't do without them. The following spring we were married. It was just as well. After I had not become pregnant by either Maximus or Julius I had rather assumed I must be barren, especially since Maximus had fathered children before. Nature works in mysterious ways, though. By the time I married Lucius I was already distinctly swollen about the waist. I feared my father would be shocked, but he was actually amused.

"Really, Helena!" he scolded jokingly. "Fancy getting caught out at your age, and you a woman of the world!"

It was only later I realised how much he had been afraid of dying without seeing any grandchildren. He has seen three now — Kynan's new wife has also produced a son — and shows no signs of dying just yet.

We had a strange conversation one day just before my marriage. He was talking about my mother, which he seldom did.

"I miss having her grave nearby," he said. "I used to go and talk to her there, you know."

"I know."

"Once, years ago, I went out at night. It was when Maximus and the elder Theodosius were staying with us. Maximus had mentioned his wife, who had recently died, and we had all drunk a little too much. I got rather maudlin, I'm afraid, and went out to sit on her grave in the middle of the night. Suddenly, I began to weep like a baby. Me, a grown man! I had never really done that since her death. Once I'd started I couldn't stop — went on blubbing for ages."

I said nothing, but squeezed his hand. That was one mystery which might never have been solved. The child who heard him thought it was Maximus, and the woman who married Maximus

289

couldn't understand why he would weep for one whom he had considered so treacherous and sinful. They were both wrong; Maximus never wept for people. I saw him weep when he heard about Valens's dreadful defeat in the East, but the tears were not for Valens. They were for his beloved Empire, his dream of a strong and united Rome, the standard bearer of civilisation for the whole world.

Dreamers are dangerous. The ones I have known have plunged the world into war and their families into despair. If those are dreams, I would rather stay rooted in reality, in the here and now and the good earth.

"Come on, father," I said. "I have a dinner to cook."

Historical note

"The Dream of Macsen Gwledig" is a Welsh legend which is tenuously based on known historical events. According to the tale, Macsen was Emperor in Rome when he had a mysterious dream of a beautiful girl in a palace by the sea, with a great island visible offshore. He promptly fell in love with her and sent envoys all over the world to identify the girl and the place. They eventually found her to be Helen, daughter of King Eudav of Arfon in north-west Wales, close to the island of Anglesey. According to the story, Macsen conquered the whole of Britain just to win her hand. It is a typical Celtic legend, heavy with heroism and romance, and historically wildly inaccurate.

The political events which form the background to this story have been gleaned from various sources, and are accurate as far as historians know. Macsen/Maximus definitely did exist, and held several senior military appointments in Britain. In the year 383 he was proclaimed Emperor by the troops in Britain and invaded Gaul, killing the Emperor Gratian and being recognised by Theodosius as co-Emperor. The details of Maximus's private life are almost all conjectural. He apparently came from Spain, and is thought to have married a high-born British woman whose name is not known. I have taken her name from the Welsh tale, but Latinised it to Helena. History records the name of Maximus's son, but not those of his two daughters or his mother. Theodosius's gallant treatment of Maximus's female relatives is recorded, however, as is the hunting down of his son by Arbogastes. Arbogastes himself later led an unsuccessful rebellion, and committed suicide to avoid capture.

It is recorded that at Aquileia Theodosius wanted to show mercy, and might have pardoned his old friend but for the intervention of his own generals, who dragged Maximus away and beheaded him on the spot. Some other ringleaders were apparently executed, and the massacre of his Moorish guard in the heat of the moment is also recorded. The rest of Maximus's soldiers are said to have been well treated, but not allowed to go home and foment further rebellion. Their fate is not known for certain, but there is a tradition in Armorica – modern Brittany and Normandy – that they were resettled there under the leadership of

Cynan (or Kynan) Meriadauc, whom I have identified with Helena's brother. For centuries Armorica was known as "Lesser Britain" and place names of British origin abound there. To this day the Breton language remains so similar to Welsh that speakers of the two languages can often understand each other.

Fourth century place names can be confusing, as most large towns were given a Latin name by the Roman occupiers, and at least one British name (sometimes more) by the natives. To complicate matters, some names in both languages were applied to more than one town. The most relevant are:

Roman Name	British Name	Modern Name
Cataracta	Catraeth	Catterick
Deva	Cair Legion	Chester
Eburacum	Cair Ebrauc	York
Londinium	Cair Lundein	London
Mona	Mon	Anglesey
Segontium	Cair Segeint, Cair-yn-Arfon	Caernarvon
Venta		Winchester

The Roman province of Gaul included not only modern France but also modern Belgium and parts of western Germany. Other Continental place names are:

Roman Name	Modern Name
Aquileia	Aquilo (near Trieste)
Arelate	Arles
Armorica	Brittany and parts of Normandy
Augusta Treverorum	Trier
Lugdunum	Lyons
Mediolanum	Milan
Mosella	River Moselle

Padus	River Po
Pannonia	Slovenia
Rhenus	River Rhine
Savus	River Sava
Sequana	River Seine

Some other Roman terms used are:

Augustus	Emperor; at this period there were up to three co-emperors
Caesar	The Emperor's deputy; usually his son or other chosen successor
Comes ("co-mays")	Literally "Companion", the highest rank after Augustus and Caesar.
Domina(e)	Mistress(es)
Domine/Dominus	Master (form of address)/Master (third person)
Dominula	"Little Mistress", an endearment used by Helena's nurse
Dux	Literally "Leader", a senior military commander roughly equivalent to Field Marshal.
vicarius	Civilian governor

If you have enjoyed this book, please consider writing a review for the Amazon website where you bought it, or on Goodreads (https://www.goodreads.com/).

And please visit my website at raforde.com for details of other published and forthcoming books.

You can follow me on Twitter: @ra_forde

Or on Facebook: https://www.facebook.com/R-A-Forde-writer-551262948707263

Printed in Great Britain
by Amazon

58483393R10159